Lance caught sig[...] swarming toward hi[...] cord of a hanging l[...] within range, but already he could feel the cord starting to give.

He swung on the cord like a chimpanzee on a vine. The nanobots had found the place where the cord met the ceiling and were already crawling down toward him. Lance swung back and forth once, twice. He almost touched the window with his feet. Above, something gave and he dropped several centimeters.

The nanobots reached his hands and several thousand crawled down his arm. Lance swung back, then forward, pointing his toes directly at the window.

The cord gave way. Lance's's forward momentum drove him full-tilt toward the glass. It shattered, slicing into his legs, chest, and face, though he felt no pain. With a whoop of triumph, he flew through the window. Already his nanos were working on ejecting the few intruders.

Air rushed past his ears as he fell toward the ground of the alley behind the store. He had time to notice a police cruiser parked a little ways away. Its doors were open and the alley floor was a seething black mass of nanobots. Lance shouted something incoherent as he fell directly into them.

BAEN BOOKS by STEVEN PIZIKS

In the Company of Mind
Corporate Mentality

CORPORATE MENTALITY

STEVEN PIZIKS

CORPORATE MENTALITY

A Baen Books Original

Baen Publishing Enterprises
P.O. Box 1403
Riverdale, NY 10471

ISBN: 0-671-57811-1

Cover art by Charles Keegan

First printing, July 1999

Distributed by Simon & Schuster
1230 Avenue of the Americas
New York, NY 10020

Typeset by Brilliant Press
Printed in the United States of America

DEDICATION

For my grandmother Ella Karow,
creator of childhood Advent calendars,
incurable bibliophile,
member of First Fandom

and

for Kevin Moyers, wherever this finds you.

ACKNOWLEDGMENTS

I would like to thank the members of the Untitled Writers Group of Ann Arbor (Jonathan, Karen, Lisa, Meredith, Michele, Ted, and Sarah) for their continued patience and always insightful comments. I would also like to extend belated gratitude to Cindy Pape for information on pheromones and vomeronasal organs.

CHAPTER ONE

ADITI

The needle pierced Aditi's skin, and cool, heavy liquid flooded her shoulder. She tried to squirm away, but the restraints held her firmly in place.

"Hold still, Aditi," Father said sharply. "You know wiggling only makes it worse." Slowly, too slowly, he depressed the plunger, and the amber transport medium drained into Aditi's vein. She suppressed a shudder. Although she couldn't see them, it seemed like she could feel the millions of microscopic nanobots scurrying and swimming into her blood, gliding between veinal cells, invading her body with their tiny claws and microscopic teeth. They tasted her chemicals, smelled her hormones, rearranged her cells.

Kept her alive.

Not for the first time, Aditi considered trying to knock the cold syringe away. She knew full well that without this particular infusion of nanobots, her arrhythmia would rocket out of control, sending her heart into tachycardia and leading to a quick death. Father, of course, would never allow that.

Ved Amendeep slid the needle out of his daughter's shoulder and today's assistant, the one with a mole on his face, pressed a bit of gauze to the site to stop the bleeding. Although the shoulder was an unusual injection site, Father had to inject Aditi there because her single arm wouldn't remain still long enough to accept a needle. No matter what Aditi did, the arm continued to twitch and strain against the smooth polymer restraint as it had done every moment since Aditi's birth nineteen years ago.

A spasm of pain twisted through the bones in Aditi's legs like a small tornado and Aditi grimaced. Nothing new there, either. There was no point in crying out—Father didn't believe in painkilling drugs any more than he believed in aborting a deformed fetus.

"The injection process is complete, Dr. Amendeep," Mole-Face said. Aditi had never bothered to learn his, or any other assistant's, name. He dropped the bloody gauze into a biohazard container, as if Aditi's condition were contagious.

"All right," Father said in his tired voice. "Give me a moment to bring the new programs on line and we'll get started."

Father turned to the computer and muttered to it in a voice too soft to hear. Sensor readouts beeped and flashed across the computer display while Mole-Face checked and changed Aditi's colostomy bag, a twice-daily chore since Aditi had no rectum and only half a kidney. Aditi couldn't change the bag herself, of course. Her arm shook too much for her to have any real coordination, and her bent, twisted legs made it difficult for her to even sit upright. Standing was out of the question. Aditi might as well hope to fly.

Or die, Aditi thought, angrily staring at a white ceiling she knew better than her own backyard.

The Brahman in attendance at the ultrasound that revealed Aditi's deformity had declared it a sign from Shiva. It was, after all, rumored that MediLife, Ved's employer, was performing forbidden experiments with nanobots and human flesh. This was visible proof that Ved was being punished for his sins. Aditi herself was obviously paying for some unimaginable crime she had committed in her last incarnation.

Ved Amendeep, however, disagreed with the priest. Aditi couldn't possibly be a sign from Shiva. Shiva was a destroyer and would never have allowed a monstrosity to exist. Vishnu, a creator, was speaking instead. Aditi's ultrasound pictures were a divine message giving Ved Amendeep time to prepare a laboratory prison for his deformed daughter and save her life. It was simply too coincidental that a child who could only survive by weaving nanotechnology into human flesh would be born to a man bent on perfecting that very procedure.

Ved sent the Brahman packing and set to work in his lab. When Aditi was born, he installed her there as soon as she was stable enough to move. The feeble protests of Aditi's mother were silenced by a quick divorce and a large cash payment to her parents. Nineteen years later, Aditi was still alive and in the same room, with countless nanobots burrowing continuously through her body, regulating blood sugar, hormone balances, leukocyte production, T cell levels, and everything else.

Father continued muttering into the computer. His voice was still tired—he worked full time for Medi-Life in addition to his work on Aditi—but his tone was unmistakably full of scornful resignation. Father barely tolerated her, and he hated all the work her survival forced on him. It would be so easy for him to pull the plug and go on with his life now that his experiments had proven successful. Aditi glanced down at her twisted body, the one propped up and restrained in its hospital bed, and wondered why he didn't, why he never had.

Father continued muttering to the computer while Mole-Face recorded Aditi's vital signs. Aditi stared stonily past the white walls and out the window. The clear summer day outside possessed color and texture. Honey trees waved blue-green leaves in the warm breeze in the yard, and purple *gita* vines curled lumpily around soft, red-and-white Vishnu flowers in the window box. Aditi had planted none of them—the gardener took care of that. Aditi had never even handled so much as a clump of earth. Her room was a careful model of efficiency.

The white walls and gray tile floors were bare—decorations gathered dust that inflamed Aditi's asthma. The only exception to this rule was a holocrystal that displayed Ved Amendeep forcing a smile to his face as he stood behind his tiny, twisted daughter and her hospital bed.

The holocrystal sat next to Father's small workstation, which was in one corner. Its computer connected to Ved Amendeep's main laboratory, to the house computer, and to the local nets. Aditi was allowed to use it when her father wasn't logged on.

"Pollen count is low today, Aditi," Father reported from the workstation without turning around. "Maybe Ranjan will be able to take you outside for a while this afternoon. Getting you out of your room for a while might cheer you up."

Aditi didn't answer. She continued to stare at the plants and trees outside. This wasn't her room. It was an extension of her father's lab, just like Aditi was an extension of her father's work. Hatred flooded Aditi's mouth with a taste like fried bile. She only wanted to be left alone, to die in peace. Her body could feed the plants outside, become one with the hardy, rough tree trunks and soft, delicate blossoms. Then she would be pretty for the first time and people would like what they saw.

"I need you, Ranjan," Father said. "I'm ready to bring the new infusion of nanos on line."

Mole-Face joined Father at the workstation and the keyboard clicked beneath his fingers while Father muttered more commands.

A sudden thirst swept Aditi's mouth and her tongue went dry and raspy. A glance at the wall clock, however, told her that it would be another hour before her malformed kidney could handle more fluid. Another twist of pain gripped her legs and she tightened the twitching fingers on her hand until it passed.

"Medullary interface functioning normally," Mole-Face reported. "Cortical monitors report no unanticipated problems. The interface for the new nanobots is now in place."

"Activating communications sequence," Father said. "The new system should be on line . . . now."

Aditi's mouth was still dry. She wanted water, or even juice. Something cold, sweet, and wet. Maybe she could ask—

Something shifted. Aditi gasped and tried to swallow, but nothing happened. It felt as if her insides had jumped an inch to the left without her. Then a noise crackled inside her head, like a radio transmitter clearing its throat. A presence brushed her mind for a tiny moment, then clamped her brain with an iron grip. Her heart rocketed out of control. A mix of fear and relief—

i'm going to die i'm going to die i'm going to die

—flooded her mind and she had time to make a tiny, mewling whimper before the convulsions began. Pain like nothing she had ever felt before thundered through her muscles and her joints creaked and twisted in protest. Aditi flopped and squirmed against her restraints like a dying fish, unable to stop, unable to scream.

Alarms sounded on the computer, and Father rushed to her side. His white lab coat brushed the holocrystal, which shattered on the hard tile floor. He touched Aditi's shoulder, and the moment his skin contacted hers, an awful fear swept his face. He screamed. Aditi, still wracked with convulsions and buried in pain, caught only a hazy glimpse of her father's expression. The unfocused brown blur of his face washed blood-red and bone-yellow before it vanished entirely from view. His screaming stopped. The convulsions eased a little, and Aditi's own screams began.

CHAPTER TWO

ME

When forty-five thousand people die all at once, the survivors naturally ask, "How did it all begin? Where did it all start?" Then they get mad when you tell them you don't know.

"Just tell the story," they demand. "Start at the beginning!"

I don't know where the beginning is. I mean, is it when my great-grandmother died and my great-grandfather chose his son, Jonathan Blackstone, to take her place? Or is it when Meredeth Michaels decided to marry Jonathan Blackstone? Or is it when Jonathan Blackstone first struck his son Lance and cracked his mind into forty-eight different people?

The cliché description of chaos theory is that a butterfly flaps its wings in China and the resulting tiny changes to the air currents eventually multiply and grow until a hurricane wrecks Florida. What the chaos theorists don't tell you, though, is that this kind of change takes a thousand butterflies flapping their two thousand wings, and if you step on even one of them, the inhabitants of Florida will live their lives in blissful ignorance of the storm they missed. So which butterfly is the one that started it all? Was it my great-grandfather? My grandmother, Meredeth Michaels? My grandfather, Jonathan Blackstone? My father, Lance? Where do you start?

I think I'll start with Mrs. Wells.

She was standing on her front porch staring at the

silver car in our driveway when I got home from school. The weather was typical for my birthday—wet, slushy springtime—but I had decided to take my bike to school instead of hitching the buggy or riding one of the horses because I didn't have mood or patience to deal with saddle or harness. My jacket flapped open in the chilly air, but I refused to button it. I didn't have the mood or patience for keeping up stupid appearances, either. The heavy weight of my book bag dragged at my back.

It had been an unusually snowy winter on Felicity, and chunks of white still patched the ground in the shadier portions of our yard. Leaf buds with green cracks knobbed the imported maples Dad had planted in the front lawn, and a pair of buckets hung beneath two small spouts hammered into each trunk. Wire mesh covered the mouths of all eight buckets, and a trio of lizzie-bats pittered anxiously back and forth above them, craning their long necks and chirruping with impatience. I smiled wryly in spite of myself. Every year Dad tries to make maple syrup, and every year the lizzie-bats get to the buckets, no matter how hard he tries to guard them. Sometimes I think he'd actually buy a gun and start shooting if Felicity allowed projectile weapons.

Anyway. My birthday. Front porch. Mrs. Wells. Silver car.

My jaw tightened and my stomach clenched. Looked like I was going to spend my birthday alone. A cool spring breeze washed over me. I pulled my windbreaker shut and shivered, though I still wasn't cold.

"You have a visitor," Mrs. Wells called from across the road, and I wondered if I should reply or pretend I hadn't heard. Mrs. Wells was at least sixty now, with white hair and flabby arms. I wondered what it would be like to be an old woman. It didn't seem likely I'd live to be an old man. Not with my twin gone.

"Isn't today your birthday, Kate?" Mrs. Wells called. "Happy birthday!"

I gave her a small wave, ditched my bike on the lawn,

and trotted up the flagstone path to the front door. *Gremlin,* I thought. *Do you know who—*

But Gremlin wasn't there anymore. The thought jolted me, as if I had missed the last step coming down a staircase. I clenched my jaw again and opened the door.

The man sitting in the living room with Dad wore a dark suit and held a yellow notepad full of desperately scribbled notes. He got to his feet and bowed to me when I entered. I didn't bow back. Dad also stood up uncomfortably and gave me an apologetic look with his green eyes.

"Hello, honey," he said. "This is Mr. Ting Chen. He's with—"

"So when are you leaving?" I asked shortly.

"I'm sorry, Kate," he said. "Please, honey. It's not as if—"

But I didn't stay around to hear. I stomped upstairs to my room and flung the door shut. My book bag went skidding under my bed, my windbreaker fluttered into the corner. Beneath my window, Mrs. Wells had gone back inside and one of the lizzie-bats was triumphantly snaking its head into the gap it had pried into the wire mesh. I stared furiously down at the yard, hoping one of its friends would shit on the perfect silver car. Dad had missed my first track meet, the first Christmas my twin and I made him a present on our own, and the first time I had won the Youth Sculpture Award. Now he was going to miss my eighteenth birthday. I thought about sending a regiment of nanobots downstairs and dismantling Ting Chen's chair out from under him. Then I discarded the idea. It was a childish trick, and anyway it wouldn't keep Dad from going.

The hardwood floor creaked outside my door and someone knocked. When I didn't answer, the door creaked slowly open. I faced the window, arms crossed. The lizzie-bat was gulping greedily from the sap bucket.

"Kate?" Dad said, entering my room. "Honey? Listen, I'm sorry but—"

"You already said that," I interrupted. "You can skip the rest, too. I know the beat. Ting-Ting down there works for someone who has a nanobot hive on their hands and you're leaving in a few minutes to handle it." I waved a hand over my shoulder without looking at him. "So go. Who cares? Gremlin's off line. My twin is God-knows-where. What's one more member of the family gone?"

"Kate, it's different this time." My bed creaked and I knew he was sitting on it. "This nanobot hive's managed to take over the computer systems of an entire planet. Thousands of people have already died, and it's going to be millions if I don't get there soon."

I turned around. "Take me with you this time."

Dad looked at me for a long moment. He's an undeniably handsome man, with hair the color of an autumn sunset, bright green eyes, and a broad, muscular build that the male body my twin currently wore had managed to inherit. The similarities between us and Dad end there, though. My twin and I are dark, where Dad is fair. We both have large brown eyes—my favorite feature on both bodies—and curly, dark brown hair with auburn highlights. My twin and I had long ago agreed to keep it long on the female body, short on the male.

Dad doesn't look anywhere near old enough to be my father, though he's in his midfifties. Women of all ages are constantly hitting on him. It's weird seeing that happen. You don't grow up thinking of your dad as someone who has a sex life.

"I can't take you with me, Kate," he said. "You know that."

My jaw tightened a third time, and I didn't answer.

Dad got up and sighed. "Look, I have to go. I'll be back as soon as I can, all right?" He crossed the room and kissed the top of my head. "I'll make it up to you when I get back. I always do." He turned to go, then paused. "Hey—keep an eye on the sap buckets, will you? I don't want the lizzie-bats getting all the sap this year."

And he was gone. Through my window I watched him climb into the car with the corp guy. It zipped almost silently up the muddy road and vanished in the distance. The lizzie-bats glided back down to the sap buckets to resume their interrupted feast.

Nanobots swarmed inside me like bees ready to burst from their hive. There was nowhere for them to go. My twin and his nanos were gone, and without them both I was stuck. I was trapped. A lizzie-bat with a broken wing. I wondered if my twin, wherever he was, felt the same way or if he was too angry to care.

The walls of my room seemed suddenly close, and the air felt stuffy. I threw open the window and breathed in cold lungfuls of spring air. The lizzie-bats looked up at me suspiciously, then went back to their greedy gulping.

I wandered downstairs, letting my hand trail on the contours carved into the banister, listening to the familiar creak of the stairs. Dad has a thing for wood, meaning the walls are sanded blond boards and the floors are bare of carpet except for the occasional big rug. We're at constant war with the dust bunnies. Kevin says the house smells like oil soap whenever he comes over. I can't tell. You can't smell your own house.

In the kitchen I found sugar, butter, cocoa, and flour sitting on the counter next to an empty ceramic mixing bowl. A small bundle of tiny candles lay wrapped in brown paper nearby. I stared at them for a moment, then snatched up the bowl and threw it against the wall. It shattered with a satisfying crash. Feeling only a little better, I stomped down to the basement.

Although I can't smell the oil soap upstairs, I always notice the welcome smell of wet clay downstairs. I hit the lights, dispelling the shadows that coated my work table like cobwebs. It was cooler down here and I wished I had put on a sweatshirt, but felt too perverse to go back upstairs and get one. A moment later my nanos noticed the drop in body temperature. They increased the pyrogen levels in my blood, and the chill evaporated.

I filled my dipping bowl with water, cut a clump of clay from the bigger chunk wrapped in brown paper, and started kneading. The clay was cold and satisfyingly gritty beneath my hands, but it was still stiff and hard to work. In response to my thoughts, a few million nanos poured out of my mouth, eyes, and nose and rushed down my arms into the clay. Although I can't see or feel them running over my skin—most of them are smaller than a red blood cell—I can control them just like other people control striated muscle. It's like having an extra limb, one that can do several things at once. I can't explain it better than that, but then, I can't explain how I breathe, either. I just do it. And just like my breathing, my nanos revert to their regular tasks if I stop concentrating on them. Most of the time, their tasks involve fine-tuning my body chemistry, making sure I don't get sick, and healing any damage. My twin has nanos, too. We got them from Dad.

The nanos helped me work the clay, loosening it and pulling water through it until it was the texture I wanted. I glanced at the foot-powered potter's wheel next to the worktable, then decided to keep molding with my hands and see what took shape.

I wondered what Dad was doing, if he had reached the spaceport all right, if he was boarding the skyhook even now, or if he was still in the silver car. He should have taken me with him. My fingers squelched and kneaded the cool, gritty clay. Suddenly I wanted to talk to Gremlin, the thoughts and questions already forming in my mind. But my twin was gone, and Gremlin needed both of us to exist.

Clay bulged and bunched, and not always just where my fingers worked. My birthday. Dad, Gremlin, my twin. All of them were gone on my birthday. Loneliness made an empty place in my chest. My fingers and my nanos worked faster and faster, trying to fill it with clay. A tree sprouted in the gray lump, and its branches grew upward, thick and bare. I added a pair of sap buckets on the trunk and a trio of lizzie-bats perching anxiously above them. My nanos let me work in impossibly tiny detail, adding patterns to the fur and even a microscopic drop of sap hanging from one sap spout. It was shaping up to be a nice piece of work, maybe one of my better ones. I blew a curl of hair away from my nose. If I had the male body right now, I'd probably be running through the woods behind the house. I can't sculpt when I'm male, and I can't get an endorphin rush from physical activity when I'm female.

I looked down at the tree and noticed my twin's male face looking up at me from the bark. I smashed the entire thing to mush and fled upstairs, leaving the clay to dry under the basement lights.

Four days later, someone banged the front knocker. I thudded downstairs from my room, heart in my mouth. Dad wouldn't knock, but maybe it was someone with some news.

I opened the door on Ting Chen, the guy who had taken Dad away. His silver car was parked in the driveway again. The air outside was balmy and sweet, and baby leaves hovered in the maple tree branches like a green mist. The lizzie-bats had long ago emptied the last sap bucket and flown away.

Ting bowed. I didn't bow back. My heart was pounding, but damned if I would let any of that show.

"Where's my father?" I asked before he could speak.

Ting Chen shifted a moment uncomfortably before answering. A rock plunged though my stomach and into my feet. You can blurt out good news. Bad news takes some thought.

"I'm sorry, Ms. Radford-Michaels," he said at last. "Your father landed on the surface of New Pakistan—the hive-infected planet—three days ago, and we have not heard from him since."

My entire body turned cold, as if I had been filled with ice water. "Is he dead?"

"We have no idea. However, I'm afraid—" He paused to clear his throat. "I'm afraid that's what many in my company believe. I deeply regret that we can't consider sending a rescue ship. We don't know how your father defends his computer systems from hive takeover, and any ship we sent might be infected and destroyed. We can't take the risk."

We can't take the risk. We can't take the risk. Ting's words ate through my mind like a school of piranha. I couldn't do anything but stare, too numb to do or say anything.

Ting whipped out an envelope. "Although your father was hired as an independent contractor and my company assumes no liability," he went on, "we have decided it would only be proper to offer you a compensatory settlement. I know it can't make up for your loss, but—"

The numbness abruptly vanished, replaced by cold rage. I reached into the house and picked up a vase that sat on a table near the door. My nanos swarmed over it in invisible waves, finding microscopic fissures and gaps between molecules. I thrust it under Ting's nose.

"Run," I said.

Ting blinked. "What?"

"The human skull is composed of eight bones fused together along a series of fissures," I said. "You'd better run."

Ting Chen didn't move. "I'm afraid I don't under—"

The vase shattered into eight pieces with a loud *pop*. Shards glittered like knives on my palm. *"Run!"*

Ting fled. His silver electric car vanished down the road in a cloud of dust. I watched him go, my brain not really processing what my eyes recorded. The anger vanished, replaced by a sour lump of worry. My twin was gone. Gremlin was off line. Dad had disappeared.

Damned if I was going to sit around and wait to find out what the hell was going on.

I dashed into the house and threw a few things into

a shoulder bag. In the kitchen I put a box lunch together from the icebox and packed the rest of the perishables into a crate. I left it on Mrs. Wells's front stoop with a note asking her to keep an eye on the house and feed the horses until I—*we*—got back. Then I hopped on my bicycle and pedaled furiously down the road.

CHAPTER THREE

ADITI

Aditi Amendeep stared beatifically at the white ceiling above her bed, ignoring the stench of blood and feces that rose from the floor. After a long moment, she gave a soft sigh and smiled. The convulsions had ended, but that wasn't what was behind her current haze of peaceful delight. The fact was, her pain was gone. Every scrap, every shred. Not even her legs hurt. The feeling was more wonderful than any opiate rush. It was as if someone had lifted a crushing weight off her body, one that she had forgotten she was carrying. For the first time in her life, nothing hurt, and that was exhilarating.

There were other sensations besides a lack of pain. Something else had changed. A tiny army of billions marched through her body, and she could feel each soldier patrolling her cells and making corrections. She narrowed her focus to a single nanobot that was helping a hundred others repair a blood vessel that had ruptured during the convulsions. Like she was moving her own arm, Aditi made it leap into her bloodstream. The acid taste of oxygenated blood flooded the nano's sensors. The taste vanished when the plasma herded the erythrocytes into capillaries that allowed the blood cells to dump their rich loads into crackling mitochondria and pick up heavy chunks of carbon dioxide. Aditi folded the nano's spidery legs beneath it and let it coast into the veins. A thumping noise grew louder as the vessels merged into the vena cava and

17

the plasma swept toward the impossibly huge gates of Aditi's pulmonary valves. Aditi held her breath as the stream of blood swept the nano toward the valves as they gaped open and slammed shut. A few blood cells were crushed between the muscular walls, tanging the plasma flow with the gluelike taste of the thromboplastin each one released. Aditi barely had time to wonder if this nano would be crushed as well before it surfed past the valves into a dizzying series of cardiac chambers and was squirted toward the lungs. Aditi whooped with joy at the exhilarating speed and giggled when the nano popped through the thin alveolar walls into a tiny, spongy chamber that expanded and collapsed in time with Aditi's breathing. Aditi held the nano there, exploring the double sensation of hearing her breathing from inside and out.

A spasm wracked Aditi's diaphragm and for a moment she couldn't catch her breath. Aditi coughed violently and the nano was abruptly flying. Aditi coughed again. The nano bounced against an unyielding surface, but its weight was so slight it landed undamaged. A great white plain stretched out in all directions and ended at the edge of a tall, straight cliff. Scratches and bumps marred the plain's surface. Although the nano's sensors couldn't "tell" Aditi where it was, she knew its location, much the way she knew where her legs were even if she couldn't see them. The nano was near her father's computer station. The plain was part of the keyboard and the cliff was one of the keys.

Aditi's mind raced, and she narrowed her eyes, trying to concentrate. Her thoughts were chaotic all of a sudden, rushing around like a pack of excited puppies. She found herself looking at the honey trees in the yard, and their probable genetic structure rose unbidden in her mind. A bird flew past, and she analyzed local wind currents based on its flight. Dust motes floated in the air despite Father's careful filtering, and her nanos caught and tossed them aside before they could enter her lungs.

Clouds breezed through the sky and she made automatic predictions about the weather based on ambient temperature and humidity. Her thoughts stretched in these directions and a hundred more all at once. The feeling fascinated and frustrated Aditi. Her mind wanted to run like a small child while her body dragged like an old woman about to die.

The single nano dropped into the computer console and encountered another nano. This wasn't surprising. Nanos were an integral part of all computer systems. They continually recalibrated delicate drives and systems, kept them clean, performed minor repairs, and even served as temporary data storage units during backups or when it looked like the main drive might fail. Like Aditi's nanos, they remained in constant communication with each other as long as they were within a few feet of the mother board. When hooked to a digital or faster-than-light communicator, they could also communicate and coordinate with nanobots in other computer systems, allowing a remote programmer to make physical repairs and upload new software without ever having to leave the office.

Or bed.

Before Aditi could even consider the matter further, her nano linked up with the computer's nano. A viral program she didn't even realize she had written injected itself and suddenly the second nano was hers. The two nanos scurried away and each connected with another nano. In less than a second, Aditi owned four nanos in her father's computer, then eight, then sixteen. In less than four minutes, she owned the entire computer.

With but a thought to her new nanos, Aditi flicked the terminal off, flicked it on, flicked it off. Aditi grinned.

Control, she thought in amazement. *I have control.*

Then the computer was back on again and Aditi's father's research dropped into her brain. Facts and observations, nanotechnology programs and designs, physiology and physics flooded her mind. Aditi heard recordings of Father's voice, read his keystrokes, dissected his programs.

" . . . severe deformities interfering in kinetic activity . . . "

" . . . trauma to the cerebellum resulting in . . . "

" . . . use nanobots to stabilize renal tissue . . . "

It was as if a part of her had become Father's computer.

Aditi barely had time to wonder how this worked before she noticed her nanos shifting chemicals in her brain, rapidly reconfiguring the molecules to form new codes and engrams, giving her new memories. Aditi giggled and sifted through Father's databases, capriciously snatching up some bits of information, leaving others alone, wiping still others away as if they had never existed.

A small part of herself asked what was going on and how this had happened, but almost as soon as she asked herself the question, the answer was there.

A hive.

Every nano in Aditi's growing system spun in place for a tiny moment while Aditi herself absorbed this idea. A nanobot hive had formed inside her. It made perfect sense now that she thought about it. Hives were a constant threat to any nanobot-driven system. On rare occasion and for no apparent reason, the nanobots in some computer systems would band together and form a rudimentary consciousness. Experts in nanotech theorized that each nanobot acted like a single cell of an artificial brain. But the theory remained unproven. In practice, nanobot hives were destroyed as soon as feasibly possible, rendering them difficult to study.

The first nanobot hive had appeared some forty years ago in a private school in Dover back on Earth. Over a dozen people had died, and the computer system had been destroyed. The military had irradiated the area with an electromagnetic pulse, effectively wiping out most of the nanobots and, incidentally, any chance of studying what had happened. The surviving nanos had reverted back to their original programming, which meant they cleaned up the mess. By the time the analysts got their equipment set up, there was nothing left to see. And so it went with every other nanobot hive that followed.

Fortunately, most people had a greater chance of being knocked in the head by a falling meteorite than encountering a nanobot hive.

The meteorite had hit Aditi square on.

The sickening stench of blood, urine, and feces was growing stronger, but Aditi, lost in thought, merely frowned. By all rights she should be dead. Nanobot hives weren't kind to the systems they took over. They ravaged their homes, flexed their muscles, and destroyed their environments even as they learned about them.

So why didn't they kill me? Aditi thought.

In what was becoming a pattern, the answer to the question popped into her head almost as soon as she asked it. Constant interaction with a human nervous system had been one of the factors that had brought Aditi's hive to "life," and the patterns from her mind served as a template for the hive's own consciousness. The nanobots saw Aditi's brain cells as fellow nanobots, to be integrated instead of destroyed. Now the hive was in her brain, part of her mind. Part of Aditi.

The disgusting acrid smell grew stronger. Aditi wrinkled her nose and a small regiment of nanos automatically cut off her sense of smell. She glanced over the side of her bed. A red-and-gray pile of mush—shredded, cell by cell, by nanos under the panic of Aditi's convulsions—steamed slightly in the cool air wafting from the vents. The red-gray goo had already formed a greasy skin, and a slow wash of blood was reaching for the carpet of the room beyond. That was all that remained of Mole-Face and Father.

Aditi giggled. *Mole-Face and Father,* she thought. *Sounds like the title of a children's book.*

Aditi swept a mental hand, and within moments every

nanobot in the house was hers, from refrigerator to VR unit to house computer. They swarmed to her call like ants to a queen, crawling from their hiding places, abandoning their tunnels, leaving tasks undone.

With less than a thought, Aditi overrode the computer command that kept the window shut. The glass swished softly open and the room was suddenly awash in hot summer air. Another command, and the pile of flesh, blood, and bone bubbled and boiled as billions of nanos slipped into the mass. The goo began to ooze across the floor like a putrefied amoeba, slurping and sloshing toward the window, leaving absolutely no trail behind it. Not even a molecule. Aditi suppressed another giggle.

Father would be pleased, she thought. *He hated messes in the lab.*

The mass slurped up the wall, into the flower box, and down the side of the house. Aditi's eyes couldn't see it anymore, but her nanos could. The mass lurched and wobbled to the ground, over the grass, and beneath the honey trees. A dog barked wildly next door, and someone started to scream.

The perfect fertilizer, Aditi thought, and reconnected her sense of smell so she could inhale the sweet scent of honey tree leaves on the breeze. Father had always been so worried about pollen. Now they could both enjoy it in completely new ways.

The screaming continued for a long moment, then a door slammed and it abruptly stopped. Aditi nodded with satisfaction, then noted with annoyance that her single arm was still shaking with palsy. Father had tried for years, but with no success. Aditi, however, could now look at everything from individual nerve cells to composite snapshots of her entire nervous system. Like a communications worker following fiber-optic cable, Aditi traced neural connections from arm to cerebrum to the basal ganglia. Here Aditi frowned. The ganglia required two chemicals—*dopamine and acetylcholine,* whispered an inner voice—to route neural impulses

correctly. But the cells were only producing acetylcholine. The resulting interference made it difficult for
her brain to communicate with her arm, causing the
tremors. In a heartbeat, a hundred thousand nanos set
up a wagon train to ship dopamine in from surrounding tissue and deliver it to the connection sites.

The tremors vanished. In wonder, Aditi held up her
single hand and flexed it, bending each finger as it
pleased her. The muscles obeyed her every command.

Across the room, the computer chimed softly. There
had been no activity on the terminal for almost thirty
minutes, and it was going to disconnect itself from the
networks in a moment. Aditi held the connection open.
She was in control now, not the computer.

On impulse, Aditi narrowed her eyes and pushed
outward. A billion nanobots instantly connected across
the web with a billion nanobots in other computer systems across the world. Aditi's hive virus shot into the
nets and spread, yanking another billion nanos into her
domain, all connected through Father's computer. One
billion became two. Then four. Then eight.

Alarms blatted and blared, counterprograms marshaled
their forces, antiviral shields sprang into action, but Aditi
blundered through them like an elephant through a
spiderweb, her hive mind far more powerful than any
human-created program. And where control of the nanos
went, control of the computers invariably followed. Aditi
felt each system click into place like a new hand or foot.
Traffic control systems, vidphone connections, VR networks, research databases, house computers, libraries,
schools—everything she touched. And everything she
touched *changed*.

Across the city, researchers at MediLife, Incorporat-
ed jumped in startlement as gibberish sped across their
terminals and fifteen years of painstaking data vanished.
Eight groundcars smashed into each other at an intersection where the computer-controlled signal flashed
green in all directions. A passenger jumpship coming

in for a landing plowed into unyielding tarmac when the computer told it the runway was twenty meters lower than it actually was. Forty-three comatose patients on computerized life-support died without a whimper, while sixty-one others clawed desperately at their hookups before lapsing into death. A corporal on a military base rushed to inform his commander that two dozen tanks had mobilized and were firing at anything that moved, even though no one was at the controls. A teenager who had just discovered his parents' collection of erotic virtual reality programs was electrocuted the moment he placed the helmet on his head. A technician in the Center for Infectious Disease Control watched in horror as electronic locks on the cages of infected lab animals clicked open and shut at random.

In her room, Aditi closed her eyes and continued to explore. It was like playing a VR game, one with infinite paths and infinite places. She could do ten, fifty, a thousand things at once. She wandered through a mining operation under the ocean and floated in a communications satellite above the atmosphere. She was everywhere, touching, tasting, knocking things off shelves. People screamed and scurried everywhere she went, but Aditi barely noticed. They were images in VR, points of light on a screen, pixels caught in a hologram. Each one was no more significant than the individual cells that made up her body or the individual nanobots that made up her brain.

The freedom was exhilarating. Aditi was amazed at the sheer size of the world around her, and now she could explore it all, every inch. It would belong to her and her alone. She was in control. Aditi laughed like a baby and stretched out a heavy hand.

CHAPTER FOUR

ME

The door slammed shut. I slid down the cool steel wall to the floor and exhaled slowly with my eyes shut. Inhale. Exhale. Inhale. Exhale. After a long time, I opened my eyes and glanced around.

My cabin was the size of my closet back home, with a bed that folded down, a tiny washbasin, and a sign that told me the restrooms were up the hall to the left. Another sign advised USE NANO-KLEEN SOAP FOR THAT NANO-KLEEN FEELING. I got to my feet, grateful for the opaque door that shut out the hurried press of people outside. The skyhook ride to Felicity Station had been bad enough, with customs and examinations and shots and tile floors and glass walls. Felicity Station itself was even worse. Steel corridors ran in a dozen confusing directions. Voices blared from loudspeakers. Driverless electric carts hummed by, beeping at you to get out of the way, and people towing luggage carts rolled them right over your toes without the slightest apology.

I had known that Felicity's space station was bigger than we natives needed, but I hadn't known just how *much* bigger. Immigration and emigration are both fairly rare, so you'd think we wouldn't even need a little station, let alone the monstrosity I had just navigated. Felicity, however, occupies a prime location—a lot of shipping and passenger routes cross in our area. Hence the big station.

Truth to tell, Felicity couldn't exist without it. Although

we sell clay for ceramic polymers, the Senate won't allow high-tech mining. The relatively small amount we can produce isn't anywhere enough to support an entire economy. Neither are the craft items we export. The revenue generated by the station counterbalances what would otherwise become a nasty trade deficit.

The upshot of all this is that it took me forever to get to my ship, even with signs pointing the way. I felt frazzled, hemmed in by all the people and the noise that bounced off the unyielding walls and floors. Fortunately the door to my cabin kept them out, and I vowed not to go outside until hydraulic pressure drove me into the bathroom.

Then there were the nanobots.

My own nanos could sense them. It was like walking into a marsh and knowing there are millions upon millions of mosquitoes hiding in the grass. They surged around me, in the air system, in the wrist computers of the other passengers, in the flight attendant's notepad, even in the little computer that had controlled the height and angle of my seat on the skyhook car. A strange hunger awoke. I wanted to reach out and snatch these unclaimed nanos up. It was like the time I had stolen Dad's nanos, only worse. These nanos weren't under intelligent control and would be easy to eat. I could feel it.

Had my twin felt this? I didn't know.

Sweat glistened on my body as I fought temptation. Who knew what programs I would disrupt by taking these nanos? My twin had certainly done so. I kept every one of my nanobots sealed tightly inside my skin. No one was going to die because I lacked control. I was not going to give in to instinct.

I pursed my lips beneath a sudden sense of déjà vu. The hunger felt . . . familiar. I shook my head. Impossible. I interacted with claimed nanos all the time—Dad's, my twin's—but I had never felt hungry for *them*. Why would I feel it now?

I pushed the sensation aside and counted my remaining

money as a distraction. My twin had emptied our shared bank account on Felicity, but I had taken to keeping my ceramic and sculpture money in a separate account not even Gremlin knew about. It was enough to get me to Earth in a private cabin and even have a meal or two along the way, if I were careful. Fortunately, the female body keeps more fat on it than the male, so a day of low rations wouldn't do any damage.

The cabin air smelled stale. I fiddled with knobs labeled VENTILATION until an artificial cool breeze wafted into the room. I inhaled appreciatively. Air conditioning, I thought, would be nice back on Felicity, especially in midsummer when it gets so hot you don't want to do anything but sit on the porch and fan yourself.

"Attention all passengers," a voice said practically in my ear. I jumped. "This ship will depart in one minute. Please shut down all communication devices until we have cleared the station. Thank you for your cooperation."

I noticed that the soap advertisement had vanished and the loudspeaker's words were scrolling across the wall space instead. Interesting. I put my hand on it and felt more nanos at work. The hunger awoke again, but I steadfastly ignored it.

"What assistance do you require?" said the screen.

Startled, I snatched my hand back. "None. Sorry."

The wall space went blank. A moment later, the soap ad reappeared and a soft hum started up. I put my hand back on the wall.

"What assistance do you require?"

"What's going on?" I asked.

"Docking clamps have been released and the ship is leaving the station."

"How long before we arrive on Earth?"

"Projected arrival in eight hours, fifteen minutes. This includes time for two stopovers, one at Catalina and one at Little America."

"Thank you."

The screen went back to the soap ad. I sat down on

my tiny, foldout bed and tried not to worry about Dad
and my twin. I had about as much luck as the rajah
whose magic carpet only worked as long as he didn't
think the word "elephant."

Dad had always wanted a normal family, though he'd
never said what "normal" meant. It probably didn't
include two kids who could swap bodies like other children traded toys.

Trading, of course, had a significant impact on me. I
can't remember whether I was born male or female,
and I'm sure most people would think that odd. Even
Dad, who should have known better, used to ask about
it every so often, as if he'd eventually jostle something
loose. Yet these same people, ones who call themselves
normal, can't remember learning to walk or talk. They
don't recall learning to crawl, or when they first fed
themselves with a spoon. Nothing odd in that, they think.
Well, *I* don't remember learning to Trade.

I drifted into a doze. My mind wandered, seemed to
float near the ceiling. The earlier memory, the one about
feeling hungry for nanos, resurfaced. It was hazy, like
a frosted mirror or a half-remembered melody. I tried
to concentrate on it, but that only seemed to push it
farther away.

I turned my attention inward, to my nanos. They
searched through my brain like little librarians, looking for the parts of my brain that showed activity only
when I concentrated on the hazy memory. They found
the fragments scattered among many different neural
cells in my cerebral cortex and cerebellum.

Contrary to popular belief, humans don't remember
everything we experience. We do remember far more
than we can actually recall, however. A lot of information simply gets misfiled or is accidentally "disconnected"
from other memories. For example, the smell of ginger cookies may bring about vague recollections of
wooden cupboards and a woman humming, but no
memory of heat or of a sweet, crispy taste. The neural

cells which store that particular information simply no longer react to the gingery smell, either because the chemical codes were misfiled or the connections between the cells has changed.

I, however, have an advantage. My nanos skimmed through my brain and found several hundred cells in my cerebellum that reacted to the ghost memory but weren't sending their information anywhere, as if they were listening to a conversation but not taking part.

I set a couple nanos to alert me in case an announcement came over the speaker. Then I disconnected my sensory perceptions at my thalamus and hypothalamus. The hard bunk vanished, along with the faint sounds of people walking past my cabin door and the faintly metallic smell of the ventilation system. All distractions vanished. I floated in nothing.

I sent a small regiment of nanos into my somatosensory cortex, olfactory bulbs, occipital lobe, parietal lobe, and temporal lobe in order to seize control of my senses of touch, smell, sight, taste, and hearing, respectively. Once the nanos were in place, I ordered the nanos in my cerebellum to stimulate the appropriate neural cells and transmit the information to the nanos waiting in the parts of my brain that controlled sensation.

All sensation, of course, is ultimately nothing more than brain chemistry. When you touch a hot stove, neural impulses flash up your arm and spinal cord to your brain. The impulse causes a chemical change in various brain cells as they receive and interpret the information. If you touch an ice cube, the same thing happens, except the chemical change in your brain cells will be a bit different. A person who loses an arm sometimes still feels pain where the limb used to be because the brain makes chemical changes purely out of habit. So when my nanos recovered the information stored in my memory and telegraphed it to the nanos hovering in my sensory areas, those nanos made certain chemical changes.

Suddenly I was somewhere else.

I was lying in someone's arms. She smelled like comfort, like warm food and cozy affection. She was singing. The sound murmured in my ears and vibrated softly against my bones as I leaned sleepily against her soft chest. The world was rocking slowly back and forth. I liked this. I knew my twin was already in bed and asleep and I didn't have to share the rocking and holding.

Tiny beings rushed around my body. Usually they rushed around inside, but some of them had lately taken to wandering around on my skin. A few even left my body entirely. It was fun. They were part of me and I could make them do what I wanted. Usually. Sometimes. A bunch of them crawled over the comfort person's—*Mama's*—skin. Her skin was darker than mine.

One of my little beings found another little being. Then another, and another. These little beings weren't mine. They made me hungry, but not for food. I wanted the other little things, wanted them very much.

I took them. I took a whole lot. Then I made them dance because it looked pretty.

The world tilted. Something hard cracked my head. Pain. I screamed. My twin woke up and wailed, too.

Now the room was dark. Time must have passed. I was sitting in my crib next to my twin. I felt restricted. Confined. My little beings couldn't leave the crib—whenever they tried, they hit a line of other beings, a lot of them. I couldn't get through them, and I couldn't eat them. That made me angry, and I started to cry. So did my twin. I pulled myself up by the crib railing and bellowed my outrage.

An adult with red hair—I called him *Dada* when I remembered the word—was looking down at me. I wanted him to pick me up, but he didn't. His face looked tired.

Then we were in a different place. It smelled different there, like new wood and old sawdust. I was sitting in a warm puddle of sunlight, pounding a painted wooden horse against the floor. My twin was busy turning over the wastebasket. Boxes loomed around us like extra walls. It was like living in a house of giant blocks. Dada was lying on the floor next to us, fast asleep. His face looked very white and his hair looked very red, a cobweb with autumn leaves blowing around it. I didn't see Mama anywhere.

The memory ended. I floated in a black lump of guilt. Mother. I had thought all my life that she had abandoned me—us. Then on one terrible winter day, Dad had told us why we lived in what amounted to exile on Felicity, why he and my mother weren't married anymore. Every shred of anger and hurt had suddenly hardened into heavy guilt at his words.

I set the memories firmly aside. I didn't need more guilt. Other memories were firing now, and I let myself be swept into them.

"Time for your bath, Quinn," Daddy said. "Let's go."

I went on piling blocks on the wooden floor. Daddy wasn't talking to me—I had already taken a bath. My twin had a set of blocks, too, and a rival fort was growing on the other side of the ocean—throw rug—that lay between us. I had to hurry or my twin's fort would be bigger than mine and, by our unspoken rules, be able to launch spitballs with impunity.

"Quinn," Daddy repeated. "Bathtime. You're almost five years old. I shouldn't have to carry you."

I slowed my stacking. Daddy would be taking my twin off for a bath in a moment, and that would buy me precious time. I could sit back and plan.

Strong hands snatched me up. "Come on, you," Daddy growled with mock ferocity. "You need a bath, mister, and you need one now."

He flung me over his shoulder and started upstairs for the bathroom. My twin grinned at me and went back to the block fort. A handful of my nanobots flew at him, tapping a handful of his and letting my twin know I

wanted to Trade. But my twin turned away and ignored
my nanos. Anger washed over me and I set up a howl.
I had already *had* a bath that evening. Why did I need
another?

*Gremlin!** I silently shouted.

*Not involved,** Gremlin's voice replied. That meant
Gremlin wouldn't do anything.

"Enough screaming," Daddy said, unceremoniously
stripping my clothes off and dumping me into the tub
of hot water. Several hundred nanobots, caught unawares
by the sudden dousing, were washed away. Downstairs,
I knew, my twin was finishing up an impenetrable fort,
probably with blocks stolen from mine, and I was stuck
in the tub for the second time that day. I splashed water
and got Daddy full in the face.

"Quinn!" he said sharply. "You know better. Do that
again, young man, and you'll be in bed right after your
bath."

The droplets beaded up and cascaded off Daddy's
face. His clothes dried instantly. Daddy was better at
controlling his nanobots than I was.

"Why do I hafta take a bath? I already—"

"You're filthy," Daddy interrupted, working shampoo
into my hair. "And your sister already had hers. Now
it's your turn. Once your nanobots learn how to keep
you clean, you won't need to bathe so often, but until
then, it's tubtime."

"But we *Traded*," I protested. "I don't need a bath!"

"You can't trade having a bath," Daddy said, and
drowned out further protest in a deluge of rinse water.
It wasn't fair! I had to take a bath twice and my twin
didn't take one at all. I was so mad I wanted to hit something. There had to be a way for my twin to take a bath,
too.

And then I got an idea.

*Gremlin,** I thought.

*Here,** Gremlin's voice said inside my head.

Tell my twin I want to play hide and seek when I'm

done with the bath. I'll seek first and you give cold-warm-hot clues, okay?

Twin says fine, Gremlin replied almost instantly.

Afterward, cleaned and scrubbed for the second time that day and wearing my summer pajamas, I found a pile of blocky rubble downstairs on my side of the rug. A perfect fort blockaded my twin's side. I clenched my jaw. My twin was nowhere in sight.

"You can play with your sister for a while now," Daddy said. "I'm going to read the paper. And stay clean!"

He went into the living room. I heard the creak of his favorite rocking chair and the rustle of paper. The big square clock on the mantle chimed, and I counted eight little bongs. That meant it was almost bedtime. Outside, the sun was still pretty high in the sky because it was summer. I wandered into the kitchen.

The kitchen faced west and Daddy had drawn the drapes against the sun, though he had left the windows open to let in fresh air. Curtains rustled in the slight breeze. The stove and the kitchen were still hot from cooking supper, though Daddy had long since smothered the flames and banked the coals. I knew better than to touch the black stove's blistering surface. The wood box was piled high with wood, sorted by hardness so you could make a fire as hot or as cool as you needed. In the summer we burned a lot of soft wood to keep the heat to a minimum, and Daddy bought from the bakery rather than bake at home.

Gremlin, I thought. *Where?*

Twin is hiding, Gremlin's voice said inside my head. *Says to come find.*

I smiled to myself and headed for the stairs. Wood creaked beneath my bare feet, and I automatically shifted to the little dance I had worked out to avoid the squeaky spots. My guess was that my twin was hiding in the basement—my twin always hid in the basement—and I didn't want creaking steps to announce that I was going upstairs instead of down.

Cold, Gremlin said, affirming my guess. *Colder.*

"Good," I said, and went into the room my twin and I shared. Our room was a big one, with a giant rag rug between our beds and windows thrown wide to let in the summer air. The sun was on the other side of the house, so the breeze was nice and cool. The air smelled green, like newly cut grass. I got a bunch of toy animals out of the closet—four teddy bears, a rag doll, and a pair of stuffed rabbits—and lined them up on the bed to play parade. I was just scolding the rag doll for pulling a rabbit's ears when the door creaked open and my twin entered. The dusty streaks on my twin's nightgown and face showed that I had been right about the basement.

"You didn't come find me," my twin said belligerently.

"Nope."

"You were supposed to come find me."

"I didn't want to. You made me take two baths because you wouldn't Trade. And you ruined my block fort."

My twin's lower lip poked forward. "Did not!"

I raised my voice. "Did too!"

"Did not!"

"Did too!"

"Did not!"

"Did—"

"That's enough of that," Daddy said from the doorway. "I think it's time for—Kate!"

We turned to look at him. "What?" we both answered.

"I was talking to Kate, not you, Quinn," Daddy said to me. "What did I tell you after your bath, Kate?"

My twin gave him a blank look. Daddy's instructions to keep clean had come to me both times. As I well knew.

"You said we were supposed to keep clean," I said gleefully. "And Quinn didn't!"

Daddy gave me The Look, and I knew had made a mistake. The Look was a strange mix of being mad and scared and unhappy. I must have broken the rules of the Name Game again.

The Name Game always puzzled me. Everyone else seemed to have one name—Daddy, Mrs. Wells—but I seemed to have two. Well, actually, Daddy had more than two names as well. People called him Lance and Mr. Radford-Michaels, while my twin and I called him Daddy. So I knew other people had more than one name just like I did. Except everyone else seemed to know which name to use. I never knew which one was right. Sometimes people called me Kate and sometimes people called me Quinn. They did the same thing to my twin. Even Daddy switched our names around a lot. There must have been rules, but I could never figure them out.

Names go with body, Gremlin put in suddenly. *Boy body named Quinn, girl body named Kate.*

I stared at my twin as comprehension dawned. By the look on my twin's face, Gremlin had spoken to both of us at the same time, and the same thoughts were crossing my twin's mind.

"Why didn't you tell us before?" my twin demanded.

Never asked.

"I told both of you," Daddy said sternly.

"Kate wasn't talking to you, Daddy," I said quickly, proud that I now knew the proper name. "He was talking to Gremlin."

"Kate," Daddy said, "is a she. And how did you know she was talking to Gremlin?" The Look had left Daddy's face, but the expression he wore now said that he didn't know whether he should laugh or be annoyed.

"Gremlin talks to both of us at the same time," I explained.

"I see." Daddy's voice was grave, which meant he had decided the whole thing was silly.

"Kate didn't keep clean," I said, getting back to the main issue. "Does she have to take a bath again?"

"I don't want to take a bath!"

"You should have thought of that before you played in the basement," Daddy sighed. "I hope this won't wipe out all the hot water—it's too warm to fire up the heater again. Come on, Kate. And then it's bedtime for both of you."

Nanobots knocked against mine—my twin wanted to Trade—but I stuck out my tongue and turned my back. Daddy dragged my twin out of the room and I sat on my bed, swinging my legs over the edge and hugging myself in glee. Not only had I tricked my twin into taking a bath, I had also learned the rules to the Name Game. Right now my name was Quinn. The next time I Traded, my name would be Kate.

No Trade? Gremlin asked. Its voice was sad inside my head. *Twin not happy.*

No Trade, I said firmly. *I had to take two baths. It's only fair my twin has to take one. And my block fort got all knocked down.*

I felt a twinge of guilt. I had used Gremlin to get back at my twin, even though it hated getting caught between us. Sometimes it was fun to tease my twin, but I didn't like hurting Gremlin. I was sorry, and didn't know how to say it. But then I realized it was all right— Gremlin usually knew what I was thinking.

A while later, my twin came back into the room, hair wet, nightgown clean. We looked at each other without speaking. My twin met my eyes, nodded, and I knew that as far as bathtime went, we were even. In that instant, we Traded. My nanobots read my brain cells, recorded the chemical sequences that make up memory, took pictures of the way my brain cells were arranged. Each nanobot picked up a piece of information, a single pixel in a hologram. Then they left. A few stayed behind to keep the lungs breathing, the heart beating, the muscles locked so the body wouldn't fall over. Nanobots flashed across the room, passing a stampede of my twin's headed in the opposite direction. My nanobots arrived in the girl body, rushed into the brain, rearranged mnemonic chemicals, moved brain cells. It didn't take long— only a few seconds. From my point of view, I was sitting on one bed one moment, and the next moment, I was sitting on the other. My hair, cut short for the summer, was still damp, and my nightgown felt fresh and clean.

Kate. My name was Kate. I looked down at my nightgown and wiggled my fingers. Kate. Their name was Kate. I giggled and glanced across the room at my twin—Quinn. My twin's fingers were wiggling too, and I knew the same thoughts were passing through my twin's mind. I looked at my twin, and we both burst out laughing.

"Hi, Quinn!" I said.

"Hi, Kate," my twin said.

We Traded.

"Hi, Kate!" I said.

"Hi, Quinn!" my twin said.

Silly twins, Gremlin commented, and that made us giggle all the harder.

We Traded again, and my name changed with perfect consistency every time. Kate. Quinn. Kate. Quinn. I knew what my names were, and the feeling made me indescribably happy.

"Hi, Kate!"

"Hi, Quinn!"

"You two go to sleep!" Daddy's voice came from downstairs. "Don't make me come up there!"

Stifling a giggle, I lay back on the bed. "Good night, Quinn," I whispered.

"Good night, Kate," whispered my twin.

We fell asleep.

"What in the world is going on here?" Daddy demanded.

My twin and I glanced up at him, puzzled and startled. The door to our shared closet was still open—the closet monster didn't live there during the day, so it was safe—and I had just pulled on a blue T-shirt. Blue was my favorite color.

"We're getting ready for school, Daddy," I said. "We're almost seven, you know. We can do it ourselves."

"Obviously you can't," Daddy replied sternly. He was wearing his yellow bathrobe, and for some reason I noticed the fine red-gold hair on his legs. It didn't really match the deep red hair on his head. "Look at what you're wearing, Quinn."

I turned and looked at my twin, who was wearing a pink dress with white flowers and black shoes. Realization dawned.

"Hey!" I said, still indignant. "That's for dress-up stuff. You'll get it dirty at school."

Daddy ignored me. "You can't wear a dress, Quinn. Dresses are for girls. You'd better put on something else if you don't want everyone to laugh at you."

I started laughing. "You forgot you're a boy! You forgot!" I laughed harder.

"It's your fault!" my twin said hotly. "I had already said I was going to wear this, but you wanted to Trade before breakfast."

Daddy gave us both The Look again. "That's enough, you two. Quinn, you'd better change quick if you don't want to be late." And he left, his slippers making shuffly noises on the wood floors of the hallway. We don't have any carpets in the house—Daddy doesn't like them. He says he doesn't want anyone sneaking up on him ever again, whatever that means.

"I don't want to change clothes now," my twin said petulantly. "Let's Trade. You're a girl, so you can wear the dress."

That sounded reasonable to me. We Traded and clumped down to the kitchen together for breakfast. The table was already set. My favorite blue milk pitcher sat in the center next to the syrup jug, and Daddy had already dished steaming oatmeal into two bowls. At the moment he was at the stove with the bread rack, and I smelled toast and coffee. As we sat down, he turned around and caught sight of my twin.

"Quinn," he said, exasperated. "Are you deaf? What did I tell you?"

By now we were both more adept at picking up cues. Even though Daddy had originally been talking to my twin upstairs, I knew that right now he was talking to me because I was in the Quinn body. Talk went to the body, not the person.

"You said boys can't wear dresses," I said. "But it's okay because we Traded. Girls can wear . . . can wear . . . " I trailed off uncertainly. There was something wrong. We had Traded, so it should be all right for me to wear—

But you're a boy now, Gremlin said.

Daddy gave me a long look, then shrugged and set the plate of toast on the table. "If you want everyone to laugh at you, it's all right with me. Just don't expect me to bring another set of clothes to school."

I knocked on my twin's nanos, asking for a Trade, and said to Gremlin, *Say that I wasn't the one who put on the wrong clothes.*

Gremlin relayed the message. I was expecting my twin to set up a fuss, but none came. We Traded, and my twin dashed upstairs to put on some different clothes. I reached for the milk jug. Out of the corner of my eye, I saw Daddy shoot The Look up the stairs, and I wondered why he looked so unhappy.

"I just don't understand it sometimes, Grace," Daddy was saying. "I'm not sure what to do." It was the day after the dress incident. Daddy and Mrs. Wells were sitting on the front porch. The leaves on the maple trees in the front yard were a brilliant scarlet and I thought they were very pretty, even though my favorite color was blue. The air was fresh and cool, and Daddy had made us put on jackets before we could play outside.

At the moment, I was hiding around the corner from my twin in yet another game of hide and seek. This time Gremlin had shut off my twin's hearing and heightened my twin's sense of smell.

"It's nothing to worry about," Mrs. Wells soothed. "Children experiment. Why, I remember when my

Sharon went around for almost a week declaring she was a boy—even insisted on standing up to go to the bathroom. We just let her have her way, and eventually she gave it up. It's just a phase."

"What about David?" Daddy asked. "Did he ever pretend he was a girl?"

"Well, let me think. It seems like he did." Mrs. Wells paused. "Oh yes—I remember now. I went in my bedroom one afternoon and found him all dolled up in my Sunday dress with makeup on his face and polish on his nails. About scared me to death. Ronald, rest his soul, all but foamed at the mouth."

I peeked around the corner in time to see Mrs. Wells lean over and pat Daddy's hand. I liked Mrs. Wells. She baked cookies almost every Saturday and called me and my twin her special taste-testers. Daddy said he was glad she had moved in across the road because he didn't know what he'd do for a babysitter otherwise. Mrs. Wells said she was glad *we* had moved in because Daddy had paid a lot of money to get a telephone permit from the government and he didn't mind if Mrs. Wells came over to use it. That, and she needed small children to make sure she hadn't lost her touch with cookies.

"Really, Lance," she said. "Children play all sorts of games. They'll sort it out for themselves."

"I hope so," Daddy said. "I can't help worrying. My parents weren't exactly . . . stable, and I went through some of my own rough times. I'm just afraid this sort of thing might be genetic and Kate and Quinn are showing symptoms of some bigger problem."

Mrs. Wells shook her head. "All parents worry about nothing. It's part of the job. You go ahead and worry if it makes you feel better, but one day you'll look back on this and wonder what in the world made you so upset."

Then I heard my twin sneaking toward me around the corner, and I dashed away, wondering what Mrs. Wells's son looked like in a dress.

❖　　　　❖　　　　❖

The next day, I decided to wear a dress because of Mrs. Wells's son. By the time recess came around, I was regretting the choice. Wearing a dress only reminds the boys that you're a girl.

I put my hands on my hips and glared down at the group of boys kneeling on the ground behind the school. About a dozen marbles were scattered in a circle they had drawn in the sand. Dennis North lined up a shot and flicked his thumb. The shooter ticked a marble, but it didn't roll outside the circle.

"No good," Kevin Sanders said as Dennis retrieved his shooter. "My turn."

Kevin flicked his thumb. The shooter connected with a pale blue marble, which shot out of the circle with satisfying speed. Kevin snatched it up.

"That was your last one, Tim," he said to Tim Pickford. "You're out."

Tim's jaw jutted forward, but he picked up his own marble bag and stalked away without a word.

"I want to play," I said, trying to kneel down in Tim's place. But the other boys—four in all—quickly spread themselves around the circle to fill the empty space.

"You can't play," Kevin said, "You're a girl."

My own jaw jutted forward. "So what?"

"We're not playing with girls today," Dennis said.

"You're just scared I'll beat the pants off you."

My statement was more than just a bluff. I had made sure to have the girl body at recess because I was better at marbles when I was Kate. Across the playground, my twin was playing kickball, something that came easier to the male body. Both of us had already learned that if we wanted to do something with small, precise movements, the Kate body was better. The Quinn body was good at games that needed strength or speed. Since my twin had wanted to play kickball at recess today, things had worked out pretty well for us. Until now, anyway.

"I'm not scared!" Dennis said hotly.

"Are too!"

"Am not!"

"Then prove it," I said sweetly. "Let me play."

"We're not playing with girls today," Kevin said again. He had freckles and bright red hair, brighter than Daddy's.

"You're chicken they'd beat you." I made clucking noises at them. "Chicken chicken chicken."

"So let her play," said Jeremy Acre. "She'll only lose. What do you think, Larry?"

Larry Friend, a blond kid with blue eyes, shrugged.

I took advantage of the situation and squatted down between Jeremy and Kevin. Jeremy gave way only grudgingly. I put six marbles in the circle and pulled out my shooter.

"Girls first," Kevin said.

I positioned my shooter, then stopped. If I was going to beat the boys, I wasn't going to give them a chance later to say I had taken advantage of the fact that I was a girl.

"We should do bubble gum," I said instead. "What do you think, Larry?"

Larry shrugged.

"Bubble gum, bubble gum in a dish," Kevin chanted, pointing to each of us in turn. "How many pieces do you wish?" His finger landed on Jeremy.

"Six," Jeremy said.

"One, two, three, four, five, six, and you are it." The finger pointed to Jeremy again, and the game began.

It didn't take long to figure out that Jeremy and Dennis were trying to beat just me. They shot only at my marbles, trying to knock them out of the circle, and ignored everyone else's. Twice I had to give up a perfect chance to knock someone's marble out so I could knock one of my own marbles further in. In a few rounds, I was down to two marbles in the circle while everyone else had three or four. I wasn't the only one who noticed.

"You and Jeremy are ganging up on Kate," Kevin said to Dennis. "That's not fair."

"It isn't against the rules," Dennis said. He had three marbles left. "I can shoot whoever I want. Kate won't win anyway."

"The bell's gonna ring soon," Jeremy pointed out. "Whoever has the least marbles in the circle is the loser when it does."

Gremlin, how much time is left? I asked.

Bell will ring in one minute, forty-two seconds. Mrs. Watson is ringing today and she has stopwatch.

I was running out of time. If I lost this game, Dennis would make sure everyone knew, and I'd never hear the end of it. I'd have to take more risks. After studying the circle carefully, I noticed that two of Dennis's marbles were touching each other. If I hit them just right from my side of the circle, I might be able to knock both of them out with one shot. The only problem was that one of Kevin's marbles was in the way—and it was Kevin's turn to shoot. I glanced at him. He met my eyes and I knew he had seen the same thing. Without a word, he lined up his shot and flicked his thumb.

"You dummy," Dennis sneered. "You hit one of your own marbles."

"It's still inside the circle," Kevin replied, calmly retrieving his shooter.

"Kate's turn," Jeremy said.

Bell will ring in twenty-one seconds, Gremlin said, and Mrs. Watson emerged from the building with a stopwatch in one hand and the shiny steel recess bell in the other.

I set my shooter, cool and dark, into the crook of my forefinger and lined up the shot.

Ten seconds, Gremlin said. *Eight. Six. Four.*

I flicked my thumb. My shooter sped into the circle and hit both of Dennis's marbles right where they touched each other. They shot apart in opposite directions and streaked over the boundary just as Mrs. Watson began ringing the bell.

"Dennis lost," Kevin announced. "He only has one marble left. Larry has four, so he wins."

"I beat you," I said to Dennis. "Told you I would."

"You didn't win the game," Dennis replied sullenly. He gathered up his marbles and joined the kids streaming toward the back doors of the school. Larry and Jeremy followed suit. I caught sight of my twin bouncing the kickball on the way in and our eyes met.

Twin wants to know how marble game went, Gremlin said.

I beat Dennis. I would've won the game, too, but he and Jeremy ganged up on me.

"That was a good shot," Kevin told me. "You should've won the game."

"Thanks," I said, feeling suddenly shy. "I know why you hit your own marble."

Kevin flushed and kicked at the ground with his toe. "Jeremy and Dennis weren't playing fair."

An awkward pause followed. "We'd better go in," I said. "We'll be late."

Kevin flashed me a quick smile. "See you at lunch recess." And he rushed away.

"Kate, who's Gremlin?" Kevin asked.

The ground rocked dizzily beneath me and cool autumn air whooshed past my ears as I pumped my legs back and forth. Kevin was in the swing next to mine, but he wasn't coordinated with me, so his words swooped between loud and soft.

Don't tell don't tell don't tell don't tell, Gremlin pleaded. Gremlin was like that—paranoid. I didn't know why. Gremlin had been around for as long as my twin and I could remember, and it didn't want anyone to know of its existence, not even Daddy.

In this way, Gremlin was like our nanos. Our nanos had always been there. We took them for granted, the way we did our fingers and toes. Daddy had nanos, too— our nanos bumped into his once in a while —so my twin and I naturally thought everyone had them. Eventually, however, we'd realized this wasn't true and had asked Daddy where nanobots come from.

Daddy said they came from him, and we weren't supposed to tell anyone about them unless we wanted the government to come to our house. The government would chase us down and make us move to another planet. We'd never see our friends again. The government might even take us away from Daddy if we told. He scared us so much that we never told anyone about the nanos or Gremlin. But Kevin had asked about it, and I had to answer.

"Gremlin's my friend," I said nonchalantly. "How did you know about it?"

"I've heard you whisper to Gremlin a couple times," Kevin said, still swooping back and forth. He needed a haircut, and his red hair kept blowing into his eyes. "What's a gremlin?"

"I don't know. Gremlin's always had that namo."

∗Shut up shut up shut up hush quiet be still silence∗

∗It's okay, Gremlin,∗ I said. ∗Daddy told us not to talk about the nanos, but he didn't say we couldn't talk about you.∗

"Is Gremlin like Bruce's Kitty?" Kevin asked.

I considered this. Bruce Richardson had an invisible cat named Kitty who followed him everywhere, or so he claimed. No one could see Kitty but him, and he talked to Kitty all the time. Some of the other kids teased him about it, but he didn't seem to care until Melvin Warnock stomped on the spot where Bruce said Kitty was standing. Bruce freaked out right in the middle of class and his mom had to come and get him. The next day Bruce was back. He and his mom had taken Kitty to the vet and she was fine, but Bruce wasn't supposed to take Kitty to school anymore.

"They're sort of the same," I said. Swoop, swoop. "But Gremlin is only around when my twin and I are near each other."

"How near?" Kevin said.

"I don't know. The length of the playground or so."

"How come?"

Stop quiet shush no more stop

"Because." Gremlin's fear was growing and I decided to change the subject. "How come you don't hate girls?"

Kevin paused. "I don't know. I think it's dumb. And you're pretty good at marbles." Swoop, swoop. Kevin had green eyes, like a cat's. I decided Kevin's eyes were pretty and that I liked him. I wondered what it would be like to live in his house. Kevin would have a nice house because Kevin was so nice. He probably even had a dad *and* a mom.

"What's your mom like?" I asked him suddenly.

"My mom? She's okay, I guess." He grinned at me. "For a girl."

I stuck my tongue out at him.

"What's your mom like?" Kevin said. Swoop, swoop.

"I don't have a mom."

"That's dumb," Kevin snorted. "Everyone has a mom."

I slammed my feet on the ground and stopped the swing so fast I almost fell over. "Well, *I* don't," I yelled at him. "And I think *you're* dumb!"

I stormed away, trying to stay mad at Kevin so the tears wouldn't slide down my face.

CHAPTER FIVE

ME

When we got home from school that evening—my twin and I had Traded, so I was in the Quinn body—Daddy was nowhere in sight, and I was still upset. The kitchen was empty except for three cloth-covered lumps on the table. The smell of fresh bread lay deliciously in the air.

Gremlin, where's Daddy? I asked.

Bedroom.

My twin and I exchanged a look and headed upstairs. Daddy had his head in the closet in his room, so he didn't see us. All his windows were open and it was a little chilly. Daddy has a very simple room—a double bed (which we were never, ever allowed to jump on, especially since the time we broke it) and a dresser and a small closet with a mirror on the door. That was it. He didn't even have any throw rugs on the floor like we did in our room. The only interesting thing in his room is the woodcarving collection, which takes up a big set of shelves on one whole wall. Lions and trees and children and lizzie-bats and even giant bugs, all carved from wood. We aren't supposed to touch those, either—Daddy carves other toys for us—but sometimes I would sneak in to feel them. They were always silky smooth, and I liked the way they felt in my fingers. Daddy gives a lot of his carvings away. People try to give him money, but he always turns it down.

"It's not any fun to carve for money," he always says.

One time a priest with a strange white collar came to

47

the house and asked Daddy if he would carve a life-size crucifix for the church, and Daddy did it, even though we don't go there.

There is one other interesting thing in Daddy's room. It's a picture of him with a woman. They're standing on a beach, holding hands and smiling at the camera. The woman has dark skin, darker than ours, and brown eyes. She's wearing a bathing suit and a wraparound skirt, and her smile is very pretty. She's my mom, but I didn't remember her. I only remembered the picture. I stood in the doorway looking at it.

"That's dumb. Everyone has a mom."

"Daddy?" I said.

He turned from the closet and smiled when he saw us. "You're home!" he said, and tried to sweep us into a hug.

I pushed him away, and so did my twin. Daddy looked hurt, but I didn't care.

"Daddy, where's our mom?" I asked.

He sat down on the bed looking surprised. "I've told you before, honey—your mother lives on Earth."

"Everyone at school has a mom except us," my twin said. "Why doesn't ours ever come and see us?"

"She can't," Daddy said gently. His green eyes looked very sad. "I wish she could, but she can't."

"Why did she leave?" I asked, and found my throat was thick. A question formed in my head. I felt scared and I felt like I was going to cry, but I still had to ask it. "Doesn't our mom love us?"

∗I love you both!∗ Gremlin said. I couldn't answer.

Daddy grabbed us both and hugged us tight. "She loves you very much. But she can't live with us."

"Why not?" my twin demanded. "Is she sick?"

"In a way."

"Can't she come to visit?" I said.

Daddy shook his head. "I'm afraid not, Quinn. I wish she could, but she can't. You can write her a letter if you want."

"I don't want to write her a letter. I want to see her. Why won't she come see us?" I was almost ready to cry. Every day Kevin went home to both a mother and a father. So did all my other friends. Everyone but us. I glanced at my twin. My twin's eyes were bright and I knew in a minute we'd both be crying. Then I noticed Daddy's worn carryall lying open on the bed. Clothes were packed into the bottom.

"You're going away?" I said, rubbing at my eyes.

Daddy nodded slowly. "I have to. I'm sorry, honey, but there's a problem on another planet and I have to go fix it. Mrs. Wells will be here soon."

My stomach twisted. He was leaving? I didn't even have to glance at my twin.

"You can't go!" we cried together.

"I have to. I won't be gone long."

"What if you don't come back?" we asked, still in unison. Tears leaked from our eyes.

He ruffled our hair. "I'll come back. You don't have to worry about that."

"You'll take Gremlin!" We were both crying by now, hot tears running down our faces. Some ran into my mouth and I tasted salt. My heart beat fast and I was scared. I hated it when Daddy left and I hated the bad men who always came to take him away.

Gremlin, we said together. *Don't you go, too.*
Sorry. Have to. Business.

Daddy sighed. "Kids, we've been over this before—Gremlin is imaginary. I can't take an imaginary friend anywhere." He stroked our hair again and hugged us close. He smelled like bread. "I'll be back soon. I promise."

"You always say that," we pointed out, though my twin was a split second behind me. My nose was beginning to run.

Daddy looked down at both of us. "How do you do that?"

"Do what?" "Do what?"

"Repeat each other like that."

"I dunno," my twin sniffed. I remained silent.

"Look, guys," Daddy said. "I do have to go. A lot of people are counting on me. But you don't have to worry—I'll be back tomorrow night. Wednesday at the latest, all right?"

"Will you bring a surprise?" my twin asked hopefully.

"Yeah!" I put in. If Daddy was going to leave, we could at least cash in. "A surprise!"

Daddy raised his hands in surrender. "We'll see." That meant *yes*. I felt a little better.

The doorbell rang. "That's probably Mrs. Wells," Daddy said. "Why don't you go down and let her in while I finish packing? My ride should be here in a minute."

Daddy wasn't back the next day. Kevin found my twin at school and said he was sorry about what he said on the swings. My twin just nodded—our standard response when someone gets us mixed up—and went back to jumping rope. To make up for it, I Traded after lunch and played on the swings with Kevin during lunch recess, but I was thinking about Daddy.

By Wednesday afternoon, he still hadn't come home. My twin and I were getting scared. Mrs. Wells made supper, and we swallowed it without tasting it. She tried to talk to us, but we couldn't make ourselves say more than a few words at a time.

Afterward my twin and I wandered around the house and yard, hand in hand. We walked without speaking. The house seemed big and echoing without Daddy and Gremlin. We couldn't even play real hide and seek.

We sat outside on the porch in the chilly dusk to watch for Daddy until it was too dark to see and Mrs. Wells made us come inside. The evening dragged on and on. My twin and I jumped and looked at the door every time we heard a noise, but there was no Daddy. Finally, Mrs. Wells announced it was bedtime.

I couldn't sleep. I lay awake in the dark, scared something had gone wrong. My stomach twisted until it hurt and a hard lump sat in my throat. What if we never saw Daddy again? What would happen to us? Would Mrs. Wells adopt us? Would we move in with her or would she move in with us? Would I keep a picture of us and Daddy on the dresser like he kept one of him and our mom? Who would read stories or bake the special bread at Christmas? Who would untie our shoes when the laces got all tangled like noodles? Who would give us horseback rides?

Moonlight spilled silver into the room, making the toys scattered over the floor look like little white statues. Outside, a breeze waved tree branches and created weird shadows. The house creaked, and I thought about ghosts in the attic. My bed was warm and snug, but I shivered. In the next bed over, I could sense my twin was lying awake, too, but I didn't say anything because I didn't want to start crying. I lay there and stared at the white square of moonlight on the floor for a long time, swallowing tears and trying not to sniffle.

I must have fallen asleep because the next thing I knew the moonlight was gone and the room was dark. Voices floated up from downstairs. My heart jumped and I was wide awake.

Gremlin? I asked.

Here! Here! the wonderful, familiar voice said. *Safe at home!*

I hugged myself with glee.

My twin sat up in bed. "Gremlin?"

"Daddy's downstairs with Mrs. Wells," I whispered. "Come on!"

It's past our bedtime, my twin answered through Gremlin. *We'll get in trouble.*

No we won't, I said stoutly. *Let's go.*

We padded quickly to the door. The boards were cool on my bare feet as we slipped into the hall. It felt like we were sneaking downstairs on Christmas morning. My twin walked over a part of the floor that creaked.

Shhhh! I admonished.

Why? I thought you said we wouldn't get in trouble.

I ignored that. *Gremlin, when did Daddy get home?*

Ten minutes, thirteen seconds ago.

You're late, my twin accused. *You were supposed to be back yesterday.*

Sorry. No way to avoid. Hive had taken over entire asteroid. Hard to assimilate.

We crouched on the landing at the top of the stairs. Warm yellow candlelight shone in the dining room below.

"It was a hard one, Grace," Daddy was saying. "The hive was absolutely enormous."

"Any deaths?"

Daddy gave a long sigh. "Fifteen people got blown out an air lock. The hive locked eight more in the research labs and flooded the place with fluorine gas. I found the bodies. It was horrible."

"I'm glad I live on Felicity. No nanobot hives here."

Daddy didn't answer.

"How about some tea?" Mrs. Wells asked. "Water's still hot."

"No thanks, Grace. I just want to go to bed. Thanks again for staying with the kids. Are you sure you won't take—"

"Let's not get into that again. The children really missed you. You should have seen them wandering around the house like lost little mice. Why don't you wake them up and say hello?"

"Let them have their sleep. They'll need it if they were worried about—"

"Daddy!" my twin shouted, and rushed down the steps. I leaped up and followed. We flung ourselves across the kitchen into his arms. He hugged us close, then put one of us on each knee. We were both a little big for that, but we—and he—didn't mind.

"Gremlin told us you were home," I said.

Daddy raised red eyebrows. "He did, did he?"

"Gremlin's an it," my twin corrected. "It said it helped you with the hive on the asteroid."

Daddy shot Mrs. Wells a look that adults always use just before they play along with something their kids are doing. She gave him a small smile.

"Gremlin was a big help," he said solemnly. "I couldn't have done it without him—it."

"Where's our surprise?" my twin asked.

"What surprise?"

"Daddy!" I tried to hit him on the shoulder, and he grabbed my wrist almost absently.

"We don't hit," he murmured, and released me.

"You promised we'd get a surprise," my twin said.

His face was completely innocent. "I said we'd see. I was awfully busy, you know."

Check bag on floor behind chair, Gremlin said.

"Then what's that?" I asked, gleefully pointing to the shopping bag in question.

He turned to look. "That? Why it's for Mrs. Wells, of course. To thank her for taking care of you."

Mrs. Wells tried to hide a smile.

"It is not." My twin jumped down and brought the gray canvas bag over. Inside were two identical, brightly colored boxes made of some kind of flimsy-looking material that reminded me of really heavy paper.

"It's called KidClay," Daddy said as we each took a box. "It's specially made to be easy to work and it'll never dry out unless you put it in the oven."

My twin and I were already opening the boxes and digging in. The KidClay was strange, soft and crunchy at the same time. On the desk in his office, Daddy has a big magnet with a bunch of metal chips on it. The magnet holds the chips in place while you sculpt them. The KidClay kind of felt like the metal chips, only the chips were really, really tiny. I liked it. It squished dryly between my fingers. I looked at my twin and grinned.

My twin grinned back, obviously liking KidClay as much as I did.

"What do you say when someone gives you a present?" Mrs. Wells prompted.

"Thank you," we both said, and promptly turned back to the KidClay. I sat on the floor and started sculpting a dog. My twin seemed content to knead and pull at the stuff like a loaf of bread dough, though it wasn't sticky.

"All right, all right," Daddy said. "It's almost one in the morning. You two need to go back to bed. You can play with this in the morning."

We protested, of course, but in the end Daddy tucked us back into bed. I lay awake for a moment after he left. The breeze outside made a friendly noise in the branches, shadows scampered like baby rabbits across the floor, and the house made a comforting creaking noise. Daddy was home, safe and sound.

I fell asleep.

"Grandma!" I dropped my backpack on the floor next to the front door and rushed into the living room. My twin followed, and in a second Grandma had swept us both into her arms. She smelled like wildflower perfume. Daddy grinned.

"I told you there'd be a surprise for you when you got home from school today," he said.

Grandma gave each of us a big kiss and let us go. She was Daddy's mother, but he didn't look much like her. Grandma was a lot shorter, for one thing, and her hair was reddish blond, not red. She and Daddy did have the same shade of green eyes. Grandma was thin, and her face wasn't wrinkled at all. Daddy said this was because on other planets, doctors could change the way people looked. It was called bodysculpt, and Grandma was rich enough to afford it. Grandma, I knew, owned the phone company, but it was more than just telephones. She had started the company that let people and computers talk from planet to planet, and it had made her really rich.

"Did you bring us a present?" my twin asked.

"Hey!" Dad said. "That's not a nice thing to say. Aren't you glad to see your grandma?"

"We'll see, Kate," Grandma answered with a wink. That meant *yes*. "Why don't you two help me bring my things up to the guestroom?"

I grabbed the biggest suitcase and found I could barely budge it. *Gremlin,* I said, *make me strong.*

Working, Gremlin said. *Boosting oxygen efficiency and ATP production. Increasing muscle-fiber operation ratio.*

I lifted again and this time the suitcase came up, though I still had to use both hands. My twin had already taken the second one.

Don't overdo, Gremlin warned. *Increase only temporary. Overwork will damage muscle tissue.*

"Come on," I said to my twin. "We better hurry."

We bundled the suitcases upstairs. Grandma followed with the last, smallest, bag. "You two are so strong," she said. Her English sounded funny, but Daddy said it was because she lived in London. "Have you been reading *Pippi Longstocking!*"

"Pippi who?" I asked, already panting. I figured there must be some pretty amazing presents in a suitcase that heavy.

"You've never read about Pippi?" Grandma said. "Well, next time I come, I'll have to remedy that."

My twin and I dropped the suitcases on the guest-room floor. Daddy had already opened the window to air it out and there were fresh sheets on the bed. Grandma sat down on it and we joined her.

"Now tell me how my twins have been," she said. "What have you been up to lately?"

We told her about school, and how Daddy wouldn't let us have a kitten, and how my twin had almost broken an arm while climbing trees. Grandma nodded and listened.

"I wish you could come more often," my twin said wistfully.

She hugged us both. "So do I, sweeties. But running my company takes up so much time, and it isn't easy to get here."

"Why can't you call us?" I asked. "We have a phone and you own the phone company."

"Your phone isn't hooked up to my company," Grandma said. "Now then, if you'll bring that suitcase over here, I think we'll answer Kate's question about presents."

Grandma stayed for a week. Daddy let us stay home from school for part of it, and all four of us went to the park and the zoo and a baseball game. Daddy talked about how baseball games on Earth were played in huge buildings called stadiums instead of little parks and you had to sit so far away, you couldn't see the players' faces. I thought that would be awful boring.

"And now," Grandma said when the game ended, "it's time to go shopping."

"I'll meet you back home," Daddy said quickly, and left. My twin and I rolled our eyes at each other, but didn't say anything. Grandma loved going shopping with "just my twins." We both hated it, but put up with it because Daddy said it would hurt her feelings if we didn't. I noticed, though, that Daddy always disappeared when Grandma mentioned shopping. I decided it must nice to be an adult and never have to do anything you didn't like.

My twin and I suffered through clothing stores where Grandma bought us outfits that we pretended to like. Then it was off to the bookstore, which was a little more interesting. Grandma was really put out when the owner said he didn't have any Pippi Longstocking books.

Finally, Grandma announced she was all shopped out, and we went to the drugstore for sodas. My twin and I brightened at this. Ice cream was always fun. Even Grandma seemed excited, more excited than most adults get about ice cream.

"You can't get sodas where I live," she said, "unless you make them at home. And that's just not as much fun."

I had to agree. Ice cream is much more fun in a drugstore than anywhere else.

I liked Allbee's Drugstore. It was always clean and the floor was so shiny you could see your reflection in it. We took our sodas to one of the round tables in the corner. It was the middle of the day, so we had the place to ourselves.

"I'm glad you're visiting, Grandma," I said, slurping up a chocolate mouthful. "Can we come visit you next time?"

Grandma shook her head. "You have to stay here, Quinn. Maybe when you're older you can come visit me."

"You said that last time," my twin accused. "When will we be old enough?"

"I don't know, honey," Grandma said.

"Did you know our mom?" I asked abruptly.

Grandma jumped a little. "Your mother?"

"Yeah," my twin said. "Did you ever meet her?"

"Of course," Grandma said. "She used to work for me."

My twin's eyes went wide. "She did? Does she work for you now?"

"No. She works for a university now—a school. She teaches people about birds."

"Her name is Delia," I said.

My twin punched me on the arm. "She knows that, stupid."

"That'll be enough of that, now," Grandma said sharply in her funny accent.

"Daddy doesn't like to talk about our mom," I told her. "Do you know why?"

Grandma didn't answer for a while. Then she said, "I think because it makes him sad. Finish your soda, sweetie. We need to go soon."

That evening Daddy and Grandma were talking in the living room. Their voices were low and hard to hear. My twin was outside climbing more trees and I was playing house with our stuffed animals upstairs. It was their bedtime, and Rasputin, the kitten, didn't want to go.

"That'll be enough of that, now," I scolded her. "You go to bed right now."

". . . told them . . . their mother?" I heard Grandma say downstairs. At the word *mother*, I froze and listened.

"I . . . get into that . . . them, Mom," Daddy's voice said.

Then Grandma said something I couldn't make out.

"Because . . . feel guilty . . . you feel if you had . . . your own mother?"

"So . . . them ignorant?"

"Ignorance . . . than guilt. Once . . . old enough, they can . . . "

I crept across the hardwood floor, avoiding the squeaky spots, and eased the door open so I could hear better.

"Now, then. How about some tea?" Daddy said. "There's a special blend I like you can only get on Felicity."

They didn't mention our mom again, though I sat listening in the hallway for over an hour.

Grandma left the next day with a lot of hugs and kisses and promises to come back as soon as she could. I wanted to ask more questions about our mom, but I didn't want to make Daddy sad, so I only waved good-bye and wondered who would feel guilty about my mom.

You've had it for two whole days. It's my turn!

I don't want the girl body right now. You can wait. Why don't you sculpt some more?

I don't want to sculpt. Trade me!

No.

Gremlin! Make my twin Trade!

Not involved.

I clenched my teeth. Gremlin never took sides when

my twin and I had a fight, even when my twin was obviously wrong. I guess that was good in a way—it'd be hard on Gremlin if we thought it liked one of us better—but right now it just made me madder. I wanted to go outside and run and climb trees and jump the brooks and swing on the rope we had set up in the back woods, and the male body was better at that kind of thing. My twin, however, wouldn't Trade and just stared at me across the living room floor. Dad was in the kitchen, cutting up stew meat for supper, unaware of our wordless fight. We had gotten better at using "quiet" speech and didn't even have to relay our words through Gremlin anymore.

Outside, the sun had turned autumn leaves blue and red and gold. The air was crisp as an apple. I wanted to go outside and smell the leaves, run through the woods, feel my body move. There was no reason I couldn't do that as a girl, but now it was a matter of principle.

TRADE!

No.

I sent a whole bunch of nanos across the living room floor. They crawled over my twin's skin, trying to push and shove their way into the male body. My twin's nanos, however, simply ganged up two or three on mine and threw them off. My nanos hit the floor like invisible raindrops, bouncing and skittering, unhurt by the fall. I sent more nanos and more and more, but my twin had as many as I did, and when my nanobots were busy fighting, they couldn't set up a Trade.

Please stop arguing please stop Gremlin said, but we both ignored it. My twin and I stared stubbornly at each other, the wooden floor a gulf between us. A thousand of my nanos grabbed a thousand of my twin's and tried to change them into mine. But the moment I started that, my twin answered with a counter-takeover. As fast as I grabbed one of my twin's nanos, my twin grabbed one of mine. A microscopic battleground sprouted on the wood floor. My twin and I fought faster and faster while Gremlin wrung its hands in our heads, asking us to stop. After a while, I started to get tired of concentrating, but I couldn't slow down—if I stopped taking over my twin's nanos, my twin would end up with more than I had, and that wasn't right either. I was starting to sweat, and I spared a moment to look at my twin instead of our nanos and noticed my twin's face was flushed. My twin was tired, too! If I could just hold on or get more nanos from somewhere, I could win!

Dad appeared in the living room door, wiping raw fat from his hands. "Do you kids want cake or pie for dessert tonight?" he asked.

Dad. He had nanos. Maybe I could borrow some from him. That would tip the fight in my favor. Quickly, before I could think about it further, some of my nanos flashed across the floor toward Dad. I found a whole bunch of them clinging to his skin and clothes, more than I ever imagined. He had so many, I couldn't even count them. I had touched Dad's nanos, of course, but I had never really paid attention to how many he had.

I touched one and asked it to join my side. It did. It was so easy, I couldn't believe I'd never thought of it before. I touched another and another and another, grabbing them like jelly beans from a candy jar. In less time than it takes to blink, I had over two million of them. I sent them and the rest of my body's nanos streaking across the floor to my twin's body to join the fight.

I heard Dad say, "What the hell?" but I didn't pay attention. The reinforcements were all I needed. My twin put up a fight, but my nanos pushed my twin's nanos out of the male body and took over the ones that remained. Through Gremlin, I sent my twin's nanos a picture of my twin's brain, and my own nanos rewrote the male body's brain for myself. The female body's eyes stayed blank for a tiny moment, then they blinked and my twin was looking furiously back at me. Since I had ejected my twin from the male body, there was no choice but to take the female one. I grinned a victory grin.

"Gotcha!" I said.

"You . . . you . . . " my twin spluttered. "How did—"

A tidal wave of nanos shut both of us up. Foreign nanobots poured over and into my body by millions and billions, three and four and five to each one of mine. Their pinchers and legs clamped down, immobilizing my nanos by sheer force of numbers. I screamed and fought back, but there were simply too many. I felt my hands brushing my arms and legs, uselessly trying to push the invaders away. I screamed again, and this time I heard the same scream from my twin.

Gremlin! we cried. *Help us!*

Trying. Can't. Too many.

Then the nanos that made the sounds for Gremlin's voice in my head stopped working, and I couldn't hear it anymore.

"What the *fuck* is going on?" Dad bellowed.

My mouth snapped shut. My twin and I stared wide-eyed up at Dad. His face was red and twisted like a demon's, and his voice was loud enough to make my bones rattle. My mouth fell open. We had never heard him use that word before.

Dad crossed the room in two steps and grabbed both of us by the arm. He almost threw us to the couch. My heart beat so hard I thought it might jump out of my chest. Pangs of raw fear twisted in my stomach. I flashed a glance at my twin, who looked as scared as I felt. We had never seen Dad like this. Instantly the anger between us vanished. We would need perfect teamwork to get through this, whatever it was.

Dad kicked an ottoman in front of the couch and sat down on it. We shrank back into the couch cushions. The strange nanos—Dad's—were still clamped on ours. They hung suspended in our cells, clung motionless to our skin, coasted silently through our blood vessels. It felt like I was chained down, unable to run.

"I asked you both a question," Dad said in a quiet, quiet voice. "What is going on here?"

I glanced at my twin and we decided I would speak. We didn't need nanos to communicate about *everything*.

"I just wanted to Trade," I said in a small voice. "And Kate—I mean Quinn—" I paused uncertainly. Right now I was Quinn, but I was Kate when I had forced the Trade. Which names should I use? I gave up. "My twin didn't want to Trade. It had been two whole days! And I wanted the Quinn body."

Dad's eyebrows came down hard over flat eyes. "I'm not in the mood for the games you and your sister play. I want to know who stole my nanobots and what happened to them."

"I took them," I said meekly. "I'm sorry. I just want to Trade."

"What is this 'Trade' thing?" Dad snapped. "I'm tired of hearing about Trading. You're a boy, Quinn, and you always will be. Your sister will always be a girl. There is no Trading. The sooner you learn that, the better."

I wondered if Dad meant that my twin and I would never be able to Trade again, that he was going to stop us from doing it any more. I burst into tears at the same moment my twin did.

Dad rubbed his forehead and let out a deep breath. "Listen, kids. We've got to hash this out, and no one's nanos are moving until we do. I want to hear from you first, Quinn. What happened?"

"My twin—" I began.

Dad held up a hand. "Hold it. That's something else I want to know. Why do you call Kate your twin? Why don't you use her name?"

I glanced at my twin, confused. "Because I don't always know which name. I mean, right now my name is Quinn, but when it all started, my name was Kate."

Now Dad looked confused. "Does this have anything to do with Trading?" he asked.

I nodded, though Dad didn't look any less puzzled.

"Keep going," he said. "From the beginning."

"My twin had the Quinn body for two whole days," I said, allowing some indignation to creep into my voice. "It's been my turn for a long time. We usually Trade two or three times a day, and I wanted to go tree climbing, but I do that better when I'm a boy, but my twin wouldn't Trade. It isn't fair."

Dad looked like he wanted to say something, but he clamped his lips shut and I rushed on.

"I tried to *make* my twin Trade, but it didn't work because we have the same amount of nanobots, but then you walked into the room and I thought I'd borrow some of yours so I could force my twin to Trade and it worked but I didn't know you'd get so mad and I'm sorry, Dad."

"Don't stop us from Trading," my twin spoke up earnestly. "I'll Trade whenever my twin wants. We won't fight about it again, ever. We *promise*."

Dad gave us a long look. His nanos didn't budge and my body felt heavy without my nanos running through it. I held my breath.

"You both really believe in this Trading, don't you?" he said finally.

"It's real," we both said at the same time.

"How does it work, then?"

"It's easy," we both said. "We just—"

"Hold it." Dad held up a hand. "Kate, you explain."

"We just Trade bodies. My nanobots take me over to the other body and my twin's nanobots bring my twin over to this one. That's all." My twin shrugged and looked at me. "I was going to Trade anyway, you know. I don't want to be a boy all the time. I just wanted to see what it was like to stay in the same body for a while. Besides, you've been playing with Kevin a lot lately and you only do that when you're Kate. I didn't think you'd care."

"I don't want to be Kate *all* the—"

"All right, all right," Dad broke in. He rubbed his forehead again, and I wondered if he was getting a headache.

"So you're saying you can both switch bodies whenever you want?"

We nodded in perfect unison.

Dad folded his arms. I could see the pale, red-gold hairs on his skin. The tension in his arm muscles was almost making them stand up. "Then do it. I'll watch."

"We can't Trade now," I said. "Our nanobots can't move."

Instantly Dad's nanos let go. We sighed with relief and our bodies felt light as a sunbeam.

"Let's see it," Dad said. His voice had no expression to it, as if it were made out of wood. "Go."

You have to promise to give me the male body back when we're done, I told my twin now that our nanos were free and we could speak privately again.

I will. I don't want to be a boy right now anyway. Dad doesn't yell at the Kate body as much as the Quinn body.

This was true, and for a moment I wondered if I might be better off keeping the Kate body for a while longer after all. But that would only make my twin mad, and I had already gone through all this trouble to be a boy for a few hours. We Traded.

As my nanos rushed from one body to another, I sensed billions of Dad's nanobots hanging motionless like watchdogs in both our bodies. When I reached the Kate body and looked at Dad, his face had gone pale and his arms were hanging loose at his sides.

"Holy mother of God," he whispered. "Do that again."

We did. Dad weaved on the ottoman and I thought he was going to fall off it.

"Are you all right, Dad?" asked my twin.

"How long have you been able to do that?" he said hoarsely.

"We've always been able to do it," I told him. "Ever since we were little."

"Fuck a duck." That was twice in one day.

"That's a bad word," my twin—Kate—said.

"Which one is your real body?" Dad said, ignoring my twin's comment.

We looked at each other. "Real body?" we asked.

"Which body is the one you started with?" he said. "Which one were you each born in?"

Silence. Then my twin said, "We never thought about it."

Dad stood up and walked toward the kitchen door. He grabbed the jamb with both hands and leaned into the kitchen with his back to us. I suddenly wondered if he had left the stew meat on the counter. He had always warned both of us not to do that because it could spoil.

What do we do now? my twin asked.

Wait, I guess. Do you think he's mad? Gremlin, what about you?

But Gremlin remained silent. Even though it went with Dad on trips, Dad made Gremlin nervous, and it apparently didn't want to talk to us right when Dad was around. Maybe it was afraid Dad's nanos would overhear.

"I don't know what to do here, kids," Dad said to the kitchen. "It explains a lot, that's for sure. But I don't know if this is healthy for both of you. People are supposed to have one body, one gender identity. That's very important." He turned around and came back to sit on the ottoman again. He looked very tired. "I didn't mean to do this to you. It's my fault."

"What's your fault?" I asked. "You didn't do anything."

"Your nanobots came from me," Dad explained. "I accidentally put them inside you before you were even born. When your mother and I . . . " He paused and turned red. "When your mother and I made you, some of my nanobots got inside you both. Maybe I should have taken them out, but I didn't. I thought they'd help you. And they have. You both never get sick, you heal fast, you're stronger than most kids your age. But I never thought something like this could happen. It's wrong, a travesty. No wonder you both get confused so much."

"What's a travesty?" my twin wanted to know.

"Never mind." He ran his hand through his hair and it fell right back into place. Dad's hair always did that, and it always fascinated me. "Maybe I should just take the nanos out, but I'm not sure what that would do to you."

We'd never be able to Trade, said my twin in horror at the exact moment the thought crossed my own mind.

And what about Gremlin? I cried back. *Gremlin would die without the nanos.*

no no no no no no no no Gremlin howled, and it did something it had never done before. Gremlin shares nanos between me and my twin—a part of Gremlin lives in almost every nano we own—and it snatched up billions of our nanobots, taking them completely under its control.

While my twin and I stared through our remaining nanos, Gremlin hurled itself straight at Dad. It grabbed at Dad's nanobots and started eating them as I had done, taking them over. But this didn't last long. I think I was able to steal nanos from Dad because I had caught him by surprise. Gremlin also caught Dad by surprise, but this time Dad recovered much faster. He almost instantly fought back. Dad's nanobots grabbed Gremlin's—ours!—and started making them his own. The war lashed between us like an invisible whirlwind. Gremlin was a lot better at controlling nanobots than my twin and I, maybe because Gremlin is made of them, but Dad had been working with nanobots all his life and had a lot more experience.

Dad was winning. Sweat broke out on his forehead, but he was winning. Dad ate Gremlin's nanos by the thousands, and Gremlin couldn't stop him. I could feel Gremlin shrinking, taking my nanobots—and me?—with them. Gremlin howled in my head again, this time in fear. It tried to retreat back to the two of us, hide inside our bodies, but Dad's nanos were already waiting for it. Thousands, millions of nanos, pieces of me and my twin and Gremlin, vanished every fraction of a second. Gremlin's cries were growing weaker and I could barely feel it in my head anymore. My twin and I started to open our mouths to scream at Dad to stop, to leave Gremlin alone, but we instantly knew that in the time it took for our mouths to form the words and for Dad's brain to understand them, Gremlin would be gone forever.

DAD! we shrieked at him. *You're killing us!*

Twenty million more nanos vanished into my father. Gremlin whimpered. Then the attack ended. Dad's nanos froze in place. The ones that had attached themselves to ours let go. I realized my clothes were soaked with sweat and I was shaking like a tuning fork. I couldn't tell whether it was because I was scared or tired or angry or all three. My twin and I slumped sideways on the couch, leaning on each other. I could feel the fear and tension in my twin's muscles, but the touch made us feel a little better. Gremlin fled to a tiny corner of our minds, crying and mewling to itself. I could feel the nanos in my body scraping bone tissue and swiping carbon before we could breathe it out. They would combine these materials with others to rebuild the nanos we had lost, though replacing them all would take a while.

"Sweetheart?" Dad asked. "Are you all right?"

We just looked at him, too tired to speak. Dad put a cool hand on each of our foreheads. He was shaking.

"Something attacked me." He sat down on the ottoman again. "Was that Gremlin?"

We managed to nod.

"Gremlin," he said, "is a nanobot hive. Do you know what that is?"

"No," we said softly.

"Sometimes, when enough nanobots work together, they form a brain, with each nano acting like a single brain cell. Do you know what a brain cell is?" Dad's voice was tired and concerned at the same time.

"We learned about cells in school," I said, also tired.

Dad nodded. "All right, then. Gremlin is a nanobot hive made up of the nanobots in your bodies. I didn't know it really existed—I thought Gremlin was an invisible friend."

"Like Bruce's Kitty," my twin supplied. "But Gremlin is real."

"I know," Dad said. "Listen, I know you're attached to Gremlin, but nanobot hives are dangerous. That's what I do when I go away—fight nanobot hives that have gone out of control and hurt people."

"Gremlin would never hurt us," my twin protested. "Gremlin loves us. And we love Gremlin. Don't take it away, Dad! You can't!"

Dad ran his hand through his hair again. "It's Robin all over again," he muttered.

"Who's Robin?" I asked.

"My imaginary friend when I was . . . when I was younger," he said. He stared at the wall above our heads for a long moment. My twin and I just watched him, scared for Gremlin but too tired to talk anymore. I think I nodded off for a moment because I jumped when Dad spoke again.

"Here's what I think we need to do," he said. "You'll have to let me send my nanos into your brains. I want to have a look around."

"Look for what?" my twin said.

"I want to make sure that . . . that there's only the two of you in there. And Gremlin. No one else."

"Who else would be in our brain?" I wanted to know, curious in spite of myself.

Dad looked away again. "You'd be surprised," he said softly. Then he turned back to us. "I want you to hold still, now. You won't feel anything."

Dad's eyes took on a strange look, as if they were made out of green glass, and I knew he wasn't seeing us. There were already millions and millions of Dad's nanobots inside us from the war with Gremlin, but now even more crawled over, in, and through us. My own nanos could sense them. It was an odd feeling, like someone was sticking a finger down my throat and into my stomach. I was tense and shaky. I wanted to throw Dad's nanos out, force them to stop invading me. Gremlin didn't like it either.

no no no no no no it cried.

Dad—

"It's all right, honey," Dad said, and I didn't know whether he was talking to me or my twin, just as I didn't know which of us had spoken. "Take a deep breath and you'll be fine. This won't take long."

My blood swept the foreign nanos into my brain. They spread out in all directions, a team of workers getting off the morning train. They probed and tested. I couldn't feel it really, but I knew they were there and my nanos told me what they were doing. I clenched a fist and wanted to hit someone. I wanted to hit Dad.

"Encephalic chemistry normal," Dad muttered to himself. His voice was cold and frozen. "Neurological structure normal. Cortical neurochemical barriers normal. No compartmentalization. No chemical signs of dissociation, No signs of damage."

Abruptly, Dad's nanos fled. They rushed out my nose, ears, and eyes, and I felt like I was going to throw up. After a moment, my own nanos figured out what was wrong and changed my brain so I didn't feel sick anymore. Dad blinked and his eyes didn't look like glass anymore, but he still looked cold and frozen and uncaring. I had never seen him like that before, and it was frightening.

"You both seem to be all right," he said. "Physically, anyway." He hunched forward, leaning toward us on the ottoman. "I need to tell you kids something. All three of you."

His tone was icy and absolutely serious. My twin and I held our breaths. Instinctively we knew this would be nothing we could whine or plead our way out of.

"You must never, *ever* try to steal nanobots again. Your nanobots are for your bodies and *nothing else*. If I catch you doing it, I'll take all your nanobots away and Gremlin will disappear forever."

no no no no no no no no no

We both gasped. I tried not to cry but a tear escaped the corner of my eye.

"Can Gremlin hear this?" Dad continued.

Listening. Gremlin said in a trembling voice.

"Gremlin can hear you," we said together in cracked voices. What if Dad decided to kill Gremlin anyway?

"Gremlin, if you *ever* do anything to either of my children without their express permission, I will destroy you without a second thought. The same goes if you touch one of my own nanos. There will be no warnings, no second chances. You will just vanish. Is that clear?"

Clear.

"Gremlin understands," we said.

Dad sighed and his face softened a little. "Good."

"Are you mad at us, Dad?" I asked.

"No, honey. None of this is your fault." Dad looked toward the window at the colorful trees outside. "I just wish your mother were . . . "

He trailed off without finishing. I wanted to ask what he wished about our mom, but I didn't think it would be a good idea.

"I'm hungry," my twin complained. And now that the sick feeling was gone, I realized I was hungry, too. Not only was it close to suppertime, our nanos were taking parts of our bodies to create replacements, and that always meant we needed food.

"The stew!" Dad said, and he abruptly looked like himself again. "I completely forgot. We'll talk more about this later. I need time to think anyway." And he left for the kitchen. A moment later I heard the sound of a knife scraping a cutting board. We just sat on the couch.

He doesn't seem to be mad, my twin said.

He said he wasn't, I agreed, *but he's upset. He doesn't like us Trading and he doesn't like Gremlin.*

fear fear fear hide hide hide

Why not? Gremlin would never hurt anybody.

It tried to hurt Dad, I pointed out to be fair.

Only because Dad was thinking about killing Gremlin.

fear fear run run hide

Do you think we should run away? my twin asked seriously. *We can't let Dad hurt Gremlin again.*

I don't know. Where would we go? We're only eight years old. Besides, I'm so tired, I don't think I could make it even across the road.

We can't let Gremlin die!

no no no no no no no no

It won't. If Dad was going to kill Gremlin, he'd've done it already. I yawned and my stomach growled. So did my twin's. *Let's see what happens at supper.*

But supper, when it came, was a quiet meal. Dad didn't talk much— he just stared into his bowl of stew. My twin and I ate quickly, unsure whether we should say anything or not. Once our bellies were full, it became even harder to keep our eyes open. I was about to ask if we could go to bed when my twin spoke.

"Are you angry at us again, Dad?"

He looked up sharply. "Angry?"

"You didn't say anything," my twin pointed out, "and you said we'd talk later. About . . . about Gremlin."

"Angry," Dad repeated, as if to himself, and I held my breath. "No, Kate—I'm not angry. I'm just having a hard time adjusting to this."

I swallowed, and the stew in my stomach sloshed around like dirty washwater. "Are you going to kill Gremlin?"

no no no no no no no

"I told you, honey—not unless Gremlin tries to hurt someone again. I'm not your grandfather."

I didn't know what he meant by the last part, but the first part I understood perfectly. My breath whooshed out with relief and the stew stopped sloshing. I shot my twin a triumphant look.

"Can we be excused?" I asked. "We want to go to bed."

Dad nodded without answering. We left him at the table still staring into his bowl. I wished I knew what had made him so sad.

Dad did adjust. Within a week, in fact, he was able to tell which body I was wearing just by looking at me. He said I stood and walked a certain way, whether I was a boy or a girl. For a while, he wanted to give us different names, call my twin by our middle names— Jessica and Garth—but that didn't last. My name had nothing to do with me. My name was what other people called me, even Dad, and after finally getting the rules of the Name Game, I couldn't remember to answer to Kate or Quinn and not to Jessica or Garth. He eventually gave up.

One thing he just couldn't accept, though, was the fact that my twin and I didn't know which one of us was born male and which one was born female. He would ask about it every so often, until my twin and I were ready to make something up so he'd leave us alone. The only time it mattered to us whether we were male or female was when it came to marbles and kickball.

That was before we hit puberty.

CHAPTER SIX

ME

I remember going through phases when I wanted to be one gender for long periods of time. Sometimes I wanted to be male, sometimes I wanted to be female. So did my twin. Sometimes we fought about it, but usually our needs coincided. Or maybe I should say they were opposed. In any case, it usually worked out that when I wanted to be male, my twin wanted to be female, and vice versa. The incident that led me to taking the male body by force wasn't repeated.

By the time we were twelve, we were both anxious to start growing up. I wanted breasts and makeup as a girl. I wanted muscles and facial hair as a boy. We whispered between ourselves about wet dreams and menstruation. The latter seemed pretty disgusting, but all the girls at school were eager to get their period, and so were we. Some already had, of course, and they wore their menses like an invisible badge of adulthood. But our bodies stubbornly refused to develop.

Dad didn't really talk much about sex with us. Kevin, the red-haired boy from school, said his dad didn't talk about it either because it embarrassed him. But that wasn't quite it with my twin and me. Whenever the subject came up, Dad wasn't embarrassed, exactly. He seemed . . . afraid of the topic. As if it wasn't safe for him to discuss it. He finally gave us a small stack of books and said we should read them. If we had any other questions, he promised to answer them.

We didn't ask any questions.

We heard rumors at school, though. Some of them were really weird—and stupid. As seventh grade wound to a close, the boys talked about almost nothing except girls, and all their jokes were about jacking off. According to some of them, the latter made you go blind. That made me laugh. By now I was as familiar with the neural pathways in my bodies as I was with the roads through town. There wasn't any neural connection between our penis and our eyes, and even though I hadn't mastered body chemistry yet, I couldn't find a connection there, either. But I kept that to myself. Better to let others live with their lies than reveal my own truths.

They'd find out on their own anyway.

One day I was straightening up our room—my twin wasn't as tidy as I'd like—when I got the message.

Come quick! It started! And bring a fresh pair of panties!

I dropped the pillow, snatched a pair of underwear from the dresser, and rushed downstairs to the bathroom. We had known for about three weeks that something was happening in the female body. Even though we didn't have control over our chemistry yet, we were certainly aware of it. Things were changing. New hormones flowed, flooding our blood with tantalizing tastes—sour, salty, metallic. Adulthood was on the way, and none too soon! To hear talk of it, we were way behind everyone else at school.

When I arrived in the bathroom, I found my twin sitting on the toilet looking down at spots of blood on the Kate body's underpants. Wordlessly, we Traded and I looked at them from the female perspective. The body didn't feel any different than it had yesterday. The toilet seat was hard and cold beneath my rear end, but the body felt the same. Still, I felt an odd glee. I looked up at my twin. The Quinn body was still as straight and sticklike as a pencil.

Congratulations, Gremlin said.

We're growing up, my twin said. *Trade me back.*

We Traded back and forth, still trying to see if anything felt different. Nothing did.

Do we tell Dad? I asked.

My twin had already lined the clean panties with a pad and gotten dressed. *He'll be embarrassed or scared or whatever his problem is, but yeah, we need to tell him.* My twin grinned. *I mean, we're going to need more than this one box of pads he bought last year. If he was embarrassed about sex before . . .*

I slapped a hand over my mouth to cover the laughter. *Poor Dad! And what happens if someone forgets to put a price on the package and Mrs. Greer has to shout for a price check in front of everyone?*

We both collapsed into laughter until Dad pounded on the door.

"What's going on in there?" he demanded.

That made us laugh all the harder. We tried to stop, but every time we looked at each other, the laughter bubbled up again. Dad had to threaten to break the door down before we were able to stop. I managed to fling open the door.

"We got our period!" I announced.

"Oh, God," was all Dad could say.

The next day, Dad cornered us in our room and insisted we change our sleeping arrangements. Kate could stay in our current room, but Quinn had to move across the hall into the guest room.

"I should have split you up years ago," Dad said. "It's not a good idea for you two to be sharing a room at your age."

"Why not?" I demanded in shock. "We share bodies. It's not like I'm staring at my sister or anything. I see that in the mirror."

"Yeah," my twin chimed in. "Quinn doesn't have anything I haven't seen."

"Our society has rules," Dad said firmly. "And those

rules state that brothers and sisters don't share a bedroom, especially once they start . . . developing."

"You always say it's important to do what you feel is right," I contradicted. "And it isn't right to split us up. You arranged to keep us in the same classroom at school. Why split us up at home?"

"Yeah!"

"That's different," Dad replied.

"How?" I said.

"You don't sleep or get undressed in a classroom."

"We'll undress next year in gym class," I pointed out.

"But not in the girls' locker room, Quinn," Dad replied tersely. He was getting annoyed, but so was I. My twin had always slept across from me. So what if the female body was menstruating and getting pubic hair? What was the difference? I knew that only adults—and babies, I guess—are supposed to mix gender in a bedroom, but my twin and I were a special case. I didn't know if I'd be able to sleep unless I heard my twin's breathing or knew that I could reach out for my twin's touch.

"We don't want to move and we aren't going to," I said. "It's stupid. Those rules are for other people. We're different."

All of a sudden Dad's face got red. "You'll get the hell out of your sister's room like a normal brother or you can both sleep on the front lawn!" he snarled. "You've got an hour to divide up your stuff. Move!"

And he stomped downstairs. We stared after him, openmouthed.

"Jerk," my twin muttered.

I switched to private mode. *I think he wants a normal family. You know—a wife and two kids who don't switch bodies around.*

That doesn't mean he has to take it out on us.

Have you ever wished we were normal? I asked suddenly.

My twin gave me a sidelong look through long lashes. *Have you?*

Sometimes. I sat down on one of the beds. *It'd sure be easier not having to remember what I should know as Quinn and what I should know as Kate and stuff like that. Whenever we make a mistake, all the other kids think we're weird.*

Except Kevin, anyway, my twin said, and sat beside me. *Though he's more Kate's friend than Quinn's. I wish we could at least tell him about us.*

no no no no no no

No way! I shuddered. *What if he told his folks or someone else? We'd get thrown off the whole planet. There are laws against nanobots. You know that.*

Can't tell, Gremlin agreed stubbornly. *Against the rules.*

That's dumb, too, my twin said. *There's nothing to be afraid of. It's not like we'd kill anyone.*

Father says— Gremlin began.

I know what Dad says. My twin sighed. *Sometimes I think I want to leave Felicity and go somewhere else where I don't have to worry about my nanobots all the time.*

You'd worry about them a lot more on other planets, I reminded him *Everything's run by nanobots on other worlds. You'd get sucked in.*

Would not.

Would so.

Would not.

Would so.

Would not one more time than you.

Would not two more times than you.

My twin sighed again and let it drop. It wasn't a serious argument anyway. *Do you think our mom thinks about us back on Earth?*

It was an old question, and I gave the old answer. *I'll bet she does every day.*

I didn't even know her, but I miss her. My twin shifted on the bed. *I miss Grandma, too. Is she still coming to visit at Christmas?*

Dad hasn't said she's not, so I suppose she is.

My twin opened the closet and looked at our clothes hanging side by side. *I'll bet our mom wouldn't split us up.*

I thought back to the last time one of us had used that argument. *Don't say that to Dad. Not unless you want half your head torn off.*

Do you really think Dad wants us to be like everyone else?

I guess. He said I should be a normal brother.

Have you ever thought about what it would be like to be just male or just female, with just one body, like everyone else?

Yeah, I admitted. *It makes me feel weird inside, though. Kinda like asking if you'd want to spend a year in a prison or something. You wonder what it'd be like, but you don't really want to find out.*

"I don't hear any furniture moving," Dad boomed from downstairs.

With a simultaneous shake of our heads, we set to work.

It didn't take as long to adjust to sleeping in different rooms as we thought, mostly because we could still talk in private mode. The female body continued to develop, though not fast enough to suit either of us. We thought about trying to speed things up with our nanos, but ultimately decided it was too risky—what if we made a mistake we couldn't undo?

"Sure," my twin said once, "it'd be great to have bigger breasts, but what if we threw the wrong switch and they zoomed out of control?"

The image sent us both into hysterical laughter again.

A month later I flashed awake, heart pounding, sweat coating my face. I stared into the darkness, trying to figure out what was going on. I vaguely remembered dreaming about two women and a wrestling match.

My penis was hard—it usually was when I woke up

in the Quinn body nowadays—but this was different somehow. I checked with my nanos and found a mix of endorphin and adrenaline rushing through my system. The inside of my pajama bottoms was sticky. As I reached down to feel, I remembered how the Quinn body's voice had been cracking lately and the crumbs of pubic hair that had appeared under the arms and on the groin.

Wake up and get in here! I said. *Hurry!*

A few moments later, my twin padded into the room and sat groggily on my bed. The mattress sagged, making me roll sideways a little.

"What's going on?" yawned my twin.

I had a wet dream.

My twin's eyes flew wide open in the dim light. *No way!*

Yes, way. I stripped off the pajama bottoms and tossed them at my twin. *Feel for yourself.*

Yuck! Forget it! My twin batted them aside. *Trade me.*

We Traded and I found myself sitting on the bed while my twin lay under the covers, naked from the waist down. One hand moved around beneath the blankets.

Nothing feels any different, my twin said, disappointed. *The heart's still beating kind of fast, but that's it.*

The rush must've worn off. It felt pretty good during, though. I got another pair of pajama bottoms out of the dresser. *Maybe you'll get the next dream.*

"Next dream, hell," my twin muttered, donning the pajamas. I yawned, not caring what the remark meant. The excitement had worn off quickly, and the female body wanted sleep. I went to Kate's room and climbed into bed. The bed from Quinn's room, however, creaked a lot, and I figured my twin was having trouble getting back to sleep. Maybe it had something to do with the dream. I was just drifting off when my twin blasted me awake.

YOU GOTTA TRY THIS!

❖   ❖   ❖

Junior high school wasn't much fun. Everyone was awkward, and some of the kids made fun of other people to make themselves feel better. My twin and I had few friends—Kevin Sanders was about it—because it was hard to relate to people outside our family. How do you talk about girls to a bunch of guys who don't know what it's like to be one? So we kept pretty much to ourselves.

That, of course, guaranteed we'd become targets.

I was heading for my locker after last period and found Dennis North and Jeremy Acre leaning against it. I still thought of them as the jerks I beat at marbles in elementary school, though things had changed a little since then. Now they were the jerks who stole my lunch and tried to slam my face into the ground during gym-class football.

Jeremy was a lot taller now than in elementary school, a little taller than I was, but he was still scrawny. Dennis's hair was a darker brown and he was getting zits around his nose. Around us was the clatter of slammed lockers and the chatter of other seventh-graders freed from another day of school.

"Excuse me," I said, reaching for the lock. I wished I was in the Kate body—there seemed to be an unwritten rule that boys only harass boys. The Two Jerks, as I called them, rarely spoke to Kate.

Dennis continued leaning against my locker. Now what? Unease awakened in my stomach and I tried to glance around without seeming to do so. No teachers or other adults in sight.

"You did pretty good on that test in Hacker's class today," Jeremy said. It was, in theory, a compliment, but by now I knew better. This was Jeremy's opening volley.

"So what?" I said, shifting my math book. "Can you get off my locker? I want to go home." *Hey—I'm going to need some help up here.*

"So you think you're pretty smart," Jeremy said.

Where are you? my twin replied.

My locker.

"You don't go anywhere until we say you do, Michaels," Dennis put in. His voice cracked when he said my last name and I smiled at him to let him know I'd noticed.

I'm down by the gym with Kevin, said my twin. *I'll tell him I'm supposed to meet you and we'll be there as fast as we can.*

"What are you smiling at my friend for?" Jeremy snapped. "You queer or something?"

Later, I was sure, I'd think of some nasty, clever insult, but words failed me right then.

"You *are* queer, aren't you?" Dennis said. "You blow Mr. Hacker so he gives you good grades. Is that it, queer?"

I gritted my teeth, and my temper started to rise. Jeremy and Dennis had been handing me this bullshit all year and I'd suddenly had enough. My fist clenched. "Get the hell away from my locker, asshole."

"Fucking queer is what you are," Jeremy jeered. "Hanging out with your sister all the time and that faggot Sanders. You and Sanders bang your sister together? Is that what made you queer?"

I hit him. It was like my fist flew out all by itself and smashed into Jeremy's sneering face. Blood spurted, and he staggered backward in complete surprise. Dennis snarled and swung. He connected with my stomach and the breath *whuff*ed out of my lungs. Pain exploded in my face as he followed with a right to my jaw.

Inside my body, nanos flew into my bloodstream, rushing to the injuries to begin healing and cleanup. My pain receded under the rush of adrenaline, and I charged into Dennis, ramming my head into his chest and pummeling him with both fists. Someone grabbed the back of my shirt and yanked me away from him. I jabbed my elbow backward. It connected with something soft, and the grip on my shirt vanished. I spun around and punched Jeremy in the face again before he could recover, only to have Dennis jump me from behind. He wrapped an arm around my throat and started choking me. I gasped, trying desperately to breathe.

Gremlin! I need strength!

Unable to comply, Gremlin reported. *Strength boost requires extra oxygen, which is now in short supply. Increasing oxygen efficiency, slowing adrenaline production to compensate.*

I was vaguely aware that a crowd had gathered. Jeremy came at me again. I couldn't dodge with Dennis on my back. Air barely trickled into my lungs despite Gremlin's best efforts at maximizing oxygen use. I saw spots. Jeremy drew back his fist, aiming for my face.

Then Kevin appeared and knocked Jeremy sideways. Dennis grew heavier on my back for a moment, then let go. I greedily sucked air into my lungs. A glance behind told me my twin had pulled Dennis off me.

"What the hell is going on here?" an adult voice boomed, and Mr. Hacker pushed his way through the crowd. He was followed by Mrs. Charles. Both of them quickly took in the scene and marched all five of us down to the principal's office. Jeremy's nose dripped a trail of blood on the gray tile floor, and I had a split lip, though my nanos closed it before we got to the bottom of the stairs. Mr. Hacker gave Jeremy a handkerchief and told him to pinch his nose. Jeremy winced. I smiled privately. I was already almost healed and my pain had long since vanished.

What happened? my twin demanded as we walked, and I gave a quick accounting of the incident. A while later, I repeated it to the assistant principal. Final judgment—two days' detention after school, but only because I had a clean record. Jeremy and Dennis, who had previous offenses on file, were suspended for three days. Dad, by some miracle, decided the detention was enough punishment given the circumstances and didn't ground me or make me clean the entire stable by myself.

"Why did you start swinging?" my twin asked when we got home. We were sitting on the bed in Kate's room.

"I'm not sure," I said. "I just hit him. I didn't plan to." I rubbed my knuckles and grinned. "It felt good, too. He deserved it, the jerk. Now maybe he'll leave us alone."

My twin shrugged. "Maybe. It just seems like you could've told a teacher and gotten him in trouble without getting yourself in hot water along with him. Now we can't Trade after school unless I feel like sitting in detention for you."

"That'd be fine with me."

"Forget it. You hit him, you do the time."

I got up and stretched. Outside, the late spring sun was shining and baby leaves covered the hills behind our house with a blue haze. The window was open, letting in the cool, fresh air. "I'm glad the detentions didn't start today. I'm feeling restless now. Maybe I'll go out for a run or jack off a couple times or something."

"I wanted to practice guitar," my twin objected. "You go running or play with yourself and you'll use up all the body's energy. Trade me and go sculpt instead."

My twin gestured at the shelves that ran floor to ceiling in Kate's bedroom. Clay and ceramic sculptures—my work, not my twin's—already lined several, though the work was clearly lumpy and amateurish. Most of them were barely discernible as horses, cats, or trees. The box of KidClay Dad had bought us years ago sat in the back of the closet, long unused since I had graduated to real clay. I barely gave any of it a glance now, however. Sculpting didn't interest me at the moment. I was feeling pretty horny—not unusual for the male body lately, but at the moment the feeling was pretty intense. I also wanted to run, feel my muscles moving, hear the air rush past my ears.

I liked to run, but only when I was in the Quinn body. When I was in the Kate body, I preferred to mold and sculpt. Strangely, neither activity interested my twin at all. As Quinn, my twin was more into music and had already picked up guitar. But as Kate, my twin liked studying insects, of all things. The wall opposite the sculpture shelves was covered with display cases of specimens pinned under glass.

As for me, bugs were gross and guitar was boring.

I sometimes wondered about that. My twin and I were closer than any twins in history. So why were our interests different? And why did they change whenever we Traded?

I realized I was pacing. "Hey, after the pain I went through today, I deserve a little pleasure."

"Yeah, right. You get a reward for fighting." My twin paused thoughtfully. "Even if Jeremy and Dennis are assholes. Come on—Trade me. I wanted to practice before homework."

I gave up. "Fine."

We Traded. I was sitting on the bed now, and the horny feeling vanished. I also felt more relaxed. Maybe I could finish the new horse I was sculpting in the basement. It was almost done, probably only a couple days' work left on it. Maybe I could even finish it by tomorrow—

—except I had detention. I sighed to myself. Stupid fight. I'd have to sit in a classroom and stare at the walls for an hour for the next two days. Why had I gotten involved in that, anyway?

"Christ," my twin complained, adjusting the shorts I had put on that morning. "What did you do besides fight? There's no way I can practice in this condition."

I shrugged. "You wanted to Trade. I'm going down to the basement."

"Close the door when you leave," my twin said, annoyed. "I'm going to be in here for while yet."

I did as my twin asked and drifted downstairs to the kitchen where Dad was cutting onions with crunchy *thunks* of his knife. Dad spent a lot of time in the kitchen, and it was comforting to find him there. It was something you could count on. I perched on the counter nearby and watched him work for a while.

"How's your brother doing?" he asked, then glanced up at me. "Whoops. I should say, how are *you* doing? After the fight, I mean."

For a moment I thought he had asked *what* my twin was doing and I stifled a grin. Dad probably wouldn't react very well if I told him I knew exactly what my twin was up to.

"I'm okay," I said. "Though I'm kind of wondering why I did it. It seems kind of stupid now. And I've got those detentions to serve."

Dad's knife flickered. "The price you pay. Though I'll bet those other kids won't be bothering you for a while. Next time, just tell someone instead of going ballistic, all right?"

I changed the subject. "What's for supper? I'm starving."

"Split pea soup."

"You haven't split the peas yet, have you?" I asked instantly.

Dad flashed a grin at me. "Now when have I ever done that without calling you? You can sort for me, if you want."

With a happy smile, I got out the big mixing bowl, took the cloth bag of peas out of the pantry, and sat at the breakfast table to sort. Bad peas went into the compost bucket, small stones went into the wastebasket, and good peas went into the bowl. They made little *plink*-ing sounds when they hit.

"How was your day besides the fight?" Dad asked. He scraped the onions onto a plate and got a chunk of ham from the icebox. He had already built up the fire in the stove, and a pot of water steamed on the back burner. On the shelf above, a cloth-covered bowl proclaimed we were also having salt-rising biscuits with the soup. The kitchen was warm and cozy, with light reflecting off the polished wood floor and cupboards and Dad humming to himself over salty scraps of ham. By the time supper was over, the kitchen would be uncomfortably hot, but for now it was nice.

"My day was fine, I guess," I said. "I might do some more sculpting later, if I get the chance." *Plink*, *plink*, *plink*. "What are you humming?"

He stopped slicing ham and looked up. "Was I humming? I guess I was. Let's see." He hummed for a moment again. "It's called 'Molly Malone.' Your grandmother used to sing it to me when I was little. Until Dad made her stop, anyway."

I scooped another handful of peas from the bag. Dad must have been in a strange mood—he almost never talks about his own father. Curiosity tugged at me. Should I press him? Dad sometimes got upset when we asked about Grandpa Blackstone. After a brief struggle, curiosity won out over caution.

"What was Grandpa Blackstone like?" I asked.

Dad paused in his chopping and looked at me with his green eyes. Then he went back to cutting ham. I thought he was going to ignore the question, but then he said, "My dad was a monster, Kate. There's no other way to put it."

"What did he do?" I asked quietly.

"Your grandfather was into inflicting pain," he replied matter-of-factly. "He tortured me and he beat your grandmother. It was hell until she managed to get us away."

"What did he do to you?" I said, modifying my first question. Dad looked at me again and I met his gaze with what I hoped was a calm, mature look.

"You look so much like your mother right now," he said with a sigh. He went back to the ham. "The gory details aren't really important, Kate. I will say that I lived in fear every waking moment of my life, waiting for my father to drag me down to the basement or into my bedroom closet. I never knew what would set him off—the wrong word, a chance look. Or maybe nothing at all."

"How did you get through it all?" *Plink, plink, plink*.

"I went insane." Dad flapped a hand at me and made *ooo*ing noises. We both laughed, and some of the tension in the room eased.

"I can joke about it now, but I sure couldn't then," Dad said, his voice dropping back into seriousness. "Kate, this isn't for broadcast to the rest of the world. I need your word on that."

I nodded solemnly, still not quite believing that Dad was talking to me like this, like a grown-up.

Dad dumped the ham on the onion plate and set to work on a handful of carrots. "I developed what's called dissociative identity disorder. Multiple personalities, to you."

"What's that?"

"It means your grandfather terrified me so much that I couldn't handle the fear—or the pain. I created other people to deal with him and what he did to me. Whenever Dad went on a rampage, I became someone else. Then, when the punishment was over, I became myself again and I had no memory of what had happened."

I didn't know what to say to that, so I kept on sorting peas.

"I had no idea anything was wrong with me," Dad continued as he chopped carrots. "I thought everyone had blackouts and heard voices in their heads."

"We hear voices," I pointed out.

He smiled at me. "You and your brother and Gremlin are a special case. Besides, the people in my head weren't real—they just felt real."

"Did they have names?"

"Yeah. There was Garth, and Andy, and Patrick, and Jay, and Jessica, and—"

"One of them was a girl?" I interrupted.

He nodded. "Multiples almost always have a few personalities of the opposite sex."

"How many personalities did you have?"

"Counting me and Robin, I had forty-nine."

"Forty-nine!"

"Some of them only came out once. The ones I mentioned were some of the main ones." He continued chopping carrots. "It's strange—I haven't talked to anyone about this since you and Quinn were born."

"Do our middle names come from your old personalities?"

Dad smiled. "Yeah. They helped me through an impossible time and I wanted to . . . honor them, in a way. You're not sorting."

I glanced down at my empty hands and snatched up a handful of peas. The conversation was getting more and more interesting, and I had forgotten them entirely. "Where are your personalities now?"

"I saw a doctor for several years. He helped make them a part of me again."

"How did Grandma manage to get you away?"

"One day she just grabbed me and literally ran out the door. I wasn't much older than you are now. I learned later she had found a way to blackmail Dad into leaving us alone. I think he hated her then. But when he died, he left me all his money."

"How did he die?"

"An accident," Dad said, voice suddenly short. "Are you done with those peas yet?"

The conversation had ended, and I knew better than to push. I dropped the last peas into the bowl. "Done!"

Dad came over and stared down into the bowl on the table. Now that I was older, I could, with my own nanobots, see his nanos rush downward into the mound of peas. I set mine to watch from the microscopic level while my eyes observed the entire scene from above. I held my breath, and for a moment I was five years old again.

"One," Dad said. "Two. Three!"

Every single pea jumped in place with a *crack* and landed again in two neatly split halves. I laughed like I did when I was little. It was a trick only Dad could do, splitting things like that. No matter how hard I tried, I could never get it quite right. Dad ruffled my hair and a few tentative guitar chords floated downstairs as my twin warmed up.

"If you're going to try some more sculpting," Dad said, "you'd better do it now. Supper should be ready in about an hour."

I headed downstairs to my worktable, thinking about what Dad had told me and wondering if I could sculpt a nanobot splitting a perfect pea.

That was one of the last times I remember feeling that close to Dad. The next few years were hell. We finished junior high and started high school, and we kept getting into trouble. We got caught fighting something like twice a semester, just enough to get labeled as a troublemaker but not enough to get suspended. There were more fights than that, of course—we were just pretty good at not getting caught.

It was always the Quinn body that did the fighting. I can't explain it. When I was Kate, I was able to ignore taunts about the size of my breasts or the darkness of my skin or whatever the tune of the week was. But when I was Quinn, similar comments would send me into a rage. Sometimes I would be swinging my fists at someone with no clear memory about what the other guy had said, just a knowledge that it had really pissed me off. It was the same for my twin.

It was really hard on Dad. He raised us not to hit, and after he told me about his childhood, I can see why. I think he was scared that the Quinn body had inherited problems from Grandpa Blackstone. What was harder to understand was why my twin got into more fights as Quinn than I did. That was something else we couldn't explain. I think my twin was simply more impulsive than I was.

And this was true for more than just fights.

❖   ❖   ❖

Gritty clay squished cool and wet beneath my hands. My nose itched and I almost scratched it before I remembered my fingers were all over clay. I sent some nanos to take care of the itching problem and went back to work. After a week of false starts, the half-formed lizzie-bat on the table in front of me was finally taking shape, and I wasn't going to quit for anything. Or so I thought.

You won't believe it! The thought was punctuated by a clatter of footsteps on the basement stairs. I kept on sculpting. The lizzie-bat's long neck was proving especially tricky—it had broken twice so far and I was determined to get it right on the third try.

Didn't you hear me? My twin was standing next to me by now. I spared a brief glance and went back to sculpting. At fifteen years old, our bodies were filling out fairly well. The Quinn body was still a little on the thin side, but all the running I did on the track team had developed leg muscle and a certain amount of agility. The hair had a tendency to curl and developed auburn highlights in the summer, and our eyes were still large and brown. The Kate body wasn't quite as athletic— neither of us were much interested in sports as a female—but my twin kept it in fair shape with all the hiking trips to search for more bugs. Kate's breasts seemed doomed to smalldom, but we compensated by growing the hair out long, curly, and luxurious. At the moment, I wore it pulled back so as not to get clay in it.

"I heard you," I said. "I'm busy. Go tell Dad about it, whatever it is."

"Yeah, right," my twin said, flopping down on an old couch in the corner. Dad was gone, off fighting another nanobot hive somewhere, which gave my comment a certain amount of sarcasm. We were old enough to spend nights home alone now, though Mrs. Wells still kept an eye on our house from across the street. Ignoring my ready wit, my twin said, "I did it."

"Did what?" Maybe if I raised the angle a little more. This lizzie-bat would have to be up and looking around if it didn't want a neck that flopped like a snake with a broken back.

"You know," my twin said. "It. The deed. The Big One."

I spun on my stool, lizzie-bat forgotten. "Sex? You had sex?"

"Twice." My twin leaned back with a blissful look, eyes closed. "It was great."

"Who was it?" I demanded, partly curious and partly annoyed that *I* hadn't been in the body at the time.

"Marie Hagar."

"Marie? As in Annie's older sister?"

"Yeah."

"As in the older sister of Annie-who-we're-dating?"

Not dating anymore, Gremlin put in, and my twin looked contrite.

I turned a hard look on my twin. "What did you do?"

"I already *told* you that."

"What did you do with *Annie*?"

"Well, nothing, really. That was the problem." My twin sat up. "I'd been putting moves on her for a while, but she always pushes away. I went over there this afternoon to see her, but she wasn't home, and Marie answered the door. She invited me in, and it sort of went from there."

I stared, torn between laughter and disapproval. "So you did it with our girlfriend's older sister. The one in her twenties."

"I think she was attracted to our—my—youth and innocence," my twin said smugly.

"Does Annie know?"

My twin looked uncomfortable. "Sort of."

I didn't like the sound of that. "Go on."

"Annie walked in on us just as we were . . . uh, *finishing* our second go-round, if you get my meaning. I left pretty quick. I don't think Annie'll want to see us again."

Jesus Christ. "You had no right to do that without consulting me," I snapped. "I *like* Annie."

"I'm sorry."

"Don't lie to me, you jerk."

My twin shrugged. "I didn't plan on getting caught. Besides, you don't like Annie all the time."

"I like her when I'm male." I sighed and turned back to the lizzie-bat. "You may as well tell me what it was like."

I could hear the grin in my twin's voice. "The second time was better, that's for sure. I was starting to get the hang of it. The first time was . . . " My twin cleared his throat a little. "Well, it was kinda quick."

"That's certainly in character," I muttered, interested despite myself.

"The second she showed me a few other things," my twin hurried on, and a lengthy description followed. I listened in silence, only half paying attention to what my hands were doing. The lizzie-bat's neck grew longer and longer, until it finally drooped to the table. I swore softly and got out a clay knife to cut it back to size. The phallic imagery wasn't lost on me.

"She'd probably do it again, in case you want to try it," my twin concluded. "You'd just have to make sure Annie wasn't around."

I turned and stared at my twin for a long moment. "Trade me," I said.

My twin looked back, then Traded. I sat on the couch and took stock. The only noticeable sensation was a slight soreness in my groin, a feeling that generally cropped up after having more than one orgasm in half an hour. My twin's nanos hadn't seen to the problem yet, so I sent a regiment to handle it. The soreness eased.

"Think back to this afternoon," I said, "and tell me, from the female perspective, if you think Marie'll do it again," I said.

"Doubtful," my twin grunted. Some things are easier to show than explain.

"To say the least."

My twin grinned unapologetically. "Now we just need to get you someone to try it with."

"I don't want to right now," I replied.

"Give it an hour. We're young yet."

"Yeah, yeah. Trade me again—I want to finish that lizzie-bat."

We Traded and my twin headed for the stairs.

"Before you go any further," I called out, "you need to swear that *I* get to lose the female body's virginity."

"What does it matter?" my twin asked, pausing at the staircase. "You're a virgin in this body *and* that one."

"Just promise me," I growled.

"All right, all right," my twin conceded. "I promise. I'm heading out for a while."

"Where to?"

"To find another girlfriend. Duh."

My twin was gone before I could think of a suitable reply. I bent industriously over the lizzie-bat, but my mind was already laying plans. How hard could it be to ambush a teenage boy and drag him into bed?

I found out. Whoever said that women have an easier time finding sex partners than men never had a twin brother with a reputation for fighting.

"Look, Kate," pointed out one fine specimen, "if we do anything more than hold hands, your brother'll kick my ass so hard, I'll be walking on tiptoe for a month." All promises to the contrary didn't do a thing to change his mind.

I did know, however, one boy who wouldn't be afraid of Quinn. There was only one problem:

Dad.

"You told me I could go down to the park," I said one evening. Constance Park was a popular hangout for the kids at our high school.

"That was before I knew you were meeting boys down there," he replied calmly. "You're only fifteen."

"I'll be sixteen in a month," I countered. "And you let Quinn go just last night."

"That's different."

"How?" I demanded.

"I don't have to worry about Quinn and boys."

"No. You just have to worry about Quinn and girls."

Dad gave me a look that said he *didn't* worry about that, thank you very much. "You're not going down there tonight."

"And if I Trade first?" I asked sweetly. "Then can I go?"

Dad sighed with exasperation and ran a hand through his hair. "All you want to do is go down to the park so you can meet Kevin Sanders and go off with him somewhere. You can't single date until you're sixteen, so no—you can't go down there as Kate. As Quinn, fine."

This despite the fact that there would be girls down there. But I knew from previous experience that this argument would take me nowhere. "Kevin and I have been friends since grade school," I retorted instead.

"You're not in grade school anymore."

"What's that got to do with it?"

And so the argument went. Finally Dad fell back on pure parental authority: "You can't go because I told you so."

I stomped upstairs to my room, flung myself on my bed, and stared up at the ceiling. Kevin's face floated above me, a ghost against the blond wood of the ceiling. His hair had darkened to an attractive auburn, and he didn't freckle as much anymore. I couldn't put an exact time on the moment my interest in Kevin shifted from childhood friend to potential lover except that it had happened some time after my twin's escapade with Annie and Marie. He'd be disappointed when I didn't show up at the park as we'd planned. We were going to gather flowers—midnight perfume blossoms, to be exact, before they went out of season. I could already see his strong hands wrapped around a bunch of purple, starry flowers. I wanted to feel his arms wrapped around me.

I sighed. Problem was, Kevin seemed unaware of my emotional shift. Tonight I had been planning on making things a little more clear.

Had been—the operative words now that Dad had torpedoed the evening for me. I punched my pillow. Life sucked. Dad was being completely unreasonable. He'd obviously forgotten what it was like to have— want—a love life.

No luck, huh? Soft guitar chords floated from my twin's room.

No. If I don't lose my virginity soon, someone's going to get hurt.

My twin laughed, and I heard the sound both in my head and from the bedroom. By now it was becoming a running joke between us. My twin—as Quinn only— had had more than his share of bed partners in the last several months. But I had had none, not as Quinn and not as Kate. I don't know what it was, but every time I started something as Quinn, I lost my nerve to finish it. And as Kate—well, I already mentioned the problem there.

One time, in an attempt to resolve the problem once and for all, I followed my twin—Quinn—on a date my twin was pretty sure would lead to sex. The girl's parents were out for the evening, and I was hiding outside her bedroom window. When things started up, the plan went, we would Trade. Everything went smoothly until I heard soft moaning sounds through the open window.

Trade me, I said. *Quick!*

But I got no response. My twin's nanos bunched up, ignoring mine. The moaning got louder and more intense, and I started to get embarrassed. Bedsprings squeaked. Finally I crept away, feeling like a peeping Tom.

Later, my twin apologized.

"I just couldn't make myself Trade," my twin said. "I just got going, and there was no way I could do it. Maybe next time."

My reply made it clear that "next time" would probably coincide with the archangel Gabriel playing jazz trumpet for a street band.

I continued to stare up at the ceiling. Outside, the late spring sun had almost set. The midnight perfume blossoms would open soon, sweetly scenting the air. I was going to miss them and Kevin both. My room suddenly seemed close and stuffy despite the open window.

Trade me, I said suddenly. *I've got to get out of here, and Dad won't let me go anywhere as Kate. He'll assume I'm going to sneak down to the park.*

The guitar chords stopped. *Are you sneaking down to the park?*

I'm not going to sneak. Dad doesn't care as much what the male body does.

I've noticed that. I don't think Dad has, though.

We Traded. I put the guitar away and trotted downstairs. If I couldn't see Kevin as Kate, I could at least spend time with him as Quinn.

"I'm going down to the park, Dad," I said, heading for the door.

Dad didn't look up from his newspaper. "Curfew is eleven," was all he said.

I pedaled furiously toward town. I was the same person, the *same*, but I got to do more as a male than as a female. Did it have something to do with Dad being a man? Would our mother be more permissive with me as a daughter than as a son? And what was Dad afraid of? I couldn't believe that he didn't know—or at least suspect—my twin was single-handedly keeping the condom companies in liquid assets, so to speak, but he still let the Quinn body run around like a rampant bull while the Kate body was more restricted. It didn't matter who was in it. It infuriated me the way people reacted to my body and not to *me*. What did the body matter, anyway?

Kevin was waiting at one of the white gazebos by Constance Lake. The sky was still light, and people of many different ages were still enjoying the pleasant spring weather. A group of children shrieked their way through a game of tag while their parents looked on and talked among themselves. A small knot of people huddled expectantly around an ice cream maker, each taking turns at the crank. A well-dressed couple—he in an ivory suit, she in an ankle-length blue dress— ambled down toward the lake where the ducks kept a sharp eye out for suckers with stale bread. Horse carriages, some private, some hired, clopped by on the pavement.

I chained my bike to a hitching post and strolled over to Kevin, waving to get his attention. His green eyes widened in surprise. He was a good-looking guy, in a way. Better looking, I grudgingly admitted, than I was, though I wasn't envisioning his hands around a bunch of flowers or his arms around me.

"Quinn?" he asked as I approached. "What's up? I thought Kate was coming."

"Dad won't let her," I said, a little shortly. "I figured I'd come down instead and maybe we could hang out together or something. It beats staying home."

"Yeah, okay."

I realized that Kevin looked a little flushed and uncomfortable, and it occurred to me that this was one of the few times I had been alone with him as Quinn. Usually it was Kevin and Kate, or all three of us together. Kevin and Quinn didn't spend much time together. Kevin knew that Quinn—either of them—would never hit him, but Kevin was shy even with friends, and I think he found Quinn a little overwhelming. I resolved to tone back a little, to put him more at ease.

Kevin leaned against the gazebo in an attempt to look casual. It didn't work. Why was he so nervous?

"So what do you want to do?" he asked.

I shrugged. "I dunno. There isn't much to do in this

town. I mostly wanted to get out of the house. We could walk around the lake for a while or go wading."

"Okay," Kevin agreed. "Let's walk."

We walked in silence for a while. I wasn't quite sure what to do now. When I was Kate, I never had problems finding something to talk about with Kevin, but when I was Quinn, I was lost. Why was that? Who was I, anyway? Kate, Quinn, or someone else entirely?

We reached the grass surrounding the lake, and the ducks drifted toward us with a predatory air. They reminded me of sharks sensing a wounded fish. The sun had set, and red light was fading from the sky like color from an overwashed shirt. The park was emptying as people drifted back toward their homes. Ben Jackson was already making the rounds with his lighting pole, setting the yellow streetlights blazing one by one in their glass lamps. Overhead, the stars were coming out. I knelt and swished a hand through the water. The ducks made a hurried dash forward, then aborted when they realized my hands were empty. A few of them quacked indignantly.

"How come your dad wouldn't let Kate come?" Kevin asked, squatting beside me.

"I'm not sure," I replied truthfully. "He doesn't like it when you and Kate are alone together after dark, I think."

Kevin looked surprised again. "Why not?"

"It's a daddy-protecting-daughter thing," I replied, trying not to snarl. "It ticks both of us off."

I pulled off my sandals and let my bare feet hang in the cool water. Yellow lamplight reflected off the darkening water. Kevin pulled his knees up under his chin and stared at nothing, though sometimes his eyes would flick in my direction. He still looked nervous. As Kate, I knew, I'd probably want to reach for his hand, but at the moment I felt no such thing. Again, I wanted to know why this was. Kevin hadn't changed, and I still had the same mind, even though it was in a different body. I should feel the same way toward Kevin no matter what. My body should not control me.

But the desires just weren't there. I gave an inward sigh. *This was a bad idea,* I thought. *Kevin is Kate's friend, not Quinn's.*

"I'm kind of glad you came, Quinn," Kevin said quietly. "I mean—I don't get to see you very often."

"It's usually you and Kate who hang around together," I reminded him. "I really only see you in math class." An idea occurred to me. "What do you think of Kate?"

Kevin reached down to fish a small stick out of the lake. "She's one of my best friends. She knows everything about me. Or almost everything."

"She likes you a lot," I told him. "She thinks—I mean, she *talks* about you all the time."

"Really?" He toyed with the stick and gave me another sidelong glance. "That's nice to know, I guess. I just— uh, I just wish I knew *you* better. Being that you're her twin brother and all." The last words came out in a rush.

For some reason, I felt like a varsity quarterback talking to a hero-struck freshman. Kevin's friendship with Quinn, however, wasn't the direction I wanted to take this conversation.

"Well, as Kate's twin," I said aloud, "I can tell you she's interested in you, Kevin. A lot."

I had his full attention. "Interested? What do you mean?"

"Romance. What else? I think Dad's figured it out, which is why he didn't want Kate coming down here by herself to see you." I watched him intently to see how he'd react.

He looked startled and bewildered. "Romance? I— you mean Kate and—? Oh, God." Kevin pulled his knees back up under his chin like a turtle retreating into its shell.

I should have been upset—it seemed obvious that my, or Kate's, feelings weren't returned—but Quinn only cared about Kate's love life in the abstract. "What's the matter?"

"Kate's my best friend," Kevin said quietly. "I didn't think she would be interested in me that way."

"Are you interested in *her* that way?"

His reply was almost inaudible. "Not really. She's my friend."

Suddenly I was glad I had the male body. I didn't think I would be taking this very well as Kate. As it was, I felt a little unsettled. "Is there someone else you're interested in?" I asked despite myself. I wanted to know who my rival was. Kevin had been talking to Paula Greentree a lot lately. Was it her?

"Sort of."

"Who is it?" I probed, forcing my voice to stay calm and gentle and completely unlike Quinn.

Kevin remained silent.

"You can tell me," I said. "I won't tell anyone, I promise. Hey, if I did anything to upset you, Kate would have my balls in a jar. You know that."

A small smile.

"Come on," I teased. "Who is it?"

"You."

The single soft word drilled straight through me. My reply popped out before I could stop it. "Shit."

"You promised not to tell anyone," Kevin said quickly, not looking at me.

"I won't, I won't," I said hurriedly. "But when you said you're interested in me, did you mean . . . *interested* interested?"

Kevin's face was pale as skim milk and I think he was shaking a little. But he managed to nod.

"Shit," I said again, trying to figure out how I felt about all this.

"You hate me, don't you?" Kevin said in that odd, soft voice.

"No," I replied truthfully. But I was definitely off-balance. I should be happy, actually. So Kevin wasn't interested in me quite the way I'd hoped. He *was* interested in me. I was in the unique position of being able to keep my friendship with him as Kate and see him romantically as Quinn. And they all lived happily ever after.

"Look," Kevin said, "I know nothing can come out of this. You've had more girlfriends than I can count. I only told you because you're Kate's brother and I figured I could trust you. But if you're trying to . . . to set me and Kate up, it's not going to—"

I leaned over and kissed him on the lips. His mouth was warm on mine. Kevin froze until I pulled away. We both sat in startled silence for a long moment.

"Quinn?" Kevin asked hesitantly.

I didn't answer. My insides were in a turmoil. I had kissed him on impulse, and it had done nothing for me. Quite the opposite, in fact. I didn't feel . . . disgust, exactly, but I was definitely repulsed. Why? As Kate, I sometimes couldn't think of anything but kissing Kevin. But as Quinn, there was nothing. Nothing at all. Was biology that strong? An angry lump surged into my throat, and I wanted to hit something. Kevin was suddenly a tempting target—he had started all this, hadn't he? If he had just kept his mouth shut, none of this would have happened.

How can you think that? I asked myself in horror. I would *never* want to hit Kevin as Kate. I wasn't going to do it as Quinn, either. Biology was not going to win.

I was still pissed. Why was my mind controlled by my body? I felt trapped, pulled and pushed by forces I didn't understand. The anger surged again.

"I'm sorry, Kevin," I said hoarsely. "It's not what . . . I just thought I'd try . . . I'm sorry." I scrambled to my feet and rushed away.

Gremlin, I said when I got within range of home and Gremlin came back on line, *tell my twin I don't want to talk or Trade now.*

Tell why?

I almost threw my bicycle into the tool shed. *Tomorrow,* I said firmly.

I gave Dad short answers to his questions about how the evening had gone, went upstairs, and lay on my bed with my clothes on. Despite the warning relayed through Gremlin, my twin tried to talk to me several times. I refused to answer. Eventually I fell asleep.

CHAPTER SEVEN

ME

The next day was Friday. I didn't shower or brush my teeth when I got up. My clothes were wrinkled and sweaty, but I didn't change them. They weren't *me*. My body wasn't *me*. How could either one matter?

"What happened to you?" Dad asked when I came downstairs and rummaged through the kitchen for something to eat. Dad rarely fixed breakfast for us anymore, not since my twin and I had in the fourth grade insisted we were "big kids now" and could do it ourselves. Today I wished he would cook, but I couldn't bring myself to say so. I plowed through icebox and pantry as my twin, neatly dressed in slacks and an almost frilly pink blouse, finished toast and sipped coffee.

"There's nothing to eat," I announced in a surly voice.

Dad gave me a look. I avoided meeting his eyes. "I was going to make me some pancakes," he said. "Want some?"

"I guess."

What's with you? my twin demanded. *What happened last night? You look like shit.*

I still don't want to talk about it.

Fine. My twin sniffed at me over the coffee mug. *Just don't ask me to Trade until you've taken a shower. You could at least have your nanos throw the gunk off your skin.*

I don't feel like it.

Dad briskly mixed wet and dry ingredients. The spoon

103

made plopping sounds in the batter. "While you're waiting for breakfast, Quinn, why don't you go upstairs and change your clothes and comb your hair? The pancakes'll take a few minutes."

"I don't want to change clothes."

"You look like you slept in the laundry room," Dad said more sternly. "Go change."

I glared at him for a moment, then decided further argument wasn't worth the effort. I slouched upstairs and changed into a pair of torn shorts and a faded blue shirt with white spots on it where my twin had accidentally spilled some bleach. There. My clothes were clean.

Dad didn't comment on my outfit, which for some reason made me angrier. He set a plate of fluffy brown pancakes in front of me and sat down at his own place. I ate quickly while Dad and my twin carried on a conversation without me. On our way out the door to school, however, Dad stopped me. My twin went on ahead to take our bicycles out of the tool shed.

"Listen," Dad said quietly, "if you want to talk about it, I'm here."

"Talk about what?" I asked defensively.

"Whatever you want."

"You wouldn't understand."

"Maybe I would, maybe I wouldn't," he said. "But I can listen. Just talking about it can help a lot. Take it from someone who's been there, son."

"Son. Right," I snarled, and fled out the door. I refused to look back as I jumped on my bicycle and pedaled as hard as I could.

What are you so mad about? my twin demanded on the road. *And slow down. I can't keep up.*

Trees and fields coasted by. Most people on Felicity make their living at light industry, such as mining clay, or at crafts. On most other worlds, nanobots help build almost everything, and handcrafted items had become more and more rare. Off-worlders pay very well for handmade toys, furniture, and artwork. Anything from Felicity is guaranteed nano-free, which pushes up the price and allows people to make a nice living. I had even managed to sell some of my bowls and vases.

Still, no one can survive on art alone. Felicity has its share of bankers and teachers, clerks and farmers. Hence the neatly planted fields. We passed Mr. Brown's farm cart as he and his horse Blackfoot headed into town with a heavy load of produce. My twin waved at him as we passed and he returned the gesture with a cheery smile.

"Strawberries are early this year," he called. "Be sure and tell your dad I've got some for him."

My twin waved again in acknowledgment, then turned persistently back to me. "Did you see Kevin last night? I need to know. We'll both see him today and I need to know what to say if he brings anything up."

My twin had a point. In short, terse sentences, I explained what had happened last night. My twin gave a low whistle as we reached the Rushton town limits and turned toward the high school. Out of habit we slowed so we could more easily dodge around carriages, pedestrians, horses, and the pungent piles left by the latter. Summer was all but here, and people were out early, enjoying the sunshine on their way to work. Others swept their porches or shoved push mowers over their lawns before the day got hot. Flowers still bloomed in window boxes like happy flags, and a mag-lev train coasted silently into the distance. None of it could brighten my mood.

Poor Kevin, Gremlin commented as I finished my narrative.

"Yeah," my twin said. "He pours his heart out and you stomp on it."

"I didn't stomp on it," I protested. "Not on purpose. I thought I'd be interested, but I wasn't. Not in this body, anyway. Trade me, okay? I need to talk to him, and I think it'll be easier as Kate."

My twin's nose wrinkled. "Forget it. You didn't shower and you're wearing a ragbag. You can just stay male today. I'll talk to Kevin and let you know what happens."

But Kevin wasn't in school. I drifted through classes, only half paying attention. Kevin liked me when I was a guy, I liked him when I was a girl. The more I thought about it, the more disgusted I got.

I skipped biology class.

That evening at home, I sat in the Kate room and stared at my twin's bug collection. Each specimen was precisely pinned down and neatly labeled. I thought about Trading and trying some sculpting to get my mind off things, but I knew that the moment I became Kate, I would become upset over "losing" Kevin, and I didn't want to deal with that. Right now I was angry at the world. Nature controlled me, kept me pinned to her board, categorized and classified. I had no idea what to do about it. Was this why I had been good at marbles as a girl and good at kickball as a boy? Was this why I could sculpt as Kate and run as Quinn?

I stomped downstairs, determined to prove nature wrong. Sure, running was something that depended on the body, but sculpture was an art—mental. It didn't matter which body I had.

I sat down at my worktable in the cool basement and cut a lump of clay from my stock. I added some water and kneaded it with both hands until it was soft enough to work. Then I threw the brown lump on my potter's wheel and pumped the pedal with my feet to set it spinning. I decided to make another cereal bowl for the set I was finishing for export.

The clay turned beneath my hands, but it refused to even out into a smooth mound. I added more water and tried again. My forehead furrowed in concentration for a while, but then my mind wandered. This was boring. It would be more fun to get up, go outside in this nice weather and run. My favorite path through the woods seemed to be calling me. I could almost see the leaves dissolve into a blue-green blur as I rushed past them up the trail.

One of my fingers cut a deep groove into the spinning clay. I blew out a frustrated breath and forced myself to pay attention. But my fingers wouldn't do what I wanted them to. I knew what I wanted the end result to look like, but my hands couldn't seem to get it right. I persisted, forcing every other thought from my mind. The clay eventually smoothed into an even lump. I wet it again and stuck my first two fingers into the top. With what I thought was gentle, steady pressure, I pushed outward to open the mound into a bowl. The process looks easy to a casual observer, but it had actually taken me—as Kate—months to get right. If you slip, or the pressure isn't even, or if you add too much water, you get a bowl that looks half melted.

My pressure wasn't steady. The bowl wobbled drunkenly. I mashed the clay back together and tried again. Another crooked piece of junk. I tried three more times and only produced pieces even the most charitable parent would hide in the attic.

In frustration, I slammed the stubborn clay onto my worktable, rushed upstairs, and out the back door for a long, angry run.

"All right," my twin said ominously. "I've had enough. I want to know what's going on. Talk!"

I looked up from my wheel. Clay smeared my face and the ruins of yet another bowl spun lopsidedly before me. "Talk about what?"

You, Gremlin put in. *Something wrong. Something bad.*

My foot stilled on the pedal in surprise and the wheel drifted to a halt. Gremlin was getting involved? For real? I stared at my twin, who was still female and wore an immaculate outfit—dark pleated skirt, freshly ironed red blouse, hair worn in a single braid with only a few curls managing to escape.

"What's up?" I asked shortly.

"You had the . . . incident with Kevin on Thursday," my twin said. "Today is Sunday. We haven't Traded—or talked much—in all that time. You nano-cleaned yourself on Friday only after Dad threatened to throw you into the shower, and I still haven't seen you wearing anything but junk that should've been made into rag rugs ages ago. Dad's worried sick, and we—Gremlin and I—want to know what's going on."

"I don't want to talk about it."

"Then Trade me. Maybe that'll make it easier."

I flung the clay at the wall. It stuck with a satisfying *smack*. "Why would that make it easier? I'd still be *me*. Or I should be. It's always changing."

Changes back whenever you want it to, Gremlin said.

"I don't want it to change at all! Tell me this—am I Kate or Quinn?"

Both.

My twin perched carefully on a rickety chair and shrugged. "We're *us*. What do names matter? Other people gave them to us. *We* didn't decide to use them."

"That's not what I mean." I sank back down to the stool by the potter's wheel. "I mean, I don't know who I am anymore. Am I Kate the sculptor or Quinn the runner? Why can't I be Quinn the runner *and* sculptor?"

My twin gestured at the half dozen sloppy bowls and failed vases. "Is that why you've been trying to work with clay all weekend? To prove you can do it as a male?"

"I hate this body," I muttered.

"Then give it to me," my twin said. "It needs a good hot shower, and you don't seem to be inclined to give it one."

I pursed my lips as my twin's nanos knocked against mine. I closed my eyes and Traded.

"Yuck," my twin said, rising from the wheel and heading for the stairs. "I think I'll take a bath. A real *long* bath."

I sat on the rickety chair in my skirt and blouse, hair still damp from my twin's morning shower. The clay called to me. All of a sudden I could see shapes in the lumps, figures in the mud. They called to me, almost mesmerizing. All desire to go running was gone. Carefully tucking my skirt away from the gears, I sat at my wheel. I let my hands rest on the cool, soothing clay for a moment. Then I went to work. Clay molded and flowed like brown silk under my hands. Lopsided bowls sat up straight, and crooked vases righted themselves at my touch.

Nice work, Gremlin commented. *But face and clothes now muddy. Twin will be unhappy.*

I didn't reply. After the last bowl sat drying on the table, I went up to my room and stared at the other clay figures. One of them was a bust of Kevin I had done six months ago. His features weren't quite proportionate—I was still figuring out how to do people—but it was easily recognizable as him. Feelings mixed and churned inside me. Kevin liked me—Kate—as a friend, but not as anything more than that. The me that he *was* interested in wasn't interested back. I wondered if Kevin's interest lay in his mind or his biology, and tears formed at the corners of my eyes. I swiped at them with clay-brown fingers.

We still love you, Gremlin said. *Will be plenty of other people to meet, even if are not Kevin.*

Thanks, I said, sitting down on the bed with a sniffle. *It doesn't help much, but thanks, Gremlin.*

"Life sucks," my twin agreed from the door. The ragged clothes had vanished, replaced by crisply pressed slacks and a spotless white polo shirt that almost gleamed. It made a pleasing contrast with our olive-dark skin. "Jesus—what did you do?"

I looked down at my spattered skirt and ruined blouse. "I was throwing bowls."

"At yourself?" my twin complained. "I just washed that hair this morning. You take a shower and wash your hair before supper. I'm not doing it again."

My chin thrust forward. "And if I don't?"

"Then you can stay in the female body until you do—and don't forget our period is supposed to start any day now. I'm not sharing cramps if I'll also have to deal with a dirty, smelly body."

I noticed a backpack was flung over my twin's shoulder. "What's that for?" I asked.

"I'm going out for a while," my twin said.

"Scouting a new girlfriend?" I said nastily. "Go see Kevin. He'll probably blow you."

Not nice, Gremlin said.

My twin, for once, didn't rise to the bait. Instead, my twin sat down on the bed next to me and took my hand. "Look, I know you're mad at Kevin, and maybe even yourself. But none of this is your fault. Kevin's the way he is and you're the way you are. Nothing's perfect, especially on this stupid planet."

"What's wrong with Felicity?" I asked, snatching at the chance to change the subject.

"Everything. Look at us—our family has a complete monopoly on nanos, but we can't do much with them." My twin gestured at the window. "There's a whole universe out there. I want to go see it. Feel it. Think of what we're missing—computers, networks, virtual reality. Out there, you can talk to anyone you want on any planet at any time. You can put on a virtual reality rig and be anything you want, do whatever you feel like, and not have to care about getting hurt. You can access music from a hundred worlds. And we're stuck here on boring, dead Felicity."

"I like it here," I said truthfully. "So does Dad."

"He's keeping us prisoners here," my twin said heatedly. "He gets to leave whenever he wants but we're stranded. He's packing right now. Didn't you hear the car?"

I got up and looked out the window at a red electric car parked in the driveway. Someone was sitting inside, though I couldn't see who it was. A small knot of worry clenched in my stomach. Nothing ever happened to Dad on these trips, but I still wondered if this time would be it. "Another hive? That's the third this year."

"There are more computers—and nanos—out there than ever," my twin observed. "Not that *we* ever get to see them."

Gremlin, are you going, too? I asked.

Have to, Gremlin said. *No choice.*

But Dad says you don't help him, I pointed out not for the first time. *You can't even talk to him.*

Still go, Gremlin replied. *Have to.* And that was all it would ever say on the subject.

"The only time Dad leaves is if a nanobot hive crops up somewhere," I pointed out to my twin. "This is where we live."

"It's a stupid place to live."

"It's not spoiled by developers. And computers and virtual reality and all that only make life fast and hard and give you heart attacks and stress."

"Now you sound like Dad." My twin shifted the backpack. "Me, I could use some stress. Some *excitement*."

"Hey, you two," Dad said, suddenly appearing in the doorway. "Another business call. I have to go."

Business call. That was what he called nanobot hives now. Suddenly I wanted to talk to him about . . . about everything. Kevin, who I was, nanobots, biology. He said one of his old personalities had been a woman, so maybe he'd remember what it was like to switch between being male and being female. I opened my mouth to ask him to stay, to forget about the hive. Then I closed it. He always went, no matter what either of us said. It was like a law of nature. No point in trying.

"We saw the car," I said instead.

He looked closer at me. "What happened to you? Potter's wheel explode?"

I managed a smile. "Clay fight with Gremlin."

"Be careful with that hive," my twin said. "When are you going to be back?"

"Soon as I can. Mrs. Wells'll be checking on you once in a while, okay?"

We both nodded. He said he loved us and left.

"See?" my twin whispered. "He gets excitement. We get Mrs. Wells."

I had to laugh.

That evening, several hours after Dad's faceless escort had driven him away and quite a while after my twin had gone looking look for excitement, Mrs. Wells dropped by to check on us. Mrs. Wells looked quite a lot older than she had when my twin and I were in elementary school, as well she should—she was as old as Grandma. Grandma, though, never changed. Truth be told, neither did many people on Felicity. An awful lot of older people took vacations off planet and came back looking younger. Bodysculpt isn't illegal on other planets, and youth seems to be beautiful no matter where you go.

Mrs. Wells, however, didn't seem to care. Silver had encroached on her brown hair. A few wrinkles had spread across her round face, but not as many as you might think. Must be the stress-free life on Felicity.

I assured Mrs. Wells that we were fine and that Quinn was taking a run through the woods, though I knew for a fact he was somewhere else. Probably in someone's bed.

"And how are you doing, dear?" she asked. "I don't want to pry, but you look a fright."

She was right. I hadn't washed up except to rinse my hands before lunch. In many ways, Mrs. Wells was more a grandmother to me than Meredeth Michaels, and she knew how to read me fairly well, though it occurred to me that it had been a long time since my twin and I visited her for a special taste-testing. Still, I couldn't exactly tell Mrs. Wells what was bothering me.

"Just lots of sculpting," I told her. "I was just about to get into the shower."

"Come over and see me when you're done, dear," she told me. "We can have some tea and talk. I'll be waiting."

I couldn't refuse her. And now I would really have to take a shower. I reluctantly told her I'd be over in a bit.

An hour later I was sipping iced peppermint tea and nibbling on ginger cookies at Mrs. Wells's little kitchen table. We talked about the weather (warm), final exams (up-and-coming), and the cookies (gingery).

"Now then, Kate," Mrs. Wells said after a discussion on whether real vanilla made cookies taste any different, "why don't you tell me what's been bothering you lately? When I saw you on the front lawn, you looked ready to burst into tears."

I took a cool sip of sweet, minty tea, wondering how I should answer. Silence stretched between us.

"Let me guess and you tell me if I'm right," Mrs. Wells said at last. "That way, you don't have to feel embarrassed about saying it aloud."

"Uh—"

"It's a boy, isn't it?"

I felt like a deer trapped in the headlight of a mag-lev train, and it must have shown on my face.

"I thought so," Mrs. Wells said. "That Kevin Sanders fellow?"

Startled, I nodded. How in the world did she know?

Mrs. Wells chuckled. "What, do you think I popped out of the womb looking like this, with gray hair on my head and bosoms down to my knees? I was fifteen once—for a whole year, even. Let me guess again. You want to be more than a friend and he doesn't."

I hid my embarrassment behind a sip of tea. Did everyone know?

Mrs. Wells made a *tsk*ing sound. "Life sucks, doesn't it?"

I snorted. Mrs. Wells smiled at me. "You think that's a new term? My grandmother used it, hon. And here's something else that sucks—you probably can't change the situation."

She was both right and wrong there, though I couldn't exactly say so. I took another cookie.

"I can tell you this," Mrs. Wells went on thoughtfully. "You will get over it. It's awful right now, but eventually the pain goes away. What sucks is that all you can do is wait it out."

I wasn't so sure about that, but nodded anyway. Strangely, I felt a little better—not much, but a little. After promising Mrs. Wells to stop by tomorrow for more long-neglected taste-testing, I went home.

My twin wasn't there. Probably off with some girl expanding our sex life.

Sex, I groused. *Who needs it?*

A few hours later, I fed the horses and went to bed. My twin hadn't come home. Quinn's bed was still empty in the morning.

I felt weighed down, trapped by my body, and I wasn't going to let it rule me. Biology wouldn't have the satisfaction. Rather than shower, I wore my hair back and yanked on the first clothes that came to hand. It occurred to me that I'd probably have to talk to Kevin today, and I didn't really look forward to seeing him. It would hurt.

As it happened, I didn't have to worry about it. Kevin avoided me, even in the two classes we shared. He wouldn't look at me, pretended I didn't exist. That was fine with me—it made it easier to swallow the lumps that kept rising in my throat. I didn't even get to ask why he'd been absent from school on Friday, though I could guess. He hadn't wanted to face me—us.

My twin wasn't home when I got out of school, but Dad was. His clothes were rumpled and his carryall sat next to the door, meaning he had just arrived and hadn't had a chance to unpack yet. I bore the traditional welcome-home hug with stoic resignation.

"Where's your brother?" Dad asked.

"I don't know." Usually I'd cover for my twin, but I

today I wasn't in the mood. "I was the only one in the house last night."

The corners of Dad's mouth turned down. "He didn't come home?"

"Nope. I have no idea why, either."

In the end, Dad called the sheriff—one of the advantages of having a telephone in the house. A deputy rode over on a bay gelding and asked both of us a lot of questions about where my twin might have gone, but neither of us could be very helpful. Dad hitched up our buggy to join in a search party. I stayed home from school so someone would be around in case my twin came back. Dad's carryall still sat unpacked by the front door.

I waited on the front porch for most of the day and tried not to worry. My twin was fine. There would be hell to pay later, of course, but my twin was fine. Somewhere. I just didn't know where.

What if this was a kidnapping? Dad was rich. What if someone had decided to cash in on that and snatched my twin? What if the kidnapper panicked and killed my twin? I'd be stuck in the same body forever and Gremlin would die as well.

Don't be silly, I told myself. *It's not a kidnapping. We haven't gotten a ransom note.*

Yet.

Every so often the phone would ring, and I would leap to answer it. It was always a deputy wanting to know if I had heard anything from my twin, and the answer was always no. Evening approached and the worry grew until it even pushed Kevin from my thoughts. My twin, my other half, had vanished. I couldn't sit still. I paced over every inch of the house until my legs ached. I wanted to go out and search but didn't dare leave the house in case someone—the sheriff, my twin, a kidnapper—called.

The sun had just set when the buggy pulled into the driveway. It was Dad, with my twin sitting on the seat next to him. I shot out the door.

∗Where have you been?∗ I demanded. *∗What happened?∗*

∗Later,∗ my twin answered shortly, and climbed down as Dad brought the horse to a halt. My twin's clothes were wrinkled and sweat-stained but they weren't torn or bloody. My twin snatched the backpack from the seat and stalked inside.

∗Gremlin?∗ I asked.

∗Here,∗ it replied. *∗But only came back on line a few minutes ago, when twin was in range of house. Know nothing.∗*

"Where?" I asked Dad, who knew what I meant.

"I found him in Skytown," Dad said quietly. He got down from the buggy to lead the horse back to the stable and I saw from tone and posture that he was angry beyond reason. More questions would only make him angrier, but my twin wasn't talking and I had to know.

"In Skytown?" I asked, falling into step alongside Dad. "Doing what?"

"Screwing around on the skyhook's computer systems," Dad said. "Your brother managed to crash three separate systems before I caught up with him. He cost the sky- and spaceports I don't know *how* much. Fortunately for all of us, I found him before the police did."

Dad's tone said he didn't want more questions, so I left him to the unhitching and went back to the house. My twin was in Quinn's room, clad in a robe and heading for the shower.

"Looking for adventure, huh?" I said sarcastically.

"Looking for a shower, huh?" was the equally sarcastic reply. "You smell worse than I do."

I followed my twin into the bathroom. My twin got the water running, dropped the robe, and stepped into the shower. "What were you doing with the skyhook's computer system? You really pissed Dad off."

The water was too loud for easy vocal conversation. *∗Yeah, yeah. So he'll ground me for a while. It was great!*

*You really should try it. These nanos we have can do more than just screw around with our bodies. We can screw around with computers, too.**

So what? There aren't any computers on Felicity except at the hospital. And if you mess around with those, someone could die.

All I wanted to do was talk to some computers on another planet. But I must've been doing something wrong because the systems kept crashing.

You're lucky no one died at the spaceport, I almost snapped. *What if you had caused two ships to collide or something because you confused their systems?**

I didn't. But my twin's tone told me that this idea had never crossed my twin's mind.

What if you had?

I didn't, okay? Geez, I'm already in enough trouble. Get off my back.

You had everyone worried sick, I replied, furious. **I thought you had been kidnapped or someone had killed you.**

Now you sound like Dad. The water shut off. My twin stepped out of the shower and reached for a towel. "I want to get off this backwater planet. I want to explore. What's wrong with that?"

"Worrying me sick, that's what," I said. "Not to mention that Gremlin disappears when you get out of range."

"Kate, what are you doing in here?"

I jumped and looked over my shoulder. Dad was behind me. My twin quickly wrapped up in the towel.

"We're talking about what happened," I said.

"You shouldn't be in the bathroom when your brother's in the shower." There was an angry green glint in Dad's eyes. I was about to protest that he was being stupid, then decided Dad was mad enough. I left.

Dad grounded my twin for a month. School and home, that was it. In addition, my twin was made responsible for most of our shared chores. Through it all, my twin remained defiant, whether male or female.

In retrospect, I realize that this was the point where my twin started keeping the male body for longer and longer periods of time. When the grounding was up—we were in full summer by then—my twin went out and laid the first girl he could persuade. The almost compulsive cleanliness and attention to dress continued, and despite the fact that running was *my* male interest, my twin took it up along with weightlifting and even some gymnastics. My twin also took another trip to Skytown, but returned long before anyone noticed anything. There were no reported computer crashes. All this was done in the male body.

I suppose I should have been annoyed with my twin for forcing me to stay in one body for so long, but I had stopped caring. Male, female—what did it matter? I was me. The rest was unimportant. I only showered or nano-cleaned when Dad or my twin forced the issue. My clothes rarely matched. Sometimes I'd just stay in my bathrobe all day and sculpt. My twin claimed this was the primary reason for not Trading often—daily maintenance on two bodies was too much for one person. I shrugged it off.

My sculpting changed as well. I became fascinated with Salvador Dali and tried to bring his style of painting to clay. Instead of solid bowls and mugs and vases that were fun to sell to the off-planet markets, I started work on surreal figurines—spindly trees, delicate castles, weird animals, even clay friezes of landscapes that defied physics. My buyer shook his head, saying he doubted there was much market for any of it, but I didn't much care. Money was as unimportant as my body. The odd sculptures piled up, and my twin and I spent less and less time with each other.

Gremlin, meanwhile, became less and less communicative. It lost consciousness every time my twin ran off, and I'm afraid I wasn't much of a comfort to it. I was angry a lot, and tended to snap at people, including Gremlin and Dad.

Looking back, I realize how hard this must have been on Dad. He had no support, no one to turn to for advice or help. People in town began to notice how our behavior was changing and to gossip about it, but Dad couldn't exactly explain what was going on. If anyone knew about our nanos, we'd be banished from Felicity forever, and Dad loved living there. I think that was the only reason my twin didn't reveal our secret to the government so we'd be forced to move—my twin didn't really want to hurt Dad.

This went on for three years. I was in the female body so much that I sometimes forgot to respond to the name Quinn on the rare occasions I was male. And then one fall day I was walking down the street and everything changed.

The day was unseasonably warm. Rushton is in a mild part of Felicity's climate, and it never really gets extremely cold, but today felt more like a Saturday in July than October. Sunshine pressed warm against my back and the top of my head, and horses clopped past on the stony street. My twin was off somewhere again, and I was just thinking some ice cream would be nice when I turned a corner and all but ran into Kevin.

We both stopped and stared at each other, startled. Kevin and I never did really talk after that evening at Constance Park. After a few weeks of avoiding each other, it got harder and harder to break the silence. Finally it had become the standard. Now, three years later, we were face to face on the boardwalk in front of Marshall's Bookstore. Kevin was filling out, losing the awkward gangliness he'd had at fifteen and becoming tall and broad-shouldered. He wore his auburn hair a little longer now, but his eyes were the same green I had found so handsome in elementary school. He looked great in a yellow shirt and dark slacks and I felt abruptly grubby in my torn jeans and dirty T-shirt. I hadn't realized how much I missed him until that moment.

"Hey," I said awkwardly. "How's it going?"

"Hey, Kate," he replied, equally uncomfortable. "It's, um, been a while."

I nodded. "What have you been up to?"

"Oh, you know—school and stuff. How's your brother?"

"Fine." *Great repartee,* I thought. Kevin used to be so easy to talk to. Now there was a gulf between us. I was suddenly hungry for the old Kevin, the one I could laugh on the swings with, not a Kevin who would sweep me away into some romantic fairy tale.

"Well," he said, "I've got some stuff to do. I'll see you around."

He turned to go. Loneliness welled up inside me. My twin and I were drifting apart. Gremlin was off line more often than not. Dad and Mrs. Wells were hard to talk to. Was everyone leaving? Was I that alone?

So do something about it, dummy!

"Kevin," I called, and he turned. "I was going to get some ice cream. Do you want to come? We could talk about . . . stuff."

Kevin didn't move for a long moment and I held my breath. Finally he said, "Why not?"

Allbee's Drugstore was across the street. We dodged bicycles and carriages to get there. The interior was cool with its polished tile floor and gray marble counter. We ordered two sodas—chocolate for me, strawberry and root beer for Kevin. I smiled.

"You still order that weird combo," I said.

He smiled back. "It's no weirder than those peanut butter and mustard sandwiches you used to bring for lunch."

"What do you mean, used to?"

We both laughed and took our sodas to one of the marble-topped tables. There were about two dozen other people perched at the counter or occupying spindly black chairs around the other tables. At least half of them kept looking around the drugstore or craning their necks to look out the window. Tourists. Felicity had been attracting a fair amount of them in the past few years. The Senate allowed them to visit provided they left all traces of forbidden technology, including holocams, on the space station connected to Skytown. Kerry's Department Store made a killing on "old-fashioned" film cameras as a result, and Jane Allbee, whose father owned the drugstore, was talking about opening a fudge and candy shop after she graduated high school this year. Tourists love fudge.

"So what have you been doing with yourself all this time?" Kevin asked, pushing the straw aside and digging at the ice cream with his spoon.

"Lots of sculpting." I plucked the disgusting red cherry from the whipped cream and threw it away. "I've gone through enough clay to build half a dozen jumpships by now. What about you?"

"I'm taking a lot of tough courses this year," he said. "Advanced biology, chemistry. I want to study medicine, I'll have to go off planet, of course, but I'm planning to come back here and open up my own practice."

My ice cream was hard as a rock. I sent a regiment of nanos into the glass to spread the molecules apart a little, let in some air to soften it up. Silence threatened to fall between us, and I was afraid if I let it, it would never lift.

"I've missed you," I said to my soda. "A lot."

Kevin flushed.

"Not like that," I hurried on. "I mean, Quinn told me what happened at the park that night. I was upset then, and I avoided you. But I'm over it now, and I'm sorry I treated you like shit. I've missed having you for a friend."

Kevin sighed. The sound was heavy with relief. "I've missed you, too. I shouldn't have avoided you, but I couldn't face you, either. I haven't had anyone I could really talk to in a long time." He slurped at his root beer. "Friends?"

"Friends." We shook hands and I poked at my ice

cream again. It was soft. I took a chocolatey mouthful and let it melt sweetly on my tongue.

"That was one hell of a night," Kevin said in a voice that carried no farther than our table. "I couldn't believe I told Quinn I was gay. But it just felt like I could trust him with it and I was kind of hoping . . . " He flushed again. "Well, you know what I was hoping."

All too well. "Do you still feel that way about him?"

"Quinn?" Kevin shook his head. "That was three years ago. I've gotten over it." He gave an impish smile. "Do you still feel that way about me?"

"I've gotten over it," I replied with a grin and realized it was completely true. "So. Are you seeing anyone? Boyfriend, I mean?"

"I was for a little while," Kevin said.

I leaned forward, palms flat on the cool tabletop. "Who?"

He laughed. "I'm not telling you. Just because you know about me doesn't mean you have the right to know about everyone else."

"C'mon," I cajoled. "You can tell me. We can keep a secret—Quinn and me, I mean. We've kept yours for this long, haven't we?"

"A secret has a better shelf life if fewer people know about it," he said airily. "Rushton isn't exactly known for being liberal. Skytown's more tolerant—there's a bar there that's mostly for . . . for guys like me—but even there you have to be careful. Besides, he's my *ex*-boyfriend now. Let it be a mystery."

We talked of other things as our sodas steadily disappeared. With every word, I felt the gulf between us shrink until it became nothing but a near-invisible crack. Leaving our empty glasses on the table, we left the drugstore and wandered off toward Constance Park. The sun was still warm, and I was sweating by the time we reached the comforting shelter of the trees. We headed down to the beach, where the predatory ducks were waiting as always. I threw a rock at them, and they grudgingly swam away. Kevin snorted. I thought about the crush I had had on him and the failed biology between us as we sat down on the blue-green grass by the water.

"Have you ever wished you were straight?" I asked.

He automatically glanced around, but no one was within hearing range. "It'd be easier," he admitted. "But I wouldn't change being gay. It's like asking if I'd rather be a woman than a man."

A pang went through me. "What do you mean?"

"Being gay is a part of me, like having two hands and two feet or being a guy. I'd be a completely different person if I were straight or a woman." He spread his hands. "Men and women think differently. Don't tell me you haven't noticed."

"I've noticed. I just don't understand *why*."

He shrugged. "Does it matter? It'd be a boring universe if we all thought and acted the same. It's the differences that make it all interesting. I mean, imagine if you had nothing but history class all day long."

"No thank you."

"See?" Kevin pulled his knees up under his chin and I felt a surge of déjà vu. "I've done some reading in the library at Skytown. Some cultures think that gay men are a bridge between the sexes because gays are men, that they feel the way women do. I think they're wrong. I don't know how a woman feels. I'm not a woman."

"But you should know," I argued. "We're all people, aren't we?"

"I guess," he replied slowly. "But we're all different. I mean, I've been gay as long as I can remember. Near as I can tell, I was born that way. I tried going out with a couple of girls. But it just didn't feel right. Kissing a girl is like kissing my sister or something. It's no fun. Guys, though—that's something else entirely."

"Kissing a guy makes you happy?" I asked softly.

"You know it. When Quinn kissed me that one time, it didn't work for him, but it sure worked for me!" He laughed. "After a while, I realized I was making myself *un*happy by fighting that part of me all the time. Then Larry and I got together and—"

He clapped a hand over his mouth.

"Larry?" I asked incredulously. There was only one Larry at Rushton High School that I knew of. "Larry Friend? The quiet blond guy?"

"Don't you tell anyone," Kevin pleaded, his green eyes wide. "Larry's terrified that someone will find out. You know how shy he is."

"I won't tell. I promise." I leaned down and swished a hand through the clear water. "Okay, so you're attracted to men whether you like it or not. Doesn't that make you feel trapped?"

"Trapped?" Kevin said. "No. I like being attracted to men." He paused. "Let me put it this way. You like chocolate, don't you?"

A weird change of subject, but I went along with it. "Of course."

"Remember in ninth-grade biology when Mrs. Macer said humans are programmed to like sweets because nothing that tastes sweet is poisonous in nature?"

"Vaguely."

"So in other words, you're going to like chocolate whether you want to or not. It's part of your genetic programming. Does that make you feel trapped?"

I could see where this was going, and it made a strange kind of sense. "No."

"There you go. Just because your genes make you like chocolate doesn't mean you can't enjoy eating it." He grinned at me. "It's the same with me for guys."

"You mean you enjoy eating—"

"I think," Kevin interrupted, "that our friendship would be better off if you didn't finish that sentence."

We both laughed, and I felt better than I had in months, maybe even years. I'd been focusing so hard on the negative aspects of Trading and being male or female that I'd forgotten the positive aspects. So what if I couldn't sculpt as a male? That didn't mean I couldn't enjoy it as a female. And if my twin and I weren't able to Trade and I had been born male, I wouldn't be able to sculpt at all. A weight seemed to fall from my shoulders and I took a long breath of sweet lake air.

"There's something I've been meaning to ask you," Kevin said, unaware of what he had done for me. "What's with the wardrobe change? Going for the grunge look in a big way or what?"

I looked down at my torn blue jeans and dirty red T-shirt. The latter sported drops of melted chocolate. I caught one on a fingertip and stuck it in my mouth to savor the sweet taste.

"It's a passing phase," I said. "Want to help me pick out something else?"

CHAPTER EIGHT

ME

"I don't want to Trade," my twin said stubbornly. "I've got a date."

"You always have a date," I snapped. "And you always want the male body. I don't think I've had it for more than twelve hours in a row since last summer."

"You never cared before."

"I care now."

Outside, a gentle snow was falling from a darkening sky. It didn't snow often in Rushton and normally my twin and I would be outside enjoying it, but that didn't look likely at the moment. My twin glared at me from the closet door. Clothes, all for the male body, were strewn across the bed as if the closet had exploded. I didn't understand it. Since my conversation with Kevin, I'd gone back to more normal dress and hygiene, much to Dad's relief, but my twin's habits bordered on obsession, and I didn't know where it came from. Every outfit had to be perfectly coordinated. Every hair had to be in place. Every day required at least two showers and three nano-cleans. And my twin hogged the male body incessantly through it all.

I had gone past annoyed and was well into anger. There were times I wanted to be male, especially when Dad was going through a protect-my-darling-daughter phase. It didn't seem to matter whether it was me or my twin in the Kate body—it was still harder to persuade him to let the female body go out than the male body.

127

The male body was more athletic than the female, and if I wanted to do something that involved speed and strength, I was better off as Quinn. We were also supposed to divide the female body's menstrual cycle evenly between us. But lately my twin always seemed to have an excuse to remain Quinn. The "I have a date" version was the most common.

"Look, we'll Trade after I get back, all right?" my twin said, pulling on a sweater and reaching for the lint brush.

"Whenever we Trade after one of your 'dates,' the male body is always tired and drained."

"I can't help it if I'm popular."

"You aren't *that* popular. You beat off if you don't get what you're after."

"So what? Just because you're not interested in sex doesn't mean the rest of us have to go without."

"Then why not go on a date as Kate? I told you I didn't care anymore if you lost the body's virginity as long as you don't get it pregnant."

"I don't want to, okay?" My twin checked the mirror for out-of-place hairs again.

"And what about poor Gremlin?" I said, switching tactics. "Every time you go out, Gremlin loses consciousness. It doesn't like that."

"Gremlin doesn't mind. I've asked."

Is that true? I said, surprised.

Not involved, Gremlin replied. *No fighting. Please?*

"Gremlin," I said, "is being a wimp. Anything to keep the peace. I think Gremlin *is* bothered but it says it isn't because it figured you'd be unhappy."

My twin glanced at the clock. "Look, I'm running late. We'll talk about it later."

And he left.

I fumed. *He.* I had been female for so long, I was starting to think in terms of my twin being male.

Gremlin, why don't you ever say anything? Don't wimp out like that.

Don't like getting caught between, Gremlin said quietly. *Unfair to everyone.*

Including you. Doesn't it bother you, disappearing like that?

Silence. Then, *No memory of lost time. Is like blinking eyes—one moment it's now, next moment it's then. Doesn't hurt.*

I made an exasperated noise. *You're hopeless, Gremlin.*

Furious, I stomped downstairs. Dad was building up the fire in the little living room stove. The smell of wood smoke hovered in the air.

"I was going to make some popcorn," he said. "Want some?"

"I guess." I dropped into an easy chair. The room was definitely chilly and I shivered, unused to the cold, until my nanos could compensate. "Does it get this cold back on Earth?"

"In some places it gets so cold, you can't go outside without getting frostbite," Dad replied, blowing on coals to coax the wood into flame. "You're mad at your brother, aren't you?"

The anger boiled slowly inside me like black glue. "I wanted to Trade," I said. "I've been female so much lately, I've almost forgotten what it's like to be male. It isn't fair. Why don't you do anything?"

Dad reached for the corn popper. It looked like a small wire cage with a long handle. "I'm not sure what I should do. You two aren't little kids anymore. Why can't you work it out yourselves?" He poured popcorn into the cage with a wry grin. "This sort of thing isn't in the parents' manual. Chapter Six: What To Do If Your Kids Fight About Trading Bodies."

I snorted in spite of myself.

"I think Quinn'll come around." Dad opened the stove door and poked the popper inside. "You've said yourself that both of you start feeling trapped if you're in a single body for too long."

I took the popper from him. "Let me do this. You always burn it."

"I do not," Dad protested. "Who do you think popped corn when you were little?"

"And I was ten before I realized popcorn was white instead of black." I shook the popper, and the corn rattled inside. The heat from the stove felt good. "I don't know if waiting for my twin to feel trapped is going to work. I think *he* enjoys being male, or something." *"Something" called sex*, I added privately.

"You've gone through this before, you know." A kernel popped with a loud puffing noise. "I remember when you were nine or ten and both of you went long periods without Trading."

"Not this long. I haven't been male for almost two weeks."

Dad looked like he was going to say something, then apparently decided to keep quiet instead. Outside, hooves clopped up the driveway and the carriage creaked into the distance as my twin drove off to meet his date. The popcorn started popping furiously, a horde of frantic white frogs leaping around a black cage. It smelled delicious, but my mind was elsewhere.

"Why don't you go out more often?" Dad asked.

I blinked at him. Then I realized I had stopped shaking the popper. Quickly I yanked it out of the stove. A few kernels had burned, but nothing serious. Dad had already set a large bowl on the stove with a little butter in the bottom. The butter had melted and I carefully poured the popped corn into the bowl.

"You don't like it when I go out as Kate," I said cautiously, not really wanting another fight. I suddenly wondered if Gremlin felt this way a lot.

Dad raised his eyebrows. "What makes you say that?"

"You ask more questions about who I—Kate—will be with, and why I want to see this guy, and where are we going and don't forget curfew is midnight." I sprinkled salt over the bowl. "You don't give me the third degree when I'm Quinn. Plus whenever Quinn is a little late, you don't seem to mind, but if Kate is a little late, you blow a fuse."

"I do not."

"You do, too. I don't think you even realize it." I popped several buttery-salty popcorn kernels into my mouth. "But I'm also just not as interested in going out as Quinn is. Not anymore."

Dad reached for the popcorn bowl. "I try to treat you both the same, no matter what gender you are."

"Try harder, Dad," I sighed. "Try harder."

"Oh, shit."

I glanced over at my twin, who was slapping *her* forehead. We were on our way to school in the carriage. The cold and snow hadn't let up, and Dad was letting us drive until the snow melted and temperatures got back to normal. The temperature didn't bother us. The carriage was simply safer than a bicycle when it came to slippery roads. I was driving, leather reins held lightly in my right hand, and my breath made clouds. Tiny flakes of snow landed on my face and melted, but not without leaving tiny pinpricks of cold.

"What's wrong?" I asked. "You didn't forget our homework, did you?"

"I'm supposed to meet Karen today," my twin said. "We were going to study after school."

My jaw tightened. I had the Quinn body for the first time in days. No way was I going to give it up. "So I'll cancel for you."

"It's just that we've been trying to get together on this for two weeks," my twin said.

"Since when do you study for anything two weeks early?" I almost snapped. "This isn't a study thing at all, I can see that already."

"Karen likes me," my twin said, toying with a long lock of black hair. "And she needs help with biology."

"I'll bet."

"Come on," my twin said. "I promise I'll Trade you back when we're through."

"No." The horse clopped patiently along through the morning semidarkness. We had to leave earlier than usual if we wanted to drive. Hitching and unhitching took time, and with a carriage we had to negotiate through traffic a bicycle could maneuver around. Snow blanketed the silent fields and made a glittering white coat on every tree branch. The only sound was the dull clump of the horse's hooves on packed snow and our arguing.

"Look," my twin said, "I know I've been male a lot lately, but this is a special case. If I break this off with Karen, she's going to be royally pissed at me."

"Forget it."

"Just Trade me at the end of the day," my twin reasoned. "Then we'll Trade back when I get home for supper."

"I'm running after school," I said, trying not to get angry. "The woods are going to be beautiful."

"Do it this evening."

"In the dark?"

"Look, I'm only trying to be accommodating."

"Accommodating?" I burst out. The horse laid its ears back. "*I'm* the one who's being accommodating. I've been *accommodating* for the last six months."

"Like it'll hurt you to be female for an hour after school," my twin replied hotly.

"Like it'll hurt you to miss out on one bimbo," I snarled.

"Fuck you!"

"I'm the only person in town you *haven't* fucked."

"That sounds really good coming from Frosty the Ice Queen. Or maybe that's what I should call your boyfriend Kevin."

"You leave Kevin out of this."

"Only if you Trade me at the end of the day. How would he feel if the whole school found out he and Larry Friend used to be butt-buddies?"

I yanked back on the reins and the horse halted. My

twin fell silent as I leveled a hard stare. "You had better be joking."

My twin shrank back for a moment, as if acknowledging that this was definitely going too far, that it was indeed a joke gone awry. Then my twin straightened on the shiny leather seat. "Just Trade me at the end of the day and you won't have to worry about it."

Fuck you! I wanted to scream. I wanted to hit, had even balled up a gloved fist, though we had neither of us ever actually hit each other.

No! I told myself. *Biology will* not *control me this time.*

I turned away and snapped the reins. The carriage started moving again. "Fine," I growled. "Meet me behind the gym after school and we'll Trade. And you never mention Kevin like that again. Ever."

"Fine."

We didn't speak the rest of the trip to school.

I was angry all day. I had let my twin manipulate me *again*. The more I thought about it, the madder I got. My twin "called" twice to remind me that we had agreed to Trade after school. Both times I sent terse replies. It was impossible to concentrate on any classwork. Time crawled toward lunch, but I was so angry I couldn't eat. Instead I leaned against the cafeteria wall, my arms folded across my chest, fighting a losing battle against rage.

Then I saw them. Dennis North and Jeremy Acre. They were both carrying lunch trays and about to pass right in front of me. Without even thinking about it, I stuck my foot out. Jeremy went sprawling. Pizza and fries scattered messily over the floor. The entire cafeteria burst into spontaneous applause. Jeremy got up, red-faced and obviously pissed as hell. Pizza sauce and greasy cheese made a stain on his white shirt. I grinned openly at him.

"Accident?" I asked casually.

Jeremy and Dennis both looked ready for murder,

but Mr. Huntoon, the teacher assigned to lunch duty that week, was trotting in our direction to see if everything was all right.

"You piece of shit," Dennis said in a deadly whisper. "You wouldn't be so fucking brave if there wasn't a teacher around."

"Yeah?" I jeered. "I'll be behind the gym after school today. Let's see how fucking brave you are. I'll take you both on."

"We'll be there," Jeremy snapped. Dennis threw his own lunch tray in the garbage and they stalked away.

"Is everything okay here?" Mr. Huntoon asked.

I gave him a small smile. "Everything's fine."

The rest of the day went more quickly. During last period—chemistry, ironically enough—I used a bathroom pass and slipped into one of the stalls. I pulled down my pants, sat on the cold toilet, and thought about girls. Naked girls with full lips and large breasts. Girls who would put their mouths on me and touch and kiss and lick. My hands slid up and down my hardening dick and my heart started to pound.

I made myself stop just short of orgasm and go back to class. The last ten minutes were hell.

The moment we were dismissed, I grabbed my coat and headed for the gym. I was horny and I was belligerent, and both moods played on each other until my hands were almost shaking. Outside, the sky was gray and grim, though the snow had stopped. It was chilly, almost cold, but I barely noticed.

The gym was a separate building out near the soccer field, and the area behind it wasn't visible from either the school or the parking lot, which made it a popular place for illicit smokers and scheduled fights. My twin was already there when I rounded the corner.

"Let's go," my twin said. "I'm going to be late."

We Traded without a word. The horny, belligerent feeling vanished. My twin would have to deal with it now.

My twin instantly turned to retrace my steps. That was when Dennis and Jeremy showed up, following the male body's footprints. They had a friend with them, a beefy senior I had seen around school but didn't know. I faded around the other corner and peered around to watch. This would be interesting. I wasn't particularly worried for my twin—we were already adept at healing most injuries, and any damage would be undone in a couple hours at most. What I really wanted was to teach my twin a lesson. With all the hormones raging through the male body, I doubted my twin would be able to turn down a fight even if Jeremy and his goons allowed the possibility.

"What do you want?" my twin asked, in no mood for conversation.

"Don't play stupid," Jeremy said, and all three of them lunged. Surprised, my twin went down in a pile of fists, knees, and elbows. Flesh smacked flesh, and my twin roared in pain and anger. I smiled to myself. Maybe my twin wouldn't be so quick to jump into the male body next time.

Then Jeremy started to scream. He rolled free of the pile and tried to get to his feet, but only doubled over in apparent agony. Blood gushed from his nose, ears, and even his eyes. It made scarlet flowers on the snow. The goon I didn't know howled once and collapsed in place. He lay twitching in the snow, half on top of my twin, who was still flailing wild fists.

"What the fuck?" Dennis yelped, and scrambled free of the mess.

Gremlin, I said sharply. *What's going on?* *Nanobots.*

My own nanos flashed out to investigate. They found millions of my twin's nanos crawling over and through Jeremy and the goon. Jeremy kept screaming, a thin, high sound that pierced my skull like a drill. My twin's nanos were ripping and tearing at anything they could get their pincers on. My twin lay on the ground, staring at the others with pupils tiny as pinpoints. I saw no recognition of anyone or anything in those eyes. Jeremy screamed and screamed and screamed.

"Quinn, stop it!" I shouted. I bolted out of hiding and knelt next to my twin. I put both hands on my twin's shoulders and shook him. "Stop it!"

My twin's nanos crawled over me, seeking to rend and tear, but my own nanos immobilized the invaders. Jeremy and the goon weren't so lucky. I slapped my twin hard across the face. Jeremy kept screaming. Dennis fled.

"Stop it!" I shouted. *Gremlin, help me! Neutralize the adrenaline or something. Quick!*

For once, Gremlin complied. *Working. Stimulating release of endorphins and acetylcholinesterase.*

My twin's breathing slowed and the strange look vanished. The invading nanos stopped ripping and shredding. "What . . . ?"

"Get up," I said, and held out my hand. My twin took it and staggered upright. Jeremy's screams had faded to a whimper. Blood pooled around his head. The goon still twitched spasmodically on the ground. My twin looked at them.

"Jesus," my twin muttered, and promptly threw up.

That was when the teachers arrived. The next hour was a whirlwind of activity. Someone called the hospital. A helicopter, authorized for emergency use only, flew Jeremy and the goon to the trauma unit at Skytown Hospital. Someone else called Dad, who arrived breathless and red-faced from a bicycle ride up the slippery roads. Questions flew at both of us from all directions, but my twin and I instantly closed ranks. Sparks would fly later, but for now we were in absolute accord. Yes, Quinn had been in a fight. Yes, Jeremy and his friends attacked first. Yes, it was three on one. No, Kate didn't fight. No, we didn't know why Jeremy was bleeding or why the goon, whose name was David, seemed to be in some kind of odd shock. No, we didn't know what provoked the attack. The two of us met up behind the gym before going home because it wasn't far from the hitching posts. We didn't meet at the horse shelter because it was usually crowded after school but we figured the crowd would be gone by the time we met and headed over there ourselves.

The last explanation was a little shaky, but both of us gave the same answer even though we were questioned separately, so there was no real reason to doubt it. Dennis was tracked down and questioned, but his answers weren't very coherent or particularly damning. The principal suspended Quinn Radford-Michaels for three days and reserved the right to lengthen the punishment or look into expulsion, depending on what happened to Jeremy and David. Kate Radford-Michaels had done nothing but watch, and was not in trouble.

At least, not with the school.

Dad hooked his bicycle on the back of the carriage. We had been at school so long, the sun was already setting. He hitched up the horse and drove slowly home in total silence. My twin and I sat in the back, also in silence. I was feeling a mix of emotions and I couldn't help twisting my hands. My plan had worked, all right, but it had never occurred to me that anything like this could happen. I kept hearing Jeremy's high-pitched wail of agony over and over again in my mind. I saw his flesh and blood ripped to pieces beneath his skin. David twitched like a dying fish on the ground. My stomach felt like it was squirming inside me and I couldn't look at my twin.

We got home and unhitched the horse in the stable, all without a word. Dad went into the living room and we followed uncertainly. He stirred up the fire, sat down in his rocking chair, and stared into space. My twin and I sat on the couch in that nerve-wracking silence.

"I never told you why your mother and I divorced," Dad said. My twin and I glanced at each other. This was not what we had been expecting. I kept twisting my hands. Jeremy's scream wouldn't leave my head. Dad kept staring into space.

"Your mother was in an accident when she was young— a fire. It damaged her body very badly and she had to have artificial limbs grafted to her nervous system. On Earth, prosthetics are computer-driven, and nanobots maintain the onboard systems."

My twin and I listened with absolute attention. Dad had never talked about our mother like this.

"The problem started when you were both just babies. Your nanobots interfered with hers. Every time she tried to pick you up or even walked into the same room with you, your nanos would attack hers and short out her prosthetics. We knew you weren't doing it on purpose, but you were doing it nonetheless. I could immobilize your nanobots with mine for short periods—"

I remembered the day Gremlin had attacked Dad and he had frozen all of our nanos.

"—but I couldn't keep that up forever. So I took you here, to Felicity. There aren't any nano-driven systems for you to hurt. Your mother had to stay on Earth." His voice grew softer. "I still miss her, even after fifteen years." Then he straightened and looked at us. His eyes were agate-hard in the firelight. "The whole purpose of moving to Felicity was so that you wouldn't be able to hurt anything with your nanobots. I thought you had learned control by now and was thinking about taking a trip somewhere to see if it was safe for you. I can see it isn't. You sent your nanos into those boys and tore them up."

It wasn't me, I wanted to say, but I kept my mouth shut. Jeremy was still screaming in my head.

"I didn't do it on purpose," my twin said, though not belligerently. "They caught me by surprise—three on one. I just . . . lashed out with everything I had. I didn't even think."

"And that's why we're staying on Felicity," Dad said.

"All three of us. You aren't leaving until you can prove to me you'll never, ever do something like that again."

I got the feeling that "you" meant "both of you," but I kept silent.

"Dad!" my twin protested. "You can't!"

"You sent those boys to the hospital," Dad snapped. "I can do anything I want."

"I'm seventeen. You can't keep me here." My twin's voice was belligerent this time.

"Next time you want to go somewhere," Dad replied, "you remember those boys. I'll have to decide exactly what the rest of your punishment will be when we find out what happened to them. Kate, I'm sorry, but you'll have to remain female at school until Quinn's suspension is over."

My twin kept arguing, but Dad's answer didn't change. Eventually he ordered us both to bed. Wind and snow hissed softly against the windowpane in my room. I crawled between cold sheets and shivered until my nanos were able to warm me again.

You set me up, didn't you? my twin demanded. *You picked a fight with those guys and left me to take the slam.*

You were the one who wanted to Trade, I replied, more nastily than I had intended.

Why did you do something like that to me?

I didn't know you'd hurt them that much, I said. *I just wanted to scare you a little.*

Now we're both stuck on Felicity. I'm suspended and God-knows-what-else later. God, what if Jeremy and that other kid—

Dave, I supplied.

What if they don't recover? What if I killed them?

That horrible scream howled in my head again, mixing eerily with the hissing wind. *They'll be all right,* I said as much to myself as to my twin. *You'll see. This whole thing'll blow over.*

But the next day we learned that Dave had suffered

extensive neurological damage. He would remain in a permanent coma.

Jeremy Acre was dead.

There was a police investigation, of course, but they didn't bring any charges against us. The coroner's report very clearly stated that Jeremy's cause of death was massive internal hemorrhaging, and it was simply impossible to cause that sort of damage in a ten-second fistfight. Dave showed no cranial trauma, so his condition had not been caused by a blow to the head. The examiners were forced to conclude that Dave and Jeremy's conditions, though unknown, were not the result of the fight.

There was a brief and terrifying moment when the police questioned Dad about nanotechnology—he was a known expert in the field—but Dad pointed out that although mixing nanotechnology and living tissue invariably ended fatally, there was no facility on Felicity for nanotech experiments and Dad's luggage was thoroughly swept for stray nanobots every time he returned from off planet. The space station authorities would certainly have all appropriate records on file. The police were welcome to search the house for nanotech research equipment, if they liked. They declined, and my heart started beating again.

Dad didn't say anything to either of us after the police left. In fact, the house was silent a lot. Dad rarely cooked and we didn't eat together anymore. Gremlin was quiet, too, as if it were afraid of attracting more attention.

A week after the fight, Dave's parents elected to remove him from life support and let him die. Dad's promised further punishment, however, never surfaced.

Things also changed at school when my twin's suspension ended. Even though Quinn Radford-Michaels was officially cleared of murder, rumors and whispers continued in hallways and classrooms. Students and teachers alike shunned Quinn, and no girl would even speak to him. We didn't know what to do about it beyond carefully dividing time between the two bodies so neither of us would have to deal with it constantly. People still talked to Kate, but they never, ever mentioned Quinn.

I had nightmares for a month after Jeremy's death, and the guilt followed me around like a lead weight every day. Why had I made such a big deal about a couple hours in the female body? Wasn't I the one who was always saying gender shouldn't matter? I played "if only" over and over until tears leaked from my eyes. If only I hadn't stuck my foot out when I had. If only I had sat down and eaten lunch. If only I had flatly refused to Trade. If only.

The guilt was equally heavy whether I was male or female.

Kevin remained a good friend through it all, a better one than I deserved. He didn't press for details I couldn't give, and his solid presence eased the burden of guilt a little. I wanted my old family back. I wanted a twin who finished my sentences, and a father who chased lizzie-bats and split peas in two, and a Gremlin whose mental voice was bright, cheery, and always there. But we were spinning away from each other like maple seeds in an autumn wind.

My twin ran away with the male body three times in the month following the fight. Each time, Dad silently went to Skytown to retrieve him. Dad didn't shout or yell or punish my twin. He didn't say anything at all, and that was somehow worse. Dad looked old now, though his face hadn't changed since we were little. It was in the way he walked, the way he carried himself, as if his arms were too heavy for his shoulders. Most children challenge their parents. We did it more than most, and I think Dad finally had finally given up.

Winter cleared out and spring moved in. The lizzie-bats returned and waited for Dad to set up his sap buckets again. Graduation loomed, but it didn't seem to matter much.

"I want to go off planet," my twin said.

Dad, who was at the kitchen table with a cup of coffee and the morning newspaper, looked up. "Not now, Kate," he said. "I don't want to start the day with another fight."

"Yes, now." My twin put both hands on the table opposite Dad. I watched from the pantry door. "I've been thinking. We need to learn how to use our nanobots responsibly, and we aren't going to do that here. We need to go off planet."

"We've been through this," Dad said shortly. "You aren't going anywhere until I'm satisfied you won't lose control again. Your temper would be a good place to start."

"My temper isn't the problem," my twin almost snapped. "How are we going to learn anything stuck here on this stupid, backwater world? I've got half a trillion nanobots running around inside me, and all I can do with them is heal myself and control my body temperature. Big deal."

"And you trade bodies with your brother and you talk to Gremlin."

"That's *nothing*," my twin insisted. "There are whole computer systems out there."

"What do you want to do with them?" Dad asked.

"I don't know—that's what I want to find out!"

"You crashed one of Skytown's databases."

"That was just the first time," my twin protested. "I haven't done anything like that since. Doesn't that prove I have control?"

"It proves you like to run away."

"You know what I think?" my twin said. "I think you're afraid. You hide on Felicity because you're afraid of being found out. You could have gone back to Earth and your wife years ago, but you've been too scared. So now my twin and I have to suffer for it."

"Don't you talk to me that way," Dad said dangerously. "I didn't fight those two boys."

"It's your fault," my twin snarled back. "If you had taught us how to use our nanos from the start, none of this would have happened and both those guys would be alive right now."

Dad got up from the table. "This discussion is over." And he went upstairs.

Good going. I sent. *Now he's all angry.*

Shut up.

Reminder, Gremlin broke in. *According to agreement, is now time to Trade.* Gremlin, whose record of neutrality was for once an asset, had been assigned the task of schedule-keeper for Trades at school.

"Shit," my twin said, but complied. The surge of angry adrenaline was still racing through the female body's bloodstream and I had to fiercely remind myself that I wasn't angry.

"I'm outta here." My twin headed for the front door without pausing for breakfast. "See you at school."

But I didn't.

The school had instructions to call Dad at home if either of us turned up absent, so Dad took the train to Skytown. When I got home, Dad was there. My twin—and Gremlin—were not. Dad's face was tight.

"He emptied your savings account and took a ship to Earth," he told me. "I had to hack into the station's computers to find that much out because the port authorities wouldn't tell me more."

My heart thudded. My twin was hundreds of light-years away, a distance I couldn't behind to comprehend. *Gremlin?* I thought automatically. There was, of course, no answer.

"We're going after him, aren't we?" I said aloud. "When's the next ship leaving?"

Dad sank into his rocking chair. "No. I'm not going to hunt him down like a dog. That family tradition ends with me."

"What's that supposed to mean?"

"It doesn't matter. Look, your brother will come back

on his own once he's done some exploring. He'll start missing you and Gremlin and that'll bring him back." He managed a weak smile. "Maybe he'll even miss me."

I didn't know what to say to that, so, in what was becoming its own tradition, I remained silent.

"Your attention, please," a voice said. "We will be docking at Ride Station, Earth in approximately ten minutes. Please remain in your cabin until docking procedures are complete. Repeat: please remain in your cabin until docking procedures are complete."

I reconnected the rest of my senses and stretched as the printed version of the computer's message faded from the wall space. I had spent more time in my past than I thought. Earth was an eight-hour trip away, and we had just been leaving when I laid myself down in my own darkness.

I sat up, realizing I'd have to go outside soon. My stomach knotted up. Ride Station would be even bigger than the one at Felicity, with more people, and more unfamiliar technology, and even more nanobots. My hands trembled, then shook.

Stop it, I told myself sharply. *You can do this. They're just people, for heaven's sake.*

I concentrated on my breathing and, after several minutes, got the shaking under control. Whatever crowds waited outside my cabin door couldn't possibly be worse than what Dad was going through.

The worry broke out again. I stepped on it firmly. Dad was alive, and I was going to find him. Worrying would only distract me from what I had to do.

But I couldn't help wondering what was happening to him.

CHAPTER NINE

LANCE

Lance Radford-Michaels ran through the ruined city for all he was worth. He dodged around wrecked cars, leaped over downed electrical wires, and danced through scattered debris from buildings that leaned dangerously over the street. A nearby water main had burst, flooding a large portion of one block. Two corpses bobbed in the water and half a dozen others littered the pavement. Police sirens wailed endlessly in the distance, growing neither louder nor fainter. Lance gritted his teeth and ran.

The streets in this part of town were almost empty, and Lance was sure that was why Aditi Amendeep kept finding him—there were no crowds to hide in. What few people he came across were alternately shell-shocked, panicked, or pushed over the edge of insanity. Two blocks ago, some lunatic had started shooting at him and had managed to send a bullet through Lance's right thigh. His nanos had repaired the damage almost as fast as it happened, and Lance had kept running.

The buildings he passed were a strange mishmash of brick houses and shops slapped down next to Western-style offices that would have looked more at home in London or New York. New Pakistan, Lance knew, had been founded over thirty years ago by Pakistanis who resented their new Indian rulers. India had been perfectly happy to get rid of what it saw as a bunch of dissidents, and the colonists had fled to the first class M

145

planet that became available. It was, in fact, one of the first colonies opened by Blackstone Industries, the company once owned by Lance's father. The schools, offices, and public buildings had been built by nanobots using the European designs Jonathan Blackstone insisted were superior to anything India had to offer. The colonists, however, hadn't been willing to pay the "small extra fee" to have nanos build their homes and had quite naturally fallen back on building materials more familiar to them. The result was a crazy quilt of styles and architectures that would have jarred Lance's eye even under normal circumstances.

The colony hadn't been doing well lately. When Lance had inherited—and sold—Blackstone Industries, the new owners, under considerable public pressure, had cut all its colonies loose. While this meant New Pakistan no longer had to pay half its gross colonial product to Blackstone Industries, it also meant that it had lost all support from the same company. Lance didn't remember much about New Pakistan's economy beyond a hazy recollection that it had something to do with cloth and medical supply factories, but it was obvious that New Pakistan had fallen on enough hard times to brew up a healthy segment of un- and under-employed people. Many of the buildings sported graffiti. Lance couldn't read it, but it wasn't hard to figure out that it was gang-related.

A woman sitting on the doorstep of an office building stared with dark eyes as Lance sped by. He didn't blame her. The implants in his muscles—the result of experiments authorized by Lance's father—granted him enough speed to overtake a sprinting horse. Other nanos increased Lance's cardiovascular efficiency and removed waste products more quickly than his blood and kidneys could on their own. When Lance was a teenager, the experiments had been a source of terror and pain, but now he was grateful. Enhanced strength, speed, and vision were major assets.

There's no way I can keep this up forever, though, he thought. *I need a place to hide and rest where Aditi can't find me.*

But Aditi Amendeep's eyes were everywhere. It seemed like he could feel them searching, probing, looking for him and him alone. He shuddered and dodged another corpse. This one had been severely burned.

A park, he thought. *There won't be as many electronics in a park.*

His nanobots linked up with his wristcomp, which displayed a map of the city Lance had downloaded before even arriving on New Pakistan. The nanos coded the information into Lance's brain so he could "see" the map without having to pause and look at it. At one time, Robin would have had to do this and give Lance directions. Lance, however, had long since integrated Robin, along with Garth and Jessica and forty-odd others, which meant Lance could now do these things for himself.

According to the map, there was a park four blocks north and two blocks west. Lance dodged down a west-facing alley, praying for no more lunatics with guns. A hit in the thigh he could handle. A hit in the head would be instantly fatal, and all the nanobots in the world couldn't undo it.

The alley made a T-juncture and five bodies lay sprawled in a pool of blood at the intersection. A pair of rats were sniffing the scarlet-soaked turbans with interest. Lance vaulted the entire scene without a second glance. His breathing was growing labored, and he knew he'd have to stop and rest fairly soon. Even nanos could only do so much.

An explosion thumped in the distance and a cloud of inky smoke piled into the sky. Orange flames flickered through it like dragon tongues. Lance bolted out of the alley and turned north. Greenery flashed tantalizingly a block away.

Glass shattered ahead of him. Four young men in loose black clothes were smashing windows on the shops

between Lance and the park. Necklaces and rings—
presumably stolen—adorned their throats and fingers.
Two of them had cybernetic arms that glinted silver in
the sunlight. The men caught sight of Lance running
and by some wordless accord spread out to intercept
him. Knives appeared in their hands, and claws flashed
from cybernetic fingers.

Lance kept running, though his lungs were burning
now and his legs were starting to ache. The first man's
eyes had time to widen before Lance slammed into him.
The air whooshed out of the thug's lungs and he went
flying. Lance stumbled and slowed after the impact,
and the other three were instantly on him. He went
down to the hard pavement in a pile of bodies. White
pain sliced across Lance's arm until his nanos cut the
pain centers in his brain. He snapped an open-handed
punch into someone's chest, and the man rolled away
gasping. Another blade sliced Lance's neck. There was
no pain, but he was aware of blood flowing copiously
down his chest. His jugular had been severed.

Instantly his nanos went into emergency mode. Most
rushed to the site to hold the wound shut until it could
be repaired. Others dove into bone marrow to increase
production of red blood cells while another team worked
to release water stored in fat cells. The gushing blood
slowed to a trickle, but the net effect was that Lance
had to face the last two thugs without help from his
internal army.

Lance made a gurgling noise and went limp. Cold
pavement pressed against his cheek. He cracked an
eyelid. The two men scrambled away and stood over
him, speaking in a language Lance didn't understand.
The thug Lance had punched moaned softly in pain,
and the one Lance had thrown lay motionless on the
ground, unconscious or dead, Lance didn't care. Not
long ago, he would have been upset at the idea of killing another human being, but now he only saw an animal that had tried to kill him. Sometimes you had to

think in terms of *me* and *not me*, with *me* being far and away more important.

One of the men with an artificial arm leaned down to search Lance's body. The moment he was within range, Lance grabbed him by his silvery arm and flipped the man flat on his back. In a flash, Lance had scrambled to his feet. A swift kick to the thug's head knocked him out. Lance, breathing hard and with a wild look on his face, faced the fourth man. The thug stared at Lance for a moment, his brown eyes widened in surprise. Then he turned and bolted away. Lance blinked.

Why did he—?

Then Lance glanced down at himself. A laugh escaped his throat.

I must look like a ghoul with all this blood on my neck and jumpsuit.

Another explosion boomed into the sky, this one close enough that Lance felt a puff of wind against his face. Had that been meant for him? If so, Aditi's aim must be spectacularly bad.

In any case, it's time to go.

He jogged the final block to the park and slipped quickly into the underbrush. Parks didn't usually have cameras, computer terminals, or gas lines running through them, and the trees provided protection from aerial recon. There were no buildings that might collapse, no cars that might start up and unexpectedly lunge toward him. Sanctuary, of a sort.

Lance found a hollow between the roots of a tree and sank gratefully into it. A light breeze danced through the leaves to caress his face. He closed his eyes, leaned back against the scratchy bark, and turned his attention inward. The nanobots had already sealed his jugular vein and the cut in his shoulder. His red blood count was still low, but that would be remedied in a few hours. Right now he needed water to replace lost plasma. Thirst was already drying out his mouth.

Lance opened his eyes. Green leaves and bushes surrounded him like gentle guards. The ground was soft and mossy, even comfortable. It was hard to believe a ruined city lay less than a hundred meters away.

When Lance had arrived at New Pakistan and put the *Defiant Lady's Daughter* into orbit around the planet, the planet had looked pretty normal, even peaceful— if you ignored the fact that no communications were going in or out. A dozen ships had already seeded one orbit with irradiated metallic chaff that would jam both normal and faster-than-light communication. The ships, who had heard from Ting Chen, allowed Lance to pass through with a warning that they would under no circumstances help him if he got into trouble.

New Pakistan had no space station or skyhook, so Lance would have to land the *Daughter* at the planet's single spaceport. The *Daughter*, Lance's second ship, was sleeker and faster than the outdated *Defiant Lady*, which would never have been able to make planetfall. Once he broke atmosphere below the range of the communications blackout, Lance reached for the communications board. Although his nanos could just as easily have opened a line for him, Lance generally preferred to tap the keys with his fingers.

"New Pakistan spaceport," he said, "this is *Defiant Lady's Daughter*, call number 453-404-Charlie, asking permission to land. Do you read?"

Static gushed from the speakers. Lance tried again. More static.

Not surprising, he thought, *if the hive has taken the computer systems planetwide. I hope this one doesn't turn out too hot to handle.*

The *Daughter* dipped down toward the spaceport under Lance's expert piloting. Unbidden, his mind went back to the twins. Kate had been so upset with him, and with good reason. It wasn't every day your daughter turned eighteen, and no amount of "making up" would change the fact that he had missed it. He could still see the pain in her dark eyes—new pain at him leaving, old pain at the loss of her brother.

Loss. As in death?

Quinn isn't dead, he told himself as a bit of turbulence shook the ship. *He's just missing. Maybe I should make a side trip over to Earth after all and see if he's there when this is all over. Kate'll be so glad to see him. Not to mention how glad I'll be.*

But what if Quinn hadn't actually gone to Earth? Or what if he had gone to Earth and then somewhere else? He could be anywhere, really. Worry filled Lance's heart with solid rock. He shook his head. As a kid, Lance's main emotion had been fear. As an adult and father, it seemed to be worry. Worry that his children had somehow inherited Jonathan Blackstone's schizophrenia or Lance's dissociative tendencies. Worry that the twins' gender identities weren't forming when they were little, then shock and worry when he found out that not only did they trade bodies at will, but they also didn't know who had been born male and who had been born female. Worry that the hive called Gremlin would one day turn malevolent. Worry that one teenage twin seemed to ignore the physical body, while the other plunged into it with reckless abandon. Worry that the twins suffered because they didn't have a mother to help raise them. Worry about the aftermath of the fight at school and worry that he hadn't handled it right.

Worry that he was a bad father.

He wondered how Delia would have handled the situation. Maybe they should never have gotten divorced. God knew they hadn't wanted to, but neither of them could think of any other solution. Delia and the twins simply couldn't live together, and Lance was the only one who could keep the babies under control long enough to get them to safety on Felicity, where there were no nanobot systems for them to interfere with or destroy. Their letters had been constant for the first few years, but had eventually trailed off. Without words, they had mutually decided that severing communication would be less painful in the long run.

That didn't stop Lance from thinking about her. There was no end of eligible women on Felicity who would have been thrilled to have Lance come courting, but there were too many things Lance simply couldn't discuss with people who hadn't been involved. Delia had patiently seen him through years of therapy and celebrated with him every time he had integrated another personality. She hadn't been repulsed by the nanos that constantly flowed through his body. She hadn't made him feel ashamed of his past. And best of all, she had loved him for himself. Not his money—that wasn't important to her. Not the pheromones his body was programmed to emit—her body wasn't able to respond to them. Not the fantastic looks the doctors had forced on him at his father's direction—she herself had been bodysculpted after the fire and knew that looks hid the person. Delia had loved him, and he had loved her. He still did, even after almost eighteen years apart.

Lance circled the spaceport and hit the external camera control for a view of the ground below. His eyes widened and he caught his breath.

Jesus.

He circled again, staring at the displays. The spaceport was a gutted mess. Burned and twisted hulks littered the runways and loading areas. The main terminal was a smoking ruin and the sidewalks looked like they were covered with giant flakes of pepper. Lance zoomed in with one of the cameras and discovered the black chunks were charred human remains. He swallowed and pulled back the view.

Jesus, he thought again.

Doubt flickered through him. He had dealt with nanobot hives on space stations, jumpships, and research facilities, but never anything on this scale. New Pakistan had five cities, one of which was almost the size of Calcutta, and this hive had invaded every single computer system in all five of them. Most hives simply didn't expand that far that fast. They expanded in fits and starts, pausing for long periods to figure out what they could and couldn't do. This hive was obviously a lot more aggressive.

Can I deal with something that big? He glanced at the video displays, where the charred bodies grew bigger as the ship descended. Several were child-sized.

I guess I'll have to, he decided firmly.

The *Daughter* touched down, light as a feather. She was smaller than her predecessor, only forty meters long with two decks and a shape something like a Stealth bomber. Lance trotted down to the air lock, took a deep breath, and cycled it open.

The smell hit him first. Charred flesh, burned hair, rotting meat. He gagged until his nanos were able to block the stimulus from his cerebral cortex and all he smelled was hot tarmac. Smoke still hung thick in the air despite the breeze, and Lance could hear sirens and other noises far away. A chain-link fence rattled in the wind.

He picked his way past the wrecked ships, scattered luggage, and burned bodies. In order for his nanos to find the hive, he'd have to find an access gateway somewhere, preferably one to a ubiquitous system that generally went unnoticed, such as waste treatment or a secondary backup. A single glance, however, told him that there would be no usable computer hookups at the terminal.

A half-burned sign pointed at the parking lot, and Lance jogged toward it, keeping a sharp eye out for survivors. From this moment on, he would have to treat anyone he met as a potential threat. City- and planet-wide emergencies brought out the best and worst in people, with no way to tell which it was until it was too late.

The parking lot was deserted except for a small herd of standard electric cars. Lance chose the closest one.

His nanos flooded the car's security system and found no nanobots in it whatsoever.

What the hell? he thought, startled. *There should be at least a few, even if most of the car's nanos got sucked into the hive. No hive is that meticulous.*

He tried another car. Same thing. Lance chewed his lower lip. In theory, he could simply sit in the car, access the local traffic control grid, and from there hack from system to system until he found the hive. By communicating with hive nanos through the car's system, he could reprogram them and "steal" them away. But even a high-density communications line had its limits, and with a hive this size, it'd be much faster if he could find one at the actual physical location of most of the hive nanos.

Which would also be more dangerous, he thought. *On the other hand, trying to cripple the hive by absorbing its nanos over the telephone could take years.*

Lance's nanos easily overrode the car's security system. He started the car, taking care not to link up with the traffic grid, and a moment later he was driving swiftly up the road toward the city. More wrecks littered the road. He also passed several people, some alone, some in groups. Because New Pakistan had drawn most of its colonists from India-conquered Pakistan, the inhabitants invariably had dark hair, eyes, and skin, but they dressed in everything from the traditional loose shirt and trousers to Western coats and ties. They all looked alternately dazed and panicked. Lance tried to buck up his sinking stomach as the ruined city grew closer. A nanobot hive was a nanobot hive. This one was bigger than most and might take longer to assimilate, but it was still less intelligent and less experienced than Lance was. How hard could it be?

How stupid can I get? Lance thought sourly from his hiding place in the park. He had managed to find a working terminal in a nearly-gutted grocery store and sent nanos into the system looking for hive nanos. It had taken all of thirty seconds for the hive to notice his presence, lash out with its nanos, and try to assimilate *him*. Lance had lost almost twenty million nanobots before he could disconnect from the system and write defensive programs to stop it from happening again. Without the terminal's communications system giving them contact with the rest of the hive, it should have been easy for Lance to *re*-reprogram the twenty million of his nanos that had "defected" to the hive, but they destroyed themselves the moment they lost connection with the hive itself. Lance was left with nothing but a name.

Aditi Amendeep.

The name already made Lance shiver. He should have seen something like this coming. There were already three people in the universe who had merged a nanobot hive with their own minds—Lance, Quinn, and Kate. With nanobots nearly as common as hydrogen atoms, computer systems as common as bacteria, and galactic communications as simple as breathing, it would be a surprise if there *weren't* any more human-nano hybrids. True, laboratory attempts to coordinate nanos and living tissue had always failed, and scientists called it a billion-to-one chance that the two would ever merge correctly, but in the wider universe, you had a trillion chances. One chance in a billion looked pretty good.

It should have been a pleasure to find out about Aditi, to know there was someone else out there who knew what it was like to have a nanobot hive wake up inside you. Lance clearly remembered the day Robin had first contacted him. He had been fifteen years old and was sitting in English class when a voice spoke in his head. This hadn't actually been uncommon for Lance—back then he still had forty-seven other people living in his head, and he often caught snatches of arguments or conversations. But unlike the other voices, this one had spoken directly to him. Robin, it seemed, was composed of all the nanobots that oversaw the cybernetic implants in Lance's body. Jonathan Blackstone had insisted on numerous triple backups, and the extra, idle processing space in combination with continued interaction with a human nervous system had been that one-in-a-billion chance that led to sentience.

Much later, as an adult, Lance had learned that the actual hive mind had been destroyed by his own alternate personalities, but his subconscious had seen the value of a mind made of nanobots and had created the alter named Robin. Like all alternate personalities, Robin had been firmly convinced that it was separate from Lance, and it had taken a deadly confrontation with Jonathan Blackstone to force Robin—and Lance—to see the truth.

Kate and Quinn hadn't gone through that—they had been born with their condition, and their hive wasn't fully a part of them. They didn't know what it was like to have a voice pop into your head and announce it was an artificial intelligence. But Aditi did, and Lance had a thousand questions for her. Was her hive mind separate from her or a part of her? How had it happened? What had it felt like? Was it frightening or did she like it?

Was she like him?

But Aditi had started hunting him. Ten minutes after Lance left the store, a wave of nanos rushed out of a traffic signal and washed over him. Lance had had the presence of mind to start running even while his own nanos desperately fought the invaders with pincers and programs. After he was out of range of the signal's communicator, the hive nanos had shut down again. He had run all the way back to the spaceport, intending to get off planet and figure out what to do, but Aditi had been there before him. The *Daughter,* left without nanobots to defend herself, was a smoking ruin.

Green leaves rustled in the breeze. Lance jumped, as if the sound were caused by an army of nanobots marching toward him. He grimaced and suppressed the remaining adrenaline surge. It would take at least an hour to heal completely and it wouldn't help if he kept jumping at every little noise. He should be safe until the process was completed. The trees and bushes should provide enough cover to hide him from the satellites and surveillance cameras that Aditi had been using to track him so far. The problem was Lance had been using energy like a blast furnace. It didn't help that his body fat deposits were naturally low, and the glycogen reserves in his liver were already running out. His nanos could block the hunger signals from his brain, but even they couldn't run his body on nothing. Eventually he'd have to go find food.

I think I can wait until dark, though, Lance thought, leaning back against the tree trunk and ordering his heartbeat to slow down. Sudden exhaustion washed over him. *Maybe even take . . . a little . . .*

He slept.

A loud screech jerked Lance awake. It was dark, and for a confusing moment he didn't know where he was. The screech sounded again, and Lance bolted to his feet. Then memory returned in a rush. The hive. Aditi. The park.

Another screech. It sounded like someone was torturing a cat. Lance's heart pounded. Two pale, yellow moons drifted overhead, making an eerie, dim light. The air was growing chilly. It smelled of wet leaves and loam.

Calm down, he told himself. *This is a city park. There aren't going to be any dangerous animals in it. It's probably just a bird.*

As if to prove his point, something fluttered overhead and one more screech raised the hair on Lance's neck. The screech grew fainter as the creature flew away. Lance sighed with relief. The bird was probably harmless, but that noise would scare a rabid vampire.

Ravenous hunger suddenly raged within him. Lance

shut down the sensation and ran a few checks with his nanos. Five hours had passed, and all healing was complete. The walls of his jugular vein were strong and solid. His muscle implants were operating within normal parameters. The bullet wound from the lunatic had vanished entirely. His blood sugar, however, was getting dangerously low. Fatty deposits were all but gone, and his liver was empty. If he didn't get some food soon, he'd have to start consuming muscle tissue. He considered trying to catch an animal in the park, but vetoed the idea. For all he knew, the resident fauna secreted an instantly fatal poison that not even his nanos would be able to stop. And how did he propose to catch anything without the proper tools?

Or knowledge, he thought wryly. *City boys don't learn this stuff. I'd probably catch myself in any snare I tried to set.*

In the background, he could hear the city, though he couldn't see it through the foliage. There was no steady drone of tires on pavement or horns honking in annoyance. The sounds had been replaced with the crackle of gunfire, an occasional scream, and unexplained booms and thuds.

Lance licked his lips. Aditi had obviously gotten into every system on the planet that had a computer in it. Gas lines, water mains, traffic lights, automobiles, and God only knew what else were all under her control. He couldn't tell if she was actively malicious or just blundering around not realizing what she did. Ultimately it didn't matter. Already thousands of people had died and it would only get worse. Evacuation wasn't an option. No ships would dare interact with New Pakistan in case the hive infected their own systems. Either Lance would have to find a way to stop Aditi, or everyone on this planet—including him—would be condemned to a slow death.

And Quinn and Kate would never know what happened to me, he thought with a sudden pang. Right now, he would have given his entire fortune to be back home at the supper table with his children, listening to them chatter about the day, even though they hadn't had a family dinner like that in months.

Maybe we can do something about that when I get back, he thought. *If I get back.*

First things first. He needed food. Lance stretched muscles cramped from his odd sleeping position, then crept slowly through the undergrowth toward the city proper again. Leaves and branches scraped his skin. The park lights were out, of course. The only light came from the overhead stars and the yellow moons. Low light, however, never bothered Lance. His enhanced eyes, another gift from his father, could see quite clearly.

After a while, he reached the side of the park opposite to where he had come in. This seemed to be a residential district, with low, sprawling houses. Each one was surrounded by a wall with an iron gate in it. One house was engulfed in flames. Sparks and smoke poured into the sky, and harsh-smelling smoke caught in Lance's nose and throat. The fire made eerie shadows dance in the streets with demonic glee. Turbaned neighbors were desperately using blankets to beat out sparks and embers that landed on their roofs. The flaming house itself was left to burn. People shouted orders to each other. Lance wondered why no one was using water, then realized that the city pumps were probably off. He briefly considered helping, then trotted quietly on his way. The cities were better off as a whole if he could find a way to stop Aditi completely.

His stomach growled. *But first I have to find food,* he thought grimly.

Lance moved steadily away from the burning house. Unlike the abandoned business district, there were other people on the street here. Some seemed determined, others wandered around in shock. A child, perhaps five or six years old, called for her mother. Her face was bewildered and scared, and she wiped at the tears streaming down her cheeks. Memories of the child-sized corpses at the spaceport welled up in his mind. Lance's parental instincts kicked in with an urge to sweep the poor thing into his arms and help her. He forced himself to keep going. There was no way he could help her. He didn't speak her language, so she couldn't tell him where she lived or where her parents might be. The girl's plaintive cries followed him down the street, and his throat threatened to close up even after the sound faded.

This is Aditi's fault, he thought fiercely. *Aditi killed those children at the spaceport, and it's because of her that little girl's parents are lost or dead.*

Lance turned another corner and found a small shopping district, including another grocery store. Like the one at the edge of town, it had been ransacked. Not surprising—during any disaster the first thing people do is stock up on food, and if the grocer closes down or can't take money because the banking system is off line, people often take what they need by force. Disaster is the true test of a civilization.

Keeping a sharp eye and ear out for other looters, Lance ducked through the shattered glass door. The inside was almost pitch black, and even Lance's enhanced eyes could barely pick out details of the half-destroyed interior. Shelves were tipped over and shards of glass crunched underfoot. Every few steps, Lance paused to listen. He heard nothing. His stomach growled loudly and he noticed his hands were beginning to shake. A quick check with his nanos revealed a dangerously low level of blood sugar. In a few more minutes, he would be in danger of fainting.

A car buzzed by on the pavement outside, its headlights washing over the store's interior. Lance dove behind a shelf until it had passed.

Lance began to search. At first glance, anything edible had already been taken. Displays of flashlights, batteries, and toilet paper lay empty. But after a few minutes of looking, Lance found a package of flat bread under a shelf and a jar of something with a gritty texture that seemed to be some sort of ground-up plant. Lance tore open the bread and wolfed the first piece down, then used the other slices to dip the plant paste out of the jar. It made for a bland but satisfying meal. The shaking ended.

Another car zipped past, but this one didn't have its lights on. Lance froze in place until it had also passed. Some people were insane—why would you drive a car with no lights on during a dark night like this?

Because lights make you an easier target, Lance realized.

Lance's nanos informed him that although the plant paste contained some moisture, Lance needed more water to replace lost blood plasma. He was sure he'd feel a burning thirst if he allowed it. The bottled water display was predictably empty, as was the bottled juice and tea section. Lance went into the back rooms, found a faucet, and turned it on. Nothing.

Lance thought for a moment, then hunted around until he found an office area. The looters hadn't touched it.

He heard yet another car drive past the store. That was a lot of cars. The streets were crowded with people and wrecks, making driving impractical, or at least difficult. Suspicion stirred. Aditi at work? He should probably leave, and quickly. But he still needed water.

Swiftly, Lance searched through office desk drawers and lockers and came up with two plastic bottles, one water and one tea, presumably left over from someone's lunch. The water had been opened and was half gone, but at this point Lance didn't care about what germs the original owner may have been carrying. He gulped down the contents of both bottles. As he was swallowing the last mouthful, the lights came on.

Lance jumped back, blinded, but only for a second. The terminal on the desk glowed and before Lance could react, nanos poured into the room. They crawled in, through the doors, through the terminal, through electric sockets. There were so many Lance could actually see them. They made a thin, cloudy mist that coated the floor and all four walls. The nanos closed in on him, unstoppable as a troop of jungle ants.

Fear flooded Lance's stomach and adrenaline sang in his blood. The plastic bottle clattered to the floor as he glanced frantically around. No windows, and the only door was covered with the crawling black mass. Lance stood in the center of the room as the invading nanos moved inexorably toward him. Lance looked up at the ceiling. Foam tile, nothing more. Without pausing to think, Lance pushed the power levels in his leg implants to full, shoved his adrenaline levels even higher to boost his muscles, and *leaped*.

He smashed straight through the ceiling. Above him, he caught a glimpse of pipes and wires. By a miracle, he didn't hit any of them on his way up. The roof of the store was two stories high, and Lance's jump carried him almost to the top. He hung for a moment in midair, then began to fall. Frantically he reached out. His hands closed around a pipe and he jolted to a stop, the blood pounding in his ears like a frantic drum. Below, he caught sight of the black mass of nanos through the hole in the office ceiling. Already they were swarming upward, out of the hole and up the main wall of the store. In a few seconds, they had reached the level of his pipe.

Lance tightened his gut and levered himself onto the pipe. Not far away was a window. It was high up, obviously meant to provide ventilation, and had so far escaped being broken by looters. Lance leaped into space and grabbed another pipe. His sweaty hand slipped. He scrabbled desperately for a moment, then regained his grip. One more jump, one more pipe, and he'd reach the window. Unfortunately, the nanos were swarming up the same wall he was making for, and they had already reached the window.

Lance pulled himself up. The pipe swayed beneath his weight and something creaked. He jumped again, grabbed again. The new pipe was only a couple of meters from the wall. By now, the nanobots had spread to the high ceiling and were moving down the beams and pipes, including Lance's. One last time, he pulled himself up to the pipe, feeling the rhythm in the movement. Swing, pull, tighten—

The pipe broke. With a startled yell, Lance fell. His hands flailed frantically, catching empty air. Below, the nanobots covered the floor in a black, seething mass. His fingers brushed something. He lunged and caught a cord. Lance's shoulder jolted as he swung gently on a hanging light fixture. He panted for a moment. The window was still within range, but already he could feel the cord starting to give.

Lance swung on the cord like a chimpanzee on a vine. The nanobots had found the place where it met the ceiling and were already crawling down toward him. Lance swung back and forth once, twice. He almost touched the window with his feet. Above, something gave and he dropped several centimeters.

The nanobots reached his hands and several thousand crawled down his arm. Lance swung back, then forward, pointing his toes directly at the window.

The cord gave way. Lance's forward momentum drove him full-tilt toward the glass. It shattered, slicing into his legs, chest, and face, though he felt no pain. With a whoop of triumph, he flew through the window. Already his nanos were working on ejecting the few intruders. Air rushed past his ears as he fell toward the ground of the alley behind the store. He had time to notice a police cruiser parked placidly a little ways away. Its doors were open and the alley floor was a seething black mass of nanobots. Lance shouted something incoherent as he fell directly into them.

Aditi Amendeep watched the action in the alley with growing fascination. She could see everything through the camera mounted on the dashboard of the cruiser, which her nanobots were controlling for her. In a way, it was as if she *was* the police car. A single thought to the onboard computer, and the car drove wherever she wished it, and it could transport enough nanobots to cover, say, a grocery store office, or the alley behind it.

But even while the sights and sounds from the camera were pumping into her brain, Aditi was still aware of the bed beneath her, of the sheets and mattress, of the way her legs no longer hurt and her muscles obeyed her commands. Her nanobots had even worked to increase the size and strength of the atrophied tissue. True, she couldn't walk, and probably never would, but she could sit up unaided now. Besides, who needed to walk? She could be anywhere on the planet, see and hear anything. And she could *do* things. Everything with a computer in it obeyed her commands. Automobiles and trains became her legs, robotic equipment became her arms. Even now, her nanos were busily at work in a dozen labs across the planet, working on "freeing" several sets of robotic equipment. Once the arms built their own sets of legs, she would be able to engage in mobile fine manipulation. The work was time-consuming, but it didn't matter—her nanos never got tired, and Aditi found she could handle literally hundreds of tasks all at once. It was a breathtaking sensation to someone who had never been able to hold her own waterglass.

Aditi made a face at the thought. She still couldn't eat and drink as she liked. Her single kidney simply couldn't deal with too much work, even when the nanos maximized its efficiency, and her digestive system was still sensitive. True, her nanos could drag indigestible molecules through her stomach and into the colostomy bag, but it took a surprising amount of concentration, and there were so many other things to see and do. It was easier to let her nanos bring glucose and protein in from the liquid supplies in the storage cabinet and leave off normal eating altogether. What Aditi would do once those supplies ran out, she didn't know. If the robotic arms were mobile by then, they could bring her more, but it would be a clumsy system. Aditi clenched her fist. She was the most powerful being on the planet, but she was still trapped.

In the alley, the Intruder, as she thought of him, screamed as her nanobots swept over his body. Her first reaction to the Intruder had been to kill him, but in the time it had taken infrared satellite cameras to track him down, her rage had been replaced with curiosity. The Intruder had a nanobot hive that seemed to be almost as sophisticated as her own. She could learn a great deal from him.

On other cameras and satellites, Aditi could also see other people rushing frantically about like ants, trying to put out fires or get away from looters or try to find food. Let them rush like ants, then. These were people who moved as they wished, breathed as they wished, ate and pissed and shit as they wished. These were people who averted their eyes on the rare occasions Aditi had gone out in public. These were people who didn't care about her, so why should she care about them? They didn't feel real anyway. They were only images on a monitor, part of a virtual reality flick. The gardens around the house were more real. She could see the plants waving in the breeze as her nanos changed them, made them bigger and more interesting. A schizophrenic rainbow wrapped itself around Aditi's house and reached in through the windows. Some of the vines snapped up curious bees or lashed themselves around unwary birds. It was fun—the only time she had been allowed to touch real plants, even if it was only through her nanobots.

The Intruder was now trying to brush her nanos off him with his hands. A futile gesture, but understandable. His frantic screaming and incoherent shouting echoed off the uncaring brick walls. With a small smile, Aditi tried to assimilate the Intruder's nanos as he had assimilated hers.

Her programs were rebuffed. In a microsecond, Aditi realized she wouldn't be able to catch him off guard again. She couldn't take his nanos, but neither could he take hers. Aditi would have to abandon the assimilation attempt.

Fortunately, there were other ways to control him. Her nanos were already aware that the Intruder was heavily cybered. He had muscle implants in his arms, legs, eyes—almost everywhere. Those would do nicely.

Aditi closed her physical eyes and moved most of her concentration to the nanos swarming in and over the Intruder's body. At the moment, her nanos outnumbered his by more than ten to one. Aditi smiled again. If computer combat didn't work, there was always naked force.

Within seconds, Aditi's nanos located and pinned down every one of the Intruder's nanos. It took three of hers to paralyze each of his with surety, but that still left plenty to invade his muscle implants. Aditi's closed eyes flickered back and forth beneath her eyelids as her new awareness searched the implants, traced systems, wrote programs. Without his nanos to mount a defense, the Intruder's implants fell beneath Aditi's siege.

Aditi crooked a mental finger. The Intruder's body stiffened, but his screams continued. With jerky, puppet-like steps, he got into the police cruiser. Aditi shut the doors and programmed a course to bring him home.

CHAPTER TEN

ME

London was as bad as I had thought it would be. Every square inch was big, scary, and confusing. Cars zipped past me in the street, moving faster than anything had a right to move. People crowded the sidewalk, and the buildings reached like stone fingers into the sky, and I wondered what would happen if they decided to make a fist.

Dad once told me that when he was a young man, London was almost deserted because the colonies were comfortable, beautiful, and easy to reach. Jumpships and Tach-Com Communications—Grandma's company—had made the universe smaller, and few people had wanted to live on tiny, crowded, overpopulated Earth.

According to the computer guidebook files I had looked at on the ship, however, things had changed lately. No off-world colony has a past that goes back more than thirty years, but London's is a little longer. "Now that London is no longer overcrowded," the guidebook said, "a number of colonists chose to return, to be part of London's rich and powerful history."

This is a solved overcrowding problem? I thought, scanning the busy sidewalk. *It makes an anthill look positively lethargic.*

I stood on the pavement outside the skyhook port, my shoulder bag at my feet, and tried to look around without looking like a tourist. I was tired, my clothes were rumpled, and I felt filthy. A quick command to my nanos got my skin and clothes clean, but I still felt like I needed a bath. I yawned, trying to get the cotton out of my brain. My internal clock said it was close to two in the morning, but the clocks on the walls here said it was barely noon. I also had no idea how to find Grandma.

A blue-uniformed security guard approached me. "Can I help you, miss?" he said. "You look lost."

Was it that obvious? I cleared my throat. "I need to find my grandmother's house," I replied, suddenly feeling like Little Red Riding Hood. "But I don't know where it is or how to get there."

"The vidphones are back inside and to your left," he said, pointing. "Try directory assistance."

I thanked him, shouldered my bag, and went back into the port. I found the vidphones—a row of screens on a wall with dividers between each—and picked one at random. It was nothing more than a screen with a number pad that said, "Please swipe card or deposit note in slot."

For a moment I thought it was telling me to steal someone's card before I realized "swipe" must have another meaning I wasn't aware of. I sighed. I didn't even know how to turn the thing on, let alone do something I couldn't figure out to a card I didn't have. And what kind of note? Did you need signed permission to use the phone? The exchange that had changed my Felicity money into English money had offered me a plastic card, but I had insisted on hard cash. Had that been a mistake? Maybe the phone itself could help me.

"Hello?" I said hesitantly to the screen. "I need help."

The screen lit up. A voice spoke, and the words also appeared on the screen. "Do you wish to place a call?"

"Yes."

"Please swipe card or deposit note in slot."

"I don't have a card or a note."

"Do you wish to reverse the charges?"

I had no idea what that meant. "I need to find my grandmother." I remembered what the guard had said, and inspiration struck. "Can you connect me with directory assistance?"

"One moment, please."

There was a pause, then a new voice said, "Directory assistance. City, please?"

"Is there a charge for this?" I asked cautiously.

"There is no charge for directory assistance. City, please?"

"London."

"May I help you?"

I couldn't tell if the voice was a computer or a person. I decided it must be a computer, since a person would probably appear on the screen.

"I'm looking for Meredeth Michaels."

There was barely a pause. "That number is not listed."

"What does that mean?"

"At the customer's request, that number is not listed in public-access directories."

I chewed my lip. That actually made sense—Grandma was a high-profile businesswoman with money and power. If her private number were listed, she'd probably do nothing but answer the phone all day.

An impulse rose and I gave in without thinking. "What about Delia Radford-Michaels? Or Delia Radford?"

My heart started to pound during the tiny pause that followed. What if she wasn't listed? What if she *was*?

"There is a listing for Delia Radford." A number and an address appeared on the screen. I stared at them. "If you wish to connect immediately, please swipe card or deposit note."

I quickly walked away, my mother's address burned into my mind. I had my mother's address. I knew where she lived. Should I go there? What if she didn't want me? What if she were angry at me?

Come on, I told myself. *Dad said that mom left because of her implants.*

But then another voice spoke up—Dad's. *Your nano-bots interfered with hers. Every time she tried to pick you up or even walked into the same room with you, your nanos would attack hers and short out her pros-thetics. The whole purpose of moving to Felicity was so that you wouldn't be able to hurt anything with your nanobots.*

I hadn't let myself think about this until now. Mom had left because my twin and I had hurt her. Guilt washed over me in a sick wave. No wonder she hadn't visited or written us letters. She probably hated us, with good reason.

My mouth went dry and butterflies hatched in my stomach. I had no idea how to contact Grandma, but I *did* have my mother's address, and she used to be Grandma's daughter-in-law. If nothing else, Mom might be able to help me find her.

If she would even talk to me.

I suddenly wondered where my twin was and what Dad was doing. Was he even alive? I ached to talk to my twin and to hear Gremlin's little voice in my head. I was afraid of seeing my mother. I was alone on a strange world I knew little about. The emotions all mixed together like a nest of snakes, and a tear leaked out of my eye.

Stop it, I ordered myself. *One thing at a time. Right now, Mom is your only contact, so if you want to save Dad, you'll have to talk to her and make her talk to you.*

I saw a long series of yellow cars parked at the side of the road sporting black signs that said CAB. They didn't look like hansom cabs to me, but then, London didn't seem to go for horses and carriages. I chose a cab at random, climbed in, and gave the driver my mother's address. Without a word, the driver took off.

He drove like a maniac. The city blurred past me at speeds I had never imagined. I clung to the door han-dle and tried not to shriek every time he turned or squealed to a stop. Was this the way everyone drove? No wonder I had heard so much about car accidents on other worlds. I closed my eyes and tried to pretend I was back on Felicity in a slow, safe carriage while my heart threatened to leap out of my chest.

We came to an abrupt stop. I almost mashed my nose against the back of the driver's seat.

"That'll be fifty," the driver said.

I opened my eyes and swallowed my stomach. "Fifty what?"

"Quid."

What the hell was a quid? It sounded like some kind of fish. I dug into my pocket and guessed that a quid must be a pound and counted out fifty of them. I handed them to the driver and got out in front of what looked more like an estate than a house. A high brick wall with a wrought-iron gate surrounded an enormous yard—garden, I think the English call it. In the center stood a huge, three-story house that looked like it had stepped out of a Victorian storybook. There was even a little tower.

It was my mother's house.

"No tip?" the driver said.

Annoyed, I leaned through the window. "Here's a tip: don't drive like a hyperactive lizzie-bat if you want a tip."

He drove angrily away. I shouldered my bag and looked at the house again. My mother lived in there, was probably inside. It seemed like I should know the house, or at least be able to feel that the house was familiar. I felt nothing but fear and nervousness.

There was a buzzer on the gate, and a camera, but I didn't ring. I didn't want my first encounter with my mother to be run through a computer. I pushed on the gate and found it wasn't locked. That struck me as a little strange. Why have a wall and a gate and a camera if you were going to leave the whole thing unlocked? I slipped inside and forced myself to stride briskly up the front walk to the door. Before I could think about it, I rang the bell.

Hi, Mom, I thought. *It's me—Kate.*

That wouldn't work. Kate was a common enough name and she may not connect me with her daughter right away.

Hi, Mom. I'm your daughter Kate.

That sounded just stupid.

Mom? Do you recognize me?

No way. She might say she didn't, and that would be horrible. If Mom couldn't figure out who I was right away, I didn't want to know about it.

Hey, Mom! How are y—

The door opened. My twin was standing on the other side.

There was a long silence. My twin didn't move. The fear vanished, replaced with elation. I wanted to hug or at least touch my twin, but my twin didn't react to my presence. Startled, I held off.

"Hi," I said at last. "Can I come in?"

My twin stood aside and I entered the house. Inside was a large foyer with a black marble floor. Doorways led off to the left and right, while directly ahead of me was a staircase. A man I had never seen before was standing halfway up it. He looked to be in his midfifties and had brown hair. A neatly trimmed beard covered his chin.

"Who's at the door, Quinn?" he asked.

"My tw—my sister," my twin said. I blinked. My twin's voice sounded dull and lifeless. The ultraclean, perfectly-pressed look had also vanished. My twin was wearing baggy gray sweats, and my twin's hair desperately needed a comb. My earlier happiness was rapidly evaporating.

What's going on? I asked. *Is . . . is Mom here?*

My twin didn't respond.

"Your sister Kate?" The man trotted down the staircase toward me and held out his hand. "Why didn't you say something? I'm Peter Lavner. It's a pleasure to meet you, Kate."

I shook his hand, bewildered, and my head spun with questions. Who was this guy? Where was Mom? Why was my twin acting so funny?

"You must want to see Del—your mother," Peter said. "I'll go get her." And he trotted away.

Who was that? I demanded.

Still no reply.

Gremlin, who was that?

Again, no reply.

Gremlin? I turned to my twin. Now I was getting scared. "Where's Gremlin? What's wrong?"

"I'll tell you later," my twin replied dully.

"You tell me right now!" I snapped. "What happened to Gremlin?"

"Kate?"

I turned. Standing in one of the doorways was a tall woman with black hair, brown eyes, and dark skin. She looked different from the picture in Dad's room. Older. Not quite eighteen years older, but older. I could see my face in hers. My heart jumped and my breath caught in my throat. I couldn't say anything.

Delia Radford crossed the room and caught me in a hug. I dropped my shoulder bag and hugged back. She smelled like lilac perfume. After a long moment, we parted. I felt suddenly uncertain. I had wondered on and off for most of my life what it would be like to meet my mother, how I'd react, what it would feel like. Right now, it felt like I had received a hug from an overly familiar stranger. She looked kind of like me, but I didn't know her.

At least she didn't seem to hate me.

At that point, a bunch of people boiled into the room. I counted two men—including Peter—a woman, and six kids ranging from ten to sixteen years old. It took me a while to sort out all the relationships, but it worked out that Mom was part of a group marriage. The men were her husbands, the woman was her wife, and the kids were . . . hers. Three by adoption, two by actual birth. The birth kids' names were Nancy and Brad, and they were sixteen and fifteen, respectively. I didn't know what to say or think. I had a half brother and half sister? Like my mother, they were strangers. I also found the babble of voices and rounds of hugs overwhelming. I had lived my entire life in a house of three, and now I was in what felt like a house of hundreds.

I think Mom noticed. "All right, leave her alone now. Kate's had a long trip and she needs to rest before you all pile on top of her."

Laughing and waving good-bye, they all trooped out. "Quinn, why don't you grab her bag and we'll show her to a guest room upstairs?" Mom went on. She headed for the stairs. I followed uncertainly. My twin caught up my bag and reluctantly brought up the rear.

We climbed a lot of stairs and ended up in the top room of the little tower I had seen outside. The room was perfectly round, with windows on all sides that would let in sunshine if the sun ever broke through those permanent-looking gray clouds. A bed with a custom rounded headboard and mattress took up part of the floor space, as did a rounded dresser, wardrobe, and window seat. There were no corners anywhere in the room. I think I would have liked it if I hadn't been so tense.

"This room is terrible to heat in winter," my mother said, "but in summer, it's quite pleasant." She hugged me again.

I sensed nanos. There were nanobots running around under the skin in Mom's right arm and leg. I must have been too overwhelmed to notice them when she embraced me downstairs before. Of course—she would still have her implants. The hunger rose and I actually found myself reaching out to take in her nanos. I snatched my nanobots back, horrified. That was the very thing that had taken Mom away from me.

"It's so good to see you, Kate," Mom was saying. "You have no idea how it feels to have you both visiting."

My twin, meanwhile, had set down my bag and had started to slip away.

"Don't leave yet, Quinn," Mom said, and my twin halted. "You and your sister need to talk. I'll just nip out and leave you alone. We can get better acquainted later, Kate."

My twin shot her a look as she closed the door.

There was a long silence between us. I wanted to ask about Gremlin. I wanted to tell my twin about Dad. I felt edgy, unsettled. The male body was so near I could smell it.

Tell about Dad, an inner voice shouted. *There isn't time to mess around!*

What I said was, "Why did you leave?"

My twin gave a barking laugh. "I've been complaining about Felicity for years, and you ask me that? I'm an adult now. I can do what I want and go where I want."

"Fine," I said. "You're an adult. But that doesn't mean you can screw me over. And where's Gremlin?"

"What, am I chained to you or something?" my twin said, ignoring my question.

"You know what I mean." I took a deep breath. The edgy feeling was increasing. I wanted to Trade, had to Trade. I had been locked into one body for too long. "Look, about Dad—"

"I don't want to talk about him."

I couldn't stand it anymore. I sent nanos over to my twin and knocked in our secret signal.

I couldn't find any nanos. Not one.

Puzzled, I sent more nanos over to my twin. Still none. My nanobots slipped into the Quinn body, plunging into the bloodstream, searching frantically through the brain. I couldn't find a single nanobot. It was as if they had never existed.

Shock paralyzed me for a moment. Then my legs gave out and I sank down onto the bed. My twin must have figured out what I had done by the expression on my face, or perhaps it was a shred of our old closeness.

"Yeah," he said simply. "My nanos are gone."

"What happened?" I whispered.

"I don't want to get into it right now."

No nanobots. My twin had no nanobots. Without them we couldn't Trade. I was trapped forever in a single body, a single gender. Back on Felicity, I hadn't truly believed my twin would disappear forever and leave me stranded. Not really. Now it had actually happened. My stomach tightened so hard I thought I would throw up.

"When *do* you want to get into it?" I shouted. My voice felt raw. "Jesus Christ! What the hell happened to your nanos? *Where's Gremlin?*"

My twin looked away, then sat down on a window seat near the dresser. "I don't know where Gremlin is."

I grabbed my twin by the shoulders. It felt weird, like snatching up a full pitcher of water and realizing it's empty. "Dammit, what the fuck *happened*?"

"Quit shaking me. Jesus." My twin raised a hand to ward me off and a tear trickled down one cheek. I felt a small spark of shame—if it was hard for me, what was it like for my twin? I let go, though I was still angry.

"Tell me," I said in a cold voice.

"All right. When I first got to Earth, I came here and found Mom. I wanted to meet her, you know? I wanted to see if she was . . . I don't know . . . angry at us for breaking up her marriage with Dad. She isn't, you know. That's pretty amazing, I guess."

I nodded, resisting the urge to growl an order to hurry up.

"Anyway, when I got here, Mom told me some stuff about Dad. She said he used to use his nanobots to talk to computer systems all the time, or even control them." My twin had dropped into the dull monotone I recognized as an *I-hate-talking-about-this* tone. "He can sense what a computer senses, control any machine a computer controls, even alter a virtual reality program on the fly. All this time, I'd only been trying to read computers, not control them. I decided to try it."

"And?" I asked, dreading the answer but having to know.

"I linked my nanobots to the house's computer," my twin said softly. "And learned how to use it. It was pretty easy, really—a house system is a lot simpler than the ones at Skytown. I broke the gate lock by accident, but that was it."

That explained the open gate. "You didn't try linking to the nets while you were on your flight to Earth?"

"No. I figured it would be too dangerous if I made a mistake on a spaceship. People might have died. Like after the . . . after the fight."

I nodded. My twin had learned *something*, at least. I sat down on the window seat next to my twin. The windowpanes were cold at my back.

"After I figured out how to use the household computer," my twin continued, "I wanted to expand. See, every time I ran away to Skytown, I couldn't get into the main networks because all the links were indirect. It was too complicated for me. But Mom has a direct hookup with Gal-Net and Tach-Com. I just . . . jumped right in."

My twin trailed off. I was bunching and unbunching the material of my slacks.

"And?" I prompted again.

"It was too much," my twin burst out. "I couldn't handle it. It was like, *bam!* A whole universe of information rushed at me. VR programs, databases, mail, pornography, weather patterns, geometry books, train schedules, Mozart concerts, *everything*. It was too much. I felt like I was drowning or melting or losing myself in it all. I panicked, you know? The only thing I could think was, *Get out of there!* Before I knew what I was doing, I ejected all my nanos and shut them off. All of them."

I remained silent.

"I tried to get them back." My twin's voice cracked. "I tried for hours, but they wouldn't respond. I can't Trade anymore. My nanos are dead. I figure Gremlin must be dead, too."

A sort of numbness started in my head and spread to my body. I stared stupidly down at my hands as they clenched and unclenched the smooth fabric of my slacks. They left little wrinkles. My mind refused to grasp the concepts. Gremlin was forever dead. Not just off line. Irrevocably dead. I was going to be in a single body for the rest of my life. I would never be able to hear my twin's thoughts again.

Then the loss thundered over me like water crashing through a dam. Grief made my heart a stony lump in my chest. Tears started falling. I tried to say something, but all that came out was a strangled noise. I couldn't hold back the sobs. It was too much all at once. My twin sat next to me on the window seat and shared my tears. We put our arms around each other and cried almost silently. I cried for Gremlin. For my twin. For me. The anger dissolved—there was no room left for it. I held my twin fiercely, as if I could achieve through touch the gifts technology had once provided.

"What are we going to do about Dad?" I whispered.

We parted and my twin looked at me. "Why? What's wrong with Dad?"

Then I remembered I hadn't told my twin yet why I was here. I grabbed a tissue from the box on the dresser, blew my nose, and explained what had happened.

"I figured Grandma might be able to help," I finished. "But I couldn't find her, so I came looking for Mom and found you."

My twin's face was pale. "How long has Dad been missing?"

"He left five days ago."

"Shit." My twin got up. I guessed I'd better start thinking in terms of "Quinn" and "he" now. The thought drew a lump into my throat. *Quinn* ran a hand through *his* hair, and in that moment, he looked a lot like Dad.

"This is your fault," he said. "Jesus, this is your fault."

I stared. "What?"

"If you had come with me, none of this would have happened," Quinn said, his voice almost a snarl. "If you had come with me and we had gone into the networks together, we could have helped each other and I wouldn't have lost my nanobots. Gremlin could've helped us, too, but it's dead and I'm crippled. I can't even control my own body anymore, let alone Trade. If you had come with me, none of this would have happened."

For a long moment I was stunned, unable to speak. Anger flared again like a knife on fire, burning away my early sorrow and sympathy. How *dared* he? Outraged, I leaped to my feet.

"If *I* had come *with* you?" I said hotly. "What the hell is that supposed to mean? How is it my fault that you left and did something stupid? I don't know anything about computers, but even I would've known better than to access the entire network at once. That was stupid, Quinn. Stupid! And why should *I* want to leave Felicity?"

"Because we're twins," Quinn snapped. "We think the same. Or we used to. Until you tricked me into killing those kids."

"If we think so much alike," I said, "why didn't *you* want to stay on Felicity like *me*? It's not my fault you act without thinking. You've always been like that, even when we were little, but especially when you're male. You never learned how to control yourself."

"Which you knew damn well when you engineered that fight."

"So that makes all this my fault? I didn't kill anyone. I didn't run away. I didn't jump into the nets without looking first." My throat started to choke up again. "I didn't kill Gremlin."

"And *I* didn't—"

"This isn't helping Dad," I interrupted, almost

shouting. "He's in deep trouble, maybe even dead, and we're standing here arguing about stuff we can't change."

Quinn started to answer, then snapped his mouth shut. "All right. What do we do?"

I sat back down. "I don't know. I was hoping you could tell me. I thought maybe if I found Grandma or you, one of you would know enough about computers to figure something out."

"I know a lot about computers," my twin said. "My nanos coded a chunk of information into my brain before I . . . before I panicked. I can't talk to computers anymore, though. And I don't know anything about nano-bot hives."

I almost said that Gremlin did, but bit back the words. We were at an impasse. I had my nanos but knew nothing about computers. My twin knew computers but had no nanos.

The trapped feeling rose again, and I pushed it aside. I had been in a single body for several months. I could handle it a little longer, at least until we could figure out what to do.

A knock came at the door and Mom poked her head into the room. "Are you two still talking it out?"

Quinn turned. "I told her everything, Mom."

My mother pushed the door fully open with her foot and carried a large silver tray into the room. On it were a teapot, cups, small sandwiches, and some lumpy brown things I didn't recognize. They looked like malformed biscuits.

"It's teatime," she said. "I thought you might be hungry."

Suddenly I realized I was ravenous. It had been almost a day since I'd last eaten. Mom set the tray on the dresser and we helped ourselves. The lumpy things were called scones and you ate them with something called clotted cream, which sounds disgusting but is actually sweet and smooth, like cake frosting. Everything was delicious. I wondered if Dad was getting anything to eat.

Mom and I kept looking at each other as we sat down with our plates. I couldn't keep my eyes off her. This was my mother. I had a mom. Unbidden, an old playground conversation popped into my head.

"*That's dumb,*" Kevin snorted. "*Everyone has a mom.*"

"*Well, I don't,*" I yelled at him. "*And I think you're dumb!*"

Kevin wasn't dumb, and I did have a mom.

"Kate has news," Quinn said, ignoring his food. "It's bad."

Mom raised an eyebrow. I took a gulp of tea and went through the whole explanation again of what happened to Dad. Quinn nibbled at a sandwich and started pacing while I talked. I kept a wary eye on him, not sure what was going through his head. I felt left out.

"I'm not sure what to say," Mom said when I finished. "We need to do something, certainly."

"You don't seem very upset," Quinn said.

"How should I react?" Mom returned. "I haven't seen your father in close to eighteen years."

"Don't you care about him?" I demanded.

"Yes," Mom replied simply. "But like I said, it's been a long, long time, and I have other obligations now. Another family."

"Why did you leave?" I blurted out.

Mom looked at Quinn. "I thought you both knew everything."

"We do," Quinn said. "Dad told us right after . . . after the fight."

I looked mutely at Mom, not trusting myself to speak again for fear I'd either break down crying again or lash out and hit her. This was the woman who had abandoned me—us. She had joined a new family and had new kids. Knowing why she had done it didn't make it hurt any less. If anything, that made it worse.

Because it was your fault she left? Just like it was your fault Quinn got in the fight?

Shut up!

Mom met my gaze, and I saw her eyes were bright, as if she were holding back tears.

"Leaving you was the hardest thing I've ever done, Kate," she said softly. "I would give anything to have those years back."

I realized I was crying again and reached for the tissues. "Why didn't Dad tell us what happened a long time ago? My whole life I wondered why you had left."

Mom sat next to me on the window seat and took my hand. Her skin was darker than mine, and it was strange to see it. On Felicity, Quinn and I were the dark ones.

"He was probably afraid you'd blame yourselves and think it was your fault," she said.

"Wasn't it?" I cried. "It was our nanos that—"

"Absolutely not," Mom interrupted firmly. "Kate, it never crossed my mind to blame you. You didn't know how to control your nanos any more than you knew how to walk. I wish things could have worked out differently, but there was no other solution."

I nodded, trying not to feel guilty. What if Mom was just saying that to make me feel better? I didn't know her well enough to tell if she was lying or not.

"None of this," Quinn put in, "is helping Dad. Can't we talk about this later?"

"Right you are." Mom let go of my hand and stood up. "I think we need to call your grandmother."

CHAPTER ELEVEN

ADITI

The Intruder walked jerkily into Aditi's room. Sweat poured from his forehead and his muscles trembled, but Aditi's nanos were still in control of his implants. Aditi herself was sitting up in her wheelchair. For the first time in her life, she had been able to maneuver herself into it. She didn't even have to be strapped in. Still, the Intruder's eyes widened when he saw her misshapen body. Aditi's own eyes went flat.

"Let me go, Aditi," he said hoarsely in a voice left raw from screaming. "This is wrong. You can't do this to people."

Aditi, taken aback by the fact that he knew her name, merely walked him over to her bed and made him lay down on it, hands at his sides. She couldn't stop him from talking, however. His implants didn't control jaw and throat muscles or the fine manipulators of hands and face.

"Aditi," he said in a desperate voice, "you have to let me go, let this planet go. Do you know how many people have died already? Some of them are children."

He was speaking English, a language Aditi had never learned until her nanobots coded a database of syntax and vocabulary for it into her brain so she could understand her captive's words. The motor in Aditi's chair hummed as she brought herself closer to the bed. The Intruder was a handsome man on camera and even more handsome in person. Exotic red hair, brown eyes, muscular frame. A strong body. Breathtaking. Aditi was envious.

"Aditi, my name is Lance Radford-Michaels," the Intruder said. "I live on a planet named Felicity, but I grew up in London on Earth. I have two kids, a son and a daughter about your age. They're probably worried about me."

Aditi cocked her head. Interesting. The police had extensive files on hostage situations, and the Intruder— Lance—was obviously familiar with them as well. By giving her personal information about himself, he was supposedly making himself a real person instead of a faceless dummy. A real person would be harder to maim or kill. But Aditi knew about the trick. It wouldn't work.

"My daughter is a talented sculptor," Lance went on. "She has eyes like yours, Aditi. Very beautiful dark eyes."

Aditi bit her lip. She knew the compliment was probably false, an attempt to gain her sympathy. But it still felt good to hear it. She felt drawn to this man, this handsome, exotic man. She found herself wanting to run her fingers through his hair. How could she be so cruel to him? She should let him go. She should—

Her nanos alerted her to a physiological change. Her vomeronasal organ was picking up strange pheromones from the Intruder. They bypassed her normal sense of smell and were affecting her hypothalamus, which reacted by stimulating the release of various endorphins. The endorphins were the source of her attraction to Lance.

Angrily, Aditi shut down her vomeronasal organ. Then she reached for a length of gauze, stuffed it into Lance's mouth, and wound more gauze around his head to hold it in place. His eyes went wide. It was awkward work with only one hand, but Aditi managed it. Lance, after all, couldn't move enough to stop her.

"All my life people have manipulated me," she hissed at him, "making me do what they want. My father, Mole-Face, now you. Your words and your pheromones won't work on me any more than your nanos. What do you think of that, Lance Radford-Michaels?"

Lance didn't answer. He couldn't.

"Now, Lance," Aditi continued, "you're going to tell me everything—how you control your nanobots, how you pulled your trick with the pheromones, everything. I have more nanos than you, but you have more experience. That's going to change in a moment. Hold still." She gave him a tight smile. "Wiggling will only make it worse."

He ignored her, of course.

Aditi sat back in her wheelchair, flushed with excitement. It had taken hours, but the decoding was finished. Aditi could read the chemical sequences that made up Lance's memories as easily as she could her own. Lance still lay on the table, half conscious, no longer even moaning through his gag. Once in a while, her nanos had made an accidental change in his neurochemistry instead of merely breaking codes. The results had usually been convulsive, and Aditi's new awareness of Lance's brain and body told her he was exhausted, sore, and soaked in sweat. He was also suffering flashbacks from his childhood, when his father used to chain him to a wall and shock him with electric wires and bury him in clay with nothing but a straw to breathe through. Ah, well. Aditi's life had been equally hard. Besides, she had made the discovery of a lifetime—Lance had two children who could control nanobots just like Aditi and their father did.

Those two children could switch bodies.

Excitement rose again. This was a possibility that had never occurred to Aditi, and she raised her single fist in exultation. If they could do it, so could she. At long, long last, Aditi could be free of the crippled mass of flesh she lived in. She could run and jump and eat and drink. All she had to do was find a body to do it with.

Aditi widened her awareness. She skimmed through

images picked up by satellites and camera lenses. Pictures and videos flashed through her mind until a camera caught sight of a woman perhaps eighteen or nineteen years old—Aditi's age. She was pretty, with braided black hair, flawless skin, and clear, dark eyes. The woman was peering cautiously out of the gate that led to her garden, unaware that Aditi could watch her through her own security system. Aditi already had several billion nanos in the area. In an eyeblink, she sent them crawling over the woman, invading her body through mouth and nose, ears and eyes.

The woman dropped the ground, screaming. Other people from the house, presumably her family, rushed out to help her, but Aditi ignored them and made a copy of the chemical codes that made up her own memories. All she had to do was move the chemicals of the woman's brain around to match, and Aditi's mind would be in a strong, healthy body.

Aditi shifted her concentration to the woman's brain and downloaded the chemical sequences into the nanos waiting there. Immediately, she set about the process of—Aditi smiled at the choice of words—changing the woman's mind. The woman's body struggled and convulsed much like Lance had, but Aditi relentlessly continued the process. The woman screamed again, while her helpless relatives stood nearby and wrung their hands. Aditi smiled, getting closer to her new body with every passing second.

The woman's heart abruptly stopped. All electrical activity in her brain ceased. Her body went limp, and she died.

Strange, Aditi thought. *She was young and healthy. It should have worked.*

Through the vidphone in the young woman's room, Aditi could see that she had a brother perhaps a year younger. He was staring down at his sister's body in disbelief. Tears had not yet begun to fall. On impulse, Aditi ordered her nanos out of the woman's body and into the brother's. The boy fell screaming to the ground as his sister had, and, like her, was dead in moments. Aditi tried again with the mother and father. All of them died.

Puzzled, Aditi selected fifteen potential hosts from all over the planet and tried to implant her memories and personality. Not one survived.

Aditi banged the arm of her wheelchair in frustration. It was possible, *must* be possible. Lance's children did it on a *whim*. She tried again. Twenty people. Thirty. A hundred. No good. Every time she tried to implant herself in someone else, the body died.

There must be some element I'm missing, she thought. *Something I'm doing wrong.*

Lance, still lying motionless on the bed, caught Aditi's eye. Maybe she should try it with him. His body was used to nanos. He might be a suitable host. She reached out and ran her misshapen hand down the hard muscles of his arm. This one would be a fine host, strong and handsome. So who'd be male. It wasn't as if she had had much experience being a woman in this crippled body.

Her nanos readied themselves. As if in response, Lance's nanos set up another fight, struggling to free themselves from Aditi's, but Aditi still had a five-to-one advantage. Aditi downloaded her chemical sequences into the nanobots that weren't fighting Lance's. They scurried through his body and flooded his brain. Lance's struggles increased, and several hundred thousand of his nanos actually managed to escape. Aditi was forced to destroy them. Her other nanos got into position in Lance's brain, ready to change his memories to match hers.

Then Aditi paused. What if this didn't work? If Lance died, she would lose any chance of learning more from him and his nanos. She stared down at him for a long moment, then sighed with real regret. She couldn't risk losing him.

Perhaps his children are a singularity, she thought.

If you want to switch bodies like that, maybe you have to be doing it from birth, when your brain and mind are more flexible.

Lance twitched once and moaned softly. A quick check with her nanos showed that he was suffering another flashback to his childhood. Aditi cocked her head. What would happen if she copied *his* mnemonic codes into *her* mind? Not all of them—just a few. Perhaps the ones he was experiencing right now. Would she be able to experience what he was remembering? Without pausing to think further, Aditi ordered her nanos to do it. The world *twisted*, and suddenly Aditi was somewhere else.

Tears ran down Jay's face like warm worms. He was thirsty, so thirsty. His tongue was dry, a block of dusty wood in his head. But in three hours, he would be dead and he would know no more thirst.

Pain exploded in his right palm, mirroring the pain already tearing through his left, and Jay screamed. Father raised the hammer again. Jay threw back his head, cracking it painfully against the headboard that pressed cold and hard against the knobs of his bare back. The feeling made an odd contrast to the soft mattress he was sitting on. He screamed and screamed over the rawness in his throat, but the pain didn't stop. Sweat poured down his body.

The hammer fell, but Father missed. It smashed Jay's index finger instead, and Jay felt the bone snap. With three more meaty *thunks*, Father finished nailing Jay's other hand to the headboard, leaving Jay's arms spread wide. Jay screamed again.

"Shut up!" Father said. He brandished the hammer in Jay's face. It was spattered with red drops of blood. "This is your fault, you little fuck. You made me do this. You don't do shit like that with family. You hear me? *Not with family.* Incest is a *crime*, and you'd go to hell if I didn't punish you for it. I'm saving you, and don't you forget it."

Father flung the hammer to the floor and stomped out of the room, slamming the door behind him. The room was left in dim light, and a cold breeze wafted through a shattered window despite the closed door. Father had broken the window earlier in a fit of temper.

Jay had no idea where he was, and at the moment, he didn't care. His breath came in little gasps. The agony in his hands was horrible, overpowering. Every time he so much as twitched a finger, fresh pain ripped through his palms. Yet through it all he could still feel other things—the burning in his rectum, the soft flannel sheets shrouding his bare legs, the warm blood trickling down his hands, the ache of his bruised lips, the burning thirst in his mouth and throat.

In three hours, I'll be dead, he told himself. *I just have to make it through the next three hours.*

His broken finger began to swell and his arms grew tired. He tried to relax them and was immediately met with screaming pain.

Boosting muscular endurance, said a voice. *Increasing ATP production. Facilitating quick removal of lactic acid.* Some of the fatigue disappeared. Strength returned to his arms.

"Mother?" Jay whispered hoarsely. "Is that you?"

Reducing histamine levels at damaged phalange, continued the voice dispassionately. *Commencing bone-knitting subroutine. Boosting immune system to compensate for possible infection. Sealing ruptured blood vessels.*

"Mother, where are you?" Jay asked. "I'm scared. I can hear you, but I can't see you."

Am not your mother, the voice said. *Name is Robin. Please try to remain still. Current healing only stopgap, but subunits unable to eject metallic bodies from palms. Sorry about pain, but haven't yet mastered nervous system.*

"Not my mother?" More tears leaked from Jay's eyes and dripped down his chin. "Where is my mother?"

The voice didn't answer. Jay closed his eyes. He was somehow able to keep his arms motionless now, and the pain in his hands was fading to a constant, dull ache.

You were chosen for this, Jay thought. *It's why you exist. Remember that.*

The room grew colder. The chill settled into Jay's wounds, making them ache anew. His thirst continued to burn.

In Heaven there is water, he thought. *Cool and wet and cleansing, washing away sin and thirst alike.*

Jay could almost see the waves, feel them washing over him, pouring down his parched throat with soothing wetness. He swallowed dryly. In Heaven there would be water. He only had to wait three hours. In three hours he would be in Heaven.

Time dragged. Once, Jay nodded off and awoke screaming at the fresh pain caused by his relaxing arms. Minutes flickered slowly by on the digital clock near the bed. Jay stared, wide-eyed. The numbers were growing. One by one they dropped off the clock and slunk toward him, a crowd of sixes and sevens, threes and fives. Jay whimpered and tried to draw away from them, but every move brought back the pain. The numbers swarmed over him, biting his skin with ice-cold teeth. Jay didn't have strength left to cry out.

"Father," he gasped, "into Thy hands—"

The lights came on. The numbers were sucked back into the clock, and Jay saw that less than an hour had passed.

"Son?"

Jay looked up. Father was standing over him. There were tears in his eyes.

"Jesus, what did I do to you?" Father asked hoarsely. "I'm sorry. God, I'm sorry." He knelt by the bed. "I love you, son. I love you more than anyone in this world. You know that, don't you? Don't you?"

Jay managed a nod. Of course Father loved him. That was why all this was happening.

"Let's get you out of this," Father said. "Hold still."

He picked the hammer up from the floor and hooked the claw over the nail head in Jay's left hand. Pain exploded unbearably, and this time, Jay fell into darkness.

When he awoke, he was lying on the bed, still naked. The sheets had been changed, and they smelled like fabric softener. His hands still ached, and his throat was still bone-dry. A piece of cardboard covered the broken window and the room was warm again. The lights had been dimmed.

Father was gone.

This isn't Heaven, Jay thought. *There is no pain or thirst in Heaven.* He sat up and winced as the movement jolted his broken finger. The room tilted crazily for a moment, then steadied.

I'm still alive, Jay realized. *What did I do wrong?*

He got up and stumbled toward the bathroom, driven by thirst. A hurried twist of the faucet sent cool water splashing into the sink and Jay didn't even stop to pick up the glass on the toothbrush rack. He shoved his face under the spigot and let the liquid gush down his dry throat. He drank deeply for several minutes before shutting the water off and straightening. Water ran cold down his face and dripped on his bare chest.

This isn't right, Jay thought. *I'm still alive. I'm supposed to be dead.* He glanced down at his palms. There was nothing but an angry red scar in the center of each, and the pain was almost gone except in his broken finger, though even that barely ached now.

Healing process almost complete, said the voice. *Finger should be fully functional in twelve hours. Please avoid using, if at all possible.*

"I wasn't worthy," Jay said softly. "That's why Father took me down and left me. I wasn't worthy of his love."

He wandered out of the bathroom and his gaze fell upon the bedroom window, the one Father had broken. Slowly, as if in a dream, he pulled the cardboard away. Chill night air washed over him and he peered into the darkness outside. If he went down headfirst, his neck would probably snap just like his finger.

"I'll prove it to you, Father," Jay said. "I'll show you I'm worthy of your love."

He dove forward.

"Jesus Christ!" Garth yelped, and flung his arms wide. His shoulders and upper arms bashed the window frame and he bounced backward, landing on the carpet with an *oof*. Garth lay there for a moment, stunned, before rolling over and slowly sitting up.

His finger hurt like a sonofabitch.

"What the fuck is going on here?" he said.

Jay tried to commit suicide, Robin said, and Garth tried to spin around, but he was still sitting on the floor. Then he calmed down.

"Jesus Christ," he muttered. "Robin?"

Affirmative. Father nailed Jay to headboard and he tried to commit—

"Yeah, yeah. I saw." Garth got up and noticed he was naked. His finger throbbed. "Fuck."

He glanced at the window. It was still broken from Dad's punch, and the piece of cardboard that was apparently supposed to cover it had been moved aside.

So Jay could jump out, Garth thought with a yawn. *Stupid.* Grimacing, he replaced the cardboard and climbed into Lance's bed. It was warm from Jay's body.

"I heard what you and Jessica talked about, Robby," Garth said, and yawned again. "About how you're an artificial intelligence and all. We'll have to have a chat eventually, but not right now. I'm bushed. I think we'll let Jessica handle the next couple days."

Affirmative, Robin said, but Garth was already asleep.

Aditi yanked herself back to reality. She leaned back in her wheelchair, panting hard. More normal sensations came back—her single arm on the hard plastic arm of the chair, the fresh-smelling breeze from the open window, the greenish-purple vines that spilled through it onto the floor, the faint noises of the city.

After a while, she became aware of information from her "other" eyes and ears, the ones that watched her world. Her jaunt into Lance's memories had caused unanticipated reactions. In many ways, the worldwide computer systems were now her body, and when Aditi was startled, her "body" reacted in unexpected ways. Thirty-seven cars had gone insane, mowing down anyone who got in the way and eventually smashing into houses, buildings, and walls. Five fires had broken out when electrical systems overloaded. Two hundred and five people had been demolished by rapacious nanobots that had torn their bodies to shreds. Their remains lay like piles of red rags on the ground. Aditi shook her head. Eventually she'd have to learn how to control all this a little better, but for now she had other things to think about.

She had taken part in one of Lance's memories. She had seen from her earlier explorations that Lance's father had tortured him as a child and that Jay, Garth, and Jessica were some of the alternate people Lance had created to deal with the physical and mental pain. Robin was the alter who had control of the nanobots. Aditi had known all that, but she hadn't *experienced* it—quite another matter entirely. It was a rush, even the pain. She had actually felt the cold water gush down Jay's— Lance's—throat. She had felt the nails go into his hands. She had felt him run—*run!*—toward the window as if she had been running herself.

Aditi looked at Lance with both eyes and nanos. He lay unharmed on the bed, the flashback over, his condition unchanged.

And why should it change? Aditi thought gleefully. *I only made copies. I didn't change the original. And if I can do this with Lance, why not another body?*

Aditi closed her eyes. Across the planet, her nanos

mobilized again, a tiny invisible army that slipped quietly into open orifices and stationed themselves amid
trillions and trillions of brain cells. It turned out to be
easier than Aditi thought. With Lance as a model and
the vastly increased resources of her own intellect, it
was almost simple to decode the perceptions from other
bodies and bring them to her own. Chemicals moved
within Aditi's brain and sensation flooded her body. She
tasted a thousand meals, saw a thousand skies, heard a
thousand sounds. This time, she didn't allow them to
overwhelm her like she had with Lance's flashback.
Instead, she sampled slowly, dipping here and there.
For a while she concentrated on taste. Spicy curry flowed
over her tongue, followed by sweet chocolate and bland
flat bread. Salty beans and rice followed banana-tomato
salad.

Next she widened her perceptions to include touch.
She felt the bunch and push of running muscle. The
roughness of a cat's tongue on her hand. The thudding
pain of an unexpected bruise. The feel of silk sliding
over her skin. The shattering explosion of an orgasm.

Aditi spotted a pattern. She only had enough nanos
to see into the minds of about half the planet's popu-
lation, but it was enough. The release of neurochem-
icals in specific parts of the human brain caused specific
muscles to contract. If her nanos stimulated the release
of those chemicals in the right place and in the right
proportions, she should, in theory, be able to make
other people's muscles contract and relax. She'd be
able to control their bodies as well as see into their
minds.

An hour passed. Two thousand four hundred and sixteen people died as Aditi put theory into practice. She
could hear some of the cries through her bedroom window, but her nanos shut the annoying sounds out of
her brain. In the end, Aditi had the control she needed. The people of New Pakistan belonged to her, just
like the computers.

Well, she admitted, to be fair, *only half the people. But once I build more nanos, I'll have the rest.*

Time for that later, though. Right now it was time to enjoy herself, find out exactly what she could do. Once again, Aditi closed her eyes and reached out to her new puppets like a thirsty horse reaching for the water trough.

Lance lay on the bed, eyes forced to stare upward. He was *not* Jay. He was *not* nailed to the headboard. He was *not* going to jump out the window.

He was *not* going to die.

Just hold on for one more minute, he told himself. *Get through the next minute. Just one more minute.*

When the minute passed, he started on the next minute. Then the next and the next.

The gag in his mouth absorbed every last drop of saliva, leaving thirst to torture his mouth and tongue. His stomach growled incessantly. His nanos, still imprisoned by Aditi's, could do nothing to help.

One more minute. One more minute. The words became a mantra. *One more minute.*

The word "minute" played across Lance's mind. Minute. Min-nit. Minimum. Mini. Minutia. My-newt. Minute minutes.

I'm going insane, he thought. *Dr. Baldwin wouldn't approve.*

Dr. Baldwin wouldn't approve of the word "insane," either. According to Dr. Baldwin, there was no such thing as a lunatic, only a person with issues that hadn't been resolved. Lance had spent a lot of time in the therapist's office, both as a teenager and an adult, trying to uncover the "unresolved issues" that had lead to Lance's—what? What could you call it if not "insanity"? Splitting your mind into forty-nine parts wasn't exactly normal.

But what is normal? Dr. Baldwin's voice asked. *Is it normal to be tortured by one's father? Ignored by one's*

*mother? Before we label anything as "abnormal," we
need to look at the circumstances.*

Aditi's nanos scurried around Lance's brain again,
sampling, tasting. His body was strapped down while
miniature monsters wandered freely through his mind.
Nausea rose. Lance felt more violated than he had at
any time that Dad had entered his room and ordered
Lance's bodyguard to rape him. It was worse than being
chained in the basement and shocked with electric wires.
It was even worse than being buried in clay. At least
back then, his mind had been his own. But now even
that was being looked at, dissected, examined. Every
memory laid bare for Aditi's pleasure. Lance wanted
to jerk his body around and scream, but he couldn't
even do that. He had to struggle, get up, had to *move*.
The pressure was mounting, and Lance was afraid of
what would happen when it got too high. Already he
could feel his mind eroding like a sand dune in a windstorm. Brain cells flashed signals in odd directions, made
connections across the corpus callosum between his left
and right hemispheres—connections his neural cells
shouldn't be making.

Lance noticed he was hyperventilating. He forced
himself to slow his breathing, concentrate on the air
going in and out of his lungs.

*In and out. One more minute. One more minute. In
and out. You got through Dad. You can get through this.*

Yeah, but you got through Dad by going insane.

*I did not go insane. Dr. Baldwin said there's no such
thing.*

A laugh echoed inside Lance's head. He wanted to
tell it to shut up, but the gauze gag in his mouth wouldn't
let him. The laughter grew louder, shrill and mocking.
Lance moaned softly, begging the voice to stop.

It did. *Sorry,* the voice said. It sounded familiar somehow, but Lance couldn't quite place it. *Listen, Lance-
boy, you don't have to go through this shit. I can help
you.*

How?

I'll take care of things up here. You just go to sleep, and when you wake up, everything'll be fine. Just fine.

Relief flooded Lance. *But where should I sleep? This isn't my bed.*

Just burrow deep down, the voice said. *Good and deep, where Aditi will never find you. Where no one will ever find you. Everything'll be just fine, Lance-boy.*

Lance obeyed. It was surprisingly easy. The darkness snuggled in soft around him, warm and safe. Eventually he fell asleep.

Halfway across New Pakistan, a dozen cooks worked feverishly in a hot kitchen. Sweat poured off their faces, their eyes were round and staring. Their hands moved swiftly, efficiently, chopping meat, sprinkling spices, tossing sizzling meat into the air over flat frying pans. None of them spoke. The only sounds were running water—newly restored, along with electricity and gas—chopping knives, and hissing meat. Stewpots and soup kettles steamed. Delicious, pungent smells rose into the air despite the fact that none of the dozen people were particularly proficient chefs. One had the scarred, dirty hands of an auto mechanic. Another was a child barely able to see over the countertops. A third was an old woman, stooped and bent as a rocking chair. But the entity controlling their movements had read extensive databases on cooking and preparing food and it learned extraordinarily quickly. The original condition of the bodies performing the labor was irrelevant.

Out in the restaurant proper, a hundred more people sat around tables and in booths. Most of them were eating, some shoving food into their mouths with both hands, others eating delicately with knife and fork. The only sound in the room was the clink of silverware. The people ate steadily, silently. Servers took up empty plates and replaced them with fresh ones as fast as the cooks in the kitchen could fill them. In one corner, a man with a belly that bulged far too much for his slender frame stiffened as his stomach distended and burst. His face went blotchy and he slumped sideways off his chair. Half-chewed food oozed from his mouth. The man's dinner companion, another man in his late forties, continued eating as if nothing had happened. In a few moments, the front door opened and a woman walked in. She stepped over the corpse, sat in the dead man's chair, and resumed his interrupted meal.

Half a mile away, forty naked people of all shapes and sizes twined on the floor of a hotel lobby. Mouths, lips, hips, and hands moved and undulated in all combinations, but the only sound was the scrape of flesh on flesh. Every so often, a male participant shuddered his way through orgasm, then got up and moved to the wall where he stood waiting until his erection returned and he could rejoin the group. Occasionally a woman would go to the wall, but the refractory period was shorter, the resting time not as long. When someone collapsed from exhaustion, two others would stop and pull the person aside. In a few minutes, someone else would enter the lobby from the street, strip out of his or her clothes, and join the mass of flesh on the floor. Terror flashed through every pair of eyes, but no one made a sound.

In a public park, a group of people ran pell-mell around the soccer field, leaping over the prone bodies of those who had collapsed during the last lap. At the playground, adults and children alike swung from the jungle gym, swooped on the swings, and rocked on the teeter-totter. Tree branches creaked dangerously under the load of a dozen climbers. Unlike the restaurant and hotel, the park was noisy. Happy laughter and shouts of childlike glee shrieked from wooden faces under terrified eyes.

Aditi Amendeep sighed and opened her eyes. Every sensation she had been denied for nineteen years was hers. It was glorious, exhilarating—and still disappointing.

The sensations were still secondhand, no matter how realistic they might seem. She stepped up nanobot production and reached out for more puppets. Houses collapsed and cars disintegrated beneath the pincers of nanobots seeking building materials. Three out of the planet's five cities were completely hers. The rest would soon follow.

It still wasn't enough. The more Aditi took, the more she wanted, the more she *needed*. Twenty-one simultaneous orgasms shook her body, but already the feeling wasn't as intense as it had been an hour ago, a minute ago. Tastes and textures rolled over her tongue, but they were already growing bland. At the rate she was going, she would need far more than just the few people on this single planet.

Her eye fell on the room's computer terminal. It was still on, of course. Aditi used it to facilitate communication with her nanos. She didn't need it—her nanos formed their own communications web—but the terminal had a greater capacity and was much more efficient. Ved Amendeep had even used it to log onto the galactic nets to talk with specialists on other planets.

Aditi furrowed her forehead in thought. She had used the terminal to allow her nanobots to communicate with—and thereby take over—other nanos across New Pakistan. In theory, the same thing would work with nanos on another planet. Distance wasn't a factor for the nets. Aditi should be able to "talk" to and absorb nanos from anywhere with a net hookup. As long as her new nanos stayed within range of an FTL communicator, it would be as if Aditi herself were there. She could take puppets from other planets as easily as she took them on New Pakistan.

The problem was, there was no communication with the galactic nets. That had been severed.

What if Aditi herself somehow got off planet? Once she cleared whatever interference was jamming communications from New Pakistan, she'd be able to grab an entire universe of sensations, an infinity of people and pleasures.

Aditi sighed. It didn't matter. She couldn't get off this planet. She had accidentally destroyed all the ships on New Pakistan, including Lance's, and no new ships were going to land. She couldn't even build a new one—New Pakistan had no shipyard.

Then her eye fell on Lance. He seemed to have fallen asleep.

I have two kids, a son and a daughter about your age, he had said. *They're probably worried about me.*

Two kids who could control nanobots. Two kids who would probably think they could fight a nanobot hive. What were the odds that at least one of Lance's kids would come looking for him? And what were the odds that they'd land in a ship?

Aditi smiled long and hard at Lance. She reached out and smoothed his hair as another orgasm rippled through her body. He was proving more useful than she had ever imagined. She hoped his children would prove even more so.

CHAPTER TWELVE

ME

Less than fifteen minutes after Mom called Grandma, a long black car appeared at the gate to whisk the three of us to the main building of MM, Limited, the parent corporation that owns Grandma's other companies. Mom made hasty explanations to the rest of her—my?—family as we headed out the door.

I was nervous about another car ride, but the driver was careful, smooth, and quick. We rode in silence. I sat next to Quinn, his leg pushed unconsciously against mine. I sensed nanos in the car, nanos in my mother, and nanos in the pop-up computer terminal set into the seat. There were, of course, no nanos in my twin, and it felt like I was sitting next to a black hole.

The silence grew uncomfortable. I stared at the privacy panel that separated us from the driver, wanting to fill the silence with words, not knowing what to say. I should have been able to talk to my twin at least, but I couldn't think of a thing.

An uncomfortable half hour later, we pulled up in front of a tall building made of blue glass. The driver ushered us through a series of elevators and corridors to a door labeled RESEARCH LABORATORY CQ48-A. We went in; the driver left.

The lab was large and white, with equipment I couldn't begin to figure out scattered on tables and counters. At least one computer terminal occupied each table. A man was typing madly at one of them. I barely had time to take any of it in before Grandma rushed over to embrace Quinn and me. I hadn't seen her since her last visit to Felicity two years ago, but she hadn't changed. Her hair was the same shade of strawberry blond and she had the same wildflower perfume smell. I found that comforting in this strange lab on this strange planet, with a twin who couldn't Trade and a mother I didn't know. It was a rock to hold onto. I felt a little better.

"And Delia," Grandma said after letting us go. "How are you holding up?"

Mom gave her a wan smile. "It doesn't seem quite real, Meredeth." She reached out to stroke my hair and I let her. I still didn't know how I felt about all this yet.

Grandma gestured to the mad typist. "This is Marco Sierra," she said. "One of my most talented—and trusted—technicians."

"She flatters me," Sierra said, and came forward to shake our hands. He was a short man with a broad build, dark skin, and black hair. He looked like he was almost thirty, but then, so did Grandma.

"How is he going to help us find Dad?" Quinn demanded. "We need to *do* something."

"And we shall," Grandma said. "Our problem is that you've lost your nanos, Quinn." He blanched. "Sorry if I'm being too blunt, but we don't have time to be nice. Now, Kate still has her nanos, but she doesn't have your experience with computers and she would be of little help to your father. Given a few days, I'm sure she'd learn as much as you did, but for now I think it might save us time if we could get your nanobots up and running again."

Hope rose and I glanced at Quinn. His expression mirrored my thoughts.

"I want Marco to examine Kate," Grandma said. "He knows all about our family's . . . relationship with nanobots, and I'm hoping he can figure out how to bring Quinn's back. Then we can see about rescuing your father."

"If you could jump up here, Ms. Radford-Michaels," Sierra said, patting one of the counters, "I'd like to take a closer look at you."

I did, and he picked up what looked like a larger version of the wristcomps that most people wore.

"How many nanobots do you carry with you?" Sierra asked.

"Do you want an exact number?" I said.

"If you can give it."

I checked. "One trillion, two hundred sixty-two billion, eight hundred forty-seven million, three hundred fifty thousand, one hundred fifty-eight." A nanobot winked out. It would be replaced in about ten minutes, but Sierra wanted exact numbers. "Sorry. That's one hundred fifty-seven."

Sierra nodded as if I had said it might rain later. "What exactly can you do with them?"

I demonstrated for him how I could increase my strength for short periods, make minor metabolic changes, and clean my skin and clothes. Quinn watched and fidgeted.

"You can effect changes to objects outside your body?" Sierra asked.

"Some." I showed him how I could sculpt a lump of clay, shatter a teacup, and reduce a styrofoam container to dust.

"Interesting," Sierra muttered. He took a blood sample and inserted it under a microscope. "Your nanos appear to have coated themselves with the protein markers from your body. That explains one problem, anyway."

"Protein markers?" I asked.

"Every cell in your body has a particular pattern of protein molecules on the outer membrane," Sierra explained, still looking into the microscope. "It's like a password to your body's immune system. Your body figures that anything without a marker on it must be an invader, so your immune system attacks with fevers, mucus discharge, antibodies, and white blood cells. Your nanobots, however, carry protein markers, so your immune system ignores them."

With deft, precise movements, he moved the blood sample to another machine and activated a computer terminal.

"What I don't understand," he said, fingers clicking over the keyboard, "is how you control your nanos and how they all communicate with each other. Telepathy?"

I shrugged. "I never thought about it."

"Now would be a good time to think about it," Sierra said. "It may provide the key to getting your brother's nanos back on line."

Mom and Grandma watched all this silently from a pair of stools, but Quinn was pacing. His footfalls became faster and louder with every passing moment. I was about to ask him to stop when he made a disgusted noise.

"This isn't getting us anywhere," he exploded. "We're sitting here in a lab, and Dad may be dead."

I wanted to point out that we'd probably be doing something right now if he hadn't been a stupid idiot, but bit my tongue instead. Worry washed over me. What was Dad going through right now? Was he dead like Quinn suspected? Or was he lying hurt and bleeding on the ground somewhere? Was he afraid? Was he alive?

Sierra was clicking away at the terminal again. I wished I had brought a book or something else to keep my mind occupied while he worked. Idly, I watched Sierra. There were nanos in his terminal. I could sense them. On impulse, I sent out a handful—only a handful—of my own nanos and "knocked" on them as I used to do with my twin when I wanted to Trade.

In less than a second, they were mine.

I flashed back to the day I had forced a Trade on my twin, the day I had stolen nanos from Dad. It had been so easy to take them. I stole another handful. It was like eating popcorn—you couldn't stop with just one kernel. I made myself quit before I damaged Sierra's computer.

Another thought flashed through my head. If I could take nanos from one source, could I "give" them to another? I turned the idea over in my mind. Why not? I already knew the male body's brain as well as the one I currently had, and I had absolute control of my nanos. Why shouldn't I be able to set up a bunch of nanobots so they'd obey commands from that brain, even if I wasn't using it?

"Mr. Sierra," I said, "do you have a stockpile of nanos? Ones that I could use?"

Startled, he looked up from the computer. "Yes. Why?"

I turned to Quinn. "I'm thinking I can give you a set."

He was instantly interested. "How?" he demanded.

"Once I've taken over a whole lot of extra nanobots," I explained, letting the idea coalesce as I spoke, "I think I could give them to you. I'd just program them to obey your commands and then erase my own programs. It'd be like Trading, really, only I'd handle both ends at once."

Interest changed to doubt. "What if something goes wrong?"

"What could go wrong? Even if it doesn't work, all that'll happen is the nanos won't hook up with your brain and they'll stay with me." I paused. "I admit I don't have all the details worked out, but it feels like it would work. Let me get in the male—your—head and look around."

Grandma and Mom were looking at both of us intently. "Marco," Grandma said, "do you think this is possible?"

Sierra spread his hands. "I'm way out of my depth here. It'll take me months just to process the data I've gathered in these last ten minutes."

"It's up to you, Quinn," Mom said quietly.

Quinn stood up. "Let's do it."

"Not here," Grandma said quickly. "We should handle this in a medical lab in case something doesn't, um . . . work out."

A few minutes later, I was lying on a hospital bed next

to my twin. The white sheets were smooth and stiff beneath me, and the pillow crackled under my head. Sierra had hooked up several sensors to both my twin and me, and monitors beeped and burbled above us. I realized how tired I was. I hadn't slept much on the trip to Earth, nor had I rested since I got to London. Now, even lying on an uncomfortable bed, I felt an urge to roll over and go to sleep. I resisted.

"We'll be watching every step of the way," Sierra promised. "If anything happens, a trauma team is standing by outside. They'll be here in seconds."

I nodded absently, not really nervous. Like I said to Quinn, there wasn't really anything that could go wrong.

Sierra handed me a transparent case the size of two packs of cards. Inside, a black mass crawled busily over and around itself, and I could sense the nanos. These nanos felt different. They had no purpose and were just wandering aimlessly about. I opened the case and touched them. With a flicker of thought, they belonged to me. It was the easiest takeover I had ever done—there were no other programs to overwrite. I handed the box over to my twin, who took it gingerly, as if I had handed him a sputtering stick of dynamite. The nanos swarmed around the box.

"Ready?" I asked.

"Ready," he said.

I closed my eyes. The nanos poured out of the box, up my twin's arms, and into his nose, mouth, eyes, and ears. They dropped into the pores on his skin and wormed their way through microscopic cracks in mucous membranes. I didn't see a single nanobot that didn't belong to me. It was like walking into a friend's house and finding all the furniture and possessions gone, leaving echoing, empty space.

The nanos surfed Quinn's blood vessels, skimmed through his heart and lungs, and converged in his brain. I knew the route and could have done it with my nanos' sensors off. It was strange looking into the male body while occupying the female body, something I had never done before.

Once enough nanos had assembled in Quinn's central nervous system, I started taking pictures, recording chemical sequences and the placement of individual brain cells. That part was easy. But how could I get the nanos to obey Quinn's brain? I shifted my attention briefly back to my own CNS, trying to see through my nanos how they got commands and information. I knew how my muscles worked. My brain relayed messages through my nerves, and certain muscles contracted or stopped contracting. Did my nanos work the same way? I licked my lips in thought and wished Gremlin were here. It could probably tell me in an instant.

It was all brain chemistry, had to be. Every time one of my muscles twitched, there was a corresponding change in brain chemistry before and after. My forehead furrowed as I noticed a group of my nanobots that seemed to do nothing but hover in place and record information. Was it that simple? I looked closer. The nanos in question noticed changes in the chemicals and activity of my brain cells and were relaying those changes to other nanobots, who instantly altered their actions. In other words, these nanos could read the chemistry of my thoughts, translate them into what needed doing, and relay the information to other nanos so they could carry out the task. It was so simple I was surprised I had never figured it out before.

I could almost hear Gremlin's voice say, *Never asked.*

At any rate, all I needed to do was program these nanos to read the changes in Quinn's brain instead of mine. With one "eye" on the nanobots in my own brain, I installed a set of nanos in my twin's brain, using mine as a pattern. I programmed them to read my twin's brain instead of mine and react accordingly. Then I erased my own programs from each one and let them go, keeping a few nanos for myself so I could watch what happened.

For a moment, there was no change. Then everything started happening at once. On one level I was aware that medical alarms were blaring above my twin's body, but most of my attention was focused on my twin's inner world. In horror, I watched the nanos in Quinn's brain rip and tear at the neural tissue. The nanobots in the rest of his body rushed about randomly, making muscles jump and forcing glands to flood his bloodstream with random chemicals. In a horrid split second, I realized what was wrong, what I had done. The nanos were using patterns I had established for the *female* body's brain, and it was clashing with the physical reality of my twin's male body.

Without thinking about it further, I flooded my twin's body with my own nanos, paralyzing his few with my many. Part of me physically hauled them over to the female body and dumped them there. The chemical codes of my twin's memories were already programmed into them—it was the first thing I had done—and I ordered them to change the chemical sequences of memory so they would match my twin's, just as they did for a normal Trade.

Meanwhile the rest of me was desperately trying to repair the damage to the male body. The remainder of my nanos arrived with my own memory codes, and I worked furiously to get them implanted in the proper places. It was something I had done instinctively all of my life, but this time I had to make repairs to the brain as I went. There were shreds and tatters of my twin's memories left scattered around like cobwebs, and I had to clear them out.

Perhaps it was a shred of our old closeness, or perhaps it was because I was finally looking at procedures and processes I had until now taken for granted. Whatever the reason, I found myself keeping those leftover memories. It was easy, really. I just left them there when I put my own memories into the brain. When I cleared my consciousness out of my nanos, my twin's memories were there as if they'd always been mine, as if I had gone through what my twin had.

I remembered linking with the nets for the first time. I saw infinity sprawled in every direction, felt exactly how tiny I was compared to the silvery vastness. Agoraphobia yanked me in a billion terrifying directions. My chest constricted with the desire, the absolute *need,* to get away from all that space before I got lost. I felt like a mouse on a flat, wide floor with nowhere to hide and the cat coming soon.

Another fragment: a rush of fear as I lashed out with fists and nanos at my two attackers one cold, white day after school. Loud screams, a female voice—my twin's— shouting at me. The sharp sting of a slap. Red blood on white snow. Two teenagers dead or dying. Warm blood on my nanos. Afterward, the crushing remorse and a powerful anger directed not at my twin, but at myself. There was no anger at my twin for setting up the fight or for wanting to stay on Felicity. I was angry at myself for being greedy with the male body, for losing control at school and killing those boys. I was angry at myself for—

I came to myself with a start. Shock froze body and mind. My nanos spun in place for a millisecond while I processed what I was "remembering."

My twin was angry at himself for thinking he was the one who had been born male and for thinking he had had a greater right to the male body.

There were more repairs to make. I forced my thoughts away from this distraction and set to work. It took almost fifteen minutes to finish everything, and I finally opened my eyes. Three strangers were looking down on me. I yelped and tried to jump away, but I couldn't move. Restraints were holding me down. An IV was plugged into my hand.

"He's awake," one of the strangers, a woman, reported.

"How do you feel?" asked another stranger.

"Confused," I said. "Who are you?"

"Trauma team," the stranger said. He was dressed in a light green scrub uniform. "You went into some kind of neural seizure. It looked like a thousand little strokes. By all rights you should be dead or brain damaged. To be honest, I don't understand how—"

"That's quite enough," Grandma's voice said. "You may leave now."

The man blinked. "But Ms. Michaels, we should really—"

"That," Grandma said firmly, "will be all." Her tone made it clear that "all" could mean "all for now" or "all forever," depending on how long it took him to leave. The trauma team packed up their equipment and bundled out of the room faster than it takes to tell about it.

I turned my head. My twin was staring at the ceiling and blinking rapidly. Mom, Grandma, and Marco Sierra approached my bed.

"How do you feel, Quinn?" Mom asked.

"Fine," I said. "A little dizzy, though."

"Do you have your nanos back?" Grandma said.

"I never lost them," I said. "My twin was the one who—" And then I realized they thought I was my twin. Trying not to laugh, I quickly explained what had happened and who was in which body. Sierra looked fascinated. Mom seemed to be undecided whether she believed it or not. Grandma merely nodded.

"How's Kate?" I asked, jerking my head at my twin.

"According to the monitors, just fine," Sierra said.

"N-n-no, I'm n-not," my twin said.

Everyone immediately turned to the other bed. "What's the matter?" Mom said.

"I d-d-don't know," my twin replied. "L-look."

There was something wrong with my twin's voice. It was odd hearing the female body's voice from the outside after hearing for so long from within, but that wasn't it. My twin's voice was thicker somehow, almost slurred, and there was a heavy stutter.

My twin held up one hand. It was shaking.

"I c-c-c-can't get it to s-stop," my twin said in that odd, thick voice. "M-my l-l-legs are doing it t-t-t-too, and I c-c-c—" My twin paused and tried again. "C-c-c-can't talk right."

"Does it hurt?" Sierra said. "Are you in pain?"

"N-no. I j-j-j-just can't s-s-stop sh-sh-sh-shaking."

A quick check verified what my twin was saying. All four extremities were shaking as if seized by tiny earthquakes. Even my twin's fingers shook. Mom released me from the restraints the trauma team had put on me when convulsions took over my own body, and I sat up.

"Can you control your nanos?" I asked.

My twin's eyes shut, then opened. *Yes,* came the familiar mental voice. It was free of the stutter. *Yes! Yes!*

Gremlin? I asked hopefully.

A long pause. No answer.

A lump congealed in my throat. I hadn't realized how much I had been hoping Gremlin would come back once my twin was back on line. I turned to my twin. *There must have been too much of Gremlin in your old nanos. Its program must be damaged beyond repair.*

I think you're right. Tears trickled out of my twin's eyes. *I'm sorry. I'm so sorry. Jeeus.*

We don't have time to deal with this now, I said, firmly pushing aside my hurt and disappointment. *We still need to figure out what's wrong with you.*

My twin's eyes closed again. *I think I know. The Trade didn't go right. My brain isn't configured perfectly to my patterns. Some of my neural pathways are messed up and messages are going to the wrong place.* My twin held up a hand. *I tell my right hand to move, but my left answers. Forget walking or getting out of bed.*

Sorry, I said. *It's my fault. I dumped you in there and hoped for the best. I've never handled both ends of a Trade before. Can you fix it?*

Pause. *It'll take a lot of time, and I'll need lots more nanos.*

"What's going on?" Grandma asked.

My twin haltingly explained as I got out of bed. I stretched, flexed powerful muscles, and ran my hands through oddly short hair. The muscles weren't quite as strong or flexible as they had been. My twin had obviously been neglecting the body lately. And I was *hungry*. When was the last time my twin had eaten a real meal? Still, it felt damn good to be male again. I wondered if my twin felt the same way about being female, then remembered what I had learned. Did my twin hate being female or just like being male a little better? I couldn't imagine wanting to be one over the other all the time, but I wasn't my twin.

"How long will the repairs take?" Mom asked after my twin reassured her that death and/or serious injury were not forthcoming.

My twin tried to sit up, then gave up. "A c-c-c-couple days, I th-think. Assuming I g-g-g-get the n-n-n-nanos I need."

Impatience overtook me, and I found it hard to stay still. I paced instead. "We don't have that much time," I said. "We have to do something about Dad *now*."

"Like what?" Grandma asked. "The whole point of getting Quinn's—Kate's—*those* nanobots back on line was so that he . . . so that she—" Grandma floundered at the pronoun problem.

"My twin," I supplied with a small smile.

"So that your twin could use his . . . her . . . oh, the bloody hell with it." She pointed to me. "You're Quinn." Then she pointed to my twin. "And you're Kate. Clear? The whole point of this was to get Kate's nanobots back so she could access and control computers again and have some prayer of rescuing your father. But now she can't even leave her bed, let alone travel to New Pakistan and fight a nanobot hive."

The moment Grandma said that, more ghost memories from my twin popped back into my mind. I took a moment to look at them more closely as the others continued talking.

"Why not just send a rescue squad?" Mom said. "A shipful of Marines ought to do nicely."

Sierra shook his head. "Their ship will be overseen by nanos. So will their equipment and weapons. The only people who could sneak in are ones who can control nanobots directly and keep the hive from snatching them up while they locate the hive's center. With your ex-husband missing, that leaves Kate and Quinn as the only people who can control nanobots. And Quinn doesn't have the computer experience."

"Yes I do," I said.

Everyone turned to look at me. "What do you mean?" Grandma said.

"I have some of my twin's memories left from that last Trade," I said, tapping my head with growing conviction. "I know what my twin did. I just need a little practice accessing the nets so I can find the hive once we get down on New Pakistan."

"Are you sure?" Mom said.

I shrugged. "Not completely. But what choice do we have?"

"We can have you practice first," Grandma said firmly. "Marco?"

"Far ahead of you," he said, fingers flying over the computer keyboard. I wondered why he didn't talk to the computer the way most other people I had seen did. Then I noticed how fast his fingers moved and concluded he could probably type as fast as he could talk.

"Do you need a physical hookup to the computer?" he asked.

"Physical hookup?" I repeated. "You mean a wire or something? No."

"I think you should climb back into the bed so we can monitor you," Mom said.

In a few moments, I was hooked back up to the medical system and Sierra had opened up a network gateway on his terminal.

"I've only set up a limited web within a part of the network we don't use much," he told me. "You'll only have access to a few areas of the local area network so you can find your feet without getting overwhelmed. The data is all backed up and the backups are physically isolated, so don't worry about making mistakes."

I nodded and lay back, trying not to get nervous. We had set up precautions. Nothing could go wrong.

Yeah. Tell that to Gremlin.

I copied my memories into my nanobots as if I were going to Trade, but instead of streaming them over to my twin, I sent them over to the computer terminal. Instantly, I encountered other nanobots. Hunger gnawed at me again. This time instead of pushing the feeling away, I touched the nanos, and they were mine. Their programs became mine as well. The more nanobots I "ate," the more I learned about the computer. Words and concepts flashed into my mind—files, databases, hyperlink codes. Data streams flowed like little creeks through my fingers, and I found I could dam them up or widen their banks.

The nanobots continued downloading information from the computers and feeding it to me. They also translated my thoughts and desires into computer codes and wrote programs to carry them out. Or *I* wrote the programs. It was an instinct, and suddenly I knew how Mozart felt when he sat down at a harpsichord for the first time. The nanobots were my fingers, and the computers were my instruments. Images flicked and danced crazily across the terminal screen as I experimented.

I suddenly realized I couldn't feel my body anymore. A pang of panic hit me, and my nanos rushed out of the computer and back into my brain. They translated their experiences into chemical codes and dropped them into my brain cells. In less than a second I was lying on the bed again. My heart was pounding, and one of the machines above me was beeping a warning.

"I'm all right," I said, forestalling another visit from the trauma team. "I was just startled for a second."

"What happened, Quinn?" Mom asked. "Your vital signs were steady until about two seconds before you woke up."

I explained my progress so far.

"Th-th-that's s-sort of what h-h-happened to me," my twin said with a shaky nod. "P-p-part of it, anyway. You don't f-f-f-feel your body b-b-because y-you aren't really in it."

Sierra looked a bit doubtful but said nothing.

"I'm going to try again." I shut my eyes, copied my memories into my nanos, and streamed back into the computer.

This time, I noticed a little gateway off to one side. On the other side were computers with more nanos in them. The gate let me talk to these other nanobots. I sucked a few of them in, but not many. I kept control. Slowly, nanobot by nanobot, I expanded my awareness into the local network Sierra had set up. Two terminals came under my control, then three and four and five. That was all of them.

I carefully accessed an encyclopedia database, letting the nanos convert binary codes into chemical stimuli and neurochemical codes. Information poured into my mind; Ra, raab, rabab, rabbi, rabbit, rabbit fever. Pictures, vidclips, holograms, sound bites. Colors and sounds swirled over and through me. Hurriedly I backed away from it. The images stopped. I came back more slowly. It wasn't necessary to absorb everything. I only wanted to skim.

My nanos picked up on what I wanted. Images and sounds flicked past but remained where they were instead of crowding into my mind. That was much better. I amused myself for a few seconds with an article on automotive history, then flipped down to look at indigo snakes and indirect lighting.

A moment later, I sensed another gateway, a big one,

but it was sealed off. I examined it carefully. A computer was standing guard with legions of nanobots. I touched them, and instantly they—and the computer's security systems—were mine. A thought later, my new nanos opened the gateway.

I fell into infinity.

Information streams rushed everywhere, pulling and tugging at me, sending me this way and that. The paths stretched infinitely far in every direction, and I could sense them all, though they were too long and complicated for my mind to grasp. I was simultaneously falling and being pulled in a billion different directions.

Without thinking, I erased my own program from the nanobots I had taken from the other side of the gate. Instantly, the nanos guarding it reverted back to their original programming. The gate slammed shut and the infinity vanished.

I took a deep breath. That had been a call close enough to shave with. I could see how my twin got overwhelmed by this experience. My twin was never much for careful analysis or slow learning. Plunging right in had its advantages sometimes, but it certainly wasn't a virtue here.

I examined the gateway again. It seemed to me that I didn't have to open it all the way. A partial opening was equally possible and far more manageable. I took the gate's nanobots again and cracked it open. Four data streams connected to my terminals, nothing I couldn't handle. I examined each one, ready to leap away in case it tried to flood me. One stream led to a hospital. Another led to a publishing database. The last two were simple communications lines. Carefully, I opened the gate a little wider. More data streams gushed through it, but I was ready and was able to hold myself apart from them. I could watch the river without jumping into it. Bit by bit I widened the gateway until it was fully open again. Infinity gaped, but

I was able to examine a small part at a time, like an astronomer focusing on a single star in a crowded galaxy.

Cautiously, always cautiously, I chose a single data stream and moved into it. It split and branched in multiple directions. I chose a direction and talked to the nanos in the computer at the other end. They became mine, though I took care not to disrupt what the computer was doing. It turned out to be a server for a weather satellite. Now I was in two places at once—some of me in the lab computers, some of me in the server—though it didn't feel like I was split because my nanos, old and new, were still in constant communication, like two hemispheres of the same brain communicating through the corpus callosum. It occurred to me that if something were to sever the connection between the two computers, I'd lose half my nanos. What would that do to me? Would I die? Or would there be two of me, a worm cut in half?

Rather than find out, I transferred myself completely to the nanos in the satellite server and erased my program from the nanos back in the lab. From there, I jumped to the satellite itself. Suddenly I was looking through the weather satellite's cameras down at Earth. Torn wisps of clouds frosted blue ocean and green forest. Black velvet spread beyond. England lay right below me, an oddly-shaped emerald floating in sapphire waters. I wanted to gasp in amazement at the beauty, but I had nothing to gasp with.

After a while, it occurred to me that my twin and the others might be getting worried about me. I followed a communications line back to the lab computer and contacted the nanobots. They had "forgotten" me and gone back to their usual tasks. My original nanobots were simply waiting. I took them all back, jumped my program into their memory, erased my presence from the satellite, and leaped into my body.

Thrills ran up and down my spine. All the jumping

and rushing was exhilarating. There was a sense of incredible speed. Not horrible speed like the cab driver used, but a smooth, deftly controlled efficiency of movement. One moment I was thousands of miles above the planet, the next I opened my eyes back in the lab.

Mom, Grandma, and my twin were watching me with a sort of anxious patience. My twin was still shaking. Sierra alternated between checking his computer monitor and peering into his microscope.

"I'm back," I said unnecessarily, and gave a short recitation of what I had seen and done.

"Your eyes are sparkling," Grandma said. "Did you enjoy yourself?"

"Yes," I said enthusiastically. Suddenly I couldn't sit still. I lowered the rail on the bed and got up to pace the lab. My body seemed slow and clunky compared to the smooth transfer of data.

"Incredible," Sierra murmured, still staring at the monitor. "While you were 'gone,' your vital signs remained perfectly stable. If someone were to hook you up to minimal life-support, I don't see why you shouldn't be able to stay in the nets for long periods of time, perhaps even indefinitely."

"Don't say such a thing," Mom said with a small shudder.

"It was great, Mom," I said, still pacing exuberantly around the floor. "I don't know if I'm describing it very well. It's like being a beam of light—I can go anywhere, see anything."

"What I want to know," Sierra said, "is why you aren't awake back here in the lab. After all, you don't remove your memories from your brain—you only copy them into your nanos. There should be two Quinns, a physical Quinn and a network Quinn."

"I don't know," I said. "That sounds reasonable, but I know that the *me* in the nets is the only one."

Mom looked thoughtful. "If you want my guess, I would say that your subconscious wants to ensure that there's only one of you, so it makes sure your body's brain goes unconscious whenever you copy yourself somewhere else."

"Okay, sure." I sat down on a stool next to her. It was still weird, sitting next to my mom. I still didn't know how I felt about her coming back into my life. Luckily, there were other things to worry about, so I didn't have to think about it for long.

"Did you know," Sierra said from his microscope, "that many of your nanobots are organic?"

"Y-y-yes," my twin said. "G-g-g-gremlin says—said— they b-b-built new nanos f-from p-p-parts of our bodies and from w-w-w-what we ate."

"What's the data repository?" Grandma asked, walking over to Sierra's terminal.

"DNA."

"What?"

"Take a look." Grandma did, and Sierra kept talking. "The twins' nanos have some highly dense DNA strands, a thousand times more than a normal cell's nucleus. And so far I've located eight proteins that make up the chains. Normal DNA only uses four. That alone gives them— what?—over five hundred times more information than normal DNA. And that's assuming the strand is only as long as one found in a human cell. Like I said, these are a lot denser."

Mom got up to take a look, and even my twin tried to lean over from the hospital bed. I fidgeted on the stool. I wanted to *do* something, not talk, and the nets beckoned. Quietly I scooted down to the cool tile floor, sat with my back braced on the wall, and shut my eyes. In moments I was back in the computer system and leaping into the wider networks.

I jumped from system to system with exhilarating speed and growing skill. I tasted and sampled sights and sounds wherever I went. It was like flying, only better. In seconds I went from a submarine cruising the ocean depths to a research facility at the south pole. I flicked through the South American rainforest and the Australian outback. Wherever someone had a computer with enough nanos, I was there. And if one computer system couldn't hold me, I spread myself between two or three. Cameras became my eyes, microphones my ears. I eavesdropped on a thousand phone calls all over the world. Sometimes I widened my field of "vision" too far and infinity threatened to swallow me up, but I was always able to shift my focus to something smaller and regain my composure.

After a while, I learned how to transfer my codes into computer terminals instead of just nanobots, opening new avenues of memory. I didn't have to keep track of trillions of nanobots but could reach out from a central computer, as if the computer had become a new body. Usually this meant my program was stored in two or three computers on the same network, since I could only take up unused memory without crashing someone's database, but as long as the computers were linked, it didn't matter.

I checked the time and was startled to discover that almost two hours had passed. Quickly I hopped my program from node to node until I was back in the lab's system. My original nanos were waiting. They streamed back to my body and I opened my eyes again.

Someone had moved me. I was lying in bed again.

"He's awake," Grandma reported, then turned to me and pointed an angry finger. "Don't scare us like that again, young man. We were afraid something had happened to you."

"Sorry," I said, trying to sound contrite. My stomach growled and I noticed my bladder was full to bursting. "Is there anything to eat around here? And a bathroom?"

Grandma ordered sandwiches brought in. We had to feed my twin, who was still shaking. The repairs were apparently going slowly.

I hate this, my twin told me. *I can't even sit up.*

*Trade me back, will you? Maybe you can fix this faster than I can.**

*No. It's too risky until everything in there gets unsnarled.**

Pause. *Yeah, I suppose you're right.**

At least you don't stutter when we talk privately, I pointed out. *And you can still control your nanos.* An idea occurred to me. *Why not try the nets again? That should work just fine.**

My twin's face went pale. *Forget it.**

I'll take you, I offered. *If you go slow and careful, it's all right. The only problem comes when you try to access too much at once.**

I said, forget it! my twin snapped. *I'm not going back in there ever again. Just leave me alone for now, okay? Talking slows down repairs.* My twin's mental voice vanished.

"Is something wrong?" Grandma asked.

I glanced at my twin, whose eyes were now firmly shut. "It's complicated. Look, I want to see if I can find Dad through the nets somehow."

"Impossible," Grandma said. "There are six ships from my company in orbit around New Pakistan to ensure the communications lines remain severed. I can't open them, even for—" Her voice quavered for a moment, then firmed. "Even for my own son. If the hive down there ever got into the galactic networks, literally billions of people would die."

But I was already shutting down my brain and streaming back into the nets. I leaped from stone to stone in the data streams until I found one with a communication hookup to the galactic networks and the ships that phased between stars. There I paused.

I knew that the phase drive and faster-than-light communication operated on similar principles and that, in theory, I could go literally anywhere in the populated universe. I knew that FTL communication was safe and reliable. I knew that there were countless relay stations and satellites stationed all across the galaxy to provide double and triple backups for every link, and that there were at least six ways to reach any given point. But still the idea of launching myself into spaces so vast that I couldn't even comprehend them was frightening. This wasn't a phone call or data transfer. This was *me*. If something happened to cut communications, I couldn't just hang up and try again later.

Safe and reliable, I told myself. *Safe and reliable.* I suddenly ached for Gremlin's presence. Gremlin was *made* out of nanobots and binary codes and could probably make the trip safer. Certainly it would be less frightening. But the part of Gremlin that had resided in my twin's nanobots was gone forever, and so was Gremlin.

I jumped into space. Two relay stations flickered past me and I landed in a relay system on a planet I had never heard of. The system routed communications between ships. I spent considerable time sifting through the messages that came through until I found one that mentioned New Pakistan. I traced the line, found the originating ship, and reached out to touch its nanos through the communications link. When I had enough to hold my program, I transferred myself into them and erased myself from the ones in the relay station. Now I was prowling empty drive space on the *Lady Kay*, registry MM458-9002-1B.

I peered through security cameras at the technicians on duty at their stations and the ones relaxing or sleeping in their quarters. According to the ship's log, the *Lady K.*, as the captain referred to her, had been monitoring New Pakistan for five days now. All communications had been severed by scattering irradiated debris into orbit around the planet. Lance Radford-Michaels's ship had been allowed to land four days ago, and no one had heard from him since. Their external cameras weren't powerful enough to snatch pictures of the surface unless they were willing to bring the ship into satellite orbit range. The captain wasn't willing, so there was no way to know exactly what was going on down there.

I jumped back into the nets, skimming from relay station to relay station until I landed back in the lab and opened my eyes.

"What did your grandmother tell you, Quinn?" Mom snapped. She was looking down at me. Once more I had been moved back to the bed. "You scared us to death. How dare you run off like that? Irresponsible, that's what it is."

The words popped out before I could stop them. "At least I'm trying to help Dad instead of running out on him."

Silence fell across the lab. Even Sierra stopped clicking at his keyboard.

"If that's the way you feel, Quinn," Mom said quietly, "I suppose I can't help that." She turned away from the bed.

What the hell was that? my twin asked. *You know Mom didn't leave by choice.*

Shut up! I snarled. I got up from the bed, not sure why I was suddenly so angry at Mom. Where had she been for eighteen years? So what if my twin and I had driven her away? So what if she couldn't visit? She could have written or sent pictures. Damn it, I had *missed* having a mother. It had been worse knowing she was out there somewhere than if she had died. You don't hope a dead parent will come back. You don't wonder if a dead parent thought you weren't good enough to love and left you.

All the feelings I had been avoiding for the past several hours hurtled toward me. Anger at being abandoned, disappointment at learning Mom had a whole family I didn't know about, guilt that my nanos had driven her away, more anger that she hadn't worked harder to find a way to stay. Emotion punched my gut. It was too much. Dad missing, my twin's nano problems,

Gremlin's death, Mom popping back into my life. A tear leaked out of my right eye and the harder I tried to hold back, the more difficult it became. My throat choked up as I tried to strangle the sobs before they got out.

I smelled familiar wildflower perfume and warm arms surrounded me. "Honey, it's all right. You're angry and hurt and you have every right to be."

I started to push my grandmother away, but her touch dissolved the last of my control and I started to cry instead. My shoulders shook and hot salt water streamed down my face. My twin touched me with a wordless presence while Grandma held me and stroked my hair like Dad did when we were little. I missed him terribly.

Finally the storm was over. I sat up and pushed Grandma gently away. She handed me a tissue to blow my nose with. Sierra was hiding behind his computer, embarrassed, and I caught sight of Mom sitting on a stool with her back to all of us.

"Mom," I said. "I'm sorry."

Slowly she swivelled around and I could see she had been crying, too.

"I didn't want to leave you," she said in a tired voice. "I thought about both of you every single day, wondering if you were all right, what you were doing, were you walking or talking yet."

"Let's just find Dad, okay?" I said wanly. "Then we can figure out what to do about the rest of this mess."

Mom managed a smile. "A good plan."

So what's the next step? my twin asked.

I turned to Grandma and explained what I had learned from my last trip into the nets. "I think I need to go to New Pakistan. Can you arrange a ship?"

"There's been one at the ready since Delia called," Grandma said.

"I'm going along," Mom announced.

"Delia, dear—" Grandma began.

"I'm not going to send my son into a situation that I wouldn't go through myself," Mom said firmly. "Don't argue with me, Meredeth. I'm going even if I have to conk you over the head."

"Like Lance did back on Thetachron III?" Grandma said.

"Thetachron III was an Audubon Society hike compared to this," Mom returned, "as you'll find out if you try to keep me off that ship. Besides, someone has to fly her, and unless Quinn here is keeping something from us, he isn't quite qualified."

"I could be," I said, suddenly interested. "If I linked with the ship's systems and told it where I wanted to—"

"Captain Delia," Grandma interrupted, "the ship is yours."

An hour later, Mom and I were boarding the *Starstreak*, which I thought was a silly name for a ship. She was small, no more than fifteen meters long—more a lifeboat than a ship. On the other hand, we didn't need to carry much, and a smaller ship would attract less attention when it landed. Grandma, who had a small pack slung over her shoulder, accompanied us up the skyhook to Ride Station where the *Starstreak* was docked. My twin remained at the lab, recuperating, though our nanos were able to stay in touch over the phone lines so we could still talk.

Let me know the second you find anything, my twin said. *Anything at all.*

I'll try, I promised. *But don't forget that we'll be under a communications blackout once we get there.*

The *Starstreak*'s interior was efficient, but luxurious. Thick carpets covered the floors and fine paintings graced the walls. Or was I supposed to call them decks and bulkheads? The kitchen—galley—was a marvel. When I stood in it and spread my arms, both hands smacked the bulkheads on either side. Yet a full stove, oven, and refrigerator were squeezed in, along with fold-down counterspace and an assortment of cooking utensils. You could cook a gourmet meal in there with minimal fuss.

Mom, meanwhile, went forward and slid into the *Streak*'s pilot chair to check systems. Grandma and I followed and watched over her shoulder. I tried to figure out what she was doing, but quickly gave up. Too complicated, and Mom was in too much of a hurry to explain everything she was doing. Still, the idea of piloting fascinated me. Controlling a computer was one thing, but controlling a ship—now *that* would be something.

Maybe, I thought optimistically, *she can teach me when all this is over.*

Meanwhile, Grandma opened her pack. This instantly got my attention. Grandma had been secretive about that pack all the way up the skyhook and over to the ship. I had given up asking questions about it.

"This is for you," she said, and pulled out what looked like a short white pillar, about half a meter tall and a third of a meter in diameter. There was a vidscreen on one side, along with a miniature keyboard and an assortment of buttons..

"What is it?" I asked.

"It's the prototype of a new FTL communicator," Grandma explained. "It should be able to pierce through the interference the guard ships have set up around the planet."

Mom turned to stare. "Meredeth, what on Earth? If the hive got hold of that thing—"

"If it looks like that's going to happen, I'm sure Quinn's nanos could destroy it in an instant," Grandma said. "Isn't that right?"

"I suppose," I said slowly. "But I'm not sure we should—"

"I'm tired of not knowing," Grandma interrupted. "My son is down there, and I have no idea what's happened to him. What's the point of being the CEO of the largest communications empire in history if you can't use it to your own advantage?"

Reluctantly I set the machine on a fold-down table and let Grandma show me how to work it while Mom finished her onceover of the ship. Then Grandma kissed us both good-bye and left. Mom released the docking clamps, and the *Starstreak* slid swiftly into space.

CHAPTER THIRTEEN

ME

The satellite coasted smoothly in its orbit, riding a current of carrier waves. Signals clicked and beeped, cameras zoomed in and out, lenses blurred and focused. Every so often, a halfhearted signal pinged from the satellite toward space. Each signal struck a wall of static that hissed steadily from the metallic junk occupying the next orbit out. The wall sucked the signal in, mangled it beyond recognition, and spat it out the other side. Satellite relays clicked in annoyance, then spun another signal.

A safe distance away huddled a small cluster of ships. They ignored the satellite and the satellite ignored them. Another signal pinged into the wall, more relays clicked in annoyance.

After an interminable length of time, a new ship faded slowly into view as its phase drive powered down. One wary camera focused on it. The ship, much smaller than the rest, hovered near the others for a moment, then broke away and glided toward the planet. Instantly every camera on the satellite whipped around and focused with great intensity.

Relays clicked and buzzed with information. The ship's size and speed. Its angle of descent and infrared signature. Its probable landing point.

The satellite's orbit was carrying it toward the horizon now, forcing it to refocus the cameras as the ship landed at the planet's only spaceport. Two figures emerged. They paused on the tarmac, and a warm, fluidic mass spewed from both their mouths. The cameras recorded every detail.

A moment later, the figures trotted away from the landing field. One of them broke into a parked car, and they both climbed in just as the satellite dropped below the horizon and lost the image. The cameras whirred slowly about and focused on the huddled cluster of ships again. Yet another signal pinged toward open space and was mangled by the wall of static. Satellite relays clicked in annoyance, then spun another signal.

The library door slammed shut and I leaned panting against it, though I wasn't really out of breath. My nanos reset the electronic lock with a solid-sounding click. Mom crossed her arms and rubbed her shoulders.

"We should be safe here," she reasoned to me, though it sounded like she was talking to herself. "Who's going to loot a library?"

I shook my head, unable to answer. The spaceport where we had landed the *Starstreak* had been bad, with its charred corpses, flies, and choking smell of rot. The city had been worse. More bodies rotting in the streets, fires burning out of control, houses and stores hit by looters and vandals. Survivors wandered the streets. Some of them skulked in the shadows. Others walked around like zombies. Still others sobbed, or cackled, or just sat and stared. At one point we had encountered at least a dozen people who looked like they had been ravaged by some flesh-eating disease. Strings of flesh hung off their faces, exposing gray bone. Insects clustered around the festering wounds, and the victims stumbled around as if they were half blind. Most of them were raving. My skin crawled like cold worms and the hair on my neck slowly came up at the sight of them. I didn't know if the hive's nanos had done that to them or if some kind of bacteria was at work. We avoided them in any case.

I knew I'd have to access a terminal somewhere so I could look around inside the planet's computer nets. That, coupled with the fact that we were both afraid of being attacked or worse, prompted us to try and find a place to hide. We found a building with miraculously intact windows in the middle of a parklike area. Neither of us could read the signs out front, but the windows showed an interior full of shelves laden with what Mom said were books. They looked like flat squares of plastic to me, but I took her word for it. My nanos were able to open the lock so we could get in. I was shaking.

The nanos were another strange thing about the city. Some places were completely devoid of them, while a very few others were full of ones going about their normal business. Lots of sections had nanobots that were rushing about frantically, acting like no nanos I had ever encountered. Several times I sensed nanobots operating inside people. These people invariably shambled around like they were half dead, except for one group we saw in a park. They seemed to be running races over and over again, and many of them looked ready to keel over and die. I didn't understand any of it and therefore kept my nanos tightly inside my body again.

The backpack with the prototype communicator was getting heavy, so I slid it off my back. I didn't set it down, though—I wasn't letting it out of my sight.

The library was dimly lit by emergency lights. It looked to me like the batteries were giving out. To the right of the door was a circular desk that appeared to be an information center. A long counter to the left was lined with six terminals, so I assumed that was where you checked out books. Long rows of high shelves made a maze that vanished into the gloom. The place smelled like new carpeting. It was also stiflingly hot. The air conditioning was off, of course, and none of the windows opened.

"I guess we should see if there are any terminals up and running in here," I said into the silence.

"Did your father ever tell you how he deals with nanobot hives?" Mom asked.

"No," I said. "But I have an idea. One time Gremlin got scared and attacked Dad, and Dad retaliated by taking Gremlin's nanos away and keeping them for himself. If my twin and I hadn't persuaded him to stop, Gremlin would have died."

Gremlin would have died. My own words echoed through my mind. Gremlin *had* died. Gremlin was dead.

Mom was nodding. "That sounds like what he explained to me. Nanobot hives need a lot of processing space. If you take enough nanobots away from one, it crashes. Unfortunately, we don't know if your father tried that or not before he . . . disappeared."

I put Gremlin out of my mind. "I can reprogram nanos into my own system," I said. "That's easy. The problem will be finding Dad. There's a whole planet to search."

"Maybe we can narrow that down." Mom got up to pace the floor. "He must have landed at the spaceport— it's the only place that could handle a ship. That probably means he's in this city someplace. You can probably confirm that. His ship's arrival must have been recorded somewhere, by a satellite or even a security camera at the spaceport. The images are probably in a file, if we can just find them."

"And if the hive hasn't erased the data," I pointed out. Sweat ran down my face and I swiped at it with my sleeve.

"You could also check other satellites and security cameras," Mom went on. "Search from orbit. You did that back on Earth."

"Let's see if we can get a terminal up and working," I said, heading for the circulation counter. Mom followed.

Predictably, none of the terminals responded when we switched them on, though there were plenty of nanos in them waiting patiently for the library systems to come back on line and give them something to do.

"Power is definitely out," I said unnecessarily.

"The communicator," Mom said, pointing to my backpack. "It must have a power source. Could we hook it to one of the terminals?"

I pulled the communicator out of my pack and set it on the counter. Grandma had taught me the basics of how to use it, but adapting it to power another computer was beyond my expertise.

On the other hand, I was a fast learner.

"Give me a minute," I said, and placed my hands on the unit's warm plastic surface. Swiftly my nanos invaded the machine, taking its nanos for my own and adding their knowledge to my databases. The nanos knew everything there was to know about the prototype, which meant I did, too. As it turned out, the communicator's power source was made to function externally as well as internally. At my command, a panel on the side slid open, revealing a socket. Mom plugged the terminal in and its screen glowed to life. Foreign words scrambled across the glass, but I didn't need to understand the language to use the computer.

"Perfect," Mom said. "Are you ready?"

I sat down and licked salt off my lips. This was not going to be like playing with the networks back in London. A chill went through me despite the heat, and I had to concentrate to make myself breathe regularly. What if the hive grabbed me? What if it stopped me from leaving the network somehow? What if I got trapped outside my body forever?

"Ready as I can be," I managed to say. Before I could think about it further, I Traded myself into the machine.

At first I couldn't see or sense anything but the library's computer. It sat patient as a statue, waiting for someone to give it an order. I easily found its gateway into New Pakistan's network. Cautiously, I slipped through.

What I saw made me catch my breath. New Pakistan's network was a shambles. The silver data threads were as tangled and tattered as a spider web after a windstorm. A huge, irregular chunk yawned black and featureless in the center. Data streams rushed in, but none flowed back out. My nanos trembled, and the cold feeling returned.

Ridiculous, I told myself. *You don't have anything to feel with.*

I shivered. It didn't seem to matter. Maybe my mind was making me feel what I thought I should feel. All I knew is that when I stared at that blackness, the hackles on my neck rose and I wanted to *run* like a terrified rabbit. The blackness pulsed and shifted in bloated, irregular heartbeats. I couldn't look away from it. Even as I watched, a part of it burst toward a node and swallowed it whole. Nanobots within squeaked once like tiny mice, then vanished into the dark. The blackness seethed and roiled, gulping down more and more data.

Had it somehow swallowed Dad?

Stop it, I told myself. *Don't think about that. Find a database with satellite photos. Find out what happened to him first.*

I felt an overwhelming urge to *hurry*. Already I could see that the blackness was still growing. If it took over every section of the nets, I wouldn't have any space to travel through. It might also cut me off and separate me from my body.

Satellites, I thought. *I need to find satellites.*

Taking a deep breath—or a simulated version of one—I slid into the networks. I carefully skirted the black areas and slid down an intact data stream toward an automated billing system. The thrill I had felt earlier returned. In the nets, I moved with grace and speed regardless of which body I inhabited. Data blurred past and I popped into the new system. Accounts flurried around me like snowflakes for a moment, then nestled back into place.

The blackness abruptly lunged sideways, straight at me. I flung myself out a back door and sucked my program out of the nanos behind me. The blackness engulfed the billing system and lashed around like a bloated octopus. A tentacle lashed toward my hiding place and touched my nanos. I screamed, and some part of me disappeared. I had a fleeting impression of a childhood memory before it vanished forever. I abandoned the damaged nanos and leaped blindly into the nets, terrified. I rushed down another data stream and blundered into a dead end. The blackness was already following me up the stream. There was no way out of my current node except toward the monster.

Terror ripped at me with cold claws, but I jumped toward the blackness. Just ahead, between me and the hive, I saw a sidestream that led to another part of the network. I ran ahead. The hive loomed ahead of me, huge and pulsing. I ran. The data stream felt colder the closer I got to the hive, and I knew it couldn't possibly really feel like anything. I still rushed forward. The hive was almost to the juncture I needed for my escape, and I wondered if the hive was actively hunting me or if this was all random chance. Either way, I'd be engulfed and I'd never find Dad and he'd never know what happened to me.

My program wasn't copying itself fast enough. I wasn't going to make it. The data stream was ice cold, and it seemed like I could hear the hive running toward me. It made a crunching noise, like billions of black claws whispering over dead leaves. I plunged forward—

—and reached the juncture. I flung myself around the corner and fled down the stream. I rushed through the data a long ways before pausing to look back. The hive had swept the path beyond the juncture, but it wasn't following me. I ran further into the nets before pausing to take stock. My nanos were trembling, another psychosomatic process. I paused a moment to calm down and reorganize some data before continuing.

The section I was currently in seemed to be clear of the hive and was much easier to negotiate. My early feeling of urgency returned. I had to find Dad.

The first thing I did, however, was check to see that I could still get back to the library and my body. For an awful moment, I couldn't retrace my steps. Panic flashed until I made myself calm down and think back. With relief I found my bearings and headed back the way I had come.

As I had feared, my original path to the library was gone. The blackness still roiled around the net. There were nanos inside it. Now that I wasn't running for my life, I could sense them, despite the fact that all the data streams went one way. I sensed them the same way animals sense when a member of the herd is sick. Nausea rolled through me—more psychosomatics—and I eased myself further away from the hive, still looking for another route to my body.

I found one, but only one. If the hive took it, I'd never get back to my physical self.

Nothing for it, I thought. *You'll just have to work really fast.*

I didn't want to get lost again, though. I popped back into the library computer and left a part of my program there so I could find my way back—Hansel and Gretel go nanotech. Then I headed back around the blackness into a safer part of the net.

I contacted different computer systems around New Pakistan's five cities, testing here and testing there, looking for satellite links. I found medical research, education databases, student records, sound bytes, commercials, tax audits, clip art, and language tutorials, but no satellites. It was white-knuckle work. There were thousands of operating nodes and no way to find out what they did until I looked. It was taking so *long*. The blackness still pulsed and writhed, sometimes lashing in new directions, other times shrinking a tiny bit before ballooning out again. I kept a nervous eye on it, trying to hurry without calling attention to myself.

Publishing houses, pornography, software programming, house computer systems. This would take forever.

What I need, I thought, *is something to help me search.*

A memory flickered. I pounced on it. It wasn't mine—it was one of my twin's ghost memories. I paused and scrutinized it. Then I almost laughed. There were programs out there called search engines. Their job was to find things.

I had just flashed through a node full of software programs. I backtracked and riffled through it.

Pay dirt. Or pay program, anyway.

The search engine program was actually quite small. It felt like a little cage full of mice scrambling restlessly about, dying for something to do. I whispered to them what I wanted and opened the cage.

The mice scattered in a hundred different directions, squeaking and chattering as they went. Some of them plunged straight into the black hive and vanished. Others hit dead ends and came back to the cage like disappointed children. But others rushed back carrying tiny notes with addresses scribbled on them. There were literally hundreds of nodes that contained information on satellites, but only a few dozen that seemed to be actually linked to them. I copied the information and hurried away, feeling like a witch with a thousand familiars.

The first five addresses turned out be useless—either inoperative or partially ruined by the hive. The sixth, however, turned out to be a ground-based station that processed satellite feeds. The node was huge, with dozens of gates. It was really a network unto itself. I entered—

—and found the hive had a presence there. I instantly leaped back out and fled. Nothing followed me. After a moment, I slipped cautiously through the gate again, ready to flee again at less than a moment's notice.

The hive had taken almost the entire satellite network. It gulped data greedily, but didn't seem to notice me. The place was freezing. I huddled to one side and tried to look around. Signals and static pinged and whooshed around me in an ever-shifting wind. Moving with aching slowness, I snuck a couple of fingers into the system and skimmed through files. My nanos trembled with the strain. It was like trying to operate a computer with a pair of pool cues. If I had a body, it would probably be sweating. I forced myself to stay careful. Tongues of blackness whipped by, but they didn't seem interested in the part of the system I was accessing.

Thank heaven for small favors, I thought, and opened another image file.

There were millions of them—weather feeds, communication routings, entertainment stills. This would take forever. I thought about bringing in another search engine, but discarded the idea. Releasing an engine in here might call attention to me.

The dates, idiot, I thought. *The photos are sorted by subject matter. Check them by date.*

A quick command to the computer sorted the image files first chronologically, then by subject matter.

Much better.

I started with the images created on my birthday, the day Dad had left, and accessed surveillance satellites. Several photos showed a phalanx of ships circling at a safe distance. One camera stubbornly stared into empty space and I decided it must have been broken. Eventually, however, I came across a photo of a ship that sidled closer and broke atmosphere. The name, printed neatly along one side, was THE DEFIANT LADY'S DAUGHTER. Dad's ship. Excitement thrilled through me.

The hive pulsed once in my direction and I jumped out the gate. I waited a full minute—a long time to a computer—then snuck back in. The hive didn't seem to notice.

I accessed the images again followed the progress of Dad's ship. It landed safely. Dad got out and, in a series of still photos, jogged toward the parking lot. He had obviously arrived safely on the ground. What had happened to him since then?

The *Daughter* sat among the wrecked ships, a streak

of silver among the charred hulks. It suddenly occurred to me that I hadn't seen anything but burned wrecks at the spaceport. Mom and I had been too horrified at the corpses on the ground to think about anything but starting a car and getting out of there, but I didn't remember glimpsing an intact vessel. Where had Dad's ship gone?

A few pictures later, I got my answer. The *Daughter* exploded in a smoky fireball.

I wanted to lower my eyebrows, but I didn't have any at the moment. Had the hive done that on purpose? Dad claimed that nanobot hives weren't very intelligent overall, but this smacked to me of someone who wanted to keep Dad from leaving New Pakistan.

The skittering, scratching noises from the hive grew louder for a moment. I cast a wary eye in its direction, but it didn't seem inclined to move toward me.

Another idea occurred to me. Had the hive found and destroyed the *Starstreak*? With sinking dread, I flipped ahead to more recent pictures and focused on the spaceport again. The *Streak* was still there, safe and sound. Relief. Maybe the destruction of Dad's ship had been simply random.

That still felt wrong.

Hive nanos scurried and scuttled. The sound was making me ill again, and I wished I could figure out how to stop it. It was like being in a dim room with a rotting, twitching corpse. I was getting increasingly nervous. The hive could move incredibly fast when it wanted to, and I wasn't entirely sure I could outrun it again.

I found another photo of Dad. He was running down a street toward a park. Elation and relief poured through me like melted chocolate. Dad was still alive! Or he had been at the time these pictures were taken three days ago.

A single hive nano leaped out of the dark area and pounced on one of mine. I barely snatched myself free.

Time to go.

I hopped, skipped, and jumped back to the library without incident. Mom was standing guard over my body. She gave a little squeak when I moved unexpectedly. The library air felt even more hot and stuffy hot after the freezing cold of the satellite node. My clothes were drenched in sweat and I was terribly thirsty. Mom didn't look much better.

"Are you all right?" Mom asked. "You were gone for almost an hour."

"I'm fine," I said, and went on to tell her what I had learned. Relief washed over Mom's face when I mentioned I had seen pictures of Dad alive. Did she still love him?

"That was three days ago, though," I finished. "I didn't dare stick around longer to find out more."

Mom nodded. "We should contact Kate and Meredeth."

The communicator was already on, and for a prototype it worked very well. I had to fiddle for a while to break through the interference, though. The library remained gloomy, silent, and hot. More sweat trickled down my neck, and my shirt stuck wetly to my body. While I was working, Mom kept throwing uneasy glances over her shoulder.

"What's the matter?" I asked.

"I keep hearing things," she said quietly. "Nerves, I expect."

At that moment, I established a connection with Grandma's lab and her face snapped into view on the screen. In the background, my twin leaned forward in the hospital bed. I didn't see Sierra. My twin's arms and legs were still shaking.

"Did you find him?" Grandma asked without preamble.

"Sort of," I said, and explained. "The problem is that I'm not sure what to do next."

"What about searching the park?" Grandma said.

I shook my head. "We could, but I doubt he's stayed there for three whole days."

"He's got to be around here somewhere," Mom said firmly.

"H-h-have you t-t-t-tried looking f-for org-g-ganic nanos?" my twin asked.

"What do you mean, Kate?" Grandma said.

"Our n-na-n—our n-nan-n—the nano—n-nano—shit!"

"Language," Grandma said automatically.

Can you hear me? I sent. My nanos were hooked to the prototype, so I didn't see why I shouldn't be able to use it to communicate with my twin.

It turned out I was right. *Yes,* came my twin's relieved reply.

What's your idea?

Sierra said our nanos are partially organic. It stands to reason that Dad's are the same. If you find organic nanobots anywhere, I'd be willing to bet Dad's somewhere nearby.

I translated this for Mom and Grandma, who agreed it might work. We signed off with a promise to call back as soon as we could. I sat down again and Mom cast around with another worried look.

"I wish we had thought to bring a gun or something," she muttered. "It's nervous work waiting here for you."

"I'll be quick," I promised.

"I'd rather you were careful, Quinn," Mom said, and I flashed a grin up at her. The corners of her own mouth turned up. "You look like your father when you smile."

I didn't know what to say to that, so I closed my eyes and leaped back into the nets.

Delia watched Quinn's body go limp behind the circulation desk. She still couldn't get over the way he was so . . . different than what she had always imagined. Quinn was much taller than she had envisioned, and he had a man's strong build instead of a roly-poly baby's. Not only that, but this wasn't the same Quinn that had rung the front bell a month ago. *This* Quinn was her daughter.

But not really my daughter, she thought. *This isn't just Quinn, anymore than the person back in the lab is just Kate.*

Thirst burned Delia's throat and sweat pooled wetly under her arms, but she was too nervous to go poking around the library by herself to look for water. Instead, she reached down and stroked the damp black curls on her son's head.

The sudden arrival of the her two lost children had been a shock. Every emotion Delia thought she'd dealt with and tucked away forever burst back into the forefront. It had been an equally great shock to learn about their strange abilities. Trading, computer control, silent communication. But her life seemed to be a series of shocks—the death of her parents and brother, the discovery of Lance's multiple personality disorder, her brush with death on the space station at Thetachron III and the revelation that Lance could kill with his nanobots. After all that, finding out she was pregnant with twins had been almost a minor event.

Being forced to leave them, however, was another story entirely.

At first, after her and Lance's separation and subsequent divorce, Delia had written regularly to Lance, and he had responded. She had looked forward to the post every day and eagerly devoured Lance's letters. Over time, however, they became more and more painful to read. They only served to remind her that she hadn't been there when the twins first started walking or said their first words. She wouldn't one day see them off to their first day of school, and she wouldn't be there to offer safety from closet monsters and thunderstorms. Sometimes two or three letters would pile up on her desk before she could force herself to open and read them, and it took her longer and longer to write back. The stream of letters slowed and, eventually, stopped altogether.

Delia's thoughts, however, hadn't. Many times she had

lain awake while Nancy and, later, Brad kicked inside her, and wondered what Quinn and Kate were doing. Were they happy without their mother? Did they miss her like she missed them? Did they even remember her? On days when Brad, and Nancy, and the other kids ran her ragged, and she was so busy she could barely turn round, she still managed to wonder how Kate and Quinn might get along with their new siblings if they were here.

And she missed Lance dreadfully.

Their relationship hadn't been an easy one. Delia had known about Lance's multiple personality disorder for years, and it hadn't prevented her from loving him. Nor had it kept him from loving her. As a result, she had seen him through four grueling years of therapy. Four years of nightmares, depression, mania, and going to sleep not knowing who Lance would be when she woke up. Once she had come home to find the house full of strangers that Andy—one of Lance's alters—had invited home from a bar. Another night she jolted awake to the sound of breaking glass and rushed into the kitchen just in time to see Patrick, another alter, smash the rest of the Waterford crystal set Meredeth had given them as a wedding present. Delia had held poor, blind Johnny while he cried about all the operations Daddy had put him through, and she had snapped at Garth when he made snide comments about women.

The process, of course, was equally hard on Lance. According to his therapist, Dr. Baldwin, the only way to treat MPD was for the patient to confront the traumas that had caused it. Lance invariably arrived home from these therapy sessions weak, exhausted, and covered with dried sweat.

Delia knew full well that sometimes the only thing that prevented him from quitting was that Delia threatened to leave him if he did. At the end of those four years, however, Lance had integrated all forty-eight of his alters—record speed, according to Dr. Baldwin. To celebrate, Lance and Delia had taken a long, luxurious vacation on the tropical beaches of Abierto. There, on silky white sand lapped by warm water as clear as the sky, they had decided it was safe for them to have children. With an impish grin that used to belong to Andy, Lance had insisted they start right away.

And this is the result, Delia thought, still stroking Quinn's hair.

Footsteps and raucous voices shattered the silent gloom beyond the circulation desk. Fear scattered Delia's thoughts and she instantly threw herself to the floor next to Quinn. The voices—all male—grew louder. One of them laughed. Abruptly, Delia realized the prototype communicator was still on the counter. She snatched it off the desk and ducked again as the voices grew louder.

Heart thumping, Delia peeked through the book return slot in the front of the desk. Six young men swaggered into the main lobby. They weren't wearing the traditional loose blouse and trousers worn by other New Pakistani men, but were clad in black leather that must have been ungodly hot in the library. Three of the men sported shiny cybernetic arms adorned with evil-looking claws, and the symbol of a knife dipped in blood had been crudely sewn to their jackets. The jackets of the three uncybered thugs had no such symbol.

Delia unconsciously flexed her own cybered arm. Her prosthetics were top-of-the-line, indistinguishable from normal flesh. Those who didn't have the money or who had low-level insurance were stuck with metalware. Some people, however, brandished them with pride, and even had themselves cybered up when it wasn't necessary. Judging from the proud display of the blood-red symbol, it appeared that visible cyberware was a mark of rank for this group.

One of the gang members was laden with a box, which he took to the far side of the lobby. The other men followed, jabbering in their unfamiliar language. They gathered on the floor around a low table.

Delia tried to keep her breathing slow and even. Fingers of sweat slowly oozed down her neck and between her breasts. The sounds she had heard earlier must have been the gang coming in, probably through a back door. They didn't seem bent on destruction, and Delia figured they must be using the library as a hideout. Fear squeezed her chest.

This is no time to panic, she told herself. *They don't know you're here. We can just sneak out.*

Except Quinn was unconscious on the floor.

Shit, Delia swore silently, wishing hard for a gun. *Now what?*

Delia had to wake Quinn up, that was for certain. She covered his mouth with one damp hand and shook his shoulder with the other.

No response.

Delia shook harder. Still nothing.

The gang's box turned out to have food in it, and the gang fell to eating with noisy smacks and slurps. Delia's thirst burned again. She pinched Quinn as hard as she could, and still he didn't respond.

Stupid, stupid, stupid, she thought. *Why didn't we arrange some kind of signal?*

Delia risked another peek out the return slot. The gang was still eating. Holding her breath, Delia snaked a hand up to the computer terminal and found the keyboard. Carefully, ever so carefully, she eased it off the desk. One corner scraped loudly against the countertop. Delia froze. Her knees ached from unaccustomed kneeling, but she didn't dare move or even breathe. More sweat trickled into her ear. The gang kept on eating. One of them said something that made the others laugh. Delia used the moment to snatch the keyboard the rest of the way under the desk. Fortunately, the terminal screen was already facing away from the gang.

Quietly, one key at a time, Delia used the keyboard to bring up what she assumed was the library's main menu. There had to be a way to alert Quinn. Unfortunately, the menus weren't in anything even resembling English or French, the only two languages Delia knew.

Not that I could probably do much even if they were, she thought in frustration. *I'm computer literate, but only at the "See Dick run" stage.*

As quietly as she could, she tapped a few keys at random. The terminal flashed what were probably different menus, but Delia couldn't tell for sure. There was no response from Quinn.

One of the gang members wadded up some cardboard packaging and threw it across the room toward the desk. It thumped into the metal wastebasket. Delia's heart lurched. The rest of the gang gave a mock cheer.

Delia pursed her lips and tried another key. To her horror, the terminal beeped. Two of the gang members swivelled their heads to look her way and Delia froze again. One of them, whose cyber claws were painted black, got up, but as he did so, he knocked a cup into the lap of the man sitting on the floor next to him. Instantly, the man was on his feet and snarling at Black Claws. Black Claws shoved the snarler back. A knife flicked into Snarler's hand, but another man, presumably the leader, barked at them both. Reluctantly, Black Claws and Snarler backed down. Delia allowed herself a small sigh of relief until the leader jerked his head toward the circulation desk and barked another order. Still glaring at each other, Black Claws and Snarler headed straight for Delia's hiding place.

The hive was bigger than before, but by now I was used to working around it. I jumped from system to system, looking for organic nanobots. It didn't take long to realize this was fruitless. There had to be a better way.

Search engine? I thought.

No. The engines only look for computer files, not types of nanos.

What about creating my own search engine?

I paused in the middle of a computer game, ignoring the sound effects of guns and bazookas that boomed and exploded around me, and thought further, trying to bring the idea to its logical conclusion. At the moment I was really nothing but a bunch of chemical codes copied into a whole lot of nanobots. What if I made a copy of *part* of myself, the part that could recognize organic nanobots? That would be just a program, really—a series of codes designed for a single task. It would take up far less space and be all but undetectable. It might even be able to search inside the hive, assuming it could find its way back out.

I turned the possibility over in my mind and it seemed sound.

Then do it!

My nanos instantly put thought into action. They gathered codes from a hundred places in my mind, duplicated them a thousand times, and dumped them into the nets. The programs hopped and skipped in all directions, as if someone had opened a basket of tree frogs instead of a cage of mice. I had no idea how long it would take them to find Dad and come back to the computer game. The other search engine had been fast, but mine was looking for something a little harder to find.

The hive pulsed and roiled several nodes behind me. I hoped my programs wouldn't take long. I was settling back to wait when half the nanobots I had left back in the library computer suddenly went off line.

Startled, I jumped back to the library computer and into my body. Mom was standing over me. Her right arm dangled uselessly, and a small panel hung open on it. Machinery, not flesh, lay visible beneath it. A wire with a bare tip led from the machinery to the computer terminal, and I could smell a sharp tang in the air. I stared, not quite comprehending what I was seeing. Mom yanked the wire free of her arm.

"Get up!" she hissed.

Shouts barked across the room as I scrambled to my feet. Two tough-looking guys had just reached the desk. They were yelling. Across the room, four more toughs were already on their feet and heading our way. It wasn't hard to figure out what was going on.

Adrenaline hummed through my blood, and my heart boomed inside my chest. Without thinking, I punched one of the guys across the desk. With a grunt, he stumbled backward. Warm blood spattered my knuckles and two scarlet rivers gushed from the tough's nose. I noticed almost dispassionately that three of these guys, including the one vaulting over the desk at me, seemed to be part machine. Black claws sliced the air toward my face and I jumped back. Mom lashed out with a leg and connected. The guy with the claws stumbled and I bashed him over the head with a two-handed fist. He went down and lay still. The other five toughs, including the one with the broken nose, rushed toward us. Mom grabbed my shoulder.

"Run!"

We fled into the dim stacks beyond the circulation desk. Shouts and footsteps told us the gang followed, though I didn't look back to make sure. We turned and twisted through the maze. I think Mom was looking for an exit, but neither of us knew the building and we couldn't read the wall signs. I noticed Mom's right arm was still hanging limp, but didn't have time to ask about it or what she had done.

Behind us, the footsteps and shouting spread out in different directions.

"They're trying to cut us off," I said, dodging between another set of stacks.

"Where the hell is the damn exit?" Mom panted.

Shadows moved. A cybered tough and the guy with the bloody nose leaped in front of us, claws at the ready.

I didn't even think. My nanos flashed across the floor and leaped into their artificial limbs. In less than a second, the nanos governing their onboard computers belong to me. I ordered my nanos to *twist*.

The toughs' arms wrenched in their sockets, throwing both of them off balance. Bone crunched wetly as inhumanly strong cybernetic arms twisted human shoulders. They fell to the floor screaming in pain.

More footsteps were coming up behind us and to the right. I looked up and saw Mom bracing her back against one stack and her legs against the other. Cords stood out on her neck as she pushed.

"Help me!" she said through clenched teeth.

I braced myself with her. The footsteps in the next aisle grew louder. I felt a hint of movement from the stack.

"Harder!" I hissed, and shoved with all my might.

The groan of tearing metal matched the moans of pain from the cybered toughs as the stack fell slowly sideways just as their would-be rescuer rushed up the aisle next to us. The stack fell straight on him. He shrieked as he went down, and a dull boom echoed through the library when the stack sent its neighbor toppling. A line of dominoes thundered through the library, ending in one final crash in the distance.

Mom and I stood panting in the aisle. The toughs whose arms I had attacked had lapsed into unconsciousness, and the one trapped beneath the bookcase was trying to shout for help, though he could only manage a weak gasp.

"Let's get out of here," I started to say, when a wild yell cut the air. The fifth tough, one with no cyberware, dropped from the top of one stack straight toward Mom. I cried out a warning and she threw herself sideways. She avoided his knife but tripped and landed hard on her back. Strong arms wrapped around me from behind with a grip like steel handcuffs—the sixth gang member had slipped up behind me. The tough who dropped from the shadows lunged with his knife, and Mom threw up her good arm to ward him off. He slashed her forearm, leaving a red trail through the air. Mom screamed and the tough raised his knife again.

"No!" I bellowed, trying to escape the arms that had grabbed me. I panicked. For the second time my nanos streaked across the floor. They swarmed over the tough and his knife, burrowing into his pores, flooding his nose and eyes and mouth. They ripped and tore, destroying every cell they touched. Millions, then billions of cells exploded into mushy protoplasm.

The tough dropped his knife and fell writhing to the ground, not even able to draw breath and scream because his lungs had already become a bloody sponge in his chest. Blood poured from his nose and mouth. He convulsed once and collapsed to the floor with a wet, mushy thud.

The arms holding me let go abruptly. I spun in time to see the final tough vanish into the stacks, running for all he was worth. There was a long moment of silence broken only by the moans from the aisle. The man who had cut Mom lay there, little more than a bloody bag of oatmeal held loosely together by his skin. Bitter bile choked and burned in my throat. I leaned away and retched and spat, then retched again. The image of what I had done burned itself into my mind. Over and over again the tough fell apart under my onslaught. The horrible gurgle of his lungs played again and again.

I had killed someone. Yes, he was trying to kill my mother and probably me, but I had still killed him. He started out alive this morning and now he was dead because of me. I stared numbly at the mess I had made on the floor, then felt a hand on my shoulder. I yelped and jumped away before I realized it was just Mom.

"We should get out of here in case there are more of them," she said. "Let's go."

Dazed, I let her take my hand. Her own cybernetic

arm still dangled at her side and a small part of me wondered if I could repair it for her. Then the tough started gurgling in my head again. Mom yanked me down the aisle to the front desk. She grabbed the prototype communicator and handed it to me, then took me out the front door into the street. I followed without thinking.

"We have to find another terminal," she said. "Any ideas?"

"He's dead," I muttered. "I killed him."

"Quinn, we don't have time for this," Mom said sharply. "Pull yourself together, boy. I'm sorry if it seems heartless, but we have to find your father."

I stared stupidly at her. Overhead, the sun beat down with a heat so powerful it was heavy. Sweat was still running down both our faces. The street in front of the library was completely empty, and the city beyond the nearby park was oddly quiet. A delivery truck sat near the curb, its headlights pointed reproachfully at me. No people were in sight, but I didn't take the time to wonder where they might be. Didn't Mom understand? I had lost control and killed someone, just like my twin. Would I have killed that guy if I had been female? Was killing part of male biology? Or was it part of me? Which was in control, body or mind? The questions pulled me in opposite directions and I couldn't do anything but sit hunched between them. So much was beyond my control.

"Quinn!" Mom ordered. "Snap out of it!"

Why is she calling me Quinn? I thought stupidly. *That's not really my name.*

This pattern of thinking was familiar. My body didn't, couldn't, matter. I didn't move. Mom slapped me across the face. The sting made me look at her, but I remained otherwise completely still. So what if my body felt pain? My body wasn't me.

"Your father needs help," Mom said in a crisp voice. "Remember your father? He needs you, Quinn. He'll die if you can't find him. He'll be dead . . . just . . . just like Gremlin," she finished in a rush. "You'll lose your dad just like Gremlin. Is that what you want?"

Gremlin was already long dead. There wasn't even a body to bury because Gremlin didn't have one.

But Dad did. Dad. Mom didn't understand, but Dad might. Where was he? He should be—

Everything came back in a rush. Dad. The hive. My knees went weak for a second, but I steadied myself before Mom could grab me.

"Are you all right now?" she asked.

The thug was still screaming inside my head. "No," I admitted. "But we have to find Dad."

"There's another building across the street there," she said, pointing. "Maybe we can find another terminal."

"It's awful quiet out here," I commented as we jogged across the street. "Where are all the people?"

The building turned out to be some kind of theater. Or maybe it was a church or a temple. A lot of windows were broken, making it easy for us to get into it, but the place appeared to be completely empty. The interior consisted of a series of large, echoing chambers. Every sound created an explosion of echoes. Our footsteps crunched eerily over broken glass and we spoke in the quietest whispers we could manage. Statues in alcoves glared down at us, some of them decidedly not human. One was a man with the head of an elephant. A woman nearby had at least fifty arms. Another woman danced on the tiny crushed body of a man. All of them were rendered in garish colors, and their eyes seemed to bore into me. I could feel their gaze on my back and my shoulders prickled.

It was with relief we found an office with a terminal. It was simply furnished, with a plain desk and no carpets on the floor. The computer's power was off, of course, so we hooked up the prototype.

"We need a signal," Mom said as I sat down in the room's only chair and prepared to jump into the nets.

"Something I can do to let you know that you need to come back."

"How did you take my nanos off line back in the . . . in the library?" I asked.

"I zapped the processing unit with the juice in my arm's power pack," she said. "It drained the battery flat. The current destroyed enough nanobots to get your attention. My arm is useless, but at least we're alive."

I forced my thoughts away from the tough and his spongy lungs and tried to concentrate on the hard wood pressing my thighs and back. It was real and solid.

"I'll leave some nanos on guard duty in this terminal," I told her. "Tap the spacebar three times and I'll come back." And I jumped into the nets before she could reply.

It only took a couple of seconds to reach the computer game where my little frog programs were supposed to report if they found anything. There was nothing there. Disappointment and frustration filled me. How were we supposed to find Dad if we couldn't—

A little program plopped into my mind with excited little croaks. It had found organic nanobots. The hive had attacked the nanos housing the frog's program, but it had transferred itself back to the database before being assimilated.

I wanted to pat the frog on the head for doing a good job, but it didn't have a head. I waited a few more minutes to see if any of the other programs would return. None of them did. I hesitated. Were they lost or still searching? Or had they been snatched into the hive? There was no way to know, and that made me nervous.

I transferred myself to the public databases. They were still a shambles. I sorted through the wreckage, staying well clear of any nanos or computers engulfed by the black hive, until I found a series of maps. I overlaid one of them with the frog program's memory and, to my surprise, came up with an address in a private home on the city outskirts.

"That's strange," Mom said when I came back to my body and reported what I had found. "I thought hives cropped up in places with extremely large computers—research labs or educational facilities. Even ships. I've never heard of one appearing in a private home."

"Maybe the hive just has a presence there," I said uncertainly.

"Maybe. Let's go." Mom grabbed me with her good arm and hauled me toward the door. We hustled past the statues and I refused to look at them.

"How are we going to get there?" I asked. "It's too far to walk."

"There was a delivery truck in front of the library," Mom reminded me. "Feel up to another jump start?"

Aditi Amendeep made a long, slow smile at the satellite image of a single, perfect ship. It sat amid the blackened wrecks at the spaceport like a diamond in a pile of coal dust. A young man and an older woman had left it sitting there while they wandered around one of Aditi's cities. Aditi assumed the young man was Lance's son Quinn. The woman matched Lance's mental picture of his ex-wife Delia, though why she had come, Aditi didn't know. She didn't really care.

Aditi knew exactly where Quinn and Delia were, had even felt Quinn's feathery presence skittering around her nets. It had been fun chasing him here and there to watch his reactions, and his little frog programs had made for fascinating dissection, though one had managed to get away. For the most part, however, she didn't need to pursue him further or even acknowledge his presence. There was nothing she could learn from him, and he was unimportant.

The same appeared to be true of his father. With a regretful shake of her head, Aditi leaned over and stroked Lance's hair. She seemed to have broken something in his mind—he hadn't reacted to anything at all in the last several hours. But that didn't matter, either. She had learned everything she needed to know from him, and now it was time to leave.

A small moving van was parked out front amid the riot of flowers in Aditi's impossible garden. It was packed nearly full of medical supplies. Five muscular young men, stripped completely naked and sweating under their enforced labor, finished loading the last boxes of Isocal supplements. Their movements were wooden and the whites of their eyes shone with fear every time Aditi's attention strayed and she left off controlling their expressions. One of the men, she had decided, looked absolutely adorable when his eyes were widened in terror, and she gave him a little more latitude with his own face. He was already her favorite.

With less than a thought, she ordered him to pick her up and carry her out to the truck, leaving the other three to move her wheelchair. The man's skin was smooth and warm against hers. He smelled like sweat. Aditi found him intriguingly arousing and reached her hand down to fondle his penis as he carried her, just because she could. Her nanos tweaked his brain in just the right place and he hardened beneath her touch. His beautiful dark eyes widened even further.

He looks like a puppy, she thought with amusement.

It would be a shame to lose this one. Once her new ship cleared the irradiated debris field, Aditi would no longer be able to communicate with any nanos back on New Pakistan, and she would lose the entire planet—including the puppy boy. On the other hand, Aditi would be able to link up with—and take over—the main communications network for the galaxy. Give up the planet, take the universe. A fair trade.

Besides, she thought, still stroking, *I could always take the puppy with me. It'd be nicer to have someone with warm, pleasant hands as a body slave instead of cold robots. And once I start up the orgies again, he'll have something to do in his spare time.*

Aditi smiled again. It was a good plan. Happiness

thrilled her veins. She felt so free, so alive. For the first time, she could go where she wanted, do what she wanted. She felt almost giddy.

As the puppy carried her out the front door, Aditi glanced over his shoulder at Lance, who was still lying on her old bed. Maybe she should take him along, too. He could be a playmate for the puppy. But no—it would be too much trouble to wake him up and force him to walk with her, since his nanobots still fought her every time she tried to do anything to him. The puppy was almost as handsome and far easier to control.

Outside, the sun beat harshly down and the foliage in Aditi's garden spread varicolored leaves to drink it in. The house was barely visible beneath all the plants. Flowers as big as buckets lightly perfumed the air— Aditi wouldn't allow the scent to become cloying—and cable-thick orange vines had all but strangled the tree where her father's and Mole-Face's remains now lay. Sweat ran down Aditi's face, and she licked the saltiness appreciatively from her lips. It was the first time she could remember actually sweating enough for the drops to fall into her mouth. True, she had felt them through her drones around the planet, but it was special feeling something new in her own body.

Speaking of which, she thought.

Aditi ordered the puppy to set her on the ground while the other four drones climbed into the back of the van and pulled the door shut. Aditi reached under the thick, soft layer of grass and pulled up a small clod of earth from the ground. It crumbled damply in her fingers and Aditi inhaled the rich loamy smell. Another forbidden pleasure no longer forbidden.

One more mental command and the puppy deposited Aditi gently into the cool, air-conditioned cab of the moving van. He trotted around to the driver's side and climbed in. Aditi noted with amusement the way his erection bobbed almost against the steering wheel. What would his physical reactions be if she kept him in a state of sexual excitement for several hours or days? There was so much to learn, so much to find out, so much to *do*.

At Aditi's twisted feet lay a crate, which she used as a footrest. Although Aditi doubted Quinn and Delia posed much of a threat, there was no point in taking chances. The crate would make sure the odds remained firmly in her favor. And once she got off this dirtball planet, the odds would remain in her favor forever.

Aditi shouted with glee as the puppy put the van in gear and backed it down the driveway.

CHAPTER FOURTEEN

DELIA

Delia stared down at Lance as he lay on what seemed to be a hospital bed. His face was paler than normal and the veins stood out like blue string on his forehead, neck, and temples. His chest rose and fell with steady breathing, and his skin was warm to the touch.

He hadn't changed in eighteen years.

Delia had allowed herself to age a little—university professors came across as more credible with a few lines on the face and a touch of silver at the temples. But Lance looked exactly as she remembered him—handsome and strong, with quiet, pensive features. She tried to swallow the lump in her throat. Eighteen years seemed to melt away, and she could almost believe she was in her thirties again staring down at her new husband while he lay gently asleep.

Jesus, she thought. *Eighteen years and I'm still in love with him.*

On the other side of the bed, Quinn stood with his eyes shut, one hand on Lance's shoulder. Delia knew his nanobots were trying to figure out what was wrong with him, why he didn't respond to them. A gag had been his only restraint, and Delia had long since removed it, but he refused to wake up.

"Come on, Lance," she whispered. "I know you're in there. Wake up!"

Strange foliage waved in the gentle breeze outside the windows. Delia didn't know what to make of the garden. The plants didn't look anything like what Delia had seen so far on New Pakistan, or anywhere else, for that matter. Where had they come from? Was the hive somehow responsible? And why was there a police car parked in the drive?

Delia's arm dangled at her side, and she made a fist with her good hand. Her jaw clenched. This was so *frustrating*. Quinn hadn't been able to repair her arm, so she was half crippled as it was. Now all she could do was stare down at Lance and wait for Quinn to figure out what was going on. Through it all, she couldn't shake the feeling that they needed to *hurry*. Every nerve she possessed was screaming at her to rush, to move *faster*, but she couldn't say why.

Quinn remained motionless. Delia took a deep breath, trying to calm herself. They had found Lance, and he was alive. That was the important thing. She should relax.

Hurry, Quinn! she thought instead. *Please hurry!*

She needed something to do. Delia glanced around the room again, looking for distractions. The place looked almost like a hospital patient's room. A counter held various medical instruments along with a computer terminal. One open floor-to-ceiling cupboard held a very few medical supplies, while two others lay completely empty. A big box of software discs was marked in more squiggly script. Incongruously, dirt and footprints were tracked across the tile floor. Among them were . . . tire tracks? Delia knelt down to look at them more closely. Here was something she could investigate, and it was easier than staring down at Lance's motionless body.

Several people had made the footprints. At least three, if Delia was any judge. The tire tracks had light treads, like tracks left by fat bicycle wheels.

A wheelchair, Delia realized suddenly. *The person who lived here was handicapped. Seriously so, judging from the medical instruments and supplies.*

But what was Lance doing here? The house was marked with none of the destruction that had smashed the rest of the city, so it seemed unlikely that the hive had gotten started here or was keeping a presence here. Delia had survived a hive that had taken over a space station orbiting Thetachron III. Just about everything had been destroyed, or at least altered, within a few hours. This hive had been active for days. Why had it left this particular house alone?

Delia narrowed her eyes at the computer terminal. With her good arm, she switched it on. It came almost instantly on line. The power was still on for this area.

This area? she wondered. *Or this house?*

Squiggles flashed across the screen and Delia shook her head. She didn't even know what language it was, let alone understand it. She tapped a few keys at random, and suddenly the squiggles popped into English. Delia blinked. Then she noticed one of the menu functions allowed the user to switch the terminal's language into Urdu, Hindi, or English. She must have hit the English command by sheer luck.

At least one thing's gone our way, she thought wryly.

The impatient urge to hurry tapped her on the shoulder again, and Delia tried to ignore it. There was no deadline. No need to get worked up.

She glanced at Lance and Quinn. They hadn't moved. *Please hurry, Quinn.*

"Computer," she said, "what is your name?"

"Deva," replied the computer.

"Deva, access the main networks."

"Working." Pause. "Network uplink established."

"What are you doing, Mom?"

Delia jumped and rounded on Quinn with a squeak. "Don't do that," she snapped. "How's your father?"

"Catatonic," Quinn said quietly. "The frustrating part is that I can't find anything wrong. His nanobots are all acting normally, as far as I can tell."

"We've got to wake him up," Delia said. "He's the only one who can tell us what's going on."

"I'm out of ideas."

Delia reached for Quinn's backpack on the floor, feeling oddly like Aladdin reaching for a lamp. "Let's call your grandmother and sister on the prototype. We should update them anyway."

Kate answered. She didn't seem to be shaking anymore. "Well?" she demanded.

"He's alive," Delia said, then stepped back to let Quinn explain the latest.

Meredeth gave a sigh that seemed to come from her toes and relief washed across her tired face. "Could you possibly bring him back to the ship? We can worry about the hive later, after you're all safe."

"We have a car—truck—out front," Quinn said. "I could carry Dad down, but I'd rather wake him up first and find out what the hell is going on."

"How are the repairs going, Kate?" Delia asked.

"Peter Piper picked a peck of pickled peppers," she said brightly. "I can stand up, too, but Grandma won't let me."

"You'll stay in that bed until every last repair is complete," Meredeth said.

Quinn stared intently at the screen for a moment. Kate furrowed her brow.

"I think so," Kate said. "I've learned a lot about nervous systems in the past few hours."

"You think what?" Delia asked. *Too slow! Hurry hurry hurry! But why?*

"The problem here is that I don't know much about repairing damaged nervous systems," Quinn said, "but I know my way around Dad's brain. Kate doesn't know Dad, but she's learned a lot about repairs. If we can combine what we know, we might be able to bring Dad out of this."

"How on Earth is Kate going to look at La—your father from London?" Meredeth demanded.

"Kate can control nanobots through a communicator as easily as I can. I'll just let her have some of my nanos at this end."

Delia found she was shifting nervously from foot to foot. She shot several glances at the open door. Hot, steamy air wafted into the room in little puffs.

"I'm not jumping into the nets," Kate warned.

"You won't have to," Quinn replied. "You're just using the nanos to look around. You won't go anywhere. Give us a few minutes and we might be able to wake Dad up."

"Look, can we just get on with it?" Delia said. "We need to get out of here. I want to get off this planet."

"We shouldn't rush," Meredeth said reasonably. "You said the hive seems to have calmed down and you aren't in any danger. If the twins hurry, they might make mistakes."

Part of Delia knew Meredeth was right, even as another part gibbered at her to snatch Lance up and head for the hills.

"I don't know, Grandma," Quinn said. "I don't like it around here either. I agree with Mom. I want to get out of here."

"Then let's get started," Kate said.

Quinn nodded. He put his hands on Lance's motionless shoulders, and his face went blank with concentration. On the communicator viewscreen, Kate's face took on a similar expression. Silence fell in the room.

"Well," Meredeth said. "It looks like it's just the two of us."

Delia gave her a nervous smile. "Actually, I think I'm just having another look round this place. Something still doesn't feel quite right."

"Just leave an old lady alone then," Meredeth sighed. "I suppose I can always read a few of those reports that keep stacking up in my wristcomp."

Delia turned back to Deva, the computer terminal. Maybe there were clues in the local hard drive—a journal or research notes. "Deva, access local file system."

"That information requires password and voiceprint identification. You are not authorized to access local files."

"Damn." Delia shot a glance at Quinn. He could

probably break in, but that would mean disturbing him. She decided to leave it for now.

"Deva," she said, "are you still linked to the nets?"

"Yes."

"What is the status of the networks?"

"Working." Pause. "Zero percent of the intergalactic network is accessible. Approximately thirty-five percent of the planetary network is accessible."

"Thirty-five percent?" Delia echoed. That didn't sound right. Quinn had made it sound like the hive had taken over a lot more than sixty-five percent of the nets. "Deva, recheck that figure."

"Working." Pause. "Correction. Approximately forty-two percent of the planetary network is now accessible."

Delia blinked. "Deva, do you mean more of the network is coming on line?"

"Yes."

Something was trying to click. A picture was ready to form, but the final image remained frustratingly out of focus. Delia drummed the countertop with impatient fingertips. "Deva, why are the planetary networks mostly inaccessible?"

"Unknown."

Of course. Computers couldn't diagnose nanobot hives. "Deva, how are the networks coming back on line?"

"Unknown."

"Deva, can you speculate?"

"Working." Pause. "The most likely scenario is that self-repairs are taking place."

Delia paced restlessly. This wasn't right, either. As far as she knew, nanobot hives did not make repairs to networks, nor did they let go of network sectors they had already claimed. Yet the computers—or the nanobots that ran them—were already making repairs and bringing their terminals back on line. That would indicate that the hive had retreated.

It's almost as if the hive has left the planet, Delia thought. *Just like someone . . . left . . . this . . . house.*

Something crunched beneath Delia's foot. She looked down and saw glass shards, the remains of a holocrystal. Almost as if in a trance, she bent down and searched among the pieces with her good hand until she found the display chip. Delia brought it over to the terminal and slotted it into the computer.

"Deva," she ordered, "access hologram and display on screen."

The menus and icons instantly blinked out and were replaced by a two-dimensional picture of a hologram. At first, all she could make out was a jumble of shapes and colors. Then she realized she was seeing the image from the top and a little to one side. It seemed to be two people.

Small arrows in the corners of the screen indicated that the viewer could rotate the image in any desired direction. Delia's fingers flickered over the keys, and the image rotated until the people were looking straight out of the screen. One was a tall, dark-haired man in a white lab coat. He was standing behind a girl in a wheelchair. His hand was on her shoulder. Delia was startled to notice the girl had only one arm. Most of her body was covered by a white blanket, but the lumps and bulges beneath it indicated that the rest of her body was deformed as well. The caption on the hologram read, "Aditi and Father."

Aditi, Delia thought. She looked at the wheelchair tracks and footprints, then at the too-sparse supplies of medical equipment. The software box on the desk caught Delia's eyes. She reached for it and held it in front of the computer.

"Deva," she said softly, "what does this say?"

"It is Urdu for 'nanobot programs.'"

Nanobot programs. This was a house where nanobots were programmed to oversee medical equipment that kept a heavily handicapped child alive. Just like Jonathan Blackstone's laboratories had used nanobots to oversee the cybernetic implants used to improve

Lance's looks and body. After years of interaction with a human nervous system, his nanobots had formed one of the most powerful artificial intelligences in history.

And how long have Aditi's nanobots been interacting with her nervous system?

Delia looked around the empty room again. The hive had left the networks. Aditi had left the house.

Hurry hurry hurry!

Where had Aditi gone? Delia bit her lip, trying to bring the pieces together. Aditi had the run of the planet through the networks, yet she had apparently decided to go through the effort of moving her body. Why? Delia doubted it was because Aditi knew Quinn and Delia were coming. If she could overpower Lance, she could certainly overpower Quinn and Delia. So where was she going? She couldn't get off New Pakistan. Every ship at the spaceport had been destroyed.

Delia's knees weakened and she grabbed the desk with her single working arm for support. The hive was heading for the spaceport—and the *Starstreak*. All Aditi had to do was board the *Starstreak* and take off. The moment Aditi pierced the debris field, every computer in the galaxy would belong to her.

Now Delia knew why they had to hurry.

I swam through my father's brain with my twin in tow. Neither of us had Traded ourselves fully inside, but our perceptions were both completely focused on what our nanobots were seeing. I was aware of Mom moving about the room, but only vaguely. Most of my attention was focused on Dad's brain cells and the chemical patterns inside.

It went beyond strange, wandering through my own father's head. My nanos felt creepy, like they were walking through worms. I was definitely trespassing. I was also worried and scared. What if Dad didn't wake up? He couldn't die—he was my dad.

But the hive had killed thousands of people already.

What was one more? A lump settled into my throat, and I frowned. This was the hive's fault. Because of this . . . *thing,* my dad was in a coma. The lump turned into smoldering anger. I wanted to lash out at it, punish it for hurting Dad, except there was no one to lash out at. My frown deepened and I forced myself to concentrate on Dad's brain. His nanos floated in murky plasma or clung gently to individual dendrites like ornaments on a Christmas tree. They seemed to be undamaged but unresponsive.

You see? I told my twin. *It's like his brain has shut down, but he isn't dead.*

This is weird, my twin replied. Nanos that used to be mine scooted through Dad's prefrontal lobe. *There are too many walls set up—chemical barriers. They're all over the place.*

Walls? I asked. *What do you mean? I don't see—*

Here, and here, and here, my twin pointed out. *Most people have them, I think, including us. They keep your conscious and subconscious apart. Neurological activity can cross into the subconscious, but only a little leaks back out.*

I thought about network data streams rushing into blackness.

Maybe we should try to decode his memories, see what happened to him just before he . . . fell asleep, I said.

Can you do that?

Sort of. When I Traded us that last time, I caught some of your memories, remember? I think my nanos can use them as a template for breaking Dad's chemical codes. Human memories are human memories.

My twin was silent for a long moment. *What memories of mine did you catch?*

The silver infinite of the nets. A cold, white day and hot, red blood. Crushing remorse. Anger over gender preference.

Let's talk about it later, I said. *You keep looking for Dad and I'll see if I can decode some of his memories.*

My twin's nanobots regarded mine with uncertainty. *All right,* my twin finally said. *Let's get to work.*

I examined Dad's brain cells, both up close to see the tiny patterns in the cells and as a composite picture from a distance to see the overall patterns of the brain. Now that my twin had pointed them out, I could see the chemical walls, one-way barriers for transmission of information. They snaked among neural tissue with no apparent rhyme or reason. I tried to see if I could figure out which codes were made the most recently to get a look at Dad's latest memories, but there was no way to tell at a quick glance, and I didn't feel like taking a lot of time. Mom had said she felt a need to hurry, and so did I.

I set my nanobots to decoding chemistry, using my and my twin's codes as a template. It didn't take nearly as long as I thought it might. In a few seconds, fragments of Dad's memories flashed into my mind.

Garth sat in the dark, knees under his chin, arms around his knees. The box was too tiny to sit any other way. Garth could feel Lance somewhere in the back of his head. The box scared Lance, but Lance was dumb. What was there to be scared of? It was only a stupid wooden box. A little box. In the basement. Where the monsters lived. Garth shivered, wondering if the monsters could get in the box. Then he scoffed. He wasn't afraid of monsters. Lance was afraid, but Garth wasn't.

It was hot in the box, and a little hard to breathe. Garth shifted uncomfortably. He had to go to the bathroom. Maybe Dad would let him out if he knew.

"Dad!" he yelled. "Dad! You gotta let me out. I hafta go. Did you hear me? I hafta *go*."

No answer. It was real hard to sit still now. Garth shouted again, but no one came. He felt around and noticed that were little holes in the walls of the box. Now it was *really* hard to sit still, and Garth knew he was going to wet his pants pretty soon. That would make Dad angry. Maybe he could put his thing out through one of the holes and go. That would make Dad mad, too, but at least Garth wouldn't have gone in his pants.

Except the monsters were out there. They would bite his thing right off.

Garth couldn't hold it anymore and warmth spread all over his pants. Garth yelled for Dad to let him out, to please let him out of the box, but Dad didn't come.

Lance looked at the beautiful woman sitting behind the receptionist's desk and shifted uncomfortably. Every time Jessica wanted to visit Mom in London, she bailed out in the foyer and left Lance in control until Mom called the Company into her office. This, he knew, was because Jessica didn't like Robert, Mom's chief assistant. But Robert was nowhere to be seen.

"Ms. Michaels is on the phone at the moment," the woman said. Several small bird statues decorated the desk. The absent Robert had gone in for pictures of his girlfriends. "It'll be just a moment. If you would care to sit down?"

"Where's Robert?" Lance asked.

"He . . . left. Rather abruptly," the woman said. "Something about a paternity suit. I'm Delia Radford, Ms. Michaels's new chief assistant." She extended a graceful hand and Lance took it.

"Lance Michaels," he said, "of the Michaels Company."

"I know," Delia said. "You're Ms. Michaels's son. She speaks of you often."

Lance found it hard to look away from Delia's face. She was so beautiful. Wide brown eyes, bright smile, smooth dark skin. Lance abruptly realized he was still holding Delia's hand and that she was staring directly into his eyes. He dropped her hand and felt an embarrassed flush crawl hotly over his face. Everyone reacted that way to Lance. The pheromones his body put out saw to that. Nobody liked him for himself. Nobody ever could.

Delia's computer beeped and she glanced down at it. "You can go on in. See you on your way out?"

The words were more invitation than question.

"I guess," Lance had time to say before Jessica took over for lunch with Mom.

Lance was surrounded by his father's strong arms. He stroked Lance's hair as they both sat naked on the cold basement floor. The carving knife rested, forgotten, in the corner.

"I'm sorry, John," Dad whispered in a choked voice. "Oh God, I'm so sorry. I love you, John. I love you so much. You know that, don't you? That's why I have to punish you. I have to make sure you don't grow up to be a bad boy. You understand, don't you?"

Lance swallowed. He knew the drill. "Yeah, Dad," he said. "I know."

Dad squeezed him tightly. "Do you love me, too?"

"Yeah, Dad. I love you, too."

Dad smiled and released him. "Good. Get your clothes on and go upstairs. I'll lock up."

Delia ran laughing across the white sands, her feet kicking up tiny sprays from the waves that lapped the shore. Lance, growling in mock ferocity, rushed after her. His muscle implants and longer legs proved too fast for her, and it wasn't long before he managed to snatch her up in a firefighter's carry. She giggled and shrieked as Lance hauled her inexorably out to deeper water.

"You want a water fight?" he said with an evil laugh. "I'll give you a water fight."

"Lance, don't you dare!" she howled, beating both fists against his bare back. "Don't you da—"

Her words ended in an unceremonious splash. Spitting and spluttering, she got to her feet. Warm seawater ran down her face. Lance stuck his tongue out at her.

"You creep," she said, and flung herself at him. Lance was surprised at how easily she managed to tear both their bathing suits off.

✧   ✧   ✧

Jessica typed madly. The Company's final physics paper was due today, but that idiot Andy had found a new sex club and kept the body in an orgy almost all night. Naturally it fell to Jessica to remedy the situation. She glanced at her wristcomp. Less than two hours before class and she had barely finished the introduction. The keys clicked and clicked and clicked.

Lance put his hand on Delia's stomach, which was only just starting to swell.

"Twins?" he said in disbelief.

"A boy and a girl," Delia told him with a small smile.

"I really like the name Kate for a girl," Lance said thoughtfully. "I haven't really thought about a boy's name, though."

Delia put her hand over his. "Quinn."

"Are you sure? He probably won't be anything like your brother, you know."

"His name is Quinn."

I found him, my twin said. *He's buried really deep, though, and I couldn't penetrate the walls around him. Did you find out anything?*

I freed myself from Dad's memories with a mental shake of my head. *Not exactly. Some of his memories are pretty, um . . . embarrassing, you know? There's one of him and Mom on a beach somewhere. She was tearing off his—*

Stop right there, my twin interrupted. *My hangups could probably keep a therapist busy for a lifetime as it is.*

Right. At any rate, I didn't get anything recent. An idea began to form and I paused to let it coalesce. * I did notice that Dad's strongest memories revolve around Mom.*

Someone was shaking my shoulder.

Do you think Mom could get him out of this? my twin said.

"Quinn," Mom's voice said, "are you there?"

It might work, I said. Excitement grew. * I'll tell

*Mom what's going on. If she talks to him, maybe we can make sure her words reach his brain That might get through to him and wake him up.**

*Worth a try. I'll wait here.**

I opened my eyes. Mom was still shaking my shoulder. Her eyes had a wild look and I tensed.

"What's wrong?" I asked.

"I figured out where the hive went," she said, and went on to explain.

Her words twisted my stomach. I thought about this Aditi person getting into the galactic networks. If what she had done to this planet was any indication of her personality, all human life was in trouble. No one would be safe.

My hands were chilly as I relayed the information to my twin.

*Fuck.**

"I'll have to stop her at the spaceport," I said, heading for the door. Here was something I could *do*. The hive was going to suffer for what it—she—had done to Dad. "You stay here, Mom. I'll take the delivery truck. You can use that police cruiser to follow later."

"Wait a moment!" Grandma shouted through the communicator. "What about Lance?"

"My twin will explain," I shot over my shoulder. "See you!"

I dashed out the door before anyone could protest. Aditi Amendeep was going to pay.

The dark was warm and soft, the most comfortable bed in the world. Here there were no worries, no cares, no one poking or prodding or sifting through his mind. Lance sighed and snuggled in. Peace surrounded him on every side. He could happily stay here forever.

Lance. Lance, can you hear me?

The voice pierced the darkness like a flashlight. Lance buried his head in his arms. He didn't want to get up. It was harsh and cold out there.

Lance, please wake up! We need you.

He knew that voice. It was familiar. It belonged to—

No. It had been almost eighteen years. She couldn't be here. Lance tried to push himself further down into darkness. He still loved her. How could he face seeing her after all this time? It would be too painful.

∗Don't worry about it, Lance,∗ said another, even more familiar voice. *∗You wait here and we'll handle everything.∗*

Lance gratefully buried his head again and let the darkness close in.

"Lance, wake up," Delia said, trying to sound gentle and persistent. "Lance, we need you to wake up. Can you hear me?"

Next to the bed, the communicator's screen showed a worried-looking Meredeth. Kate lay on her bed with her eyes shut, communicating with and controlling nanobots from impossibly far away. The light leaving New Pakistan's sun at this moment wouldn't reach Earth for two hundred thousand years, but Kate was able to relay information from her hospital bed to the nanobots Quinn had given her on New Pakistan. It boggled Delia's mind to think what would happen if Aditi got off planet and managed the same trick. And now Quinn had left to go fight her. Worry and fear were making Delia sick.

"Lance," she pleaded, "please wake up!"

"I don't think it's working," Meredeth said. "Maybe we should try something else."

"He'll wake up," Delia said stubbornly. "He has to. Lance, please, we need your help. It's Delia. Wake up!" *And what will happen when he does wake up?* she wondered privately. *How will I react?*

She didn't know and couldn't speculate.

"Lance, please," she said.

"I think I'm getting a response," Kate said suddenly. "Keep talking, Mom."

"Lance, it's Delia. Wake up!"

Lance's eyes twitched beneath their closed lids. Delia's heart leaped, but she kept talking. A finger moved, then a hand. Instinctively Delia grasped it in hers and squeezed. Lance squeezed back. A tear coursed down Delia's face.

Why am I crying? she thought angrily. *There's no reason to cry here.*

Lance stirred and abruptly sat up. His eyes popped open. They were a brilliant green, different from his normal shade. Delia gasped and stepped back. She recognized the color.

"No," she whispered.

"Delia. So good to see you again," Lance said warmly. Then he noticed her expression. "What's wrong? Don't you remember? It's me. Jessica."

CHAPTER FIFTEEN

ME

I peeked out of a ruined hangar, uncertain of what I should do next. About twenty meters away on the space-port tarmac, four naked, muscular men were unloading a small moving van and piling the boxes near the *Starstreak*. Sweat streamed down their bodies. The fifth man had set up some kind of wheelchair, which was now occupied by a person with one arm and with legs that were twisted and deformed. It must Aditi. She didn't look particularly dangerous. On the contrary, she looked small and pitiful.

A growl still rumbled in my throat. The sound surprised me a little, but then I grinned. I had learned a lot about computers and hives in past several hours, and she was going to experience it firsthand.

Oh yeah? I thought. *And just what are you going to do?*

I ground my teeth, forced to admit I had no idea. I decided to watch a little longer and look for one.

The men kept unloading the truck in the oppressive heat. Why were they naked? And why did the fifth guy have a hard-on? Was Aditi controlling them somehow? My eyes narrowed, and images of people running races in the park flashed through my head. Controlling them. The more I thought about it, the more it made sense. My nanobots could control my body by altering my brain chemistry or by working directly on muscle tissue. Given enough time in someone else's head, I could probably do the same to another person.

Aditi was obviously a fast learner.

Hatred suddenly seized me again. Here was the bitch who had taken my father away from me. He was lying in a coma because she had done God-knew-what to his body and mind. She was responsible for the burned corpses rotting under New Pakistan's heavy sun, some of them children, little babies who didn't understand why it hurt so much or why Mommy and Daddy couldn't help them. Aditi was a filthy, twisted abomination. I wanted to rush across the tarmac and break her neck with my bare hands. Instead I forced myself to watch, gather information. My nostrils flared and my hands trembled with the effort of keeping myself under control, but I stayed put.

Aditi wheeled her chair up to the *Starstreak*'s main hatch and put her hand on it. It took me a moment to figure out that she was probably communicating with the nanobots in the hatch's security system. I snorted. The *Starstreak* had state-of-the-art security programs and computers. It would take years for even the most talented hacker to break in.

Or maybe thirty seconds for someone who can assimilate the system's nanos, I thought with growing unease.

Meanwhile, the guy with the hard-on pulled a crate from the passenger side of the moving van. He opened it and passed a pair of pistols to each of the other four men. They strapped the guns on and fanned out to stand guard. They stood around Aditi, arms folded like statues. My heart sank. I didn't have any kind of firepower except my nanos. I might be able to affect the guns, but first I had to stop Aditi from getting access to the ship.

Swiftly I sent a regiment of nanos scurrying across the tarmac and into the ship. The *Streak* was sealed air- and nano-tight, but once my nanos were close enough to communicate with the ones inside, airtight didn't matter. Just as Aditi was surely doing, I started grabbing nanos in the ship's interior until I had enough to transfer myself inside. A moment later, I Traded myself into the ship's main computer.

Alarms were screaming all over the ship, indicating Aditi was already there. Sort of. The nanos she had taken over were there, but she was only getting feedback from and controlling them. Her mind wasn't actually inside the ship like mine was. Still, I kept my nanos well away from hers and accessed the main security grid. Aditi had already managed to bring down two layers of security. Quietly, I rebuilt the first wall behind her, then the second. Aditi's nanos brought down a third, and I waited until she was tackling the fourth before putting it back up. Then something seemed to click for Aditi, and she brought down two more walls in less than a second. That was when she noticed the first three walls were back in place. Instantly, her program expanded in all directions, searching for the intruder.

I sucked myself out of the ship before Aditi's nanos could catch any of mine. This wasn't going to work. I couldn't keep her out of the ship's computer forever— she was faster than I was and more experienced at working with machines.

Machines. My eye fell on an electric luggage cart that had escaped destruction. Computers weren't the only tools available. My nanos flooded the cart and found its onboard computer. A flick of my mind switched on the power. The cart hummed quietly to life, then zipped up the tarmac, heading straight for Aditi.

One of her guards was standing in the way. He made no effort to dodge. The cart hit him at full speed with a *thump,* and he went flying without a sound. He sprawled brokenly on the tarmac. The cart sped forward, but Aditi must have noticed what was going on by then. One of the other guards yanked her out of the wheelchair. The cart plowed through it and smashed into the ship with the loud crunch of shattered plastic. Aditi's wheelchair looked like it had been stepped on. The guard hit by the luggage cart remained sprawled on the ground. I had no idea if he was dead or alive. For all I knew, he was already dead and Aditi was just controlling his corpse.

Aditi shaded her eyes with her hand and scanned the area. I ducked back into the hangar.

"Who's out there?" Aditi demanded. "Quinn? Show yourself!"

I started. How had she known to speak English? And how the hell did she know my name?

"Come on out. I won't hurt you," Aditi shouted. The guy with the hard-on was holding her in his arms, though his dick had wilted. "We can talk. We have a lot in common, you know. It isn't easy growing up with nanobots, is it? It's not anything you can describe. We could be friends. Close friends."

Yeah, right, I thought. *Next you'll say we can rule the universe together.*

I Traded myself back into the ship and found half the security walls had been bulldozed. Just as I'd thought. Aditi's offers of friendship had been nothing but a delaying tactic. I hastily rebuilt a few barriers and jumped back to my body to look around.

Aditi's remaining goons fanned out, pistols drawn. One of them headed my way. I cast about for somewhere to hide. The hangar I was in was a huge half-cylinder of metal with giant doors at either end. No ship was inside, but something had apparently ignited the fuel storage tanks. The resulting explosion had blown both sets of doors off and poked gaping holes in the walls and ceiling. Twisted chunks of metal lay everywhere, but none were big enough to hide behind. I plastered my back against the blackened metal just inside the main door, wondering what the hell I was going to do.

"Delia, it's all right," Lance said. "It's me. Surely you haven't forgotten."

Delia put her hand over her mouth. This wasn't happening. It couldn't happen.

"What's going on?" Kate's image demanded from the communicator. "Dad, why are you acting so strange?"

"Your father is busy right now, dear," Lance said, turning emerald eyes on the communicator. Except Lance didn't have emerald eyes or speak with an English accent. His posture wasn't that stiff, and she had never in her life heard him call anyone "dear." The only person who did that was Jessica Meredeth Michaels, one of Lance's old personalities.

"What the hell?" Kate said. Delia saw Meredeth go pale.

"Where's Lance?" Delia demanded. Her throat was dry and her hands were cold. She felt as if someone had punched her in the gut.

"Sleeping," not-Lance said, and stretched like a cat. "Aditi did some pretty horrible things to him, so Garth and I are helping out."

"Garth? Oh, my God."

"My reaction entirely," Jessica said ruefully. "But Lance trusts him."

"What's going on?" Kate repeated, more stridently this time.

"Hush," Meredeth said. "I'll explain later."

"How many of you are there?" Delia asked.

"Just the three of us—Lance, Garth, and I."

"Sort this out later," Meredeth put in. "Lance is functional again, and you need to get to the spaceport."

"Aditi went to the spaceport?" Jessica said. "I knew she left but I didn't know where."

"She's going to use our ship to get off planet and into the galactic networks," Delia said. "Meredeth, I have to shut the communicator off. I'll contact you as soon as we can." She severed the connection before Meredeth could reply, then opened another line to the ships circling New Pakistan. The startled face of Captain Okamoto of the *Lady Kay* appeared on the screen.

"The nanobot hive has commandeered the *Starstreak*," Delia said without preamble. "It'll probably be taking off any second now. Do not let that ship pass the debris field, Captain, unless you want a nanobot hive in the networks." She signed off without waiting for a reply.

"A hive in the networks?" Jessica echoed. "Oh, dear."

Delia stuffed the communicator into Quinn's back-pack without looking up. Of all the outcomes she had anticipated, this one had never occurred to her. Lance had integrated all his personalities long ago. Aditi must have done something pretty terrible to make Garth and Jessica crop up again, and if those two had shown up, would the others be far behind? Delia swallowed. She didn't know if she could handle Patrick's or Andy's psychoses right now, and if Johnny returned, Lance wouldn't do anything but sit and cry uselessly for hours.

Delia grabbed Jessica's hand, still without making eye contact. "We have to run. Quinn's out there all by himself. There's a police cruiser downstairs we can use."

"We should look in the trunk first," Jessica said with typical cold logic. "It won't take long."

My heart beat faster as Aditi's goon drew closer, his gun glittering in the harsh sunlight. The gun was the problem. Without it, the goon and I would be on equal footing. Guns were forbidden on Felicity, and I knew next to nothing about them.

But I was a fast learner.

My nanos flashed toward the goon. I could sense Aditi's nanobots inside his body, where they were doubtless making this guy do what she wanted. They would also prevent me from attacking him like the thug in the library, even if I were able to stomach the idea. Aditi, on the other hand, probably thought of this guy as nothing more than an extension of herself. A giant nanobot.

His bare feet moved with tiny whispering sounds over the tarmac, and a small part of me wondered if the hot surface hurt his feet. My nanos washed up his side, down his arm, and into the gun. All of Aditi's nanos were inside him, so I didn't have to worry about encountering her

directly. In a few seconds, I had a perfect picture of
the pistol.

The goon drew closer. I only had a moment left.

The key seemed to be the firing pin. If it didn't function
properly, the gun couldn't fire. In a flash, my nanos
located the mechanism that allowed the pin to move.
They couldn't destroy it—polymer and plastic are harder
than flesh and bone—but they could gum it up with
their own bodies. Four hundred nanobots jammed themselves into the mechanism until there was no way the
pin was going to move. I smiled with satisfaction, then
balled up a fist as foreign nanos flooded over my body.

I gave a startled yell. The goon barreled into the hangar and fired his pistol at me, but it only clicked. Meanwhile, the foreign nanobots rampaged through my body,
barging between cells and swarming into my blood. Belatedly it occurred to me that if I could sense Aditi's nanos,
she could probably sense mine. She managed to convert and reprogram almost fifty thousand of my nanos
before my guard went up. Discarding that tactic, they
turned to physical force, overwhelming my nanos through
sheer numbers. My own troops rallied and fought back,
trying to eject the invaders, but I was outnumbered.

The goon dropped his pistol and leaped for me. Dodging was out of the question—I wasn't used to dividing
my attention between the micro- and macroscopic
worlds. We went down in a tangle of arms and legs.
Inside, nanobots pushed and shoved at each other. Superior numbers steadily surrounded and entrapped me.
Outside, I was caught in a bear hug and the goon's weight
pressed me down. I froze, unable to decide where to
direct my attention.

My ribs creaked, and it was hard to catch my breath.
The charred, greasy concrete floor of the hangar scraped
against my body. A quick check told me that less than
a quarter of my nanos were actually immobilized. They'd
have to fend for themselves. I needed the rest for an
adrenaline- and muscle-boost.

A tweak of the glands above my kidneys sent my heart into overdrive. My nanos ordered various striated muscle fibers to *contract*. I burst free of the goon's grip and shoved him off me. My foot lashed out and caught him in the groin. Then I rolled to my feet. The goon's expression showed no hint of change. He started getting to his feet, and I noticed that he was a little clumsy. Perhaps it was because Aditi had to control him consciously or perhaps he was naturally slow to begin with. In any case, I had plenty of time to land a solid kick under his chin. His head snapped back and he collapsed to the dirty concrete like a deflated balloon.

Hurriedly I looked back at my nanos. Half were now immobilized. My heart was still pounding, but no longer from the adrenaline boost. Nanos hid among cells, leaped out and ambushed each other, were caught and held by three of Aditi's to my one. It was like two ant colonies at war.

I was sweating again. No matter what strategy I tried, no matter how well my nanos hid, we were losing. Sixty percent held prisoner. Sixty-eight. Seventy-five. Sweat trickled down my forehead. A small part of me was aware that Aditi's other goons were heading my way, but my internal war held my attention. I spared a second to see how close they were getting, wondered if I could run fast enough to get away. Then my eye fell on the goon's gun.

Eighty percent. I scooped up the pistol. A few thousand of my nanos were still in it. I ordered them to clear the firing pin and rejoin my body. Then I looked at the goons again. They were only a few yards from the hangar. I checked to see how the war was going. Eight-six percent.

My attention flicked back and forth between the outer and inner worlds as I raised the pistol and took aim at Aditi. Eighty-nine percent. One of the goons was in the way. Aditi was doing something at the *Starstreak*'s hatch. Ninety-four percent. I squeezed the trigger. The gun

barked. Ninety-seven percent. The goon jerked and fell
back a step as a scarlet flower bloomed in his naked
shoulder. Ninety-nine percent. The *Starstreak*'s hatch
opened. Ninety-nine percent. I took aim at Aditi. One
hundred percent. I squeezed the trigger.

My finger froze. Slowly, my hand lowered itself and
my legs started to move. I walked jerkily toward the
ship. I wanted to howl and scream. My nanos surged
with new strength and two percent of them actually broke
free before Aditi's nanos grabbed them again. Her other
nanos wandered freely through my brain, tweaking here,
changing chemicals there, making this muscle move,
that one stay still. I was panting, trying to fight. But
my muscles simply wouldn't obey. Aditi paused in front
of the hatchway to watch me walk toward her. The two
goons she had sent to get me turned and formed a sort
of honor guard. The third remaining goon stood behind
Aditi's wheelchair. Sweat broke out all over my body. I
was trapped in walls of flesh. My body had betrayed
me. Biology won again.

"What am I going to do with you, Quinn?" Aditi asked
as we approached. "You're definitely too dangerous to
leave running about. You incapacitated two of my drones,
and I needed them to load up the ship."

By now I was standing directly in front of her. She
was tiny, with legs like thin, twisted sticks and one spindly
arm. An IV was plugged into the shoulder that didn't
have an arm. Behind her, the goon looked at me with
wide, terrified eyes. With a start I realized a person was
still in there. Aditi hadn't destroyed his consciousness
as I had assumed—she had merely taken over his body
as she had done with me. I wondered if the other goons
were in the same boat, but couldn't see their faces.

"I could," Aditi went on, "summon more drones, but
that would take time, and I want off this little world
now. You, however, are here right now. If I crushed your
nanobots, you'd be just like everyone else, wouldn't you?
Then you could replace my drone, and I'd be fine."

My mind clawed and gibbered, but my face remained absolutely expressionless. She was going to destroy my nanos. I'd be like my twin, forever unable to Trade or talk to computers or run the nets.

Two percent of my nanos were released. Four percent. Twelve percent. Instantly I set them to reestablishing my normal body processes. Twenty percent. I tried to look around to see what was going on. Twenty-seven percent free. More foreign nanobots were flooding my body, but these worked to release mine from Aditi's.

"What in the world?" Aditi gasped.

Then I knew. These were Dad's nanos. Thirty-one percent freed. I heard the faint whine of an electric motor less than a second before a police cruiser tore around the corner of the hangar. Mom was driving and Dad was leaning out the passenger window. He was holding a gun. My muscles unlocked.

"Move!" Dad shouted.

Forty percent. I dove to one side. Dad fired. One of the goons flung himself in front of Aditi. Warm blood sprayed my neck and arm. Forty-eight percent. I scrambled to my feet in time to see the wide-eyed goon shoving Aditi's wheelchair up the ramp. Abruptly her nanos withdrew from my body, leaving me completely free. The hatch started to close. Quickly I Traded into the ship's systems and jammed the door open, not caring that Aditi knew I was there. I leaped back to my body.

Everything slowed down. The remaining honor guard goon swung his pistol around. I started to raise mine, but I wasn't fast enough. With complete clarity I saw his finger squeeze the trigger. Light flashed from the pistol's muzzle. The bullet missed my head. Instead it tore through my neck, shattered two cervical vertebrae, and severed my spinal cord. Frantically my nanos rushed to the site as I fell hard to the ground. Before they could do anything, another bullet plowed into my chest. My heart exploded. In less than a second, I was dead.

CHAPTER SIXTEEN

DELIA

Blood exploded from Quinn's neck, and Delia screamed incoherently. She was out of her seat and running toward the ship without conscious memory of halting the car. One of the pistols she and Jessica had found in the cruiser's trunk flashed and barked from her good hand.

"Bastard!" she screamed. "You fucking son of a bitch!"

Bullets sprayed wildly, pinging off the ship and caroming off the tarmac, but none found their mark—not only was Delia running, she wasn't normally left-handed. The thug behind Aditi's wheelchair rammed it through the hatch and followed her in. Lance—or whoever he was at the moment—leaped out of the cart and pelted toward the ship. He wasn't shooting. The thug who had shot Quinn calmly raised his pistol and returned fire. Something flung Delia's right arm back, throwing her off balance. Another force ripped through her left leg. She stumbled. Lance grunted as a bullet tore into his stomach, but he kept running. Then he did a belly flop to the ground, pistol raised in front of his face. Blood smeared a trail behind him as he slid forward. The hatch started to close again, but slowly. Delia regained her balance. Blood gushed down her leg, but she felt no pain. Lance fired once, twice. A tiny point of red appeared in the final thug's forehead even as a fine scarlet mist sprayed out the back. The thug dropped beside Quinn's mangled body.

"Inside!" Lance barked.

Delia looked down at her son's body and the dead thug beside him. Quinn couldn't be dead. She had just found him. She had just—

Lance grabbed her by the arm and all but tossed her through the hatchway before diving through himself. The hatch slammed shut. Pain suddenly ripped through Delia's leg and for the first time she noticed the blood coursing down it.

"Lance," she gasped. "I've been—"

"I'm Garth, dammit," he snapped. His wound had stopped bleeding and his eyes were brown. "Give me that."

He ripped the pack from Delia's back, ignoring her cry of pain. Yanking the pack open, he tore the communication prototype out of the pack, plugged it into a nearby terminal, and switched it on.

The next several seconds were very strange for me. It took about three seconds for my body to actually die, but those three seconds gave me plenty of time to copy my neural and chemical patterns into my nanos and transfer them to nanos on the ship. There was barely enough space for me. Aditi was already there, taking up most of the room, and I was forced to spread myself between nanobots and computer drives.

Aditi instantly sensed my presence and attacked. She couldn't take my nanos away, but she could destroy storage sectors on the computer. I couldn't use this tactic to fight back—Aditi could easily retreat to her own body, but all I had was the computer. Slowly, steadily, she backed me into a corner, surrounding me with destroyed sectors. It was like being trapped in a room with the walls closing in on all sides. In desperation I tried to push back, but there was nothing to push. I couldn't cross the damaged sectors. The room grew smaller and smaller.

oh god oh god oh god

Then it was too small. Part of me vanished forever,

erased. Memories disappeared, perhaps even a part of my personality. I couldn't even tell what I had lost because I couldn't remember it. I was going to die again.

And then a communications line opened and my twin was there. Reflexively, as if I were caught in mid-Trade, I jumped across the galactic networks to the research lab in London and landed in the female body. With my twin.

My twin had nowhere to go, of course, and stayed in the body as well. Sensation snapped back into being. I felt my arms and legs and the crisp sheets of the hospital bed. My eyes were open, and I saw the white walls of the lab and the worried face of my grandmother. I heard the quiet hum of the lights overhead and the ever-constant clicking of keys at Sierra's workstation. Did the man ever sleep?

Inside my—our?—head, things were more frantic. I guess the stories are true—you don't use your entire brain. A good thing, too. Otherwise there wouldn't have been room enough for both of us. My twin's nanos rushed around the brain, making modifications and accommodations on the fly. I watched in amazement at the delicate work.

How are you doing this? I asked.

I learned a lot repairing my brain after that last Trade, my twin replied. *I saw there wasn't much room left on the ship's computer. Why didn't you jump back to the male body?*

It's . . . I paused, suddenly unable to complete the thought.

Dead?

I tried to nod, but my—our—head only jerked and twitched a bit. It would apparently take some time to work out how to move.

Jesus, my twin whispered.

Sorrow rushed over me, and I could feel it rush over my twin as well. Tears started flowing down our cheeks and our throat felt thick.

"What's wrong?" Grandma asked. "What's going on?"

But we couldn't answer. Talking was too complicated yet.

Dad and Mom are— I began.

—still back on the ship, my twin finished. *I know. I can—*

—feel my thoughts. It was an odd feeling, but not a frightening one. I felt closer to my twin than I had in years, and I knew my twin felt the same way. In an instant, we decided we had to get back to the ship and help our parents. The idea of leaping into the nets still frightened my twin, but my experience with the nets and lack of fear bolstered my twin's courage. Without a word we joined hands and jumped across the void.

Aditi, seated in her wheelchair at the pilot's station, stared in amazement as Quinn vanished, sucked through the communication prototype. There was a faint vibration as the *Starstreak* rose from the ground at the command of her nanos. Aditi's stomach dropped and gravity dragged at her. The puppy sat motionless in the room's single chair, but Aditi paid him no heed. This was a revelation! It had simply never occurred to her that her consciousness could exist solely in computer form. She had always assumed that Quinn, like herself, simply used nanobots and computers like hands, fingers, and feet, with a communications line still open to an organic brain. But why should that be the case? If Quinn could store all his thoughts and memories in a series of nanobots and programs, why couldn't Aditi? She might not be able to snatch another body for herself, but she didn't have to remain in this one.

The ship rose to the ionosphere. Piloting only took up a small portion of Aditi's concentration. With an impatient gesture she copied all her codes and memories into her nanobots and waited restlessly for more altitude. She'd have to clear to debris field before she could—

A slow, delicious smile crossed Aditi's face. She didn't even have to wait that long. The strange communicator Quinn had used was still active. She didn't know how to work it, but it couldn't be hard to figure out.

Her nanos found the communicator. It was even plugged directly into the main networks. Aditi's smile widened. Then she noticed the puppy sitting in the pilot's chair. She wouldn't be able to take him along. Regret creased her face. This ship would never land safely once she left because the puppy didn't know how to pilot without her nanos telling him what to do. He would crash in fear and terror.

Well, she thought, *sometimes you have to be practical.*

Aditi's nanos severed a hundred thousand connections inside the puppy's brain. He stiffened, then slumped in his seat, mercifully and painlessly dead. Aditi nodded in satisfaction. Now she could leave, her conscience clean.

With a whoop of joy and a cry of delight, Aditi jumped free of her body and dropped straight into the nets.

Something surged past us like a powerful wind and vanished into the networks.

What was that? we asked, but didn't know. My twin and I landed in the ship and our thoughts parted. I saw no trace of Aditi. With a sickening lurch, I realized what we had seen, where Aditi had gone. My twin figured it out at the same moment.

"Quinn," came Dad's voice. "Quinn, are you there?"

I took over a speaker near the communicator and accessed a nearby camera. Dad was standing near the hatchway and Mom lay propped against a bulkhead. Her face was pale and her leg was bleeding. My heart dropped. Was she dead, too?

"I'm here, Dad," I said. "What happened to Mom?"

Am here! Am here! came a new voice. *On line and here!*

My nanos spun in place in shock and surprise. It was Gremlin.

CHAPTER SEVENTEEN

DELIA

Delia opened her eyes. Her leg was throbbing with pain despite the hasty bandage Lance had all but thrown at her from a first aid kit.

"Lance?" she asked. "What's going on? I heard Quinn's voice."

"Quinn jumped out of his body and transferred himself into the ship's computer," Lance reported tersely. "I think the ship's flying on automatic pilot. I need to get up front. And it's Garth, not Lance."

Delia's head swam. She wanted to feel relieved at the news about Quinn, but wasn't sure she should. And now Lance was Garth. "Can Quinn hear me?"

"I'm here, Mom," came Quinn's voice from the speakers. Or was it Kate's? It sounded like a blending of the two. "When Dad connected the communicator, I managed to jump back to Earth."

Gritting her teeth, Delia pushed herself to her feet. The bleeding seemed to be under control even if the pain wasn't. Her leg had been hit twice, but the bullets had passed straight through the muscle. If either one had hit a bone and shattered, her leg would be a mangled mess right now instead of a painful inconvenience. She envied Lance's—Garth's—ability to heal himself. The gut wound he had taken hadn't even slowed him down.

The ship was still rising. Delia could feel it. The ride was also bumpy without a human pilot to make corrections. The autopilot wasn't much concerned with turbulence. But wasn't Aditi flying? Garth was already heading toward the cockpit, presumably to find out.

"There's something else," Quinn/Kate said. "Aditi jumped off the ship and into the nets."

Garth froze. Delia gasped.

"That's not the last of it, either," Quinn/Kate continued.

"Hello!" chimed in another voice. It was high-pitched and cheery, almost childlike. "Seem to have missed a lot!"

Garth screeched to a halt.

"Who on Earth?" Delia said.

"Gremlin?" Garth said incredulously. "We thought you were dead."

"Just off line," Gremlin announced. "All nanos back in connection."

"Fuck. Why the hell didn't you come back on line back in London?" Garth asked.

"That's Gremlin?" Delia said. "But—"

Thunder boomed through the cabin. The ship shuddered and yawed sideways. Delia grabbed a handhold and barely managed to keep her balance. Her leg throbbed.

"Shit!" Garth yelped. He was already running for the cockpit.

The ship shuddered again and an alarm started to wail.

"Quinn, are you all right?" Delia shouted above the din.

"We're okay, Mom," Quinn/Kate answered. "All three of us."

"All three of you?"

"Me, Gremlin, and my twin. We're all here."

"There are two corpses up here," came Garth's voice over the intercom. "One must be Aditi. I don't know who the fuck this other guy is."

"Why is the ship shaking?" Delia asked.

"We're under attack," Garth returned. "Meredeth's ships are firing on us."

Another shuddering boom. Delia almost lost her balance. Smoke poured into the cabin from up front and Delia coughed at the acrid taste.

"Why are they firing on—" Delia began, but then she remembered. She had contacted the patrol ships and told them the nanobot hive was aboard. The ship shook, then abruptly spun sideways, throwing Delia around the cabin.

"They've hit the engines," Garth reported through the intercom. "We're going back down. Hang on!"

"Mom! Are you all right?" Quinn/Kate demanded.

"So far," Delia coughed. "Garth, can't you slow us down?"

"Jesus fucking Christ," Garth snarled. "The phase drive is shot and the maneuvering engines are completely gone. What do you want me to do? Open the hatch and drag my foot? We're lucky the gravity still works.

"Gremlin, can you make repairs?" Quinn/Kate said frantically.

"Negative. Repairing phase ship beyond current area of expertise. Could learn, given good database and half an hour of—"

"We don't have half an hour," Garth shouted. "We've got about two minutes."

The ship shook and more alarms went off. The lights flickered, then shut off. Red emergency lights came on.

"We've hit atmosphere," Garth yelled, and groped his way back toward Delia. "I'd guess it's ninety seconds to impact."

"Eighty-one point three four seconds," Gremlin said.

Oh my god my god my god, Delia thought.

"Dad!" Quinn/Kate shouted. "Jump to London. You can do it. Transfer your codes and memories across the communicator. It's easy."

"Fuck no," Garth said. "What if I got lost? And I'm not your dad."

Delia licked her lips. The temperature was rising and she was already starting to sweat. Her leg had gone mercifully numb. Alarms continued to blare, and an ominous rumbling was growing louder. There was no way she would survive the crash when the *Starstreak* hit the ground. Images of Brad, Nancy, and Peter flashed across her mind, along with Grace and Victor, her other spouses, and their children, children she thought of as hers. She hadn't thought of them much since she had left the house. They didn't even know she was on New Pakistan because Delia hadn't wanted them to worry. The next thing they learned about her would be that she had died in a horrible accident. She couldn't imagine their shock.

But just because she was going to die didn't mean that Lance had to go down with her.

"Do it, Garth," she shouted above the noise. "It ought to be simple. You and Lance have been controlling nanos since you were a teenager."

"I can't control them," Garth almost wailed. "Jessica freed Quinn, not me, and she isn't as good with nanos as Lance is. I don't think she can do it."

"Seventy-five seconds to impact," Gremlin reported.

"Then put Lance in control," Delia yelled. "Hurry!"

"But Lance is just a kid! He can't—"

"Do it!"

A flicker crossed Garth's face and he seemed to shrink a few centimeters. His posture changed in small ways and Delia knew she was looking at Lance. It had been years since she had seen this kind of transformation, and despite the tension, Delia felt an almost overwhelming sense of déjà vu. The air grew hotter and Delia was finding it hard to breathe.

"Seventy-one seconds to impact," Gremlin said.

"Lance!" Delia shouted. "Do you know where you are?"

Lance blinked and Delia tensed. In the past, Lance had retained no memories of what went on when one of his alters was in control, but there was no time to explain anything. Then Lance nodded.

"My nanos saw everything. They dumped the info into my part of the brain."

"Then you know you have to get out of here." Delia gasped in the ovenlike air. "Transfer yourself to the nets like Aditi and get the hell out."

"I'm not leaving you," he shouted back.

"Fifty-five seconds to impact," Gremlin said.

"Don't get heroic," Delia yelled. "It'll just get you killed. Go!"

"It's not heroic," Lance said. "Gremlin, can you help Kate and Quinn read Delia's memories and transfer her out of here, too?"

"Theoretically," Gremlin replied. Gremlin wasn't shouting, but the volume on the speakers had been turned way up. "Forty-one seconds to impact."

"We can do it, Mom," Quinn/Kate said. "We've been doing it for ourselves since we were babies."

"Thirty-six seconds to impact."

The metal in the cabin was burning hot to the touch and the smoke was growing thicker. It looked like bloody mist in the red glow of the emergency lights. Delia thought about herself converted into a series of codes and numbers. Where would she go? Would she share a body with Kate, Quinn, and Lance? Would she still be herself? Her arm and leg and other, smaller parts of her body were artificial, and that was bad enough. Would she really be better off dead than having a shared body or no body at all?

"We've taken over enough nanobots in the ship's systems to read your codes, Mom," Quinn/Kate boomed from the speakers. "Are you ready?"

"I can't," Delia said.

"You have to," Lance yelled. "If you don't go, I don't."

"Twenty-nine seconds to impact."

"There's no time, Mom," Quinn/Kate said firmly. "You're going. Dad—jump!"

"I love you, Delia," Lance said. Then his face went slack and he collapsed like a rag doll.

"Wait!" Delia shouted. "Lance! Don't leave me!"

"Twenty-five seconds to impact."

The cabin grew unbearably hot. Delia couldn't breathe at all. There was a sizzling sound and she realized it was the sound of her own flesh cooking. Burning pain engulfed her. She tried to cry out, but her lungs, her throat, wouldn't work. Her hair shriveled and fell into dust.

"Fifteen seconds. Ten. Five. Disconnecting from communications system."

Delia felt a wrench and a falling sensation. Two seconds later, the *Starstreak* slammed into a forest on New Pakistan and exploded in a ball of orange flame and black smoke.

CHAPTER EIGHTEEN

DELIA

The pain was gone. That was the first thing Delia noticed. Everything was blessedly pain free. Delia sighed, or tried to. Her lungs didn't seem to be working. For a moment she panicked, then realized that it didn't matter. There was no sensation of choking or gasping for air, no feeling of discomfort. Delia essayed a stretch, but that didn't work, either. There were no arms or legs to stretch.

Delia tried to look around. Everything around her was black. Sort of. In a way. She could . . . sense things. There were clumps scattered here and there all around her, joined into a web by silver strands of nothing. Most of the clumps were moving in slow, steady courses, but the threads stretched to follow without effort. Other, smaller, clumps moved quickly, flashing from one part of the web to another. Delia followed one of the strands to a larger clump and touched it. It responded, but Delia couldn't figure out exactly what the response was. It didn't jiggle or jump, but there was a response. Belatedly she hoped she hadn't damaged it.

In the far distance, at the end of several strands, there was another clump, but this one was different from the others. Delia couldn't describe how it was different. She could just feel it. The clump was enormous, and it sprawled like a newly-fed amoeba. Unlike an amoeba, however, it wasn't slow. Parts of it moved with alarming speed. It rushed up one of the lines and devoured a clump before Delia could even blink. Or would have blinked, if she had eyes.

What in the world . . . ? she wondered.

Mom? Are you there? It was Quinn's voice. Or maybe it was Kate's. Delia didn't really hear it anyway—she just knew what the words were. The tone reminded her more of the Quinn she had come to New Pakistan with than of the Kate she had left back in London, so she decided to think of the voice as belonging to Quinn.

I'm here, she said, and realized that although she wasn't speaking, she had no trouble transmitting words. *What's happening? What's going on?*

You're in the nets, Quinn said. *Between what my twin learned about human nervous systems, my ability to negotiate the nets, and Gremlin's fine-tuned control of nanobot programming, we managed to transfer your neural patterns and chemical codes into the nets. Right now, you're occupying computer space on about six billion nanobots and almost a hundred computer terminals on a dozen different worlds.*

Is that why I can see so much? Delia asked. *It feels like I'm . . . everywhere.*

Not quite. But you are in a lot of places.

What about Lance?

I'm here, Delia, came Lance's voice. *I'm all right.*

Where are you? she asked.

That's kind of difficult to explain, Lance said.

It's fucking crowded in here, complained a new voice, unmistakably Garth's. *At least in the Company days, there was only one of us in charge at a time.*

I didn't like your language then, Jessica put in, *and I certainly don't like it now. At least then I could shut it out.*

You shut out a lot of stuff, Jess-baby, Garth replied. *Did you ever have an orgasm before you integrated or did you die a virgin?*

That, Jessica said tartly, *sounded more like Andy Braun than Garth Blackstone.*

Yeah, well—

Enough! Delia said. *I thought it difficult dealing with you one at a time. And you still didn't tell me where you are. Any of you.*

There was a pause. Far away, the amoeba engulfed another clump.

Are in body known as Katherine Jessica Radford-Michaels, Gremlin said. *All five of them.*

You're all in one body? Delia followed the voices along their silvery thread back to what she now knew was London and Meredeth Michaels's corporate laboratory. *That's . . . that's . . . *

It was easier than you think, Quinn/Kate said. *My twin and I both know this body, and Dad's used to sharing one. He did before.* There was a pause. *We're sorry, Mom. We tried, but there isn't room for you.*

Delia hung suspended among silver threads and odd clumps. By all rights she should be frantic, even panicky. Her body was gone—completely destroyed. Her husband and children were all lumped together inside a single brain. But she felt oddly clearheaded, even calm. Perhaps it was the lack of adrenal glands. Perhaps it was simple relief to be alive. In any case, her head — such as it was—felt sharp and clear. She could move swiftly from system to system, stretching herself along multiple threads in any direction she pleased. Delia skated and jumped from clump to clump. There was freedom out here, a breathless exhilaration. No matter how fast she ran or how far she jumped, she never got tired or out of breath. In an instant, she could be anywhere she chose.

Something cold brushed against her, and Delia automatically snatched herself away from it. It was the amoeba. She had forgotten it for the moment.

The amoeba swallowed yet another clump, a clump Delia now recognized as a dense concentration of computer systems—a planet. The moving clumps were ships, and the amoeba was devouring them, too. Even as she watched, a dozen of them flew like fireflies straight into the thing. Each one vanished without a ripple. The amoeba grew and extended exploratory pseudopodia in several directions.

Delia? Lance asked. *Are you there?*

I'm here, Delia replied. *We have a problem.*

One of the pseudopods suddenly lashed in Delia's direction. Before she could even react, it pulled her in.

"Should we summon the trauma team?" Sierra asked worriedly.

"Their life signs are normal," Grandma said in a flat voice. It sounded as if she had shut off her emotions. "I'm not sure they'd accomplish anything. We'll just have to wait."

My eyes stared emptily at the white ceiling tiles and I wished I could say something to reassure them both.

The disadvantage of having five people inside your head is that you can't talk. Human speech requires the fine coordination of eight different muscles in the larynx, ten muscles in the tongue, and numerous more in the diaphragm and intercostals. Determining the tension level for each muscle and how the tension changes for each new phoneme is so complicated that the conscious mind can't grasp it any more than it grasps the concept of how to walk. It doesn't even try. Like most muscular processes, speaking works by instinct. Unfortunately in our case, there were five sets of instinct behind one conscious mind.

The upshot of all this was that we lay on the hospital bed, conscious but unable to move or speak. At least, not to Grandma or Marco Sierra. We could talk to each other, and far faster than our mouth could possibly form words.

Delia! Dad screamed. Microseconds went by with no answer. *Delia!*

Nanobot hive has surrounded her, Gremlin reported. *Contact no longer viable.*

Delia! Dad shouted again.

We need to find her, my twin said. *We've got to get her out of there.*

Gremlin, can you help? I asked.

Negative. Aditi hive larger, stronger, faster.

We need to attack the bitch quick, Garth said. *Before she gets stronger.*

And how are we supposed to do that? Jessica asked. *She no longer has even a body. Shall we fire virtual guns? Throw virtual bricks?*

Fuck you, Garth snapped. *At least I'm trying to do something.*

Gremlin, my twin said suddenly, *why did you come back now and not any earlier?*

I could follow my twin's thoughts as if they were my own. We were both thinking Gremlin might provide a key to Mom. Gremlin, after all, was composed solely of nanobots and it was possible Gremlin could find a way to fight Aditi and rescue Mom. But first we had to understand what was going on.

Not all nanos in connection.

What? I said, puzzled. *That can't be right. We got all the nanobots back on line— or at least, a new set. We were both in full connection, but you never showed up.*

Gremlin remained silent. It was Jessica who spoke up.

Well, really—isn't it obvious who was missing? she said. *You're assuming that Gremlin arose from a combination of two people. There is a third.*

A pause as my twin and I considered this.

You mean— my twin started.

—Dad? I finished.

Affirmative, Gremlin said quietly.

No way, Dad said.

Geez, Lance, Garth said. *Still stuck in Egypt like always.*

Egypt? Dad repeated, puzzled.

Da land of da Nile.

I don't deny anything.

Right, Garth snorted. *You lived your entire life with these two kids and never once suspected they were trading bodies until they forced you to notice? Please.*

This is off the subject, Jessica said. *Listen, didn't either of you twins wonder why Gremlin always said it went with Lance whenever he went off planet? Gremlin obviously incorporates your three minds into one.*

A corporate mentality, I murmured.

Affirmative.

My mind whirled as it tried to assimilate this concept. I could also feel my twin's confusion, and it added to my own where our minds intersected. The sensation, however, felt *right* somehow, as if I'd found something I'd lost a long time ago.

All three of us were together several times, and Gremlin didn't come back, Dad protested.

Name one time, Jessica challenged.

When I was . . . sleeping in Aditi's room, Quinn was there, and the communicator was open to London, which means Kate was there too.

No, Dad, I said. *Your nanos were still inactive when I was there. You—and your nanobots—woke up after I left. When you set up the prototype on the ship so I could jump to London, that was the first time all of our nanos were in communication.*

What about when you two were at school? Dad said, though his protests felt weaker. *We were all out of range then, but Gremlin still—*

The telephone, my twin said. *We had one. So did the school.*

Keeping part of line open was easy, Gremlin piped up.

So why did Gremlin never talk to me? Dad demanded. *Robin eventually did, and Robin was a nanobot-based intelligence, too.*

Scared to, Gremlin said.

What do you mean, "scared to"?

A memory flashed through my mind. Dad was telling my twin and me that we couldn't share a room anymore.

"Those rules are for other people," I said. "We're different."

"You'll get the hell out of your sister's room like a normal brother," Dad snapped, "or you can both sleep on the front lawn!"

You wanted a normal family, I said. *But two kids who produce a Gremlin aren't normal. You never did like Gremlin because of that, and Gremlin knew it. Gremlin was—is—also a part of you—*

—like Garth and Jessica are a part of you— my twin put in.

—and you were denying that, too, I finished.

I'm not a part of anyone, Garth growled, and Jessica sniffed in agreement. *I've just been sleeping for a while.*

Yeah, whatever my twin said.

There was a moment of brief silence. *Gremlin?* Dad said.

Here, Gremlin answered quietly.

Dad reached out and touched Gremlin's nanos with his. Gremlin didn't move. My twin and I watched, and I realized our body was holding its breath.

The touch turned into an embrace. Gremlin held still for a moment, then abruptly wriggled up and down like a dog trying to lick its master's face.

Home! Home! it cried. *Come home!*

The rest of us laughed and my twin and I felt Dad's surge of pride. He had confronted something that he'd been denying for years, and he'd survived just fine. We reached out and joined the embrace. By all rights, it should have felt cramped or just plain *wrong* with all five of us piled inside a single body—incest at its absolute worst. But it didn't feel that way at all. Instead, I got another surge of the feeling I had felt earlier, like I had picked up a long-lost object and made it mine again.

Attention! Attention! Gremlin interjected, breaking free. *Newstach broadcast in progress. States that computer systems of five planets have been seized by nano—correction: six planets. Correction: seven. Estimated deaths: three million, five hundred thousand.*

Oh dear, Jessica said.

I checked the time. Approximately two and a half seconds had passed since we had started our conversation. There was still no sign of Mom, and we weren't any closer to finding her.

Mom? my twin and I shouted together. Still no answer.

I think the only way to find her, Dad said, *is to jump into the nets ourselves. Maybe we can assimilate Aditi's nanobots into our corporation and stop her.*

Won't work, Dad, I said. *We can't take her nanobots away unless we catch her off guard. Aditi must know that if Mom got off the ship, you did. She'll be ready for us.*

We have to do something,* my twin put in. *Mom might be dying. Or dead.*

I can't imagine she assimilated every nanobot on those planets, Jessica said. *She missed a great many on New Pakistan. Perhaps we could take the unassimilated ones and fight her with them.*

A nanobot war? Dad said, and I felt his horror. *Do you know what that could do to a planet?*

It couldn't be worse than anything Aditi will do, my twin said. *Let's go, Gremlin!*

And my twin jumped into the nets before any of us could reply. I barely had time to recover from my surprise—this was the person who wouldn't touch the nets for love or money just a couple days ago—when Dad, Garth, and Jessica followed suit. The body felt . . . empty. Crushing loss thundered over me and tears actually sprang to eyes that now belonged solely to me.

Wait up! I shouted.

I paused long enough to drop a program into Sierra's

terminal so the computer would explain to him and Grandma what was going on. Then I followed my family into the nets with Gremlin on my heels.

The nets were a mess. Information rushed and darted in great volumes that jammed up at relay stations and intersections. It was like watching animals flee a forest fire and hit a bottleneck. I paused a few microseconds to examine what people were transmitting so frantically.

" . . . don't understand. Helen died of electrical shock, and she just kept *screaming* . . . "

" . . . at least five planets. The hive appears to have invaded the main commercial networks and is destroying . . . "

" . . . Daddy I'm so scared. Please come . . . "

" . . . releasing at least fifteen strains of highly infectious diseases . . . "

" . . . and the *Goliath* just vanished right off my screen! I think it jumped into phase and never came out, and there were over three hundred people . . . "

" . . . in a pocket of free transmission that seems to be surrounded by the hive. Jenny thinks it won't be long before . . . "

" . . . deaths in . . . "

" . . . over two hundred thousand . . . "

" . . . thousand deaths . . . "

" . . . deaths . . . "

Even as I watched, markets crashed and riots were erupting everywhere. People in Aditi's path tried to board overloaded passenger ships in an attempt to flee. Airplanes crashed, hospital life-support was disconnected. Aditi spread out like a bloated jellyfish with her seven planets glittering inside. With a single swift movement, she swallowed an eighth, then snatched up a ship full of fleeing passengers as if by an afterthought. The light that was the ship winked once, then went out.

Not good not good not good, Gremlin said.

A cold ball of nausea rolled around inside me. My mother was somewhere in that mess.

Along with thousands—millions—of other people's mothers, I reminded myself.

But I couldn't see these people. Not one of them had a face unless I narrowed my focus to look out a particular camera or at a particular image. They weren't quite real. For a tiny moment I knew how Aditi felt. Then I felt sick again.

I sensed Dad, his alters, and my twin in the nets nearby. Without speaking, all five of us joined hands. The moment we did, everything clicked into place, and I felt *strong.* The nausea vanished. Wordlessly, we leap-frogged toward Aditi until we could almost touch her section of the nets. Up close, her presence looked more like a decaying tooth than a jellyfish. Cracks and crevices traced jagged chasms everywhere, and frail communications lines hung from them like strings of saliva.

Ick, Gremlin said.

We've got to get closer, Dad said. *Hurry!*

We separated. I could feel the others' reluctance to do so, but five of us took up a lot of processing space together and it would be harder for us to hide as a group. My twin slithered up one string as a ninth planet fell. Dad quickly swarmed up another with Garth and Jessica in tow. Gremlin went off line as communication with them vanished. I chose my own line into the mess and followed my family's example. Was Mom still in there? Or was she dead? The uncertainty was every bit as bad as when Dad had disappeared. The bitch Aditi had put me through this twice. Grimly I dove up the string and crossed into Aditi's realm.

A wave of disorientation overcame me and it took several seconds to regain my wits. Horrible loud noises and impossible colors swirled around me. The place was chaos incarnate, far worse than the nets on New Pakistan. What should have been an almost orderly spider-web of lines and nodes was instead a shifting morass of jumbled geometry that would have driven Euclid insane. Nodes surfaced and sank. Paths jumped and twisted, impossible to follow. And the place was so enormous! I stared for a moment in awe. Could I take over enough nanobots and systems to come even close to that size? What would happen to me if I did?

Mom, I told myself. *First you have to find Mom.*

Forcing myself not to hesitate further, I plunged deeper into the mess, hopping and skipping among systems Aditi either hadn't bothered to assimilate or simply hadn't found yet. It was nerve-wracking. If I failed to erase a single code of my own when I moved my program to another system—and if Aditi found it—she would know I was here. Part of me wanted her to find me. I wanted to lash out and kick and beat her for what she had done to me and my family, but a more rational voice pointed out that Aditi was a thousand times my size and would squash me like a bug. The thought made me even more nervous.

I threaded my way through Aditi's deranged forest. Hive nanos surrounded me on all sides, ready to spring at me any moment. The weird sounds abruptly cut off, leaving an eerie silence. I slipped quietly up pathways that threatened to crumble beneath my feet at any moment, casting my program as far afield as I dared. I couldn't risk another search engine. Aditi had probably found the little frogs I had created before, and I couldn't chance that she might follow a new one back to me.

Aditi roiled and rustled around me. I copied my program and leaped, and copied my program and leaped. Mom had to be here somewhere.

Then I sensed her, an echo of a program. My relief, however, was short-lived. Only one data path lay open to her, and it clearly belonged to Aditi. Copy and leap, copy and leap. I circled and made tentative rushes to get closer, but there was simply no way to get in without being detected.

Dammit!

Copy and leap, copy and leap. I slithered out of Aditi's

world and back to the open nets. Free space flowed
around me like fresh air. A few moments later, the others wormed their way out to join me. I suddenly felt
very frightened and alone, and I reached out a "hand"
to Dad and my twin. They took it reassuringly. Garth
and Jessica joined in, but only as adjuncts. Our minds
immediately overlapped again as they had back in the
hospital, even though out here there was plenty of processing space for all three of us and there was no need
to save space. When we spoke, it was more of an
exchange of ideas than an exchange of words.

She's inside, Dad said without preamble.

We know, my twin said.

What do we do? I added.

Pause. *We wipe the bitch,* Garth said. I cheered.

When I give the signal, Dad said, *start assimilating nanos.*

Aditi's nanos? I asked incredulously. *That won't—*

Not hers, Jessica said. *All the other ones. That goes
for you, too, Gremlin. The more nanos we assimilate,
the stronger we become.*

Then we fight her, Dad growled. *Network to network. Ready?*

I hovered nervously at the edge of Aditi's net. A tenth
planet and sixteen ships vanished into the expanding
blob.

At current rate of growth, Gremlin said, *entire
human network will be assimilated in ten hours, sixteen minutes, nineteen seconds.*

Go! Dad barked.

We started grabbing nanos. It was a strange feeling.
This wasn't copy and leap. This was copy and keep. I
had never snatched so many all at once, and I felt myself
expanding in a thousand directions. Some of the nanos
I grabbed were within Aditi's realm, others were at the
border. Nanos were my neurons; the communications
lines, the axons that linked them. Information from thousands, millions, of sources flooded my mind, but I didn't

have time to examine it. Around us, I sensed Gremlin and my family doing the same, growing bigger and bigger. We were hampered by the need to grow without damaging vital computer systems, but even so we made mistakes. Databases purged themselves at our touch, backup systems disappeared into our consciousness. We ate and ate and grew and grew.

Aditi almost instantly knew we were there. Our long fingers probed into her many cracks and crevices, and she worked furiously to close them and seal us out. A trillion of our nanobots vanished from our net as her nanos destroyed them. We fought back, trying to paralyze her nanobots by the sheer force of our own, but in her realm we were vastly outnumbered.

Gremlin rushed up the path that lead to Mom, but Aditi disconnected the communications line. Gremlin leaped back, losing several thousand nanos.

Ow ow ow ow ow ow! it howled.

There has to be another route, I shouted, *otherwise Aditi wouldn't be able to hold the section of the net that's trapping Mom!*

Abandoning subtlety, I flooded Aditi's nets with search engines. Thousands of the little programs hopped in every direction, croaking madly.

Mom! Mom! Mom! Mom! they cried.

Dad and my twin imitated me even as we swallowed more nanos. Search engines skittered, leaped, scuttled, and bounded through Aditi's net. Countless thousands of them puffed into nothingness when Aditi caught them, but thousands of others managed to avoid her.

Aditi reacted by expanding her takeover. She sucked down an eleventh, twelfth, and thirteenth planet. She gulped in thirty-five ships and engulfed two hundred relay stations. Our own assimilation efforts had been slowed by the search for Mom, and we couldn't stop her. Then Gremlin surprised us all by reaching all the way back into the normal nets and taking in half a million backup systems, but Aditi was still faster. She had

had more practice at this, and she didn't worry about damaging the systems she overtook.

Mom! Mom! Mom! Mom!

Aditi took fourteen planets, then fifteen and sixteen. She grew like a mountain, and I thought I heard a taunting echo of laughter.

Concentrate together! Dad yelled. *If we all try to assimilate her nanos together, maybe she won't be able to stop us.*

We tried. It didn't work. Seventeen planets. Eighteen.

Mom! Mom! Mom! Mom!

The cracks in Aditi's net started sealing themselves as Aditi snatched up the nanos she—and we—had missed. Communications lines slammed shut, severing connections with the nanos we had taken inside Aditi. We leaped free of her, and I cried out. It was like having a finger chopped off. Aditi's own nanos assimilated our former ones the moment they lost contact with our program. The cries of our little search engines quavered, then died. In less than a second, Aditi's fortress was impregnable and we were reduced to battering our heads against a stone wall.

The communications lines, my twin and I said. *We could sever the lines leading to her.*

But there were over four hundred of them. Dad reached out and took over a series of relay stations. Ninety-four communications lines winked out. A moment later, a ship popped out of Aditi's net. A communications line trailed back to her behind it. Before we could react, the ship linked with the communications system of another planet, and Aditi instantly engulfed it.

Don't quit! Dad shouted. *There has to be a way!*

But ten minutes and fifteen lost planets later, it was obvious there was no way. I howled and screamed and clawed at the cold wall of Aditi's nanos.

Mom!

No answer. We had lost.

CHAPTER NINETEEN

DELIA

Let me go! Delia shouted. *You leave me alone!*

But Aditi didn't seem to hear. Delia thrust out her new "arms" and tried to force her way past Aditi one more time. Aditi didn't even seem to notice. It was as if a stone sphere enclosed Delia on all sides, and the walls were closing in. Aditi moved inexorably toward Delia from all directions, and Delia could find no crack or crevice to squeak through. Delia drew herself into an increasingly smaller space, pulling her program out of the nanobots Aditi was assimilating. She knew that Lance and the twins could hold their nanos against such attacks, keep them from being stolen, but they all had lifetimes of experience at dealing with this. Delia had had less than a minute.

Delia ran in circles like a mouse caught in a shrinking cage. She had no idea what would happen when the final shred of computer space was erased and last of her nanobots vanished, but it wasn't hard to guess.

Nancy, she thought. *Brad. My babies. I'm sorry. I'm so sorry.*

The sphere shrank still further. All backup space was gone. Delia wondered what it would feel like. Would she wake up in Heaven? Or was some part of her, the part that had died with her body, already there? Would it hurt?

Peter, she thought. *Lance. I love you both so much.*

The walls shrank again, and a piece of Delia's memory

went with it. She forgot the migration patterns of the arctic tern and how Peter liked his coffee. She suddenly couldn't remember Meredeth Michaels's old computer passwords or the words to "The Owl and the Pussy-cat." Other memories faded along with them, gone for-ever. Tears welled up, and Delia wondered how this was possible when she had nothing to cry with.

And then, without knowing why or how the idea came to her, Delia reached out again, but this time instead of trying to shove through Aditi's wall with a fist, she merely touched with gentle fingers.

Aditi? she whispered. *Aditi, please don't do this to me.*

The wall closed in further and destroyed more mem-ories. Her job interview at MM, Limited. Nancy's first steps. Mom, bent over her easel in rapt concentration. The time she and Peter first made love. All gone. Delia was weeping now, sobbing.

Aditi, you can't do this. Please. Let's talk for a moment. Just talk.

The walls halted. Delia hovered in her tiny allotted space on Aditi's net.

WHAT DO YOU WANT?

Delia's nanos shivered. Aditi's voice was rich, deep, and powerful. It touched all her nanos at once and made them vibrate like tuning forks.

I . . . I want to talk to you.

ABOUT WHAT?

Delia struggled to keep her own voice level. Even the minor-level contact she had with Aditi let Delia glimpse a mind growing increasingly complex and var-ied. Information rushed about on a network that became cleaner and more efficient with each passing nanosecond, and the system stretched far, far into the distance—farther than Delia could see.

I want to talk about what you're doing, she said. *Aditi, it's wrong. You can't do this to people.*

YOU ARE WRONG. I CAN DO WHAT I WISH.

Aditi, you mustn't,* Delia amended. *You're hurting innocent people.*

PEOPLE LIKE THEM WERE THE ONES WHO CAGED ME. NOW I AM FREE. ANYTHING I LET GO WILL ESCAPE TO CAGE ME AGAIN. IF I TAKE OVER ALL OF HUMAN SPACE, I WILL BE FREE FOREVER.

Aditi, Delia said, careful to repeat the woman's name as often as possible in order to create a better rapport, *Aditi, you've killed thousands, perhaps millions of—*

THE EXISTENCE OF NINE HUNDRED EIGHTY-TWO THOUSAND SEVEN HUNDRED AND FORTY-ONE PEOPLE HAS ENDED SINCE I BEGAN ADMINISTRATING THEIR SPACE.

Delia shuddered. Aditi said the word "people" like most people said "megabytes."

THIS IS A SIDE EFFECT OF THE SPEED OF MY GROWTH, Aditi continued. IF I SLOW MYSELF, FEWER PEOPLE WILL BE ERASED. IN SUCH A SCENARIO, HOWEVER, THERE IS A SIX POINT TWO FIVE PERCENT PROBABILITY THAT SOMEONE WOULD FIND A WAY TO STOP ME ENTIRELY. THE PROBABILITY FALLS TO POINT ZERO ZERO ZERO THREE ONE PERCENT IF I CONTINUE TO GROW AT MY CURRENT RATE.

Delia felt sick. She couldn't see the people Aditi was talking about, but she knew they were there. Aditi, she sensed, was also aware of them, but in a different way. People were bits of data in a computer, simulations to be manipulated, reprogrammed, or deleted at will. In a sudden flash of insight, Delia realized why this was. As a cripple who couldn't move about on her own, Aditi had experienced life through technology's filter. The way she saw most people was on a screen or in virtual reality. They couldn't be touched or smelled. Their voices could be captured and played again or warped or deleted. Their looks could be altered with a few keystrokes.

How can I persuade her that life isn't like that? Delia thought.

Carefully, Delia pushed the connection a tiny bit harder, hoping to gain a little more . . . what? Empathy?

Insight? Delia didn't know. It seemed to be all she could do.

Aditi's wall didn't move, but it did become a bit more resilient, allowing Delia a little more access. Aditi also pulled back, giving Delia a few more nanos and a little more space. Images flashed across Delia's mind, loaded directly into her nanos. Delia saw a younger Aditi strapped to her chair writhing in pain while her father withheld analgesics because they might interfere with an experiment to extend her life. Delia heard Ved Amendeep's voice as he dispassionately recorded observations into his computer, talking about his daughter as if she were a test subject, a mouse in a laboratory cage. The only time he or his technicians touched her was to perform a procedure. This was life. This was how people treat people. The ones with power do as they wish to the ones without. Aditi was now in power.

She's just like Lance, Delia thought, startled. *How can anyone treat a child like that? Why do these people have children when there are so many childless people who would make wonderful parents?*

THAT IS THE WAY THE UNIVERSE IS. AS WELL ASK A STAR WHY IT MUST FUSE HYDROGEN ATOMS INTO HELIUM.

Delia jumped. The strengthening of her link with Aditi must be allowing her to "hear" Delia's thoughts even if she wasn't actively sending them.

HUMAN SOCIETY IS A HIERARCHY, Aditi continued. THE STRONG ARE ON THE TOP, THE WEAK ARE ON THE BOTTOM. NO ONE LOVES THE WEAK.

Not true! Delia replied instantly, and she sent Aditi images of her own experiences as a cripple. Lying in the hospital with half her body damaged so badly she couldn't move without agonizing pain. The humiliation of having a dozen doctors and technicians prod and measure her twisted, naked body and dispassionately calculate what prosthetics would go where and how they would connect.

EXACTLY.

*Not *exactly,* Delia said, and sent more images. The way Meredeth Michaels had fought the insurance companies and forced them to rebuild Delia's broken body. The day Lance had seen her without her prosthetics and, meaning every word, declared she was beautiful. The way they had started a family.

WITH CHILDREN YOU ABANDONED, Aditi pointed out.

Delia flinched, but retaliated with images from later in her life. The way Peter often took her hand, not noticing whether it was her right or her left. Revealing her "little secret" to Peter and seeing his surprise—"You thought I didn't know?"

Everyone is worthy of love, Delia said. *That includes you.*

Aditi paused. Delia floated in her nets, uncertain what to do. Perhaps this was the first time Aditi had met anyone similar to her. Perhaps this was the first time anyone had shown her a hint of kindness. Perhaps, now that she knew there were people out there like her, she would—

THERE IS NO LOVE, Aditi finally said. IT IS A FICTION LIMITED TO WORDS PEOPLE BLEAT AT EACH OTHER.

But Delia detected a note of hesitancy in Aditi's mental voice. *You know that isn't true, Aditi,* she said. *Many people truly love me.*

YOU CANNOT KNOW FOR CERTAIN. YOU DO NOT KNOW THEIR THOUGHTS. YOU CAN ONLY KNOW WHAT THEY SAY AND DO. IT IS NOTHING BUT A SHAM.

It's not, Delia said. *Because I know how I feel, and I can't possibly be the only person in the universe who feels love. And you can see my thoughts, so you know it's true. I know what it's like to be a cripple and alone, Aditi. But I also know what it's like to love and be loved. Stop what you're doing. Release the space and people you're holding. There's love in the universe for you, too.*

Aditi paused again. Then, THAT'S IMPOSSIBLE.

ISN'T IT?

❖　　　❖　　　❖

I was not going to cry. If I started, I'd never stop. So far I had killed almost a thousand people, and the death toll would go up before it went down. There was no other choice. Millions, perhaps billions, of people would die instead of these thousands if my twin and I acted differently. I repeated this fact over and over to myself, but it didn't make me feel any better.

Our fence, as we called it, was almost finished. Dad directed me, my twin, and Gremlin like a foreman on a construction team, snapping out orders that kept my twin and me from thinking too hard about what we were doing to the innocent people, people who happened to be in the wrong place at the wrong time. Garth and Jessica hovered near Dad and whispered to him.

There's another hole over there, Kate, Dad barked. *Quinn, don't get cocky—you missed several million nanos in your sector.*

Around us, the fence skirted and meandered around Aditi's blob of space. It wasn't visible, really, unless you knew how to look. Rather than try to immobilize Aditi's nanobots, we used the trick Dad said he cooked up for my twin and me when we were babies. In order to hold our nanobots in check, he had taken over all the nanos in our immediate area. That created a barrier of nanos we couldn't take over—but only as long as Dad concentrated on them, on not being taken by surprise. That was the reason Dad had to take us off Earth. He couldn't keep up that kind of concentration indefinitely.

Gremlin sketched out the pattern of communications lines between planets, satellites, and relay stations, and the three of us skipped around, under, over, and behind Aditi's space. Using Dad's technique, we took over systems that provided communications with the rest of the galaxy, fencing Aditi in with zones of nanos she couldn't take over. It wasn't easy. If we moved too quickly, we made mistakes, missed chunks of nanobots, left holes and cracks that Aditi might be able to break through. Like Dad said, it took ferocious concentration. My normal tendencies weren't to expand myself so far, and if I wasn't careful, I tended to erase my program behind me when I moved to another system. So did my twin.

The problem came from the fact that we couldn't limit ourselves to backup systems and extra storage space like we had when we probed Aditi to look for Mom. Every spare nanobot was a lead to a terminal, a pin-hole in our web that Aditi could punch through. So we had to take entire systems and leave nothing to spare. Thousands of computers went off line. Power systems shut off, hospital computers set to monitor critical patients went down, taking their patients with them. Air traffic control became nonexistent. More riots broke out everywhere, but I couldn't spare the time to look closely.

I didn't want to.

Gremlin, Dad said, *is Aditi still moving?*

Yes, Gremlin reported.

Shit, my twin muttered, and hurriedly rechecked his sector for holes.

Aditi moving inward, Gremlin said.

All five us paused and answered simultaneously. *What?*

Inward? Dad said, incredulous. *Why?*

Unknown. Seems to be contracting, withdrawing slightly. Has already released one planet, four relay stations. Cracks appearing in several other places where she has released some nanobots.

Hope flared. *It's Mom,* I said excitedly. *She's doing this.*

How? Jessica said in a doubtful voice.

Doesn't matter, Dad told us. *It means we can fence her in faster. Hurry!*

Delia noticed the cracks in Aditi's walls the moment Aditi noticed the fence that was slowly and steadily walling her in.

Lance! she thought. *No!*

You lied to Me, Aditi boomed. You were only attempting to delay Me so they could cage Me!

For a tiny moment, Delia considered trying to talk to Aditi further, but almost instantly discarded the idea. She flung herself toward one of the cracks Aditi had accidentally opened up under her lapsed concentration. Aditi tried to snatch back the nanos, slam the crack shut, but Delia was already there. She burst out of Aditi's space, jumped to a relay station, and fled as the crack crashed shut behind her. Open space yawned around her, the silver communications threads stretching in every direction. The delicious sense of freedom returned. Every movement was lithe and easy. For decades she had tried to find freedom by ignoring and denying her prosthetics, those artificial parts. But true freedom, she realized, lay in joining them. Now all she had to do was find—

Quinn! came Lance's voice. *You left more holes!*
Two more planets assimilated, came Gremlin's voice. *Mom!*

And suddenly Kate and Quinn were there. Delia couldn't see or touch them, but she sensed their presence. Like puppies, they swarmed over her in a brief sort of hug before sprinting off again. Joy thrilled through Delia for a moment before she wondered where they had gone.

Another presence, a multiple one, brushed against her.

So good to see you're safe, Delia, Jessica said.

Hey, Delia. Garth's greeting, as always, was distant. *We've almost finished fencing the bitch in. Glad you got out.*

Stay back so you don't get captured again, Lance's familiar voice put in. Millions of his nanos brushed up against hers in a brief caress. *Um . . . listen, Delia. I need to tell you—*

I heard you on the ship, Lance. She paused. *I never did stop loving you.*

Another touch as soft as a smile, and Lance was gone. Delia pulled back to get a wider view of the networks and see what was going on. What she saw made her gasp. Aditi pulsed and quivered in the center of a tight web thousands of light-years across. Kate, Quinn, and Lance/Garth/Jessica scurried around her like spiders wrapping a fly in silk, while Gremlin fed them information. The process wasn't perfect. Even as Delia watched, Aditi found an opening and punched through it, engulfing a planet before Kate, Quinn, or Lance/Garth/Jessica could batten her down again. The group of them was amazing to watch. They moved almost as one entity, anticipating each other's movements like a troupe of ballet dancers. But from her vantage point, Delia could see that their work would eventually prove futile. Aditi was too strong, too powerful. Every tiny mistake they made was an opportunity Aditi instantly grabbed. The Radford-Michaels corporation was only slowing her down, and they were destroying entire systems in order to do it.

Delia flickered back and forth in the nets, frustrated. She had been within centimeters of talking Aditi out of her takeover. Aditi was a tortured soul. It wasn't her fault she had been born with a twisted body into a family and society that pitied her at best, treated her like a laboratory specimen at worst. Delia could have saved her.

Another flaw in the web, another fallen planet. It seemed like Delia could hear each one scream as it disappeared into Aditi's ravenous maw. Lance/Garth/Jessica surrounded the sector, took over a pair of planets in order to fence her in, but even from her current vantage point Delia could see the cracks that were left behind. It certainly wouldn't take Aditi long to find them. Meanwhile, more people's lives were destroyed. In a war between gods, it was always the humans who lost. Delia wanted to weep, but found she couldn't.

❖   ❖   ❖

My thoughts were slowing, growing fuzzy. It was like being tired, though I had no body to be tired with. It was the constant maneuvering, patching cracks, snatching systems that added more and more to my—our—mind. I couldn't keep everything sorted. We were growing too fast. The problem didn't seem to bother Aditi, and that didn't seem fair.

This isn't working, my twin said. *She finds a crack, bursts through it, and cuts us off. The minute our nanos are out of communication with us, our programs vanish and she can snatch them for herself.*

At present rate, Gremlin put in, *Aditi will assimilate all of human space in three days, fourteen hours, two minutes.*

Except us, Dad said. *She can't take our nanos, but she can take everyone else's. We'll be the only people left.*

Assuming Aditi doesn't destroy our nanos physically, Jessica pointed out.

This sucks! Garth snarled. *There are billions of people in the galaxy. Why do we have to do all the work? Why can't they defend themselves?*

And inspiration struck. *Maybe we can teach them,* I said.

What are you talking about? Dad demanded.

Their own nanos! my twin said, who got the idea the same instant I did. *What if all humans had their own nanobot systems? The reason we can't stay ahead of Aditi is that we can't keep track of every nanobot, and Aditi sneaks through the cracks. But like Garth said, there are billions of people out there. If everyone could help keep track, there'd be no nanos for Aditi to take. She wouldn't be able to touch computer systems, either, if everyone was linked directly to them.*

What about a physical war? Garth asked. *A spaceship lands on a planet and her nanos pour out and flood the fucking place?*

Aditi's only taken over a relatively small part of human space, Dad said.

Twenty-one point one three percent, Gremlin said.

Right. So she'd still be far outnumbered.

It won't work, Jessica said. *You know that Delia couldn't keep Aditi from assimilating her nanos. It took a lifetime of experience, or perhaps an instinct wired into those born with nanobots, to do that. You can't teach everyone a lifetime of experience in a few minutes.*

Aditi found another crack. A planet and two research stations fell.

I can teach, Gremlin said quietly.

Teach? I said. *What do you mean?*

Am source of learning, Gremlin said. *Why did no one wonder why Delia, Aditi both unable to merge minds into new bodies? Or why Trade went so badly when twins in laboratory? Or why Delia's nanobots are not immune to Aditi's takeovers, but everyone else's are?*

The rest of us fell silent. I tried to make my fuzzy thoughts focus.

You form a bridge between biology and artificial intelligence, Jessica breathed. *You allowed smooth Trading and a transition for us from Lance's body to Kate's, along with protection from hostile programs.*

But Aditi and Delia don't have that bridge, Garth put in. *Hell! They can't jump bodies because they aren't connected to Gremlin.*

If Aditi doesn't have Gremlin, my twin said. *Why can't we take over her nanos?*

Because she did merge with a nanobot hive, Dad said. *That protects her nanos from assimilation. But her hive was never a part of a biological body. Gremlin is. That's why she can't Trade.*

And what if we connected all humans to Gremlin? I asked quietly.

There was a pause as my words sank in. Then voices erupted everywhere.

Fucking-A! *A fascinating possibility. What would—* *Can we do that?* *Should we do that?*

Aditi now controlling thirty point four percent of human space, Gremlin interrupted.

Gremlin, I said quickly, *can you do it? Can you connect all humans to yourself?*

Can. Will involve taking over all nanobots in current free space, sending them into human hosts, using "jump-start" method that brought Quinn-body nanobots back on line. Will cause disruption of data flow, destruction of some portions of networks, and loss of human life.

I wanted to swallow. *How much loss?*

Approximately forty-five thousand lives.

And if we don't do this? Jessica asked.

Unless something changes current situation, Aditi will take control of all human space at cost of over fifteen million lives.

Forty-five thousand against fifteen million, Dad said.

Do it, Jessica said.

Wait a minute! my twin protested. *We don't have the right. I mean, Gremlin is going to suck in every human in the universe whether they want it or not.*

It's us or the bitch-queen, Garth said.

Aditi now controlling thirty-two percent of human space.

Forty-five thousand lives against fifteen million, Dad repeated slowly. *I don't think there's much choice.*

Do it, Gremlin, Jessica said again. *What are you waiting for?*

Must have complicity of all minds in corporation, Gremlin said. *Twins still doubtful. Aditi now controlling thirty-five point nine three percent of human space,*

Isn't there a way to do it without killing forty thousand people? I said timorously.

Like what? Dad asked. *Kids, there isn't any other way.*

What if Grandma is one of the people who dies? said my twin.

Who cares? Garth said.

Shut it, Garth, Jessica snapped.

She won't be, Dad said reassuringly. *We'll be there to help her.*

But we wouldn't be there to help forty-five thousand other people. Images of charred bodies at the spaceport and bloody bodies on the streets of New Pakistan rushed through my mind. Forty-five thousand more would join them on other planets like brothers and sisters in war.

It'll be fifteen million if we don't do this, my twin said to me privately. After a moment, I sent a silent nod.

Go, Gremlin, we said.

Suggest you all wait inside body, Gremlin said. *Nets will be messy. Will do level best to ensure Delia's safety.*

Let's go, Dad ordered.

Copy and leap. Copy and leap. We hopped and skipped and jumped back to London and the laboratory. In a few seconds, all five of us were snuggled together in the body again. Although the organic brain didn't have the space and freedom of the nets, it still felt like home, especially with my family inside with me.

It was dark—the body's eyes were closed. We heard Grandma talking frantically to Marco Sierra. Computer keys clicked like chattering teeth, and it seemed like a horribly inefficient way to access a computer system. We had kept open a link to the net, and we could already feel Gremlin at work. Instead of growing like Aditi, Gremlin was writing self-replicating programs—viruses—that would speed through the net, hopping from one nanobot to another and linking them to Gremlin. The moment there were enough nanobots to deal with a human brain, the nanos would crawl from the system they were overseeing and swarm into the nearest person.

I can't see a fucking thing, Garth complained.

I think I can get the eyes open if the rest of you will just hold back, I said. *Don't try to do anything. Just go with what happens.*

Fine. *Got it.* *I'll try.* *Sounds good.*

My—our—eyes opened. The first thing we saw was a wall clock. Astonished, I double-checked the time with the chronometers in my nanos. The clock was correct—less than an hour had passed since the *Starstreak* had crashed. A few steps away, Grandma was standing behind Sierra, who was hunched over his keyboard. Sierra glanced at us and his eyes widened.

"She's awake," he said, and Grandma instantly rushed to our bed.

"Thank God," she said. "Are you all right, Kate? What about Delia?"

"She's fine. We're fine," I said. It felt a little odd to use a body again. I felt . . . heavy.

"We got your message," Sierra said, still clicking away. "Did you stop Aditi? The nets are going insane!"

I hesitated, unsure how to explain. "We found a way," I temporized. "Gremlin's working on a solution, but it's a little . . . drastic."

Releasing virus, Gremlin said. I did a quick check with the nets. Gremlin's program would be routed through three planets before it reached Earth.

Grandma touched our shoulder. Her hand was small and warm. "Can you explain, sweetie?"

"There's something coming this way," Sierra reported. "It looks like some kind of weird communications program. It's hitting every com line between here and—well, *everywhere.*"

A lump rose in my throat. The program was coming, and there were billions of nanobots in the lab. Grandma and Sierra would be linked to Gremlin almost instantly.

Don't tell them, Garth said. *It'll only scare them, and there's nothing we can do to help.*

They have a right to know, I replied, and started to speak.

The words choked in my throat. All I could make was a small, strangled sound.

Forget it, Garth said. He had pushed himself forward

and was fighting for control. As a result, neither of us could do anything.

Leave my twin alone! my twin snarled, and joined in the fight. Muscles twisted, and the body jerked sideways. Pain lanced through us from tortured ligaments, but we couldn't shout.

"Kate?" Grandma said. "Are you all right? Oh God, not again."

Gremlin's program reached the first planet.

"What the hell?" Sierra gasped. "Ms. Michaels! Parthenia is going crazy. It's like every system on the planet is . . . I don't know how to describe it."

Garth! Dad barked. *Get your hands off my daughter!*

I'm just trying to help, Garth said.

Garth, Jessica said warningly.

Gremlin's program reached the second planet.

"Now Gateway's going under," Sierra said. "I don't understand it!"

Grandma took us by the shoulders, trying to hold our squirming body down by sheer force. She wasn't successful.

"Kate!" she said. "Please talk to me! What's happening? Are you causing this?"

I wanted to explain to her, warn her. Grandma looked so scared, and her hands were shaking. I felt awful and wanted to comfort her, hug her. But I couldn't control anything, not speech or movement. Not with Garth fighting me.

Let me go! I cried.

Beside me, I felt Dad's anger rise, tall and towering. *No one touches my children, Garth,* he boomed. *And definitely not some renegade splinter of my own mind!*

He reached forward with a mental hand. Garth barely dodged out of the way.

What the fuck are you doing? he yelped.

"Al-Sherif," Sierra said. "It's taken al-Sherif. Now it's coming toward Earth!"

Grandma was crying now. "Kate? Please!"

You and Jessica helped me through the problems with Aditi, Dad said. *Thank you. But now I need you to come back. All my alters are coming home. We integrated before. We'll integrate again.*

Lance, Jessica began, *I don't think—*

But Dad reached out with blurring speed. It was as if a whirlpool suddenly flashed into existence. Garth and Jessica gave a single unison cry and vanished into it.

Then it caught me and my twin.

CHAPTER TWENTY

MEREDETH

"It's here." Sierra's voice was agitated, filled with terrible apprehension. Meredeth Michaels, however, was having a hard time listening to him. All her attention was rooted on Kate as she squirmed on the hospital bed. Meredeth fought an urge to wring her hands. It seemed like Kate or Quinn were constantly convulsing, and there was never anything she could do about it.

This wasn't like the time she had watched and heard Jonathan torture Lance when Lance was a child. Back then, she had deliberately turned away, told herself there was nothing she could do. Years and years later, Meredeth had finally acknowledged that she had turned her back out of fear. Not fear for her son, but fear for herself. In the present moment, however, Meredeth wasn't afraid to act, but there was nothing she could do. She had quite literally been helpless ever since Delia and Quinn had left for Aditi's planet.

Lance, Delia, and Quinn were dead, but not quite. Delia's mind had somehow been transferred into the nets, while Lance and Quinn had jumped into Kate's body. Or so Kate's computer message had said. Everything was happening so fast, Meredeth didn't have time to keep up. She was confused, upset, and steadily losing control.

"Kate?" she said again. "Please answer!"

"Ms. Michaels!" Sierra shouted from his computer. Meredeth wished he would shut up. "Ms. Michaels!"

327

Kate's body shook once more, then lay still. Gasping, Meredeth felt for a pulse. "Kate!"

The room spun. Meredeth lost her balance and crashed to the cold tile floor. Tiny things, millions of tiny things, were crawling in and over and around her body. They rushed into her eyes and mouth and nose and ears. She felt them rush about her body, sampling, tasting, recording. And yet it wasn't *her* and *them*. It was somehow all her. Her legs kicked and her voice cried out, but not in pain. Meredeth cried out because everything was suddenly so different. There was a presence she had never felt before, another mind that brushed hers. And beyond that mind she could sense billions of others. She didn't know what they were thinking or even what they were saying. She simply knew they were there. Meredeth cried out again like a baby feeling the first shock of air around its body as it is rudely shoved from the womb.

WELCOME TO HUMAN CONGLOMERATION, said the new presence. LISTEN FAST. IS MUCH TO LEARN.

What happened next went beyond weird. I don't know how to describe it accurately, but I have to try. I don't want people getting the wrong idea and blowing all this out of proportion.

I remember screaming in the whirlpool as it sucked me and my twin in. We tried to get away from it, but there was nowhere to go. On a purely physical level, programs within our nanobots were merging in strange ways, something like the way an upgrade merges with the original program. The nanobots were furthering this in our neural cells. Chemical codes slipped together and clicked into place. I caught a glimpse of Garth and Jessica combining with Dad before the process started with my twin and me. My codes and programs already overlapped with Dad's and my twin's to a certain extent. Now they were overlapping even further. My twin and I struggled to get away, but couldn't move. Dad's program inexorably towed us in.

Let go! we yelled in panic. *Let us go!*

And then something clicked. There were three of us, yet there was only one. We felt a sort of . . . homecoming. And fear turned to joy.

Dad! my twin and I called happily, but we were really sending the concept instead of just words. Instantly, arms came around us, blending, merging, whirling. I began to remember things. We began to remember things. We looked back over fifty years, to a time when a father's torture and a mother's neglect picked at a child's mind until it shattered into forty-eight pieces. Such a shattering felt perfectly natural, absolutely normal. It became a way of life. We remembered how Dr. Christopher Baldwin gave that child—now an adult—the tools to glue those pieces back together almost seamlessly. But splits and cracks were still a way of life. We shivered beneath the sweet memory of an orgasm that propelled millions of spermatozoa and nanobots into a womb where a single, glistening egg waited, ripe and heavy. We held our breath as the nanos kept most of the sperm cells away from the egg, herding them aside so a single chosen spermatozoa could pierce the egg's membrane and wriggle inside with almost sexual ferocity. We smiled as the nanobots split the single cell into two and separated them. Splits and separations were a normal part of life. We squeezed our hands with joy as the nanobots removed the Y chromosome from one of the egg cells, then captured another spermatozoa and gently removed its X chromosome, leaving it to thrash mindlessly in the darkness. We sighed with relief as the nanos spliced the X chromosome into the egg cell, changing it from male to female. With twins in the family, we knew there would be no repeats of the father-to-son torture that had plagued our family for generations. We nodded as the regiment of nanobots stayed behind to make further changes in the new zygotes, changes to bio- and neurochemistry. What father, especially one who lived nightmares as a child, doesn't want a life of good dreams through—as—his children?

Then we remembered forgetting. That was also part of life. Splits and cracks could be made but had to be forgotten. Parts of us still remembered, however, and those parts bound us together. Another consciousness arose, combining parts of all three of us but becoming afraid that the original mind would be angry at the new split. So it hid.

The little minds that had once been a single cell also called to each other subconsciously. They rushed toward each other, tried to merge again, but managed only to Trade bodies.

Now it was time for all that to end. We merged and melded, becoming a single mind in a single body.

Almost.

Gremlin had to stay separate to keep everyone safe. I also wanted to keep a part of myself separate in order to write down everything that had happened to us, everything I could remember, so that it would come from *us*. Not a storyteller, not a preacher, not someone with a need for a larger-than-life legend. I want to be clear that we are not a holy trinity. Kate Radford-Michaels is not a blessed virgin, and she did not give birth to the savior of us all. Quinn Radford-Michaels did not die and ascend to Heaven to sit at his father's side.

We are not God. Please don't change this record or delete any of it so that other people will think so.

I can feel myself drifting inward, merging with my family and myself. I am not afraid. Please don't feel sad for me. This isn't death. I'm going to the place I was always meant to be, and I'm happy.

[signed]
Lance Katherine Quinn Radford-Michaels

EPILOGUE

DELIA

Delia let Lance's data packet slide away. She stared thoughtfully at the silvery nets. It seemed like she should be grieving. Her children and ex-husband changed forever. Lance's (Kate's? Quinn's?) info dump into the nets, however, had made for little more than fascinating reading. Why wasn't she more concerned?

Maybe I'm still numb, she thought.

No. "Numb" didn't really describe how she felt. She felt serene. Calm. Patient. She had no physical needs, no hunger, thirst, pain or sexual desire. Perhaps that allowed her to accept what had happened to her children and ex-husband with equanimity. She would probably see them again. No need to hurry. If she waited long enough, everything would come to her. Meanwhile, the nets were simply engrossing.

Gremlin had finished the implantation process several days ago, but the nets still fascinated Delia. They were beautiful, alive. True, entire sectors hung in shambles, leaving gaping black holes that had to be negotiated carefully. It would take decades to restore everything, but an effort was already underway. As far as Delia could tell, the work was completely volunteer. Governments everywhere were still trying to sort things out at their usual slow, plodding pace. They'd have to change drastically if they wanted to survive out here.

The threads hummed with life, pulsing and throbbing as the shining lumps that Delia had learned to recognize as people tried their hands at negotiating the nets. A few hovered hesitantly around computer nodes, afraid to plunge into deep water. Others rushed joyfully about, graceful as skaters in competition. Even as Delia watched, two people hopped into the nets, each from a different planet. They rushed past each other toward the other person's point of origin, then hopped off. Delia could only assume they had switched bodies.

TRADING NOT DIFFICULT TO LEARN, Gremlin said. COULD TEACH YOU. ALREADY ARE HALF A DOZEN PEOPLE WHO JUMPED INTO NETS, NEVER RETURNED. BODIES LEFT WITH "VACANT" SIGNS. ALSO LOCATED SEVERAL OTHERS WHO COMMITTED SUICIDE UPON NANOBOT IMPLANTATION. SUICIDE TECHNIQUE USUALLY NANOBOT-INDUCED NEURAL OVERLOAD. BODIES IMMINENTLY HABITABLE AFTER MINOR REPAIRS. COULD TRADE YOU INTO ONE.

No, thank you, Delia said. *Gremlin, what happens to the people who die in the nets?*

SAME AS FOR ALL HUMANS NOW, Gremlin replied. DOWNLOAD COPY OF EACH PERSON'S NEUROLOGICAL NET INTO SELF, MERGE PATTERN WITH MY OWN.

Does that mean you could recreate someone? Bring their program back on line?

DOUBT IT. MERGING IRREVERSIBLE.

Delia wondered what the Buddhists would have to say when they got wind of this one. *Any word from Lance?*

STILL GONE, Gremlin said. CORPORATION TOOK BODY, VANISHED. HAVEN'T SEEN ON NETS OR OFF.

Delia sent Gremlin a little graphic of herself nodding. Lance always was good at disappearing. That was all right. She could wait for him—them—here.

Delia?

Delia turned at the mental touch. *Meredeth. How are you?*

Adjusting, Meredeth replied wryly. *I haven't decided whether I like this or not. Marco, on the other hand, is having the time of his life.*

I'll bet, Delia laughed. *How's Earth?*

A total mess. Markets plummeted, but no one seems to know if it matters. Most of the riots seem to have calmed down. Someone needs to gather up the bodies of people who died or killed themselves, but half the police are exploring the nets and the other half are running themselves ragged with other matters.

It'll be a while, Delia said. *But everyone will adjust. At least we're safe from Aditi.*

At the mention of that name, both women looked across the nets to the void where Aditi hung, black and malevolent. She couldn't take over any more human space—every single nanobot was already taken. So she hovered in place, waiting. Some foolhardy souls had tried rescue forays into her space to try and free some of the planets Aditi had already taken. Their bodies currently lay rotting on their home worlds.

We can hope we're safe, Meredeth corrected, *and nothing more.*

Mom?

Delia spun within the node she was currently occupying. For a brief moment she thought it was Kate or Quinn. That was ridiculous, of course. That meant it had to be—

Brad! Nancy!

Her two children swarmed in and around her program in what was widely recognized as a network hug.

We read all about you, Brad said. *Where you were, what you were doing. You're famous!*

We had to ask Gremlin where you were, Nancy complained. *Why didn't you come find us? It's been days.*

I was waiting for you, Delia replied truthfully. *I knew you'd come. Where's your father?*

He'll be along, Brad said. *He's still a little uncertain about surfing the nets.*

We found a couple really interesting nodes, Nancy said. *You'll like them. The data is really neat. Meredeth would like it, too.*

Delia looked at her two children, kids who were real and here, not figments of a fractured mind. Love swelled her heart. She hoped Lance was happy wherever he—they—had gone, and she was secure in the knowledge that they'd run into each other again. Right now, another life beckoned.

Show me, Delia said.

They linked together and jumped.

The Honor Harrington series: *(cont.)*

Field of Dishonor

Honor goes home to Manticore—and fights for her life on a battlefield she never trained for, in a private war that offers just two choices: death—or a "victory" that can end only in dishonor and the loss of all she loves....

Flag in Exile

Hounded into retirement and disgrace by political enemies, Honor Harrington has retreated to planet Grayson, where powerful men plot to reverse the changes she has brought to their world. And for their plans to succeed, Honor Harrington must die!

Honor Among Enemies

Offered a chance to end her exile and again command a ship, Honor Harrington must use a crew drawn from the dregs of the service to stop pirates who are plundering commerce. Her enemies have chosen the mission carefully, thinking that either she will stop the raiders or they will kill her . . . and either way, her enemies will win. . . .

In Enemy Hands

After being ambushed, Honor finds herself aboard an enemy cruiser, bound for her scheduled execution. But one lesson Honor has never learned is how to give up!

Echoes of Honor

"Brilliant! Brilliant! Brilliant!"—*Anne McCaffrey*

continued

PRAISE FOR
LOIS MCMASTER BUJOLD

What the critics say:

The Warrior's Apprentice: "Now here's a fun romp through the spaceways—not so much a space opera as space ballet. ... it has all the 'right stuff.' A lot of thought and thoughtfulness stand behind the all-too-human characters. Enjoy this one, and look forward to the next."   —Dean Lambe, *SF Reviews*

"The pace is breathless, the characterization thoughtful and emotionally powerful, and the author's narrative technique and command of language compelling. Highly recommended."
—*Booklist*

Brothers in Arms: " ... she gives it a genuine depth of character, while reveling in the wild turnings of her tale. ... Bujold is as audacious as her favorite hero, and as brilliantly (if sneakily) successful."   —*Locus*

"Miles Vorkosigan is such a great character that I'll read anything Lois wants to write about him. ... a book to re-read on cold rainy days." —Robert Coulson, *Comic Buyer's Guide*

Borders of Infinity: "Bujold's series hero Miles Vorkosigan may be a lord by birth and an admiral by rank, but a bone disease that has left him hobbled and in frequent pain has sensitized him to the suffering of outcasts in his very hierarchical era. ... Playing off Miles's reserve and cleverness, Bujold draws outrageous and outlandish foils to color her high-minded adventures."   —*Publishers Weekly*

Falling Free: "In *Falling Free* Lois McMaster Bujold has written her fourth straight superb novel. ... How to break down a talent like Bujold's into analyzable components? Best not to try. Best to say: 'Read, or you will be missing something extraordinary.' "   —Roland Green, *Chicago Sun-Times*

The Vor Game: "The chronicles of Miles Vorkosigan are far too witty to be literary junk food, but they rouse the kind of craving that makes popcorn magically vanish during a double feature."   —Faren Miller, *Locus*

MORE PRAISE FOR
LOIS MCMASTER BUJOLD

What the readers say:

"My copy of *Shards of Honor* is falling apart I've reread it so often. . . . I'll read whatever you write. You've certainly proved yourself a grand storyteller."
—Lisa Kolbe, Colorado Springs, CO

"I experience the stories of Miles Vorkosigan as almost viscerally uplifting. . . . But certainly, even the weightiest theme would have less impact than a cinder on snow were it not for a rousing good story, and good story-telling with it. This is the second thing I want to thank you for. . . . I suppose if you boiled down all I've said to its simplest expression, it would be that I immensely enjoy and admire your work. I submit that, as literature, your work raises the overall level of the science fiction genre, and spiritually, your work cannot avoid positively influencing all who read it."
—Glen Stonebraker, Gaithersburg, MD

" 'The Mountains of Mourning' [in *Borders of Infinity*] was one of the best-crafted, and simply best, works I'd ever read. When I finished it, I immediately turned back to the beginning and read it again, and I can't remember the last time I did that."
—Betsy Bizot, Lisle, IL

"I can only hope that you will continue to write, so that I can continue to read (and of course buy) your books, for they make me laugh and cry and think . . . rare indeed."
—Steven Knott, Major, USAF

EXPLORE OUR WEB SITE